THE PATHWAY

NOTE

The four books (of childhood, boyhood, youth and early manhood) making the work called *The Flax of Dream* are

The Beautiful Years
Dandelion Days
The Dream of Fair Women
The Pathway

THE PATHWAY

HENRY WILLIAMSON

'*I am the way ....*'

faber and faber

This edition first published in 2010
by Faber and Faber Ltd
Bloomsbury House, 74–77 Great Russell Street
London WC1B 3DA

Printed by CPI Antony Rowe, Eastbourne

A CIP record for this book is available from the British Library

ISBN 978–0–571–27002–6

CONTENTS

THE glacial wind pouring for so many nights and days past the manor-house of Wildernesse to the plains and sandhills of the shallow coast had polished the stars to a glitter, and deserted a land silent and blank with snow. The girl, standing by the eastern window of the gable room, could see the Great Nebula of Orion as a haze about the middle star of the sword. Betelgeuse at the right shoulder of Orion was tinged with red, and never before had she seen Rigel so hard and white. She opened wider the casement window, and the flame of the candle on the table behind her continued to burn upright and steady. Above the earth dependent for its mortal life on the light and heat of a dwarf-yellow star, a vast firmament was held in a negation of darkness, pierced in vain by its glittering night-suns.

A voice calling the name of Mary from the passage beyond the bedroom made her turn from the window, and the shadow of the candle-flame wavered away and discovered a bird huddled on the snow in the corner of the sill. She saw the tiny gleam of its eye, and took the bird in her hands swelled with chilblains, and breathed upon it. The toes of the robin's feet were drawn together, its head was tilted stiffly. Again the voice of her mother called her, and answering that she was just coming, Mary opened a drawer in the chest by the bed-head and took out her only pair of silk stockings. Quickly making a purse of one leg folded back several times over the foot, she laid the bird within, and placed it in her bodice against her breast.

9

Then taking the brass candlestick she opened the door and hurriedly went down three steps and along a corridor to the landing. Peering over the oak banister-rail she saw her mother standing below. Mrs. Ogilvie told her that the fire in the hall had burnt low, and the box by the hearth was empty, so Mary went across the landing and through another dark corridor down narrower stairs leading to the kitchen. As she opened the door, a boy leapt up from beside a dog and sat down in a chair drawn up to the table, placing hands over ears and elbows on table, and bending over a copy of Cæsar's *de Bello Gallico*.

Realizing that Mary had entered, and not his aunt, he looked up. His eyes were large and dark in a face thin and pale, not with ill-nourishment (as some thought) but with no development. His lean bony body was too short for his long feet; he was fourteen years of age. He wore a schoolboy's suit of cheap dark material, patched and repatched at the elbows and seat of the trousers.

'You can't do it in those boots, Benjamin,' said Mary, smiling at him. 'They make too much noise.'

The boy cleared his throat and said in a husky treble, 'I've read two pages, and only got to do the essay on Fiscal Reform, and I was thinking what I should write, see?'

'I see,' said Mary, opening the door to the yard outside, and going to the wood-shed. Benjamin got off the chair and sat down again beside the dog.

The dog was an old black cocker spaniel, lying before the fire, on its back, paws up in the air with a cat and her three kittens curled up against its chest. With one of the heavy hob-nailed boots hanging on his legs, he rolled the ribs of the black dog, who groaned with pleasure and closed its eyes. Displaced again, the kittens opened their blue eyes and looked for their mother, who anticipating demands upon herself stepped lightly away and jumped on the table. The kittens clawed themselves up the long hair of the spaniel, who after a series of grunts gave a long sigh and prepared to sleep again. Benjamin amused himself by pushing the kittens with the iron-shod tip of his boot, and watching their frightened efforts to cling to the dog. Tiring of doing this, he put one on his boot, and held the boot near the fire. Its hair and fur became ruddy with firelight. He began to shake his foot, and the kitten clawed frantically the thick leather of the boot.

The boy became absorbed in watching it, and shook his foot the more. The plaintive mewing of the kitten changed to its loudest wails, and only then the cat sitting on the satchel paused in the washing of its face to chirrup reassurance to its offspring. The kitten continued to wail, and Benjamin took hold of its tail, pulled it off his boot, and held it upside down. On the flags of the yard sounded the clatter of boots, and he heard the gruff voice of his grandfather talking to Mary; and listening intently in order to hear if they were talking about him, he did not notice that the other door had opened.

'What are you doing with that kitten, Benjamin?' asked Mrs. Ogilvie, and the boy's eyes opened wide.

'Only playing with it, Aunt Constance.'

'I won't have you bullying the animals. I distinctly heard that poor kitten crying in the hall. You're a nasty little bully!'

'But I was only seeing how hard it could cling to my boot, Aunt Constance.'

'That was why you were holding it up by its tail and scorching it before the fire, I suppose?'

The yard door was pushed open for Mary, who carried three elmwood logs in her arms. Immediately the black spaniel got on his legs, shaking off the kittens as though they were leaves, and limped over to the new-comer, and leapt up at him.

'What's that?' said the old man, ignoring the dog's welcome. 'Benjamin been roasting a kitten by its tail? Well, he can't be more hungry than I am. H'm. How would you like to be hung up by your tail?' addressing the boy, whose facial expression remained as when Mary had first gone into the kitchen.

'I haven't got a tail, Grandpa.'

'H'm, well the kitten's none the worse, I expect,' said the old man with a laugh to his niece Constance, as he closed the yard door and opened the breech of his ten-bore fowling piece lest he might have forgotten to remove the cartridges. Benjamin's eyes watched eagerly as he unslung a canvas bag over his shoulders, helped by Mary who had put the logs on the floor.

'Only had ten shots,' he said, as Mary unstrapped the bag and looked at the birds within.

'Three mallard, three teal, a widgeon, and what's this one? I haven't seen anything like it before.'

'I rather fancy he's an eider duck,' said her great-uncle, while she thought, peering in the bag, Oh, you've shot two golden plover.

'Ha, I got two golden plover, too!' said the wildfowler, thinking she had not seen, in a voice not personal enough to be called gruff or hearty. 'I browned 'em with both barrels and only knocked over two. Should have got more, but my eyes aren't so good as they were. H'm. Well, what's for supper, young woman?' as his kind eyes, faded and shrunken in their sockets, looked up suddenly and straightly at hers.

Sufford Calmady Chychester, esquire, was seventy-five years of age, and like many another of the English counties during the first quarter of the twentieth century, he was living the last years of his life in a house different from that in which he had been born. In the period following the death of Queen Victoria the income of his landed estate had diminished, and the liabilities of his eldest son had helped to make it considerably smaller. After the Great War, in the first year of which his three sons had been killed – the eldest with his cavalry regiment at Ypres, the second with his horse battery at Neuve

Chapelle, and the youngest with the yeomanry at Gallipoli, – he had sold the farms of his estate to their various tenants – farmers who had saved purchasing price out of their big war-time profits, whose sons, with scarce exception, had done no military service, and who had regretted the end of the War which had given them motor-cars and big bank-balances. Only the house, with its bedroom ceilings patched with damp, and a few acres of land were left. First and second mortgages had to be paid off, and money invested for an income to be paid during her lifetime to that second widow. H'm! Better to sell the place altogether, and have done with it! So Heanton Court, long-since spoiled as a residence by the railway line running in front of it, beside the estuary shore – the house with its eastern and western windows walled-in grey and blind, stood between Branton and Barum – came into the market, and the old gentleman had his clothes and guns packed up, and some of his books and pictures and sporting prints put into wooden cases, and went to live with his widowed niece Constance Ogilvie at Wildernesse, an old manor-house added-to and rebuilt in many parts since its foundation in the reign of Alfred the Great. It stood within a high wall, surrounded by trees, behind the wind-formed hills and hollows of sand, held nearly permanent by their binding growth of marram grasses, which began where the high northern ground finished its long slope, and ended at the estuary of the Two Rivers. This tract of land, covering what was anciently the river-bed, was known as the Santon Burrows.

Sufford Chychester was big-faced, long-nosed, heavy-bodied, with prominent blue eyes; his white moustaches and short beard were stained a yellowish-brown by tobacco smoke. He wore a shooting suit of Lovat tweed, with the high lapels of a bygone fashion, and the buckskin patch on his right shoulder was worn where his guns had rested. The skin of his thick neck was tanned, like his forehead, his hands and wrists, by long exposure to English weather.

He sat by the fire, and leant over to unfasten the brass buckles of the leather anklets above his boots, and sat up again. H'm!

'Benjamin,' said Mrs. Ogilvie immediately, 'take off Uncle's boots for him,' and she went out of the room.

'Don't bother, boy, I can do it,' throwing up his bearded chin so that a smile was thrown out of the blue eyes. 'Smoke first!' as his fingers drew out from a pocket a small black wooden pipe with a narrow stem. Mary was ready with a match, after which she lifted a steaming iron kettle off the hob, and went into the scullery.

'I'd like to do it,' said Benjamin, who had removed all evidence of homework, done or undone, in the satchel, and hidden it in one of the drawers of the dresser. Kneeling on the slate flags at the old man's feet, he pulled at strap and buckle. Neither spoke. He was unlacing the first boot when something flung itself against the door, and the aged black spaniel staggered to its legs, scattering the kittens again, and barking hoarsely. 'Quiet, Coalie, be quiet!' shouted Benjamin, but the hoarse barking of Coalie continued. Scratches and whines came from behind the door. The boy got up and unlatched it, when a brownish-coloured long-legged dog with long tail, ears, and body, fell into the room and bounded over the flags to Mr. Chychester. The long dog was an Irish water-spaniel, covered with short crisp curls, except for a smooth tail, and a face clothed with short hair, over which was a top-knot dropping forward to a peak. It fell sprawling at its master's feet, and laid its throat on his unfastened boot, looking up at him with eyes brown and full of intelligence. The old gentleman took not the least notice of his dog, and when Benjamin knelt again to finish his job the water-spaniel, which had retrieved every bird shot by its master that evening without breaking the smallest feather, walked away into the scullery to see if anything eatable had been thrown into the pig-bucket outside.

14

WINTER

Mary was in this room, standing at the sink, an apron round her waist, her sleeves rolled up, and her hands in a bowl of hot water. She was washing up the knives and silver and china used for tea. The room was lit by a paraffin lamp, the glass of which was sombre with a smoky film. Beside the sink, near the open door, was a pump with iron pipes leading from the well under the floor to a tank in the loft. Water was drawn through a brass tap fixed two feet up the pipe; but the pipe above the tap was ice.

Something struck her legs as she swilled out a cup, and looking down she saw that Rigmarole had greeted her with his long smooth tail as he passed on his way to the pig-bucket. The hungry dog routed in the rimed mass of potato- and sprout-peelings, taking out crusts of bread stuck with tea-leaves and flavoured with green-water. Seeing him chew a fare so poor for a faithful retriever of shot wildfowl, Mary went into the larder with the smitching lamp and surveyed the meat-safe. Within the square of wood and perforated zinc-sheeting rested a plate with a ham-bone and some scraps on it, half a cold rabbit pie, a shoulder of mutton, and a basin of brawn – all of Mary's preparation and cooking. Rigmarole stood at the entrance to the larder, his eyes two orbs of warm brown fire, his nostrils working, his tail sweeping, sweeping, sweeping! Rigmarole trusted Mary, and that is why his tail had brushed her legs as he passed so humbly to the frozen bucket. Rigmarole was given two cooked rabbit-heads and ribs out of the pie, and after the cracking and crunching he stood on his hind legs and licked her warm forearm, then padded away through the kitchen and along a twisting passage paved with flags unevenly sunken, to the hall, where he stretched himself out on an open hearth, partly on the feet of a tiny old lady trying to warm her toes at the embers of a fuming fire.

'Now, sir, that was most rude of you,' she pronounced in a sweet voice, tremulous with an effort to be firm and stern,

15

as she tried to push away the recumbent legs and body by inserting her toes under the dog's ribs. Rigmarole lay unmoving, except for a slow swelling of his ribs, which subsided as his lungs expelled a deep sigh. The wind of contentment made redder the embers and fanned a lilac flame out of a charcoal crack in the lowest brand, which leapt up and bit the wood above it. Alarmed by the nearness of the blaze to his sensitive nose, Rigmarole raised his head, stared resentfully, groaned, gathered up his tail and legs, and took himself off the slate hearth to an arm-chair against the bookshelves in a far corner, leaving Miss Edith Chychester with her toes held gleefully to catch the heat of the flames. She was eighty-seven years old, and becoming deaf.

This affliction prevented her from hearing the noise of footfalls on the hard gravel drive without the lobby, the crack of a whip, and the clear voice of a girl calling a dog by the name of Dave. Rigmarole had heard, and his ears had jerked up, and again fallen soft, a minute since. The maker of firm steps and clear sounds turned the handle and barged the heavy oaken door with her shoulder before the catch was lifted, found it solid, and ejaculated an explodent *Damn*! Pushing back the iron-studded door, she ordered the dogs within, opened the lighter lobby door with a twist of her wrist and a kick of her boot-cap, and called out, 'Anyone at home? Chaps, I've some news!'

Feeling the draught from the threshold through the grey Shetland shawl on her back, Miss Chychester turned and peered in that direction.

'Is anyone there?' she asked, pronouncing every syllable with the care of one who had neatly worn a black silk gown of a mid-Victorian fashion every Sunday to church for four decades, and not considered it old.

'I said, Is anyone there?' she repeated.

The girl came into the hearthlight.

'Hullo, Aunt Edith,' she said casually, then 'Hullo, my dear

old Rolly!' in soft caressing tones as the Irish water-spaniel
fell out of the chair and fawned upon her.

'It is Jean.'

'Where's Ron and Pam?'

'Do you not remember? They returned to school this
morning!'

'Blast, I meant to say good-bye to them.'

Miss Chychester did not hear.

'There is a draught blowing from the lobby, Jean.'

'Sorry!' shouted Jean, and strode swiftly to the doors, which
she closed. When she came back Miss Chychester was standing
up.

'Where's Mary?' shouted Jean. Miss Chychester put a hand
to an ear, and waited.

'Who is?'

'Where's Mary, I said,' bawled Jean.

'Yes, your mother is back.'

'Oh, my God,' groaned Jean. 'Nice warm weather we're
having,' she yelled into the hand. Aunt Edith replied with an
emphatic, I think so! Ignoring her great-aunt, Jean whistled
to the two dogs which had entered with her, and walked down
the passage into the kitchen.

Rigmarole followed at the heels slouching on the flagstones,
and when the door was opened three dogs tried to squeeze
past her legs. Jean flung her felt hat on the table and sat on
one corner, swinging a leg. Benjamin lifted his eyes, with their
blank dark look, from the bound volume of *The English Boy's
Annual* he had been reading so raptly in a wicker chair. The
thick cardboard covers of the quarto book rested on his knees,
his toes were turned in, and his backbone curved; his attitude
was chiefly due to the fact that the seat of the chair was broken
and stuffed with newspapers, deep among which his hind-
quarters were wedged.

'Hullo, you,' said Jean. 'Any adventures in that book?'

'Eh?' replied Benjamin, his thoughts abstracted by the

scene in which he had been wonderfully living with a mysterious hero named The Night Hawk, who hunted at and cowardly German spies in the mountains of Scotland, Switzerland, and elsewhere. Down in his hands went his cropped head, which stretched on a skinny neck out of an Eton collar too large in circumference by an inch and a half, and which bore in marking ink initials which were not his.

'Hullo!' said Jean to Mary, who came out of the scullery with two tea-cloths for drying upon the line. 'I've got something to tell you,' as she swung leg and riding whip together. 'I've had an adventure.'

'Just a minute, I must fill the kettle,' said Mary.

Many people had remarked since the early childhood of the two eldest daughters of Constance Ogilvie that two sisters so dissimilar in temperament and appearance surely could not be found anywhere in Devon. They were both tall, Jean being five feet seven and a half inches in height, and Mary half an inch taller; but while Mary's head was small and dark, Jean's was bigger, and fair. Jean had the long straight nose, the blue eyes, and the fair hair of the Saxon Chychesters; her eyes were spaced widely under a smooth brow. People – meaning most of the women and almost none of the men – in the district were fond of discussing Jean Ogilvie, and one of the nice things said about her was that if she took the trouble to dress up to her original appearance, and to be less wild in her talk and behaviour, she *could* make herself quite attractive. The expression on her face, as she stared in silence at the floor, seeming to have forgotten the adventure, was familiar to her sister Mary. Her nose seemed to have grown sharper, the lines under the eyes deeper, and the eyes themselves were clear of animation, holding a moodiness of thought. Mary understood Jean. The lips of Jean were turned down at the corners, neither leg nor whip was swinging now. Nor was she sitting upright as when Mary had gone out half a minute before to

18

fill the kettle. When Jean looked like that, her sister knew of what she was thinking.

With both hands Mary lifted the two-gallon kettle and slid its iron case, polished black outside and furred grey inside, over the circle of flame, while it dribbled on the hot iron and bubbles revolved and sizzled into steam.

'Tell us the adventure, Jeannie,' said Mary, looking at her sister with eagerness, although her mind was not so eager to hear as her expression appeared to show.

'Oh, it's nothing,' replied Jean despondently, tapping her leg with the whip.

'Where have you been? Appledore?'

'Yes. I saw Luke on Crow Island getting driftwood, and as he was going over I thought I would go over with him and see the new pups at the Prince of Wales'.' Jean's voice was very casual, and she dared not look at her sister.

'Any good?'

'One wasn't so bad. Liver and white. Dog.'

'What was the adventure?'

'Oh, that!' cried Jean, smiling so that she showed her top front teeth – long, even, and white. 'My dear, I must tell you. It happened as I was coming back, for while I was over there I thought I would go up to Howard's and see his falcons.'

Mary thought, I knew it; but she said:

'Oh, you did go there. Mother thought perhaps you had gone to Hamlyn's stables at Bideford. Anyone at The Ridge?'

'Diana and her mother, and some old general and his female belongings. Old Jig, too. And of course Howard. Very much there, was Howard – with Diana! And, my dear, I must tell you! Mrs. Shelley staring through her lorgnettes at Dave, who wouldn't stay outside. "What a peculiar dorg that is, Jean. What sort of a dorg would you call that?" "Oh, Dave's a Fixed Railway Hound," I said. "A Fixed Railway Hound?" asked Old Jig. "What does that mean?" "He's a Fixed Platelaying Dog," I replied; "aren't you, Dave?"

"Whatever is that?" "Oh," I said, feeling a damned fool, "He fixes plates with his eyes, and lays about whatever he sees on them," and at my words Dave cocked his head over her plate and licked up her bread and butter. It took me a week to think out that "joke," which of course was greeted with roars of silence. Damn and blast them!' cried Jean, scowling, and clenching her hands.

Mary saw the shine of tears in her eyes, and said, putting a hand on her shoulder:

'Jolly good joke, I call it; much too good for them to see!'

'To hell with them,' said Jean brusquely, 'I loathe the sight of them all. I'll never go there again. Will we, Dave? Dear old Dave, then, he was his mother's clever boy, wasn't he?'

The mongrel called Dave, a lurcher dog, half a greyhound, with sleek russet coat, white chest and feet, and a foxy face, stood with his forepaws on the table. He had an intermittent habit of stealing up behind the legs of visitors who came to Wildernesse, sniffing deliberately their calves, and if he did not like them, of nipping their legs. On Jean's forearm was a red scar, given by Dave in rough play a year before. Dave's companion was Jock, a thoroughbred Aberdeen terrier with legs stumpy and bowed, with whom he poached rabbits in the vast warren of the burrows.

The lurcher looked from his human companion's face – he was too independent to need a master – with his small, hard, bright eyes, and with tongue flacking and short ears cocked he gazed swiftly round the table. Seeing no food, he lost interest in the kitchen, and ran to the larder, from which, in his eighteen months since puppyhood at Wildernesse, he had stolen two chickens, seven rabbits (leaping on the tall safe to lift them off nails on the beam above), nineteen pounds of butter, several pounds of bacon, dozens of cakes and scones and buns, lapped many jugs of milk and bowls of cream, and once had eaten a mouse in a trap. Mrs. Ogilvie disliked Dave, but Jean wanted him, would have him, insisted on having him, and so he slept in her bedroom with the terrier Jock.

In spite of her declared loathing of the people at the house called The Ridge, Jean's thoughts seemed to be upon the afternoon's events, for she said:

'Well, afterwards Diana played, and of course I was out of it, especially as Dave had disgraced himself by his little trick. I said I'd better be going, and every one seemed to be damned glad to hear it –'

'Oh no, Jean,' said Mary. 'It is only your sensitiveness.'

'Me sensitive!' scoffed the younger girl. 'Nothing like that about me. How could I be, with a nose like mine?'

Mary had not what was sometimes referred to as 'the Chychester nose.' Mary's nose was small and straight. She was a Celt, as her father had been; and that vivid, charming, and irresponsible Scotsman had begotten a daughter who, taking after himself, had no resemblance to her mother. What tales had been passed on senescent female tongues in North Devon about her father! – the late Charles Sholto Pomfret Ogilvie, esquire, of Wildernesse, and lord of the manor of Santon in Devon.

Mary cried suddenly.

'Oh, the 'bin! I've forgotten my 'bin!' and put her hand in her blouse.

'You are a lad!' said Jean, looking at her sister gently unfolding the stocking. The robin lay still.

'I found him on the window sill, frozen and huddled up, the poor mite, but I do believe he'll live,' murmured Mary.

'What's that?' cried a husky treble voice. The wicker chair creaked as Benjamin wriggled out. He had left his boy heroes asleep in the turret of an old chateau, after an envied meal. They were waiting to warn The Night Hawk, having escaped at Zebrugge from a German submarine which had captured them while in their canoe fishing off the Cornish coast. Whenever Benjamin stopped reading such tales, he never read to the end of an instalment, but left off in the middle of one. If he read to the end, something always happened – a pistol shot, a guttural laugh in the cellar, buzzing blue sparks of a wireless set, the clatter of 'Uhlan's hoofs' – that made it necessary for him to turn over the pages to the next instalment, to relieve the suspense. Benjamin left the one boy friend asleep in a horse-rug before a fire, and the other on guard in the turret, and considered this a good place to stop reading; they had had a gorgeous feast of stolen German sausage and all was comfortable for the night (he hoped).

'You got a 'bin? Oh, show us,' the voice begged.

Mary folded back the stocking, holding the robin in the purse of the foot lest it fall in a weak flutter. Its eyes were open and bright, and it feebly pecked at the finger that would soothe its poll.

'Oh, give it to us,' said Benjamin.

'What for?' asked Jean. 'Another of your bird-stuffing experiments?'

'No, just to show the chaps at school. Oh, give it to us.'

'He isn't quite strong enough, Ben,' said Mary, looking shyly at the admiring eyes of Jean. 'Now wrap him up carefully and put him back, and later on he shall have some scraps of fat ham, he shall,' murmuring with eyes downcast on the bird, and returning it to the warmth.

'Why is it,' asked Jean, still staring, 'that I always feel about fifty years older than you? You haven't changed a bit since you were fourteen – and how old are you, twenty-four? It's the way you scrimp up your hair I suppose, and the out-for-a-walk-on-a-Sunday-I'm-a-big-girl-now-and-walk-behind sort of expression about you.'

'What about that adventure?' asked Mary, smiling.

'Oh yes! My dear, I must tell you. When I left The Ridge I went down to see that wooden battleship at the shipbreakers' yard, and passing The Prince of Wales', I saw three chaps coming out just before me. One of them, with red hair and

red beard, was reciting poetry, and the other two seemed
pretty well fed-up with him – '

'Poetry!' interrupted Benjamin, scornfully.

'Shut up,' retorted Jean. 'Well, at the quay they seemed
to be having a sort of quarrel, and one of them said he was
going on alone. I knew I'd seen him before somewhere, but
couldn't think where.'

'What was he like?' asked Mary.

'Quite nice. He wore no hat, and had a great stick – a
young tree it looked like – in his hand.'

'Who was it?' interrupted Benjamin.

'Wait, you fool. Well, he'd got a small brown moustache,
and a hazel nut for a head. Honestly, it was the smallest head
I'd ever seen on such a tall chap. He looked at me, such a
peculiar look in his eyes – not sad, or wondering, but sort of
between the two. Then he looked at Dave, who was stalking,
hackles raised, round a spaniel, who was holding his tail
stiff and gazing at the chap. Dave started snarling, and bit
the spaniel behind the neck – you know, the silent sneaky way
he has. Well, the chap just picked Dave up by his scruff, and
brought him to me. Dave tried to bite him, snarling like the
devil, but the chap didn't turn a hair. "I'm afraid he'll bite
me if I let go, and I don't want to hurt him by flinging him
away, so may I drop him in the water?" I said yes, and so
Dave was dropped in. When he came out the chap went
up to him and patted him, and Dave wagged his tail! It
was extraordinary. I mean, old Dave coming back quiet as
a lamb!'

'Coo yes,' said Benjamin.

Mary's mind was now eager. Colour was coming in her
cheeks. How pretty she is, thought Jean, and then, Thank
God I've got a sister I can talk to. She said, feeling suddenly
very happy:

'Well, you see, when the chap whistled his dog it made me
more puzzled, because I had heard it before, but where

I'd seen him I couldn't think. I asked Bill Baily, and he zaid he were a stranger hereabouts.' – Jean's voice changed, and she spoke in the broad burring tones of the West Country.– 'Wull, midear, I zaid, wull, I be gwin to walk right up to'n, and zay, Begging your pardon, but plaize to tell me your name, young man.'

'And did you?'

'No.'

They laughed.

'Why didn't you?' asked Benjamin.

'Shut up, you fool. As a matter of fact, when the other two men had gone over to Instow by ferry, he came up to me, and staggered me by asking how Diana Shelley was. "I know you," he said. "You were with Diana Shelley at Cryde Bay four years ago, during the summer of the long drought. Diana Shelley," he said in a soft voice, "I remember I accepted an invitation from her, and I never went. And you," he said, "had two plaits over your shoulder, and you were turning cartwheels on the sands."

'I told him who I was, and he looked quite bucked, and asked me how you were, and if you still lived on the Santon Burrows. He said he had walked from Okehampton that morning –'

'Okehampton?' said Mary. 'Why, that must be nearly forty miles!'

'I know! He said he started in the darkness, as it was so cold. Well, anyway, he said he was going to cross the estuary and walk to the cottage he hadn't seen for four years. "Well, do come and see us," I said, and he said he would. "Don't wait four years this time," I said jokingly, and he took me seriously and said, "You know, I ought to have written to Diana Shelley – I've often thought about it. She was going to play in a church somewhere."'

'St. Sabinus's,' ejaculated Benjamin.

' "Well, you come and see us," I told him, "and you'll

probably see Diana there, because she's very pally with Mary. Come to supper to-night if you like." Just then I saw Luke going down the slip, so I darted away. I thought of asking him if he would like a lift over to the Crow, but he might have thought I was trying to get off with him, or something.'

Down the passage from the distant hall came the muffled franging notes of the grandfather clock striking eight times. Seven o'clock already! In half an hour it would be supper time, and the potatoes were not even peeled. Mary had thought that morning to give them a squab pie for supper, but always there had been other things to do, and now it was too late. She opened the door of the oven, and saw that a light brown crisped skin was formed over the rice pudding in its china dish. Apples!

Taking a basket and an old brass lanthorn from the dresser she lit the candle, and went out into sparkling starlight to the woodshed, climbing the worn broad steps to the apple loft, a place of limewashed walls flaking loose into cobwebs, and rows of shelves holding apples resting on straw, each tray marked by a piece of cardboard tacked to it. There were rows of Annie Elizabeth, big yellowy-green ones; Scarlet Leadington, very red and too good for cooking; Lane's Prince Albert, which were green and would keep until April. The straw-laid trays of an entire wall were packed with pippins – Cox's Orange, Wyken, King of the Pippins. There were Newton Wonder and Cornish Gillyflower, and the big ruddy Barum Wonders, which had had a bloom. Barum Wonders it should be.

How many to take? Uncle Suff, Aunt Edith, Mother, Jean, Ben, herself. Six, and Uncle Suff and Ben might like an extra one each. Eight. Two extra in case anyone turned up, but of course no one would; and ten ruddy-brown apples were laid in the basket, the door closed, and Mary ran down the dark stairs, knowing since childhood every knot and groove in the wood. From a drawer of the dresser, where was hidden Ben's satchel, she took a tube of tinned iron sharpened at one end, pressed it through each apple, and removed the cores, filling the spaces with brown sugar; and putting them in a dish with a little water, slid them on the top shelf of the oven.

Making up the fire with coal, which burnt fiercely owing to the frost, she ran into the larder with the lanthorn, and from a basket selected knives and forks and spoons, each handle of which was engraved with a lion on a cornsheaf. These were piled on the tray, beside a platter and loaf, salt cellars and peppercorn grinders, a jar of home-made apple chutney, six glasses and Uncle Suff's pewter mug, and six table napkins in rings.

'Ben dear, fill the glass jug for me, will you?' she asked the boy as she hurried with the tray to the dining-room. A match to the pile of driftwood and sea-coal on the open hearth, and another to the wicks of the candles. A tablecloth was flung over the refectory table; she set a bare polished board with plate-mats only when ' people were coming.'

Outside in the hall Uncle Suff was reading one of his big red books on heraldry, a subject that was one of his hobbies; he was lying back in the leather chair out of which he had tipped Rigmarole. He said to her as she passed, 'I want my supper!' and made gruff genial noises, as of laughter. 'You shall, Uncle Suff, you shall!' cried Mary, as earlier that evening she had cried to Benjamin, when granting him award of a piece of cake for chopping wood, not long after that boy's tea in the kitchen.

She remembered soup in the larder, which ought not to be kept any longer, and lifting from a shelf beside the plate-rack in the scullery a blue enamel pot blackened with smoke, she poured in the soup and carried it to the stove, amidst the mewing of cats. 'Watch that soup, Ben, and stir it – don't let it burn, there's a dear,' and into the larder again, followed by the pack of cats to get the cheese.

Tetties! She had forgotten the potatoes. And she had no

excuse, for that evening she had wasted half an hour in her bedroom, sprawled on the bed and reading again the chapter at the beginning of the third volume of 'Bevis,' about the stars and the zodiac Bevis made, and the final chapter, where the 'black north wind came down,' and froze the long pond, and Bevis and Mark went skating on the ice that sometimes cracked across with a great *boom*! Afterwards she had routed in a cupboard for a pair of skates that had belonged to her elder brother Michael. Wasting time!

Mary ran out of the larder and into the yard once more with the basket, swiftly chose enough potatoes for seven, and peeled them at the sink, helped by Jean who had strolled into the kitchen. They were dropped into a pot of boiling water, instead of the usual cold water, and shoved beside the soup.

She set seven places at table, and drew a jug of cider from the hogshead in the cellar, which she put on the dining-room hearth. The fire was burning brightly. Remembering soup-plates as she leapt upstairs to tidy herself, she ran down again to the scullery, pulled them out of the rack, and put them on the range above the bodley. Telling Benjamin, who had wedged himself into the chair again and was at that moment hating a skunk in Belgian uniform saluting the Union Jack, while with pig-eyes glittering he made guttural asides about *der tag* (obviously he was the arch-spy of the Huns), not to forget to stir the soup, she hurried up the stairs once used by servants, and so to her room in the gable.

It was cold, for she had left the window open. Sirius was now above the trees by the gate, and flashing a deep blue ray and then a sudden red, but no green. The gem-like star-chord of the Pleiades twinkled never so quickly. Mary's mood when last looking out of the window was changed. Now she felt something going from herself to the night, the night above the fields and dykes she loved and knew so well. Far away she could hear an increase in the cries of wading birds on the sandbanks already covered with ice to the line of the lapsing tide. Out of the throats of curlew fell light bubbles, stringing themselves on the prolonged whistles of golden plover. Every trilling note was a star of sweet sound, as though the birds could take each point of heavenly light reflected in the earthly waters and change it into a cry of the joyful spirit. Thousands of birds were crying, thousands of stars were dropping down their music. Mary sighed with the feeling of strength come upon her spirit. Her eyes felt wide as the firmament, she was strong as Orion, who strode with a shining mace to shatter what dark unknown?

And where is Littleboy, she wondered, turning away from the night, and in her heart was a pain that she welcomed. Never dare to tell anyone of Littleboy! Littleboy with the night in his hair, and starry eyes, who with cries of delight came to her, to be taken to her heart, to be murmured over, to be cherished.

Chapter 2

MARY was about to close the window when a far-away bird-like cry made her stand still. It came again, and she could not decide whether it had come from the throat of a curlew or from the lips of a human being. The cadence was beautiful and melancholy as the frost cries which all night passed in the darkness, the quality and periods were exact, but the roughness of the long whistle was not there. She knew the whistle. She had heard it by another sea, in another year, when the haggard youth by her side had been pouring out his spirit like oil of spikenard at the feet of one who saw disfigurement thereby.

While she was remembering that walk on the Folkestone Leas towards the sunset three and a half years before, a dog gave tongue in the distance, as if chasing rabbits. In the clear cold air, whose moisture had been rime for weeks, she could hear the beat of its feet on the frozen marsh. She heard the whistle again, and was certain of it; she had an impulse to hail him; but what would her mother think if she heard her calling to a stranger from her bedroom window? He was walking on the inner sea-wall, she judged, between the keeper's cottage and the great drain. Jean had said he looked tired; and his cottage was several hours' walk distant. That derelict miner's cottage would be damp; when she had seen it in the spring, walking round the coast with Howard, the sodden thatch had been green with moss, and looking through the window, they had seen plaster fallen to the floor.

She took the lanthorn from the dressing-table and waved it out of the window. Then standing it on the sill she clasped her hands, which felt as though they were wooden, so that the palms made a hollow with an opening between the top joints of the thumbs. Against the opening she put her lips, and blew into the hollow, making the hoot of a wood owl. She listened, but only the more distant cries of the wading birds were moving in the night. Again she waved the lanthorn, and sent a quavering deep call out of her hands, while thinking, as though in answer to her mother. After all, Jean invited him to supper, and he may have lost his way. This excuse made her uneasy with herself; she was not being fair to her mother. There came an answer, startlingly near, and she could not be certain if an owl had answered.

The candle threw its beams into the darkness once more, and from the sea-wall she heard the beginning of *Hymn to the Sun,* instantly knowing that he was asking if she herself were showing the light. She wetted her lips to continue the tune from where it had stopped, but her lips were too cold to whistle. So she hooted again, and waved the lanthorn so vigorously that the candle fell from the socket and dashed its flame out against the horn sides.

I do hope he will come, she thought, as she swiftly brushed her hair by starlight, and arranged it in the way she had not varied from her seventeenth year, since when the long thick rope had been plaited only for the night. It was parted at the side, and lay on the right forehead, pressed there by a narrow fillet of black silk which encircled the knot at the back of her head. She pulled the curtains over the window, re-lit the candle, and stared at her face, thinking how true was Jean's remark about her hair. Her image smiled at her in two positions, full-face and three-quarter, and she watched herself with faint dismay, which was faithfully returned from the mirror. People said her face was like a child's face; it was plain, and small! Jean's face was more like a face should be, and when she was happy and smiling she was beautiful. Dear Jean! How glad she was that Jean was her sister.

The soup! Supper! And she was smiling at her own face in

the glass, when she had not washed her hands or changed her blouse, the collar of which was positively *grimy*. She opened a drawer and unbuttoned the brown woollen jacket she wore, throwing it on the bed and flinging the blouse after it. One clean blouse was left, thank goodness – she was behind with the washing. Clothes got hard as boards hanging in the garden.

Her numbed fingers, blue and cracked with the chilblains she so wanted to scratch and beat, fastened the buttons of the white silk blouse, and over it she pulled a thick jumper which had lain folded in the bottom drawer. It was knitted of rows of brown and grey and yellow geometrical figures, and she had made it herself while Jean had scoffed; and when it was finished Jean had liked it so much that Mary had given it to her; but before Jean had worn it Diana Shelley had come to stay with them wearing a similar jumper, so Jean had given it back to Mary.

She put her arms into the adder-marked sleeves, carefully pulled it over her head, smoothed it everywhere, and set the long pointed collar of the blouse. A last look at the mirror, no posing this time, my girl! The image looked gravely at her, until it saw the swelled red and blue fingers holding the lanthorn, and frowned, and vanished.

In the hall sat her mother with Uncle Suff and Aunt Edith near her in their own chairs. Mrs. Ogilvie was glancing at the *North Devon Herald*, Miss Chychester was reading a three-weeks-old copy of the *Church Times*, which one of her nieces regularly sent to her. As she was going into the kitchen Jean came out with a steaming tureen, and Mary felt grateful to her younger sister. Benjamin was back with his unnatural heroes, who with The Night Hawk were about to complete a tunnel from a hollow oak in a Brussels garden to a cell in the military prison, where an English secret agent, heroic and unskunklike, was waiting to be shot at dawn. Jerked from the tunnel back to the kitchen, with only rice pudding and baked apples after

soup and cold meat, Benjamin did not appreciate the import-
ance of brushing his hair and washing his hands.

'Get on with it, Ben,' said Mary, 'you know that Mother
hates to see grimy paws at the table.'

Ben muttered about there being no soap, and the water
was frozen, and he didn't want any supper.

'Ben dear,' said Mary, 'I know how nice the book is to you,
well, people being neat at table is nice for Mother, so hurry
up, and take some of the water out of the kettle, but not much.'

She took in the soup-plates by another passage that led to
the dining-room, placed them at the head of the table, and
went back to mash the potatoes and fetch in the leg of mutton
and the rabbit pie, which she put on the sideboard. She
surveyed the seven sets laid, and in a sudden panic gathered
up one and put the knives and silver with the meat, before
beating a bronze gong. The hands of the grandfather clock
in the hall pointed to twenty-five minutes past seven.

They stood behind their chairs, and Mrs. Ogilvie, seeing
that all were present, gave a glance to Benjamin, who said,
'For what we are about to receive may the Lord make us
truly thankful for Jesus Christ's sake Amen.'

The heads lifted, and Mrs. Ogilvie sat down at the head
of the table, and ladled out soup. Benjamin stood at her left
elbow, and removed each plate as it was half filled. Since
he had read that evening of The Night Hawk left hanging
to a rope inconveniently tied around his neck and the
branch of a tree, his feet two yards above the ground,
Benjamin had determined to develop wrists as powerful as
those of his hero, who had saved himself, when the Uhlans
had returned to their drunken orgies in a farm-house, by a
hand-over-hand hauling to the branch. The distribution of
soup-plates appeared to him to be a good opportunity of
testing the strength of his wrists, so each plate was gripped as
near the edge as possible by a thumb and two fingers. Miss
Edith Chychester's soup was placed before her in safety,

Mary's glided down on an inclined plane, Jean's was nearly tipped into her lap, and Mr. Chychester's wobbled as it approached at the end of an agued arm, the ague changed to curvature of the spine and paralysis, and with a husky cry of 'Oh!' the soup was spilled on the carpet.

Mrs. Ogilvie looked up, paused with the ladle in the tureen, and with a look of restrained annoyance, she said:

'What *are* you doing, Benjamin?'

'It fell out of me hand,' said Benjamin, looking at her fixedly, his face too skin-and-bony to express his alarm.

'Then why not use two hands,' said his aunt, in a conversational tone, as she ladled more soup. Mary had already given up her untouched plate to her unperturbed great-uncle, and gone for a floor-cloth, a basin of hot water, and a fresh plate. Benjamin stood by Mary while the mess was swabbed up, twice clearing his throat and volunteering to relieve her. 'You go and sit up,' said Mary; 'this won't take a second to do'; but he stood watching her.

'If you put a diluted solution of NaOH on the place, it will dissolve the grease, and by adding some diluted HCl, it will be neutralized, and you get H_2O and NaCl, which is common salt and water! See?' He looked round at his grandfather as though he expected the old man to dash his spoon into his plate, push back his chair, throw away his table napkin, and stare at the extraordinary author of this chemical discovery. Yet Mr. Chychester continued to drink soup, not out of the side of the spoon as Benjamin had been taught by his aunt, but out of all of it. The quick Jean observed the expectancy in Benjamin's wide eyes and parted teeth, and caricatured his expression by dropping her chin and gazing idiotically at him.

'Is that so?' she mimicked. 'Go on, you're ragging, I say, aren't you, Chych? You could knock me down with a traction engine. See?'

'Don't tease, Jean. Benjamin, come and sit up before you

do any more damage. You will have to have a cold plate, but it will teach you to be more careful. Come on, Mary dear, your soup's getting cold.'

'Ben can have my plate. There's another in the oven.'

Ben squeezed a 'No, that's all right, I say,' from out of the wide collar lying outside his jacket, as he began to sip from his spoon the juices of boiled vegetables and sheep's bones. Mary sat beside him, and began her soup as Mr. Chychester laid down his spoon, threw up his bearded chin, and said in a convincing tone of pleasure, 'Ha, that was good,' and handed up his plate for more.

Mrs. Ogilvie would not have the dogs in the room during meals, and they were lying in the hall, Rigmarole curled in the saddlebag arm-chair, Dave listening to a mouse gnawing the wainscoting, Jock sitting beside Coalie, and Coalie lying with head on paws and nose at the crack under the door. He heard the soft clatter of spoons being assembled and plates collected, and a noise, between a whine and a groan, oozed out of his slobbery mouth.

Benjamin used two hands for taking and handing round the plates of meat, and his abject silence annoyed Mrs. Ogilvie because it induced within herself a feeling that she was being hard on the boy, for after all, it was not his fault that he was what he was. Mrs. Ogilvie had given him a home, since his grandfather had adopted him, not on sentimental impulse, or because she deemed it her duty to do so, but because she wanted the last years of her uncle to be as happy as possible. And people – with the faculty of imagination and the instinct of curiosity which must be employed somehow (and the manner of employment reveals the personality and character) – had remarked together many things about the origin of Benjamin, his relationship to Connie Ogilvie, the perceptible likeness of face to her daughter Mary, his furtiveness, his undevelopment, his voracity at Christmas parties. (He was not invited at any other time.) He was fourteen years old, he was apparently to remain at the grammar school, and not go to a public school. It was 'known, of course, that the old man had no money.'

Benjamin took round the plates without mishap, and then seated himself and began laboriously to carve the baked head of a rabbit. He had been bold enough to ask for this delicacy because he knew that no one else would eat it, and Benjamin had read that somewhere lived a tribe which believed that by eating the brains of an animal, or a man, they acquired its cunning or wisdom. Holding the nutlike skull upright with a fork too unwieldy for his hand, he pressed the thin bone of the cranium between the eye sockets, in order to split it and dig out the valuable kernel. Repeatedly his eyes darted to the head of the table, for he dreaded lest it might slip from under the pressure of the knife and slide off the plate. Mrs. Ogilvie was unconscious of this uneasiness near her, for she was staring at the window, wondering if she had been mistaken, or had a face passed in the darkness. No, there it was again – it seemed to hesitate, and then to pass away. Once more it returned, hovered, and vanished.

'Take it on the mat, Chych,' suggested Jean, after watching Benjamin's unsuccessful attempts to split the skull. Mary took knife and fork from him, and firmly bisected it. She was handing them back to Benjamin when the four dogs behind the shut door threw their tongues together, and every one stopped still, except Aunt Edith, who with the third finger of her left hand was brushing bread-crumbs into a minute mound.

'Who can it be?' asked Mrs. Ogilvie, looking from face to face, as though unable to understand why anyone should come to the house at that time of night. She said nothing about the face she had seen, not wanting to alarm them.

'Stop the dogs, Jean,' she implored. The four animals were barking furiously.

'It's probably the man I asked to supper,' said Jean, pushing back chair and dropping napkin on the floor.

'A man?' asked Mrs. Ogilvie distinctly. 'What man?'

'Oh, a chap I met 'cross th' water,' drawled Jean. 'A sort of tramp.'

'A sort of tramp? My dear Jean, what do you mean? What does she mean, Mary?' Mrs. Ogilvie appealed to her eldest daughter, as Jean slouched out of the room. Hi, Dave, shut that beastly rattle! they heard her shouting. Down, Coalie! Damn you, Dave, will you shut up! followed by the yelp of Dave stung by the lash of one of the holly coaching whips that stood in the lobby corner.

'What has happened, Constance,' the voice of Miss Chychester demanded, as she sat still and upright, immune from the frets of life, a lace cap on her white hair so neatly combed and brushed, a white Indian shawl tightly arranged on her tiny shoulders and fastened below the high black stiff collar by a gold filigree bow-brooch. Her colourless eyes peered from her brother's face to her niece's face, thence to her great-niece. What was happening?

Having thumped, kicked, pushed, and whacked the pack into single dogs, Jean shut herself in the lobby, and pulled open the heavy front door.

'Hullo!' she said, in a clear and welcoming voice, discerning a shadow beyond with stars around its head. 'It's you, isn't it?'

A voice said softly, as if shyly, out of the shadow, 'Yes. I've got the spaniel with me. Will anyone mind if I bring him in? I'm late, I'm afraid.'

'There's only mother who doesn't like dogs much, but you needn't worry about her. You're just in time for supper. Ugh! You must be jolly cold. Come in.'

'Thanks,' said the visitor. 'Come on, Billjohn.'

'I'd better shut Dave in the kitchen, I think,' suggested Jean. 'He'll probably fight your spaniel otherwise. I wonder if you'll mind waiting in the lobby while I take him away? I shan't be a moment.'

She shut the door, seized Dave by the chestnut scruff of his

36

neck and dragged him down the uneven passage, while he thrust back with four stiff legs and tried to bite her. He was flung into the kitchen, where the cat spat and clawed at him as a threat to keep away from her kittens, as he ran past her to the larder. Feeling a sudden keen interest in her life Jean returned to the lobby, and the three remaining dogs surrounded the strange spaniel, who threw a ringing bark and sprang up at his master.

'Good note, that,' said Jean. 'Coalie and Rig won't hurt him. Shut up, Jock, you grumpy little beast. Stop it, Scotty!'

She put her boot under the Aberdeen terrier's ribs and hurled him away. The guest laid down pack and staff on an oaken chest, and followed Jean into the dining-room.

'Come along in. Mother, Mr. Maddison has come to supper.' Mrs. Ogilvie saw a tall and thin young man in a worn tweed suit, who bowed to her and smiled from the door-way behind Jean, then came forward swiftly to shake her hand.

'How do you do, Mr. Maddison. I am so sorry we have begun supper, but Jean has only just let us know of your coming. You'll forgive us, I hope. Will you sit next to Miss Chychester? Benjamin, fetch a chair, please.'

Miss Chychester shook the visitor's hand twice before clasping it in both her hands and saying, 'Your hand is very cold, my dear. Have you no overcoat? You must let me give you some cod-liver oil!'

'Oh, I'm all right,' smiled the stranger, and Miss Chychester liked his face.

'Aunt Edith's deaf,' said Jean.

'Thank you very much,' he said in her ear, since she was waiting for an answer.

'Very well, I will,' said Miss Chychester. 'Mary has gone to get you a hot soup plate. You may sit beside me.'

Mr. Chychester, who had risen from his seat when the guest entered the room, then shook him by the hand. While he was giving Mrs. Ogilvie a reply to a question about his journey asked by Miss Chychester, Benjamin lifted a chair from against the wall and staggered with it towards the table. It was of black oak, with a carved straight back nearly as tall as Benjamin, and more than a score of times his age. It was for the guest to sit upon, which he did unexpectedly, Benjamin having thrust it forward so zealously that the front edge of the seat butted the backs of the guest's knees and he subsided as though hamstrung.

'Oo, I'm so sorry, sir,' said Benjamin in a husky mutter, and his round eyes peered at his aunt, to lose their strained dark look when the guest laughed at Jean, and Jean laughed at the guest. Mrs. Ogilvie smiled to see the young people, and Mr. Chychester said H'm and Ha! out of his beard.

'That is right. Sit down and draw up your chair,' said Miss Chychester.

'Hullo,' said Mary, coming into the room, smiling, a sudden colour in her cheeks. She shook the guest's hand, and sat down, silent, and the colour went, but not from her lips.

She did not look up until he had swallowed several spoonfuls of soup, and she noticed that the hand holding the spoon was not steady. Seeing this, her own nervousness fell off, and her natural colour returned. The three other women also noticed the unsteady hand, and Mrs. Ogilvie, to put him at ease, said:

'Would you like to warm yourself by the fire, Mr. Maddison? You must be dreadfully cold!' and Miss Chychester, hearing nothing, said definitely:

'Your hand is shaky. You have caught a chill. You must have some hot honey and lemon.'

'Thank you,' said Maddison, in her ear, 'but I don't think I've caught a chill. I'm always a bit nervous in a strange house. But you all look very nice, and so my hand won't shake for long.'

'It's really because he drinks, Aunt Edith,' shouted Jean. 'I saw him tottering out of the Prince of Wales' this afternoon, with a poet with a red beard.'

'Jean, do behave yourself,' begged Mrs. Ogilvie.

Maddison smiled with a quick turn of his head to Jean. The spoon was now steady. Jean examined him with friendly eyes. She liked his hands, his even teeth, the bright alert look in his brown eyes, his fresh cheeks – he was so different from the man she had seen strolling aimlessly on the quay that afternoon in the fading light. Hardly had he laid down the soup spoon when Benjamin nipped off his chair and took away his plate.

'That's very kind of you,' said Maddison. 'What's your name?'

'Benjamin Chychester, sir.'

Maddison held out a hand.

'For God's sake don't drop that plate!' yelled Jean, seeing that Ben was about to shift it to his left hand. 'Go on, shake hands.'

'Pleased to meet you,' said Benjamin nervously, and feeling tremendous gratitude to the gentleman.

'Pleased to meet you,' echoed Jean. 'How often has your Aunt Constance told you that only low-class trippers to Combe say "Pleased to meet you." You will please your Aunt so much if you will remember to say instead, "How do you do." Won't he, Mother?'

Mrs. Ogilvie smiled wanly, trying to hide her humiliation and her dread of what might follow. Long ago she had given up hope that her daughter Jean would behave and speak as a young lady when guests came to the house. She was grieved by her profanity and looseness of talk, and always endeavoured to ignore it, as she knew to her unhappy experience that Jean, seeing her distress, would probably behave more badly.

'Can you eat rabbit pie, Mr. Maddison? Or there is cold mutton.'

'Oh, anything, thanks.'

'But which would you prefer?'

'Oh – rabbit pie, please, Mrs. Ogilvie.'

Benjamin brought him salt, pepper, apple chutney, and
bread, and was thanked with a smile and a word for every
flitting visit, so that by the time he had delivered a plate of
pie and brought the dish of potatoes to the guest's left hand
his mind was in a flurry to think out how he could serve
further. With great care he poured out a glass of cider, during
which he remembered that his finger nails, or that part of
the nails no longer used for a livelihood of root-scratching,
were black. Dreading lest the guest see them, Benjamin sat
motionless in his chair, and hid his hands under the table.

Eight candles in the twin antler-like silver candlesticks lit
the faces round the table. Mrs. Ogilvie was watching the face
of the guest, and sometimes glancing at the faces of her
daughters. She was pleased. Something touched her hand,
and looking down she saw a spaniel squatting on its hind legs,
with head held up, and one paw resting on the leg of the table.
A swishing noise came from below, and peering into the
shadow she saw the stump of a tail moving rapidly. As she
looked at the spaniel it rose half an inch and gently touched
her hand with its free paw. The swishing increased. It was
hungry, and asking her for food, so nicely. Mrs. Ogilvie gave
it a crust of bread, which it took slowly and quietly from her
fingers, and chewed on the carpet, afterwards picking up the
crumbs it had dropped from the corners of its mouth.

'What a nice dog, Mr. Maddison.'

'Yes,' he replied, leaning down to pat the dog's head.

Mary stared at his profile, and became lost in thought,
until suddenly she started. Coffee! Surely she ought to have
thought of coffee, served in Aunt Edith's cups, when a guest
was coming. Yes, her mother would allow her to leave the
table, and she went into the kitchen. The Jacobean silver
coffee-pot was locked in the chest on the landing, so she used
the pewter pot belonging to the set on the dresser. Steam
was softly hissing out of the serpent-like spout of the iron
kettle; the coffee was in the cupboard. On the bottom of the

pewter pot was a black bog covered by mildew – another of her acts of forgetfulness. No matter, scald it out and scour it with sand, and no one would know.

When all was ready she bore the tray into the hall, where Maddison on his knees with the bellows was blowing the embers into a blaze. He arranged the iron firedogs and laid the brands across, and blew slowly until sparks and flames were cracking and flapping up the wide black chimney. The fireplace had been rebuilt of beautiful grey stone, brought from a quarry on the Youldstone property of Mrs. Ogilvie's grandfather, when she had married Charles Ogilvie near the end of the nineteenth century. It was the discovery of this stone in the arch of the hearth that had finally decided her Uncle Sufford to live at Wildernesse.

Mr. Chychester said, 'Ha, this is something like a fire' to himself, as he stretched out his legs to the blaze, and opened *The Morning Post*. He never read until the evening, when his day's work was done. Mrs. Ogilvie drew the curtains over the stone mullioned windows.

'Sugar and milk?' said Jean to Maddison, and waited.

'Sugar and or milk,' she repeated.

She looked at him, levering the wooden handle of the bellows. The flames lit his face, and every line and hollow was marked with shadow. He had not heard her. Mary waited with the lowered tray, Jean with the jug and basin, beside him. The bellows ceased to blow. Why does he look so sad, thought Jean, and what is he thinking?

'I say,' said Jean, not wanting to call him Mr. Maddison.

'You with the bellows! Hi! You! I say!'

She had to touch his hand. He started, turned to her, and said:

'Oh, I am so sorry. Were you speaking to me?' He coughed, and Miss Chychester leaned over importantly and said to Jean:

41

'He would prefer some cod-liver oil, perhaps. He has a cough.'

'What did you say? Is it your bedtime? Yes, it is!' shouted Jean.

'It is . . . ?' and the old lady made two shells of her hand and ear.

'It is your bedtime, Aunt Edith!'

Miss Chychester looked disappointed, and screwed up her eyes to see the positions of the grandfather-clock hands. Unable to see them, and assuming therefore that Jean could not see them, she declared:

'It is not my bedtime yet,' and patted the head of Billjohn. 'She is a nice dog,' stroking its ears. The other dogs were asleep before the fire.

'You make good coffee,' said Maddison abruptly, turning to look at Mary. 'There are inverted flames in each of your eyes.'

In her nervousness lest the effects of this unexpected remark show in her face, she picked up a poker, and thumped a brand.

Sparks flew up the chimney, the burning brands flung out their flamy cheer, and when all the cups were empty Mary collected them and took them into the kitchen. She returned, not to the fire, but to the dining-room, and seeing her with Benjamin beginning to clear away the supper things, Maddison jumped up and would have helped them, had not Mrs. Ogilvie and Mary and Jean insisted that he should return and warm himself by the fireside. He looked at Mary framed in the doorway, wanting to be with her and yet not wanting to be a nuisance, when she clutched her bosom, and a startled look came into her eyes. Something dark appeared on the flesh below the throat exposed by the V-shaped slit of her woollen jumper, and he saw the head of a bird thrust itself out. Before she could cage it in her hands it fluttered away over the floor, uttering ticking cries of angry fright.

'My frozen 'bin,' she said, in soft shame, facing her mother.

Her lids covered her eyes, and the firelight seemed to burn in her cheeks.

'I'll guard the fireplace!' said Maddison excitedly, 'you go slowly and take it in your hands! Don't let the dogs know!'

The robin fluttered about the dark panelled hall. They tried to catch it, helped by Miss Chychester, who did not know what was happening. Maddison stood before the hearth, ready to spring and catch it if it should flutter from the dogs, now awakened by the excitement, into the fire. Jean rated and beat them away, but Billjohn avoided her, and marking the bird in a corner seized it in his mouth, turned round, and began to walk with casual steps towards his master. Jean was holding Dave and Jock, and Benjamin was astride Coalie, while at a finger-lift Rigmarole the water-spaniel had crouched at Mr. Chychester's feet.

'You give that to me, my poor boy!' said Maddison, gently and persuasively. The dog let out a rolling growl of good humour, while steadily wagging his tail. This was obviously an old game they were playing. His master knelt on one knee, and waited while the dog walked round the table, turned to the left past a chair, returned towards the door, and finally, with tail in perpetual motion, laid it into his master's hand, safe and uninjured, but pecking in anger.

'I'd like to have that dog,' said Mr. Chychester, as Maddison and Benjamin followed Mary into the kitchen. She put the redbreast in a box with some scraps of ham, and hid it in a cupboard until the morning. Afterwards she said she must clear away, and they followed her down the passage into the dining-room, finding Miss Chychester under the table with a crumb pan. Mary explained that her aunt usually brushed up the crumbs after a meal, and folded up the tablecloth after the last meal of the day. The crumbs she saved in a match-box to be kept for her bird-tray outside the window.

Maddison carried the loaded tray into the scullery, where Mary said she would wash up in the morning. They returned to the hall, and sat by the fire. At nine o'clock Jean fetched a copper warming-pan and shovelled embers into it, while Miss Chychester watched her regretfully. Jean went upstairs with the warmer, which was put in the old lady's tester bed. While she was gone Miss Edith selected her own silver candlestick, of which the engraved crest of cormorant with eel had long since been rubbed away by use and cleaning. Maddison lit it for her; she took it with a slight curtsy, and stood at the foot of the stairs, by the dog-gates. When Jean came down she shook hands with every one, saying to each, I wish you a good night; then kissing the women, she stepped upstairs, waving a pale yellow hand to Maddison. Benjamin followed her, carrying a can of hot water. At the turn of the staircase she paused, and looking over the banisters, said:

'A piece of cheese rind in my crumb-box is for your dog. The ackymals are fond of cheese-rind, but your dog deserves a reward. She shall have it at breakfast to-morrow.'

'Dear old Edith,' said Jean. 'She's a proper li'l maid, and most obedient. So tidy. A model to all young girls to-day. Never smokes, swears, drinks, or wants to get her hair bobbed. Aoough!' She yawned.

Benjamin came downstairs, only to be sent up again by Mrs. Ogilvie, who said that he knew it was his bedtime. He said a reluctant good-night and went to his room in the attic, next to the frozen water-tank. When Mr. Chychester had gone to bed Maddison suddenly rose and said good-bye in a manner that puzzled her, it was so queer.

'I'm so glad I came to-night, Mrs. Ogilvie.

"A robin redbreast in a cage,
Puts all heaven in a rage,"

but what would Blake have written if he had seen Mary's robin to-night!' Seeing the expression of bewilderment on her face, he turned to Mary and, looking down at her upturned face, he said in a lowered voice:

'You know the legend of the robin, and the thorn in the broken brow – Mary, when I see a robin in future, I shall think of you, feeling shame before us, because a robin had flown from your merciful heart. Dear Mary, your sweet charity shines in the darkness of the world.'

Mrs. Ogilvie heard but fragments of what he said, and because he had lowered his voice before her, she frowned. Maddison, mistaking her frown for disapproval of what he had said, turned to her and said seriously, 'You know, William Blake, the poet who died about a hundred years ago! He was supposed to be mad, of course – the English always deprecate, or even destroy, their best minds. Blake wrote that lovely poem which was sung in so many schools during the war – "Jerusalem":

> I shall not cease from mental fight
> Nor shall my sword sleep in my hand
> Till we have built Jerusalem
> In England's green and pleasant land

which various head masters and mistresses thought was a perfect expression of England's war aims for the annihilation of the German people. What stupidity, what blasphemy! The "dark satanic mills" of Blake's earlier verse referred to the industrial system, which began the ruin of England: and which the financial power went to war to defend against continental industrial systems, first Napoleon, and then Germany! Poor Blake, a long watch he has been keeping! The lies that were told in the war, and are still being told, about the Germans! The humiliation of their Rhineland being occupied by the conquerors who knock off the hats of civilians who forget to raise their hats to French and Belgian officers! The *agents provocateurs* who arrange clashes between the rival political parties of resurgence in order to proclaim martial law! I have just been walking through Germany,' he went on, in a rapid nervous voice, amidst complete silence, 'and I know a little about it. It

45

is terrible to see how that proud and truthful nation is brought low. The poor little starving children – why, the starvation blockade was maintained until that revengeful treaty was signed at Versailles, eight months after the fighting ceased. Their bread was half sawdust. Scores of thousands of babies have died because of starvation.'

'It is retribution,' exclaimed Mrs. Ogilvie. 'Their defeat was the judgment of God! How can anyone think otherwise?' Her face was pale, her voice trembled.

Maddison hesitated. He too was pale. He took a deep breath. 'Good-bye,' he said. 'Thank you for welcoming me to your fireside,' he added, while standing before her uncertainly, and holding out his hands to the flames. 'I feel rather deeply about the war,' he said, in a low, trembling voice.

'You are not the only one,' said Mrs. Ogilvie.

'Because, you know, it will happen again if all people do not examine themselves and see the cause of war in their own un-understanding of their neighbours. We are all war-makers, unless we know and watch ourselves.'

'I would rather not discuss it, if you do not mind,' replied Mrs. Ogilvie, putting down her needlework. 'Well, perhaps if you are passing any time again, you will call in and see us? I am sure we shall all be pleased to see you.'

'Thank you,' he said, and shook hands with them, and walked to the chest on the far side of the hall, where his pack and staff were laid. Above the chest was a stuffed hawk in a convex glass wall-case, hanging by a leg, its wings half-spread. He examined it, as though intently and exclaimed, in an attempt to break the feeling of constraint in the room,

'I say, this sparrowhawk is well set-up, Mrs. Ogilvie.'

'My boy shot it when he was sixteen,' replied Mrs. Ogilvie quietly. 'He was most interested in birds. There were several uncommon species in the Burrows, and he shot at least two very rare birds just before the War – a Greenland falcon, and a bittern.'

'Are there still bitterns in the reeds of the duckponds? I heard one booming there four years ago.'

'I am not certain, but I don't think so, I have not heard of any. Are you interested in birds, Mr. Maddison?'

'Oh yes! Once I stuffed a plover, and took it to school with me to present to a dear old man we most shamefully ragged and called Useless, who used to take us for field rambles, and whom most of us, chiefly my disgraceful self, used to rag with fool-questions, and spurious observations, such as, "Oh, sir, I have just observed a fine specimen of what I identify as a knuckle-toed bumblefinch pursuing its insect prey!" ' Why am I talking this nonsense, he thought in agitation as he picked up his hat. Mrs. Ogilvie, whose faint dislike had gone when the queer young man had resumed a less unusual conversational manner, suggested, as she had intended to do before, that the journey to Breakspears St. Flammea would be rather a long and cold one, and if he cared to stay the night, they would be most happy to put him up. He hesitated again, and Jean, who was examining his staff said:

'Of course he'll stay! And so will his poor boy. And I've left the warming pan in Aunt Edith's room. Bloody nui –' She put her hand to her mouth, and laughed at Maddison. 'I'll go up and get it!' She leapt up the wide stairs three at a time, and Mrs. Ogilvie went to the kitchen to heat her nightly glass of milk. Mary remained in the hall with the guest, holding his staff, and watching him as he rubbed away icy trees and ferns on the window pane, trying, he said, to see Orion.

"Would you rather go back to your cottage?' she asked him quickly, in a low voice, and he turned to see her dark eyes upon him.

'No, I would rather be here with you,' he said, kneeling to read the titles of books on shelves along the wall. It was too dark to see, and Mary said, 'Let me fetch the lamp.'

'No, I really don't want to read, thanks. I prefer the dim light.'

47

He went to another window, turned away from it, examined the sparrowhawk, whose body in life had stopped upon lesser birds in the very way it was hung there.

'Where is the bittern?'

'On the landing. I'll show you as we go up. Would you like some hot milk? I could get you some in a moment and it wouldn't be the smallest trouble.'

'No, thanks.'

She thought how much older he looked than when last she had met him; she had seen by the firelight many grey hairs in his dark head. And he was only twenty-five years old.

There was silence for half a minute, and then the grandfather clock struck eleven times.

'It's been like that since before Christmas,' said Mary. 'I really must adjust it.' Then she said, 'I saw the Great Nebula in Orion, for the first time to-night.'

'So did I!'

'I love the Dog-star best of all stars,' said Mary, her lips moving with the beginnings of many smiles – 'except the Morning Star.'

'I've seen her for many mornings, as I started out – "a white-gold ball of fire".'

'That's Richard Jefferies!'

'Yes. Have you read Jefferies?'

'Oh, yes. Why, I've read "Bevis" scores of times!'

'You have? How wonderful! Mary, why didn't I know it before? I've known you for years, since you were a little thing in sticking-out short skirts, and I never knew you had read Jefferies! You know, that man is not appreciated even by those who read him. A voice crying in the industrial wilderness of the nineteenth century.'

'I know what you mean by appreciation. Uncle Sufford reads Jefferies – he doesn't care for the real Jefferies, what I call the green corn spirit – he likes the matter-of-fact books, like the Southern County, and the Gamekeeper. He thinks the Story of my Heart isn't quite commonsense, somehow.'

'I say, do you remember the chapter in "Bevis" on the stars – called "Bevis' Zodiac"? I was thinking of it to-night when I was walking along the sea-wall.'

'That must have been about the time I was thinking of it!'

'And did you hear the stray cries of the curlews suddenly increase to a myriad trillings and bubblings, as though the water-shaken gleams of stars were uprising in melody? I heard swans trumpeting, and geese honking overhead as I walked up your drive.'

'Then they have come down from the north! O Willie, I do hope I shall see them. Uncle Suff will love to know it. But his love of wildfowl lies side by side with a love of shooting them. It's beastly of me to put it like that – Uncle Suff really likes birds – and I suppose we must eat.'

'I understand, Mary,' said Maddison. 'Your doubt and reproach are of the spirit; your judgment of the brain. The spirit is unworldly, the brain of the earth.'

'I wish people wouldn't shoot birds, to put them in glass cases. We've got a great bustard upstairs, shot by my grandfather in 1870, one of a flock of eight that flew here in another hard winter. Boys sliding on the Ram's-horn duckpond thought they were wild turkeys, and flung stones at them; and the whole parish went out after them with guns.'

By the stuffed sparrowhawk in the circular wall-case they stood talking with animation, a foot apart, glancing at each other's eyes made full and deep by their talk in the duskiness of the hall. Jean, coming downstairs with the ember-pan, saw her sister leaning back with her hands holding the holly staff behind her, and swaying. Maddison stood with his hands high on his ribs – she had wondered why his coat was worn threadbare there – over six feet tall, and talking rapidly. He seemed a different man – so good-looking! Mary turned and said to her:

'Was Aunt Edith asleep?'

'No, she said she had forgotten to give you some cod-liver

oil,' replied Jean, coming to Maddison and standing before him. Looking into his face, she said:

'I am ordered to give you a spoonful! So I am afraid you will have to have it.'

'Yes, I'll have it, rather!'

'I'll go and get a spoon,' said Mary.

'Don't bother, I'm going to the kitchen to get some embers off the fire. And I must go and make up your bed,' and leaving the bottle on the table, Jean went away.

'I like Jean,' said Maddison.

'She's sweet,' replied Mary. 'What a pity you didn't come last night, for you would have seen Pam and Ronnie. They went back to school this morning. I say!'

'Yes?'

'Are you going to be long in Devon?'

'I don't know. I go anywhere, at any time, and as long as I can be in the English country, I am happy.'

She ceased to sway on the staff. 'I'm glad you are happy,' she said, and immediately regretted saying it, lest he might think she was remembering the sad happenings when last she had been with him. 'Here's Mother.'

Mrs. Ogilvie returned to the hall with two glasses of milk on a tray, and saw the animation in his face.

'It did not occur to me that you might like hot milk, Mr. Maddison,' she smiled, 'but you will have a peg of whisky and soda, won't you? Mary dear, you know where the decanter and tumblers are kept.' She took a key out of her desk, and gave it to her daughter.

'Thank you,' said Maddison, 'but I believe Jean is about to give me some cod-liver oil!' Jean, having filled the warming pan, had returned again.

'I shouldn't take Aunt Edith's instructions too seriously, Mr. Maddison. You'd like a peg, wouldn't you?'

'No, thanks, Mrs. Ogilvie. I rarely drink anything except water!'

'Really?'

'Yes, thank you so much.'

'A lot of politeness flying about to-night,' remarked Jean, vaulting over the dog-gates. 'Now then, open your mouth like a good little boy, for I warn you that I am used to physicing dogs, and if you aren't good I shall have to hold your nose and stroke your throat. You've got a nasty 'acking cough, my lad.'

'See what I have for a daughter,' smiled Mrs. Ogilvie.

Yes, the dogs were indoors and the larder door shut, Mary assured her mother, after a few minutes' talk. The tiny lamp on the table was put out; the hunting prints on the wall above the staircase were illumined by four candles, one after the other; men, horses, hounds, fences, trees, fields, and foxes, faded out; and at the turn of the stairs a big bird with yellow-brown plumage, and tall varnished legs and sharp beak, and a glistening eye, stood motionless amid grasses and rushes behind glass. Gilt lettering below told that it was a bittern, and when and where shot. On the wall above the ledge whereon it stood was another case, inhabited by a still grey hawk-like bird. Gilt lettering named it a marsh harrier. Further up was a third bird, with white plumage and great eyes and talons. A snowy owl. Higher still a pair of peregrine falcons, a rough-legged buzzard, a grey shrike, and a red-necked phalarope, some of the rare visitors to the Santon Burrows shot by Michael.

And on the landing above, hung against the black oak panels, a portrait in oils of Michael himself, wearing the service uniform of an ensign of Foot Guards. Below on the gilt wood frame in black letters:– Second-Lieutenant Michael Sufford Pomfret Ogilvie, Scots Guard, killed in action before the Hohenzollern Redoubt, 27 September 1915, aged 19 years. 'Florcat Etona.'

Chapter 3

THE guest was shown his room by Mrs. Ogilvie, who, after saying that she hoped he would find all that he wanted, bade him good night and departed. A four-posted bed with a canopy of frayed red silk hanging over it stood massive and gloomy and still against one wall. The top bedding was folded back on the coverlet, and a wooden handle stuck out diagonally from the sheets. While he was trying to unhasp the casement window the spaniel whined and scratched on the door, and apparently gave it a soft double knock. He opened it, and Mary stood there, with the spaniel.

'Your poor boy wants to come in. And here's a sleeping-suit,' she whispered, and was gone.

He saw the initials M.S.P.O. sewn on the inside of the collar, and was wondering why the garments were so warm, when a tattoo of raps sounded on the panel with a voice saying, Bang-titty-bang-bang, Bang! Bang! Again he opened the door. Jean stood there.

'I've brought you a pair of pyjamas in case you haven't got any. I pinched them from Uncle Suff, but he won't mind.'

'Mary's just brought me some, thank you, Jean.'

'Oh, that's all right then. Sorry if I disturbed you.'

'You didn't. Thanks. More politeness flying about.'

'Oh, shut up! I'm sorry, I didn't mean to be rude.'

'All right. Don't get frightened just because my speech doesn't drip with bloodies. It often does. But not when I'm with one so charming as you.'

'Oh, shut up.'

'I mean it –'

But Jean had gone.

He opened the casement wide, and looked out into the night. Over the distant moor the moon was rising, wasted and pockmarked and dead, bright with the rays of a dwarf-yellow star which it reflected to the earth. Above the moon the Dogstar glittered in spiky colours. He could hear a multitude of crying birds in the estuary, and sometimes the whistle of pinions that had cast a flight-quill, and the distant honking of geese. The tide was flowing fast in the estuary, carving and sharpening the sandbanks and gravel ridges, travelling inland with its grating broken plates of ice. No longer were the star-points for the curlews' songs. Thousands of gulls were speaking as they paddled the froth of wavelet lap, clamorous and harsh and overlaying the bubble-linked sweetness of the gentler wading birds. From the sky over the house came a deep *krark!* and he peered into moonshine for the wide vanes of a heron. *Krark!* as the unseen fisher flew on.

'Christ, it's cold!' he shivered, and his breath hung in the cold air. He stooped to pick up his pack, part of a British infantry soldier's field equipment. Unfastening the leather straps of the khaki web flap, he took out a razor, a toothbrush, a comb, and a piece of soap, wrapped in a towel. Underneath were three books, two of them being printed, and the other of plain foolscap sheets, bound and covered with strawboards. Many pages were filled with small writing, scored and corrected and revised. He opened one, and read:

'There was a shining in the alcove to-night, for the Three Wise Spirits of the Earth were there. They were looking at something, and they were talking in the symbolic speech of Beyond, which being rendered with the sounds of the human tongue would be like this:

' "I saw the White Lady arise from out the Morning Star, and tread the sky-steps to the earth," said the Quill Spirit, "and I came immediately to the castle, to pay homage to the

53

Star-born. How proud and joyful I am that one of my birds has been chosen!"

' "I too saw the White Lady," said the Leaf Spirit, "and I came up the ivy, bringing brake-fern for a warm bed, and vernal grass with wildflowers for sweet breathing. These are my gifts to the Star-born."

' "Wanhope, who is strangely excited," said the Water Spirit, "came to me in the gorge with the tidings that once again the star hung in the east like a silver May-fly trailing its beams in the stream of heaven. He told also of Huquol the Shadow, whom we all dread, who had come from the darkness of ruined suns to harm the Star-born! But one mightier than Huquol the Shadow was here, a messenger of the All, and we were safe. For my gift I bring a sun-bow for the Star-born to play with; it lives in a crack in the rock by Skait's Hole, coming out in the sunlight and quivering in the spray."

' "I know it well," breathed the Leaf Spirit. "It is shaped like one of my ferns, but coloured."

' "Your ferns are shaped after my sun-bow," replied the Water Spirit. "You forget I was old before you were young." '

'It's awful,' he groaned, throwing down the manuscript, and sitting down to take off his boots. A pity to use the pyjamas for one night; it would only add to the work of washing, and it was much warmer between blankets in one's clothes.

'Warmer than that haystack last night,' he said, when in bed, and from the floor came a series of dull beats, as of a drum. 'You won't get frostbite to-night, Billjohn.' More thumps of the spaniel's tail on the pan.

The red fragment of the wick smouldered out; the shine of the moon brightened in the open window. He listened to the wildfowl, distinguishing between the flight of mallard and widgeon and teal, the hound-like baying of white-fronted geese and the honking of the solans; and as he was falling asleep a flat report followed by a rush of wings and flatter

echoes made the spaniel throw up its head and growl. Flock
after flock passed over the house, with varying cries and wing-
sounds. The report he knew to be that of a big-bore gun
fired probably from a boat, and he thought how, years ago,
he had hoped to own such a gun 'when he was big,' and pass
every night stalking the feeding flocks. How far-away and
unreal seemed those boyhood days! For an hour he turned
restlessly, pondering many things, often speaking aloud,
sometimes his eyes wet with the emotion of his peculiar ideas;
and when he awakened out of a dreamless sleep the spaniel
was curled against his neck, having crept there off the cold
copper pan eight hours previously.

Hearing footfalls in the passage outside, the spaniel cocked
its ears and growled. Something by the door was taking in a
deep breath and blowing it out of nostrils with a considerable hissing sound. Maddison got out of bed and opened the
door, and Coalie the old cocker spaniel walked in, climbed
leg by leg on to the bed, and settled to sleep in the warm
blankets.

'Let's hope he's not very lousy,' remarked Maddison to his
spaniel. He broke the ice in the ewer, and shaved and washed
and dressed. Afterwards he went downstairs, carrying his
frozen boots in his hands. The grandfather clock faintly
groaned between each *tick* and *tock*: it was half-past seven.
No one was in the hall, and he looked round the walls, at the
pates of otters and masks of foxes mounted on small wooden
shields, examining the place and date of each kill painted
under them in white letters. Over one mask, that of an ancient
dog-fox with long canines, hung several thonged hunting
whips, some old and battered and long of handle, some shorter
and stouter in the modern pattern, others small, with cane
handles, and probably belonging to Ronnie and Pam. Above,
nearer the raftered ceiling, heads of red deer, consisting of
antlers and part of the skull, were spaced around the walls.
A carved oaken boy bore on his back the Royal Arms, and a

55

small Union Jack was fixed below the figure's feet. Sixteen leather fire buckets with the Bassett coat armour in paint and varnish faded upon them, were hung in a row on another wall.

In a corner near the sparrowhawk leaned a Lochaber axe on its long handle, a broadsword, and a targe or circular shield of wood and leather decorated with brass studs and having an iron handle. In the opposite corner, behind a table bearing an Indian brass tray on which scores of dusty visiting cards were scattered, stood a suit of armour and a lance.

He sat on the floor, examining the names and titles of books. There were sets of Dickens and Scott, of Thackeray, Surtees, and Trollope. There were slimmer volumes of Kipling and books by Rider Haggard, and rows of novels by Mrs. Henry Wood, William Black, and Ouida. In another shelf were books on Natural History, including a rare and early edition of Sowerby's *Wild Flowers*, and the volumes of Morris' *British Birds*. Near a gramophone, and a pile of records, most of them worn and chipped, were rows of children's books, and editions of *Peter Pan*, *A Midsummer Night's Dream*, and Hawthorne's *Wonder Book*, illustrated by Arthur Rackham; and a miscellany of cheap editions of novels by W. J. Locke, Ian Hay, Archibald Marshall, Mrs. Humphry Ward, Beatrice Chase, John Oxenham, and other authors.

'Punk!' he said, and rising, began to jump up and down to warm his icy toes. While he was doing this a door at the other end of the hall opened, and Mary looked at him. Picking up his boots he ran over the carpet to her, and saw that her hair hung in a plait down her back. She wore a dirty apron, and her hands and forearms were black. She said she had not expected to see him there, and that she had been cleaning the bodley. He replied that when Coalie, after a steady blowing under the door, had forced him to get out of bed, and had taken possession, he had imagined that it was acting under instructions from herself.

56

'The naughty boy,' said Mary. 'He gets into any warm bed he can, and comes down only when he smells the breakfast.'

'Look here, let me light the kitchen fire for you,' he said, creeping behind her along the passage.

'I've done it, thanks. Your socks want mending. And you will get cold feet if you walk about like that.'

'I've got them already.'

The kitchen bodley was roaring.

'You'd better put on your boots.'

'I think I'll thaw them first. Oh, it doesn't matter.'

He sat on the floor and pulled on a boot.

'Don't,' said Mary, 'I will fetch you some slippers from upstairs. You'll get chilblains.'

'I don't care. I'm going to help you sweep.'

'You're not to put on those boots. Wait there a minute.'

'Really, don't bother.'

She took away one boot, put it on the range above the stove, and held out her hand for the other.

'You give it to me, my poor boy,' said Mary, imitating his voice of the night before, and smiling above him. She leaned down to take the boot, and her plait fell against his cheek. He held it there, tugging it gently, and saying it was lovely hair.

'Child,' said Mary, with reddening cheeks held away from his gaze, 'let go, I must get on with my work. Really. No, no, don't. Honestly! Mad Willie, stop it!'

He was pleased that she had called him by his school nickname.

'Give me back my boot, then. I'm going to wash up for you.'

She cried out, 'Goodness, you are sitting on a stone floor. Get up immediately! Why, you need as much looking after as Benjamin!'

She darted away for the slippers, returning with a pair discarded by Mr. Chychester.

He slouched around and got a broom, and began to sweep the floor, while Mary went outside into a gold-frosty light and fetched wood for the fire in the breakfast-room. She said as she passed him that it should have been dried last night, but she had forgotten again.

When the kettle boiled he carried it to the sink, and poured the water over the spoons and forks which she had put in a chipped enamel bowl. As the scalding stream splashed over the silver she dropped into the bowl a piece of washing soap, which became soft and jellied. He ladled it out and said she was a wasteful girl, that the proper way was to slice off a corner with a knife – so. She was pleased by the little economy, and wondered, as he dropped hot forks and spoons on the table under the plate rack, where he had learned it. As though her thought had been spoken, he replied that he had watched his old nurse Biddy paring off hundreds of slices.

'She kept the soap in a scallop shell, like the one here,' he said, and taking it, held it on his head. 'That was one of my tricks as a kid. I used to pretend, and at first I believed she was taken in by it, that it was a third ear. "Be it now," she would reply, until one day I declared that God had given me an extra ear to hear Him with, and she was so shocked at what she considered my blasphemy that she punished me by hiding Ung, my lovely companion, my self-made oddmedodd, for a whole day. To this day I remember how utterly miserable I was without Ung. You know, Mary, people never really mean to be unkind to children, or to each other; it is because they do not realize how suffering has degrees of intensity.'

' "Children's griefs are little, certainly; but so is the child, so is its endurance, so is its field of vision, while its nervous impressionability is keener than ours," ' she quoted.

'That's Francis Thompson writing of Shelley – and himself! Have *you* read Thompson?'

' . . . of course I have. Have *you* read Thompson?'

They laughed.

'A beautiful writer. Aow, this water's hot! I think I'll put in some cold.'

He drew down the iron handle, it whined, and slid easily. No water spouted.

'It's lost its fang. There's ice on the washer. Just a minute,' said Mary, 'I'll pour in some hot.'

The pump made a noise, between a sigh and a whistle, which changed to a hollow whisper sounding to him like *Oi! Woo her! – Oi, woo her!* The pump's voice was drowned in a chuckle of rising water. As the lead spout gushed he said, 'This pump is a wise old fellow. And I'm not "an icicle, whose thawing is its dying." '

'I don't know that quotation.'

Her cheeks burned again as she polished the soup-ladle bowl, and he thought, She's got a quick mind.

'I'm not getting on with the job fast enough,' he said dryly. 'I can see your cheeks positively burning with impatience.'

She smiled, and said he was getting on famously. With a cotton mop he washed the fork prongs, seeing that each prong was clear and bright, and bowls of spoons, back and front; and when the turn of the knives came, he knew that bone handles must not be put in hot water. Afterwards came the small plates, and the coffee cups; and then the dinner plates, which were not dried by cloths, but put in the rack to drain and drip.

' Wait, I must rinse them first under the pump.'

'I never bother,' said Mary. 'There isn't time, usually.'

'I know my job.'

'You know mine also,' she murmured. 'I must go and light the fire in the breakfast-room.'

'Leave it to me. I've nearly finished. Only got one more plate to rinse and a pudding dish to scrape – here, my poor boy, lick it clean,' and the waiting spaniel immediately licked.

While he cleared the ashes in the hall fire – ruddy of pine

driftwood, grey of oak, and white of elm – and laid a faggot fire, she made the morning tea, and took up four cups and dry biscuits to the lie-a-beds. Flames were arising in the hearth when she came down, and they had tea together, sitting on a stool in the ingle-nook. Afterwards, four cans of hot water, two of which he carried as far as the landing. Porridge was put on, and with pan and broom and brush, she set to work on the stairs. He insisted on helping, and this being done, just as the clock was striking nine, she flung off her apron and departed to wash before cooking the breakfast.

'You can make some toast if you like. Don't cut it too thick. Bread's in the larder.'

When she came down ten minutes later to fry bacon and tettie-cakes – as she called the flat cakes of mashed potato remaining from supper – he thought how lustrous was the dark hair hiding the ears under the plaited coils, how warm and child-like the line of cheek and neck. The feeling of companionship, of security, the heat of the fire on his legs, the look of the pure and steady eyes, filled his heart with joy, and he stroked the small smooth head, saying, 'Nice Mary, clever little Mary, compassionate little maid Mary. How nice her hair looks this way!' She would not look at him. He went on stroking the head, and hearing his tender voice the spaniel got out of the broken chair and stood on its hind legs to share the affection. Maddison scratched its ears with his other hand, and smiled to himself above her bended head.

'How's the 'bin, Mary?'

'I was wondering if you had forgotten him.'

'No, I hadn't. But I have been thinking of you.'

'The 'bin scolded me when I woke him up, and put him on the window sill with some food, and left him there. He ate it up, and flew away. Now he must look after himself.'

He thought of the journey with his dog after breakfast, and was silent. Mary said:

'Has anyone been in your cottage since you left it all those years ago?'

'I don't know. I sent a year's rent every Ladyday – thirty shillings – to Gammon, at the Nightcrow Inn.'

'But what about your blankets? And your mattress?'

'I had no mattress, and now I am justified in that economy, for it is not damp!'

'You'll probably have to get new blankets.'

'The old ones will do for me.'

Benjamin came into the kitchen, looking astonished and pleased.

'Morning, Benjamin Chychester.'

'G' morning, Mr. Maddison.'

'My name's William to you.'

'Er'r,' grinned Benjamin.

'Glad to be going to school, Benjamin?'

'Yes, thank you.'

'What, when you might be going skating or tobogganing?'

'Ooh, I'd rather do that, of course,' grinned the boy.

'Of course you would. Do they still teach you Euclid?'

'Yes, only they call it Geometry now.'

'Well, one day it'll have no name, and a good thing too, as far as children are concerned. "The sun, the wind, the trees, all these were bright: God said, Let Euclid be, and all was blight." That's a cheap imitation of Pope's epigram,' he said, turning to Mary, 'and may only indicate that I haven't a mathematical mind, thank God.'

'I hate Geometry,' confessed Benjamin.

'And do you hate all your lessons?'

'Only some of the learning part, like Algebra and Latin and History and Geography and Shakespeare. I like Woodwork. But I like being with the chaps.'

'Ah, that's the only part of school that's good,' said Maddison, remembering his own schooldays.

'Homework's too much,' said Mary, frowning.

'Of course it is! Do you know, my old Headmaster – I was a day boy at Colham School – used to trust to the honour of senior boys to do nearly three hours' homework every night. From nine in the morning until three minutes to eleven: from eleven until twenty-three minutes past twelve: from two until a quarter to five: then two and three-quarter hours in the evening! Now supposing he had trusted to our honour to swallow two and three-quarter pints of diluted carbolic acid every night, then every one, seeing the physical revulsion and distress, would see the wisdom of ignoring such an unnatural practice! Whereas the injury to the mind, sterilizing the delicate high imaginative tissues by two and three-quarter hours of mental carbolic acid, is scarcely realized!'

Mary was surprised at the way his voice and manner had changed, and into her mind came a picture of the Vicar declaiming before her mother the truth and justification of his high-church ritual. She realized what she had not done before, how deeply Mr. Garside must feel about it.

'I met my old Headmaster in London the other day. It was an ordeal. The old nervousness came upon me, and I was unable to say anything that I wanted to say. I remembered his iceberg look, "Deceitful fellow, sir, be careful, sir! You will have to leave this school if you are not careful, sir! Your standard of honour should be raised, sir," but he was gentle and charming, so unlike the Old Bird I knew as a boy. Now that man has a keen intellect, a mathematical mind, and he is saturated in Latin and Greek epics, and in our major poets. Their thought is his thought, he thinks. But in reality he is a slayer of minds! His vision is not sane. He does not realize that a great oak was first a folded green hook pushing from a crack in an acorn, and then three frail roodets below in its natural soil, and for years a thing of smallness, easily broken or twisted. He was very attentive and receptive to my feeblest remarks, but I could not say what I wanted to say. My mind was in an agony of incoherence. . . . I suppose it was the effect of the early environment . . . Damn and blast their stupidity!' he cried, beginning to pace the stone flags of the kitchen floor. 'If I had not fortified myself in isolation to follow Truth to the end, through every un-understanding and indifference and even hate, I should despair!'

Benjamin stared at him, one boot on a foot and another in his hand. Maddison stopped, and said:

'But perhaps I ought not to talk like that before you. Personal feelings should not be thrust on others,' and resumed his pacing.

Mary stood still by the stove, and looked at him with grave eyes. Again she thought of Mr. Garside: he had just the same way of taking things to heart, only they were different. She felt uneasy, and then unhappy.

'Do you think I'm merely ranting?' he asked, with an unsure smile.

She did not know how to express what she thought, or indeed what she did think: she looked on the floor, thinking of his haggard face.

'No, I don't; but –'

He waited.

'But?'

She made no reply.

'But . . .' he repeated to himself. 'Yes, that "but" is the world.'

He opened the door and went out into the yard.

Just before half-past eight Mrs. Ogilvie and Mr. Chychester came downstairs, and they went in to breakfast.

'Didn't I hear Mr. Maddison talking to you in the kitchen?' asked Mrs. Ogilvie, glancing as the vacant place.

'Yes,' replied Mary. 'I expect he'll be here in a minute,' and they began the meal.

The breakfast was like the supper, except that Miss Chychester was not present, and Benjamin did not hand round plates. The boy sat still as a water vole, to which indeed he had some resemblance, as after porridge and bacon he nibbled his bread and margarine out of a paw-like hand, his cropped brown head and collared shoulders held very still, yet taking quick glances at the faces of anyone who spoke. Immediately he had finished Mrs. Ogilvie said, You may leave, Benjamin, and the boy put paws together, sunk head nearer the starched linen collar (one that Michael had worn years before), fluttered his eyelids, and mumbled the words of Grace.

In the kitchen he strapped on a pair of leather leggings (an old pair of Jean's thrown at him for a birthday present) around his thin legs, and put on an overcoat. Mary ran out to cut him some lunch, making sandwiches of bread and butter and meat, and others of cheese and –

'Put some chutney in,' begged Benjamin. 'Oh, let me have some chutney.'

'You shall, Ben, you shall!'

'And a bigger bit'r cake to-day.'

'You can't say I gave you a small bit yesterday, Bennie!'

'Oh, make it a bit bigger,' he pleaded.

A very large slice was wrapped in a bag – Mary 'saved' all bags, smoothed and folded, in a drawer in the dresser – with a segment of treacle tart.

'There, you won't be hungry when you get that inside you.' She wound his muffler round his neck, and buttoned up his coat. On his fingers he pulled gloves, with holes between thumbs and forefingers, and picked up the satchel.

'Good-bye, Mary.'

'Good-bye. Be careful of sideslips.'

'Poof, I don't worry. Will Mr. Maddison be here when I come back?'

'I don't know. Now hurry, or you'll be late.'

Benjamin's face looked happy as he came out of the wood-shed, dragging his bicycle, an arrangement of rusty iron piping, enamelled black in patches, and connected with two wheels. This bicycle had belonged originally to Mr. Ogilvie, afterwards to Michael, and when it had been discarded by Michael, Mary, and Jean in turn, the younger children had learnt to ride upon it. It had been abandoned altogether until Benjamin came to live at Wildernesse, and had annexed it, calling it Trusty; although Jean had suggested that a better name would have been Rusty.

Mounting Trusty from a pedal like the jaws of a rabbit gin, Benjamin sat upon the decayed saddle, and with the remaining half of the only mudguard rattling over the buckled back wheel, disappeared through the yard gate on the two-mile ride to his school.

Mary went into the wood-shed, seeing Maddison sitting on the chopping block, with a pile of kindling chopped beside him.

'Breakfast?' she said. 'Aren't you coming?'

'I don't want any, thanks,' he replied, avoiding her eyes. 'But I'll help you wash up afterwards if I may. Now you go back, before your bacon gets cold.'

She waited a moment; but as he began chopping wood again she returned to the breakfast-room, where Billjohn the spaniel was being fed by Uncle Suff with bacon rind. Afterwards it was solemnly presented with a piece of cheese rind by Miss Chychester, as 'a reward for her humanity towards the robin the night before.'

Maddison came into the scullery afterwards and washed up, while Mary dried the spoons and knives. Again from the pump a hollow and water-rising whisper of *Oi! Woo her, Oi! Woo her*, and he asked her if she usually washed up alone.

'Jean sometimes helps, but she's got the dogs and The Buccaneer, her hunter, to look after.'

'Nobody helps you in the house?'

'Oh yes, I don't do it all. Mother does most of the upstairs rooms, but she's got her own political and other work to do.'

'You usually wash and dry the plates alone?'

'Yes. Why?'

65

'Oh, I thought you must have been alone.'

'Why?' asked Mary, averting her eyes.

'Because if you weren't alone, some one surely would have acted before on the advice of the pump.'

'Howard helps me sometimes,' she murmured, and her cheeks burned red. He went on with the swilling of the porridge plates. Afterwards he scrubbed the sink with soap and wood-ashes, removing all grease from the glazed earthenware, and restoring its primrose colour. He polished the brass taps, and scoured the enamel bowl, and washed out the dish-cloth. Then the kitchen table was scrubbed, and the scuttle filled with coal. He shook the mat, and was only restrained from scrubbing the floor of the scullery by being told that a film of ice would form on the stone.

'I see. Now I must pack up and go on my way. Where's your Mother?'

With an abstracted look in her eyes, she said slowly, 'I expect she's upstairs doing the bedrooms.' And as though she had just realized that he was about to go, she exclaimed:

'I'll tell her,' and he followed her into the hall, where before the fire, Mr. Chychester was standing, hands in pockets and a short pipe sticking out of his bearded face. Jean was coming down the stairs, and seeing Maddison, she said that she was going into the village to fetch the newspapers and the post, and would he like to go with her?

The dogs heard, and their eyes brightened; Rigmarole threw up his head and let out a cooing howl, which was an expression of his overwelling happiness. Jock rolled, Coalie panted, Billjohn pranced, Dave greeted a table leg like an old friend.

'Here, get out,' muttered Mr. Chychester. 'Confound the dogs.'

'Yes, I'd like to come,' said Maddison. 'I must put my boots on first.'

'Right-ho. Ready in five minutes?'

When they were ready, Jean in a thick grey tweed coat and skirt and Maddison with his holly staff, Mrs. Ogilvie came down the stairs and looked at them.

'Jean, you ought to wear a coat, my dear. And Mr. Maddison – won't you be cold?'

'Cold? I shan't be cold!' exclaimed Jean. 'Nor will our Will. Will you, Will?'

'No. I'm hardened.'

'You young people . . .' said Mrs. Ogilvie.

Miss Chychester came over to Maddison, moving like a black pawn off a chess-board, and said distinctly, 'You are not going away, I hope? Because I have not yet shown you my bird-table. A nuthatch came this morning, and took the ackymal's nuts.'

'No, he's not going. He's staying here for a year,' shouted Jean.

'Staying yurr? How nice!' and Miss Chychester looked pleased at her own lapse into dialect. 'Then I shall have time to show you my book of pressed flowers and grasses.'

'Ready?' said Jean to Maddison. 'Come on, dogs!' pulling her hunting whip from its rest on the fox's mask. 'Good-bye, chaps.'

He followed Jean out into the snow-light. After the blizzard Benjamin and Mr. Chychester had shovelled and swept the mossy drive; the stained heaps of snow were piled on its borders. Maddison had not seen the house before in daylight. It was built of grey limestone, and the two wings built on to the original farm-house gave it a look of trying to huddle from the south-west winds which sometimes swept unceasing for days over the Burrows. The thatch was doubled with dazzling snow, out of which reared the square smoke-blackened chimney tuns, each covered-in with a flake of shale to break the down-draughts. Ferns grew out of the mortar between the stones.

They walked down the drive. The trees surrounding the

house and gardens were shorn by the winds of years, only their branches stretching north-east, away from the Atlantic gales, remaining. They had the appearance of being bent inland. The leafless branches were crooked and gnarled under the burdens of drifted snow. Snow lay on the bars of the gate: the sleet had sought out every crack and cranny of the gate-posts, which were old ship's-timbers. In a trenail hole, half filled by rusty flakes of an iron pin, lay a frozen mouse; Maddison's eye saw it instantly, but he did not stop to look at it, nor did he speak of it.

Jean asked him if he would mind walking to the village over the fields, or would he prefer the sea-wall? He preferred the fields. They began to run at a slow pace to keep warm. The dogs made circles round them, barking before dashing away to hunt rabbits. Tracks of feet wandered over the snow, feet of animals and men, one half in shadow cast by the sun climbing its low arc over the south-eastern hills across the unseen river. They clambered over stone walls and frozen dykes, passing cattle shippens – low stone and cob sheds, with one side open, their roofs supported by two rounded stone pillars, their floors rugged with frozen mire. Bullocks, herding round the sheds, pushed into each other and blew through nostrils in fear of the dogs as they passed. In a gateway at the far end of one field a man with a horse and butt was bringing linseed cake and turnips for the hungry animals. Jean waved to him, and called out, 'Hullo, Jack, how be getting on, boy?' He called back some answer, and stared at them after they had passed.

'Don't turn round. He's wondering who you are,' said Jean, with satisfaction. 'Well, let him wonder.'

They crossed another dyke, and went through a clump of willows and hawthorns, which grew by a tarred wooden barn covered by a rotting thatch.

'Old Farmer Bissett, Jack's father, who lives at Burrow Farm, says he's really a Bassett – Daddy's mother was a

Bassett – and ought by rights to own all this,' said Jean, pointing to the Burrows.

'I expect he is a Basset – on the wrong side of the blanket. One of several thousand, if this county is like my own, where Maddisons, Maddsons, Middlesons, and Massons swarm. I don't know what side of what blanket our little branch came from, and I don't care.'

'Nor do I about mine,' said Jean, sincere for the moment. 'I say, I want to tell you! Something strange happened to me here.'

She hesitated.

'Well, what is it, midear?'

Jean stared at the ground, then suddenly struck her legs with the handle of her whip. She hurt herself, and groaned through set teeth. 'O my God, I am a damned fool. I start to tell you a trivial and idiotic thing, and then make a fool of myself . . . I hate and loathe myself!' and giving a yelling cheer to the dogs, she ran swiftly ahead, cracking the lash, until she slipped in the snow.

'Don't listen to me. I'm just a fool. I was born a fool. I shall commit suicide one of these days. No, I won't, for if I did, who would look after Dave? My dear, if I hadn't got Dave I don't know what I should do!' and she fell on her knees and kissed the mongrel's muzzle. He was moved by the faint colour in her cheeks, and the glisten of tears in her laughing eyes.

'Jean, tell me what you were going to say!'

But she would not say, and they walked on in silence to the inner sea-wall. A dyke ran alongside the road, and they walked on the ice binding the sapless reeds, which reminded him of rusty bayonets abandoned in an old shell-widened trench on the Somme. He stopped, remembering the frozen winter of 1916–17, and a trench near the Beauregard Dovecot before Miraumont, half filled with ice, and two faces, side by side, in the ice. Both had had leg wounds which had been roughly dressed at a first-aid post; a shell had killed

69

them as they were helping each other along the communication trench to the rear. German and Englishman, both slain by the same shell; both slain by the same false thought, by false patriotism. Yet they were great days . . . no, great only in memory, when only the glamour of stupendous and terrible scenes was recalled, and the spirit of great friendship, of love, between men who were banded together. The immense magnitude and light-thrall of a barrage seen before dawn from a hill-top behind the waiting assault! But . . . when you were crouching under the barrage, while the steel glacier rushing overhead scraped away every syllable, every fragment of a message bawled into your ear, and you were stiff and your mind was staring as in an icicle when the parapet just before zero hour began to spirt and crackle and break with machine-gun bullets! Great days! Christ! How easy to fall into false thought! . . . Ghastly days!

Jean was pointing at a yellow snail-shell under the ice. Her hand was on his shoulder.

'What are you looking at? That nice little pretty shell? You can't have it, Will – there's a little man lives in this mere, and that shell is his teapot.'

The turned-up brim of her small hat was pulled down over her ears, so that the fair hair and bright blue eyes and fresh cheeks were enclosed by an inverted horse-shoe of grey felt. She stood close to him, and he thought how pretty and lovable she was. He had already approved her legs, arms, and young bodily shape; he would like to kiss her. They looked at each other, then turned away, each smiling at the thoughts of the other. She slid away from him, cracking her whip, and holloaing to the dogs. He began to sing in a tenor voice; but an old man suddenly appeared over the sea-wall, carrying a dead sheep slung on his shoulders, and he stopped. The old man disappeared.

'That's Shiner,' whispered Jean. 'A bliddy ould thief, if I know anything about it.'

WINTER

They walked along the road for awhile, and then climbed the sea-wall. In the distance, lapped around with sandhills, stood the white stem of the Branton lighthouse, and beyond it, the houses of Appledore under the hill like a low rounded whitened pyramid.

'I feel I've known you for ages,' said Jean. 'I'm glad you came along yesterday. I was feeling rotten when I saw you. I'll tell you about it some day. Pah! Damn them! I'll never go there again! It's all right!' smiling at him, 'I'm only getting rid of a nasty memory. Jocky boy! Oi, Dave! Dave, Dave, come on all o' yer, forrads my dears, boys, come on boys and little bitches!' She ran with all her strength along the sea-wall, until she fell into the snow drifted against the slope.

The bleating of lambs rose out of a fold, where ewes were nibbling turnips in the snow. Four older lambs played together; they had been born a week before Christmas. Over the fold flew a short-eared owl, beating sedge-yellow wings as in its hunger it stared down for sight of bird or mouse. He shouted, and pointed at it.

'I wish I were an owl,' yelled Jean. 'I'd hoot all night in Old Jig's window.'

He wondered who Old Jig was, but said nothing. They got under the strands of a wire fence, and walked over snow to the outer sea-wall, which held back the spring tides in the pill, or creek, from flooding over the fields of the reclaimed marsh they had just crossed. The wall sloped down to the saltings of sea-rimed sward scored with channers and guts and pools of frozen water. Beyond the saltings was the pill, with steep sides of mud and a rocky bed held firmer by ice. The black hulks of three ketches were frozen in the ice; the pill-mouth was sealed by a barrier of ice-floes.

'Hullo,' said Jean, 'wild swans!'

Eight whooper swans, visitants from Arctic seas, had risen from the Ram's-horn duckpond behind the further sea-wall, and with necks outstretched and white wings beating a rhythm

71

in the blue air, they flew over the marsh to the estuary. He watched them until they had dropped below the line of sandhills, and ran after Jean, who had wandered on, and was standing by a low ramshackle hut below the wall.

'Luke's hut,' said Jean, and they stooped to go inside, seeing the candle-drippings on the wooden lintel supporting the sheet-iron roof. They sat on the seat, and watched the ring-plover turning and speeding over the estuary. The action of each pair of arched wings, bent back at the elbow, was identical in thrust and glide, as though one brain controlled the flock.

'Who is Old Jig?' asked Maddison. 'What has she done to you, that you should want to hoot at her?'

'Oh, lots of things.'

'Is her name Jig?'

'No, Miss Goff. She's the big pillar of our church.'

'Oh!'

'She makes it hot for poor old Glasseyes,' mused Jean.

'And who is poor old Glasseyes?'

'The Vicar. He lectures me playfully about my foul language, because Mother's put him up to it, I expect. He and Mother are great friends. As though one means half the words one says!'

'I know! Tell me about Glasseyes. Is that his real name?'

'No, Garside. He's not a bad old thing, and he does his little best. On Christmas Day, it was rather amusing. My dear, I must tell you.'

Jean's voice became liquid as she forgot herself in what she visualized. The Baptist minister was taken ill suddenly, and four men waiting to be baptized, so Glasseyes did it instead. There's been a row about it ever since. Old Jig was furious, and came to see Mother about it, and Mother stuck up for the Vicar, when Miss Goff said it was only to be expected, as he wasn't a gentleman. I told her I couldn't see it made any difference whether the men were wetted or not. Old Jig was shocked.'

WINTER

'The truth is sometimes shocking.'

'Then you agree with me?' asked Jean.

'So would anybody. Baptism is an ignorant vulgarization of an ancient select mystery.'

Jean wrinkled her nose and forehead at him. 'Sounds clever, anyway.'

'Well, you see, the baptism in the Jordan waters was entirely symbolic, and part of the mystic cult of a small and persecuted group of highly-spiritualized Jews. A man was baptized when his spiritual consciousness had got above his ordinary workday mind. It took years of meditation and aspiration before the soul was born again from above, which they called virgin-birth, partheno-genesis. Many were called, but few were chosen – genius is rare, owing to the way it is killed in childhood. Does this sound rot to you?'

'Rather not. Go on.'

'To-day, baptism is merely part of a social system in churches and chapels and other buildings of a hundred sects and denominations. Its original meaning is entirely changed and debased.'

'Then I'm damned if I'll teach any more rot in the Sunday school!'

'Oh, you mustn't take me as an authority,' he said, pleased that she had believed him; and immediately losing interest in the subject.

'But tell me why you dislike Miss Goff? Because she dislikes your Vicar?'

'No, not exactly. She – oh, she says things. She – oh, I don't care!'

She *is* pretty, he thought, looking at her; and thought of Mary, and her red cheeks when she had spoken about Howard. Well, he didn't care: Jean was sweet! They sat there talking for some time, and then, both in a state of pleasurable and semi-intimate excitement, they left to continue the way to the village.

Jean went into the toll-gate to inquire, as her mother had asked her, after the bronchitis of the marshman's wife. Maddison noticed a sack of coal inside the cottage, and seeing his glance the marshman smiled and said it had come from Miss Goff. A proper lady Miss Goff, real good to poor people! Besides the coal, she had brought a bottle of emotion for the missis. He fetched the bottle, and held it up before him. Proper physic for the missis, thaccy emotion! Apparently he meant emulsion.

After a cup of cocoa and a slice of cake each, which the marshman insisted on their having, they walked along the wall, until they came to the village, and entered the post office.

This was a room in a thatched cottage opposite the church. He was introduced to the post-mistress, Mrs. Mules, a fat, contented woman who sat at a table – when she was not doing housework – all day for six days a week for £1, with compensations of gossip and the interest of scrutinizing the letters sent and received by her neighbours.

'Well, Muley midear, how be it?' said Jean, heaving herself on to the table.

'Mustn't grumble, Miss Jean. Plaize to sit down yurr, sir, by the vire.'

'Any letters?' asked Jean.

'Yes, midear. Yurr they be,' and she began to scrutinize each one carefully.

'Here, let me see,' exclaimed Jean, taking the bundle, 'you're as blind as a dog's tail, Muley dear. H'm, two for Uncle Suff, seven for Mother, one for Mary – h'm, what's Howard writing to her about I should like to know? None for the Master of the Wildernesse Rabbit Hounds – that's me,' she said, looking at Maddison, while the post-mistress, wiping her hands that were both dry and clean on her apron, went into her kitchen. Jean laughed, and whispered to him that he was 'for it.'

'It be weest weather,' called the voice of Mrs. Mules. 'There's poor old Granfer Jimmy Mock dade, and 'a can't be buried. Hard as iron be the ground, hard as iron. John be turrible worried that 'a won't keep much longer! Hard as iron be the ground, hard as iron!'

They sat by her fire, and she cut two thick slices of saffron cake. Some one entered the other room for a stamp, and Jean broke off a piece of her cake and stealthily fed the dogs. The post-mistress returned, and urged them to have more cake.

'Don't ee deny your stummick, midear, there's plenty more out t'other house,' jerking her head towards the larder.

'No more, Muley darling,' said Jean, but Mrs. Mules insisted.

'No more, thanks; no more thanks; no more thanks; no more thanks,' said Jean.

'Won't ee, surenuff?' asked Mrs. Mules. 'Can't ee stay a bit longer? Must ee go, surenuff?'

Jean said she must go, and they went out.

'I have to have cake whenever I go there,' she explained outside, 'for Muley's got the idea we're starving "out to Big House." Hullo, here's John. Morning Jan! How be ee, Jan?'

A man in postman's trousers, but an ordinary cap and coat, shambled out of the churchyard. He carried an iron bar in his mittened hands.

'Good morning, Miss Jean, good morning midear. 'Tis turrible cold weather. Turrible cold. And poor old Granfer Jimmy Mock lying dead over a week in his coffin.' He blinked his sandy lashed eyes and scratched his red head. 'Over a week, 'tis now, Miss Jean. 'Tis turrible. Poor old Granfer Jimmy. Granfer Jimmy. He'm as stiff as a cockabell, Miss Jean, stiff as a cockabell. Poor old Jimmy Mock, I feel sorry for'n, stiff as a cockabell. Some do zay us'll have to open the coffin and salt'n in if the vrost doth hold much longer. 'Tis turrible times to-day, bant it, sir? The ground be hard as iron. Hard as iron. Hard as iron be the ground. I can't make no difference with the bar. Poor old Granfer Jimmy, waiting all this time to be put with his wife. I wouldn't be he for something.'

'You talk too much, Mules,' said Jean, pushing him in the ribs.

'Ha ha, Miss Jean. You'm a naughty maid, Miss Jean. I mind ee when you wasn't so tall as my willbarrer. 'Tis true, you wasn't so tall as my willbarrer! Naughty maid, you be, Miss Jean. You won't mind old Mules, willee, Miss Jean. Ha ha ha!'

He seemed all elbows, knobby fingers, and gentleness, and never once looked at them in the eyes.

'What shall we do now?' said Jean, when the sexton, who was also postman and verger, had clop-clopped away down the village street. 'There's nothing to see in this place. I wish it would thaw, then I could exercise the Buccaneer. He's eating his head off. I say, there's the Biscuit Box – let's hurry past – for I don't want to have to stop and talk to Old Jig.'

As they walked past the Biscuit Box, which was a Rolls-Royce car with a coupé body of polished aluminium, a big woman came out of a cottage and said pleasantly:

'Good morning, Jean.' She gave a quick glance at Maddison.

'Good morning, Miss Goff,' said Jean cordially, as though most pleased at the meeting.

'How's your Mother?' inquired Miss Goff, buttoning up her fur coat with her big hands.

'Oh, she's very well, thanks.'

'And Miss Chychester? She must be feeling the cold.'

'She's very well, thanks.'

Miss Goff removed the rug from the radiator of the car, saying:

'Oh, Jean! To save me writing, will you tell your Mother that if she is going to the Committee meeting of the Conservative Club next Wednesday, I shall be very pleased to give her a lift?'

She smiled at Maddison, who smiled at her.

'I can't give you a lift towards Down End, can I?'

'Thanks awfully,' replied Jean, 'but we're just going across the Great Field. I'll tell Mother. Thanks most awfully. Good-bye.'

As they walked down the village street Jean's feelings about the encounter were expressed by her face, over which passed a variety of frowns, smiles, scowls, and grimaces. 'The old booger!' she said, half to herself, and looked at him with half smiling anxiety.

Remembering how sympathy and friendship in the past had given him fortitude, he asked Jean to tell him what was on her mind. After several cracks of the whip she said:

'Promise you'll believe me if I tell you?'

He said he would believe her.

'Well, you saw that chap turning out roots from the butt, for the sheep? He's Jack Bissett, the son of the farmer of Burrow Farm. Well, he took me to Bampton Fair last year to see the Exmoor ponies being sold, on the back of his motor-bike. Old Jig saw us from the Biscuit Box and told Mother. So I rode the bike myself past Old Jig's house, with Jack on the carrier. She wrote a letter to Mother, saying what a lot of harm it would do me, as it was bound to be talked about, when all the time she had spread the news herself!'

'I wonder what she would say about me, if she knew I once fell in love with another man's wife!'

Jean did not answer. She walked quietly beside him, as though subdued by some thought. They passed the Parish Club-room, gift of the elderly Virginia Goff, and turning down a narrow lane came to the Branton Great Field, a white expanse of three hundred and sixty-five acres, over which flocks of plovers were wheeling and forming. A flock settled on Lower Cutabarrow, rising again before the dogs. Some of the dark green feathered bodies remained on the snow, and walking over to them, they saw that they were broken and dragged about by rats, having been pounced upon while roosting there at night, or after falling dead of hunger.

Chapter 4

JEAN threw the papers and letters on the hall table, and went upstairs; Maddison, after a glance at the *Morning Post*, picked up the letter addressed to Mary in such a neat, firm handwriting, and went to seek her in the kitchen. Mary was there, with a fire-flushed face; the wild duck shot by Mr. Chychester the night before were roasting in the oven. 'Phew, it's hot! They were very difficult to pluck!'

'I thought of you working while I was loafing,' he said, and gave her the letter. She glanced at it, and put it in the pocket of her skirt, under her apron.

'But you've been to get the post! And I'm sure that Jean was very glad to have you with her.'

He did not answer. She was peeling sprouts, and he helped her.

'When do you go out, Mary?'

'Sometimes in the afternoons.'

'Shall we go out this afternoon? Or do you think your Mother expects me to clear off? But perhaps you want to go alone, or with some one else?'

Jean came back into the kitchen, and dropped into the broken chair. After a minute of resting on the base of her spine, she struggled up, and said:

'I'm going to look at the Buccaneer. Would you like to see him?' Maddison looked at the sprouts, and at his wet hands; before he replied Jean said, 'All right, if you're busy,' and went out alone, followed by Dave.

'You stay,' said Mary. 'Unless you want to go.'

'Of course, I'd like to stay.' He spoke doubtfully. 'But doesn't Mrs. Ogilvie expect me to go?'

'I spoke to Mother this morning, and she said there was no reason as far as she was concerned why you should go, so you needn't worry any more about that.'

'I won't! Shall we go for a walk this afternoon?'

'Yes! To the estuary!'

After lunch Mr. Chychester, a stump of a pipe in his mouth, went off to his room to write his diary, taking the *English Boy's Annual* with him. Mrs. Ogilvie wrote letters. Miss Chychester sat by the hall fire working the bobbins of her lace pillow. Jean tried to read a recent birthday present, Stevenson's *Virginibus Puerisque*, and after half a page dropped it listlessly beside her as she sprawled across the arms of the leather chair opposite her great-aunt. Mary went upstairs, after clearing the dining-room table, to put on thicker clothes. While waiting for her Maddison sat on the floor and examined books. When Mary came down Jean asked her where she was going, and Mary replied, 'For a walk, to the estuary.'

'Walkees?' said Maddison to his dog, who jumped up at him, while the other dogs stirred out of various lazy attitudes.

'Come with us?' said Mary to Jean.

'Yes, do come,' said Maddison.

Mrs. Ogilvie, wearing spectacles, looked over her shoulder, said, 'Yes, why don't you go, Jean?'

'I don't expect they want me.'

'What nonsense, Jean. The walk will do you good, my dear.'

Miss Chychester, whose glances had moved from face to face, laid a little yellow hand on Maddison's pocket, and said:

'I read in the paper last week that the dreadful Bolsheviks in Russia are forcing their unhappy victims to go to the theatre, and I have been wondering ever since what would happen to him if a man could not afford to pay for his seat. A general of the Army, for instance, who is selling newspapers for a livelihood.'

'You needn't answer,' said Jean, seeing that he was getting ready to explain. Miss Chychester smiled at him, waved her little yellow hand, and returned to the bobbins of her lace pillow.

'Coming?' said Mary to her sister.

'Yes, go with them, dear,' said Mrs. Ogilvie.

'Two's company,' replied Jean.

'What nonsense you do talk, Jean,' said her mother complacently.

'Go on, you two. I'm not coming.'

'Really?'

Jean got out of the chair, and went slowly upstairs.

They set out alone. As they were trudging over a drift filling a hollow in the sandhills with its white brilliance, Maddison said, 'Mary, you are the only person I know who makes me feel that I need not explain anything I say.'

'I expect it is because we are the same.'

He shook his head, thinking she was like snow where no foot had pressed.

Over the white tower of the lighthouse, a mile distant, a flock of plovers made a black down-curved line as they turned.

'They are like an eyebrow in the sky,' he said.

'I've often thought they were just like that!'

The eyebrow sank out of sight as the birds dropped to feed on the sands. They walked on. He proposed a game of running on the peaks of the dunes and not pausing, even when a sandy precipice suddenly appeared below their feet. They clasped hands and ran, leaping over a seven-foot edge and rolling in sand and snow together. They got up laughing, and she cried out:

'Some more! Come on, Mary! I say, can't we make some skis? Or a toboggan?'

'There's an old tea-tray of hard wood,' she said doubtfully.

'Let's go back for it!'

'I've got to meet some one on the Crow.'

He wondered why she had not told him before; and

wondered if that was why she had asked Jean to go with them. Knowing what he was thinking, she blushed.

'It's Howard, and I didn't know until I got the letter this morning. He asked me to meet him there.'

He thought of his question by the pump – his foolish, foolish question! – and calling his spaniel, ran up the slope in front and over the summit.

When she reached it she saw his tracks down into the hollow beyond and over the next hillock. She came upon him kneeling in the snow with the dog beside him, holding a rabbit he had taken from a gin, with both its forepaws broken.

'Do you mind if I kill it? It's no good releasing it with both forepaws gone, is it?'

She shook her head, and calmly he grasped the kicking hind legs in his left hand and the head in his right, and stretched the body across his thigh, so that the neck was broken. He dropped it beside the gin, over which its head rolled.

'As though in a caress of forgiveness,' he said, and her lips moved in a small smile.

'Are there many traps here? I suppose there are?'

'They trap ten thousand every year on the Burrows. And the trapping rent just keeps Ronnie at school. Ten thousand screams in the darkness every year. I hear them sometimes.' She spoke very gently.

'The story of the Burrows is the story of all the world,' he said, as they walked on.

The spaniel ran back for the rabbit, and with wagging tail and bright eyes brought it to his master, and laid it at his feet.

'Don't disappoint him,' said Mary. 'The trapper won't miss just one.'

The rabbit seemed to fold itself up and drop itself into his pocket.

He began to sing a moment later, and she wanted to sing too, but felt too shy.

'Do you mind me making this noise?'

'I like to hear you.'

Realizing that she was serious, he was too shy to sing any more.

The lighthouse stood large and white before them when they had climbed the last hill before the Great Pan, a hollow nearly half a mile long and a quarter of a mile wide. Wind made a scythe-like sound in the spiky marram grasses binding the sand; it scoured the loose snow on the drifts below. Holding hands, they ran down into a drift which covered all except their heads; and while they stood there together, looking down the wind-smooth snow into the Great Pan, they heard a deep harsh croak, and instantly he said, 'Keep still!'

Knowing why he had said it, she did not speak, but remained motionless in the snow. Big black wings flapped over and around them, and after watching for nearly a minute, a bird alighted among the grasses two gunshots away, and croaked three times. It was a raven.

After many throaty mutterings, and croaks to its mate, it threw itself into the air as though in alarm, and glided over their heads. After another two doubtful minutes it walked sideways towards them, uneasily, and was approaching what it thought to be corpses when the spaniel, who had been scratching at a rabbit bury half a mile away, ran over the hill on their trail, and seeing the raven, dashed over the brittle crust of snow to attack it. The bird croaked angrily, and fearing for his dog's eyes, Maddison shouted and threw up his arms, knocking Mary on the side of the head.

'Mary, dear Mary! I'm sorry! That's the second time I've struck you on the face. The same cheek, too! Damn myself!' He struck his own head violently with his fist.

'No, no!' she cried, seizing his hand, making as if to take it to her breast, but dropping it immediately, 'you hardly touched me, really.'

He stroked the cheek with the backs of his fingers. 'Poor gentle little Mary,' he said softly, and the colour flowing in her face made it more sweet against the snow. She knew he was going to kiss her, and instantly he reacted to her startled look, and looked away, while the spaniel, whose tongue lolled in breathlessness above them, leaned down and licked his ear rapidly, twice. Filled with self-loathing, he scrambled with elbows and knees through the drift, which was shallower at the bottom of the dune against which the wind had piled it, and hurried away clenching his hands, and muttering, 'God, you fool, you bloody bloody fool!'

A beaten track beside a line of telegraph posts lay across the Great Pan, leading to the lighthouse, with lines of bicycle wheels cutting into each other beside the track. He walked along the slippery way, while she followed fifty yards behind, hands in pockets and looking at the flakes whirled by the wind over dry sand and pebbles. In front, behind a clump of rushes made still and solid with snow, a small flock of starving linnets was crouched, by the skeleton of a rabbit. The icy wind whirled grains of rock and shell against the bones of the living and the dead, with sounds of sighing and tapping inaudible in the common plaint, as though striving in blindness to mingle all in the formless sand. The birds would struggle up into flight if he continued to walk straightly, so he called his dog to heel and made a loop away from them, and when Mary came to the beginning of the loop she saw the birds and knew why he had gone round them, for she would have done the same thing herself had she been leading.

When she was walking by his side again he seemed to be away in thought, so she did not speak. Over the Great Pan they walked, seeing only sandhills and snow and sky and each other, for in the sunken plain all else was hidden.

Climbing the last range of sandhills they saw the estuary before them, and every cottage and mast in Appledore across the water. A sailing boat was waiting at the edge of the water, its foresail flapping, a man in oilskins stamping by it, and swinging his arms for warmth. Mary waved to him, and he waved back to her. On the beach Maddison asked her if he should remain away while she spoke to him.

'No, of course not. Only – well, perhaps if you leave us alone for a short while, it will be better. You see, Howard and I are very old friends, and he wants to see me particularly about something.'

'Of course, I understand. I'll just wander off and leave you alone.'

He lingered behind as they came near the water. He saw the sturdy young man in oilskins pushing the boat afloat; heard its iron keel-shoe grating on the shingle. Mary walked to the boat alone, while Maddison wandered down the shore, watching the ring-plover as they paused statue-like in their running at the tide-line, to run on again, piping faint notes, as though the stones had cried. A dull roar came sea-wards, where on the bar the long Atlantic rollers were breaking white. He was counting the buoys marking the fairway when a hail broke into his sense of loneliness. The oilskin-clad figure was beckoning, and so was Mary. He ran to them, where they stood on the loose watery gravel.

She said that he was Howard – Howard de Wychehalse. He was in rubber waders, and bare-headed. Above the broad-shouldered black shiny jacket his clean-shaven face was ruddy and wet with spray. He gripped Maddison's hand hard.

'I say, Maddison, I am most awfully sorry not to have come and met you and Mary, but the tide's ebbing fast, and if I don't shove off continually she'll be beached. I've just asked Mary to bring you over to our place one day and see my peregrine falcons.'

'Thanks very much. I've always wanted to see hawking. Are they haggards or eyesses?'

'Oh, eyesses. I got them two seasons ago, from the headland.' He pointed northwards.

'I know the breeding ledge. Did you climb down on a rope?'

'Yes. It's not so hard as it looks.'

'It looks terrible! Nearly two hundred feet of climbing, with a sheer drop of three hundred feet from the top! I should die of fright.'

'Oh, it's merely a question of being used to it, I think. Well, I think I must be getting along now, Mary. Thanks most awfully for coming. I suppose you wouldn't care for a sail?' he said to Maddison.

'Yes!' said Mary excitedly, as a wave broke over the stern of the boat.

'I've got some oilskins in the locker. Here, let me lift you in, Mary.' And putting one arm round her back and another under her knees he picked her up easily and put her over the gunwale.

'Don't you get wet feet,' he said, seeing that Maddison was measuring the distance for a spring; and as easily as he had lifted Mary he picked him up and sat him down on a thwart.

'You're very strong,' said Maddison, in his soft voice, sitting still where he had been placed.

'A mere animal!' said Howard, with a glance at Mary.

'Don't you take any notice,' replied Mary stoutly; and Maddison wondered why Howard had spoken so contemptuously of himself.

It was a sixteen-foot boat, wide in the beam, half-decked, clipper built, and 'stiff.' The name *Anjelita* had recently been carved on the mahogany backboard.

Howard lifted the spaniel into the boat, and shoved off, while Maddison and Mary seized an oar each and poled it afloat. The bow of the *Anjelita* was thrust round, the sail was hauled up, it flapped and filled, the mast creaked and leaned, they sat on the weather combing as she heeled, and behind the stern the wavelets were smoothed with bubbles and eddies. Mary took the tiller as Howard jerked the wood cover off the locker and hauled out some oilskins.

'I don't want any,' said Mary, but as the boat was put over

a wave slapped against the weather bows and threw drops over all of them. Billjohn looked over his shoulder to see if more were coming, and crept under his master's legs.

'Put 'em on,' cried Howard, throwing an amber-coloured coat to Maddison, and a black coat to Mary. She laughed at his curt command, and obeyed. Wind tore the ragged tops of waves, and the hempen rope clattered against the leaning pine mast. Splash! half a bucketful on Howard's wide back. 'Ease her up a bit, Mary!' The wave-tops were almost lipping over the combing.

Half-way across the Pool was a line of agitated and jumping jets of water in froth, where the ebbing waters of the Two Rivers met and bickered before agreeing to flow as one to the sea. The *Anjelita* slipped from Taw's ebb into Torridge's ebb, crossing the String, and soon the squally wind lessened, for they were under the hill around whose base straggled the cottages of Appledore. Howard was staring in the direction of Lundy, low and grey on the horizon beyond the bar, and knowing his mood Mary thought he might prefer to be alone. She luffed into the wind and put about the *Anjelita*, they ducked their heads to avoid the cuff of the boom, and the boat scudded back to the neck of the Crow. Howard said nothing, but stared at the western horizon.

'Good-bye,' he said, in a subdued voice, when they had jumped to the shingle, and he had poled himself afloat again, 'I'm going to sail round the Bar Buoy.'

'Howard, you're not to, on the half-ebb!' cried Mary. 'You'll get on to the North Tail!'

'And damned good riddance,' muttered Howard.

'Howard, please don't go!' begged Mary, as he shoved off, but he only laughed mirthlessly.

With sheet close-hauled the *Anjelita* tacked down the estuary faster than they could walk on the loose trickling shingle. Her captain sat still and huddled in the stern. Maddison observed that Mary glanced at the boat many times. He saw the colour in her cheeks, and wondered if it were the colour made by the wind. He ran on in front with the spaniel, and turning back, waited for her. The wind sculptured knee and thigh and breast as she walked. Her eyes met his, and he thought how her spirit was wild as the golden plover fleeing over the waves. A sweet bubbling cry from a bird's throat fell down the wind. and pain stirred in his heart.

They passed the lighthouse and the wooden groynes and piles and tarred concrete breakwaters before it. Further down, the brown iron ball was low on its post, a signal to ships in Bideford Bay that the bar was unnavigable. Below the lighthouse three fishermen with baskets were gathering shell-fish on the rocky flats left by the tide. They wore slops and ragged coats, their trousers were rolled above the knee, and water ran out of the breaks in their old boots. Seeing Mary, one of them hailed her with a cry melancholy as the cry of a gull, and threw up a steel hook on a leather forearm. They went down to him, and Maddison saw that he wore his hair long, so that it lay on his shoulders. Mary called him Luke, and afterwards told Maddison that he was a deaf and dumb fisherman who was the caretaker of the hospital ship, where he had lived alone for more than thirty years.

The afternoon grew cold and grey, but when they reached Aery Point, where the hollow growl of the bar was increased by the rollers along the shallow coast, a skyey conflagration was reflected on the glazed sands. The *Anjelita* had put back towards Appledore, her skipper's desperation becoming less than his good sense when he saw the broken water of the Hurleyburleys before him.

They left Aery Point behind them, walking in a northerly direction. Yellow dry skeins of sand were blown slanting by their feet. The skeins would twist into ropes, which broke and scattered before the carven sand-cliffs ragged with the exposed marram grass, and the black and brittle roots of dead brake-ferns. They were alone on the sand-sweeping waste, with flocks of oyster-catchers and ring-plover watching them from the margin of the sea. A big roller reared up and crashed a hundred yards away, and out of turmoil and travail a virginal foam was born.

Over the uneven sands the water rushed and leapt, overtaking the hastening flocks and driving them up into flight. When it reached their feet the foam was discoloured, and but a line of wavering froth. A formless mass of bubbles remained after the original impulse was gone, and the wind broke it up and soiled fragments were blown and scattered inland. Some rolled on, others broke up.

'Christianity,' said Maddison, and Mary did not know what he meant.

'Or any idea born in the high realm of the spirit,' he added, with a swift sidelong glance at her.

'Yes,' she said, understanding.

The pied oyster-catchers had settled two hundred yards along the coast, looking like music notes on the sand. They flew away with piping cries over the sea. Mary and Maddison walked on, the wind urging them before it, while the winter sun fell below the clouds and cast a red fire on the distant sea. The sands and the surf took on a purple tinge. Dark objects stood in the great level stretch before them. A wooden ship had been wrecked there years before, and only its ribs remained in a pool. It had been there ever since Mary could remember; the Wildernesse children called it the Dutchman's Wreck. Seaweed hung on the timbers, and gave them fantastic forms, which shook in the wind, like shapeless gestures of elemental wood-spirits. Mary touched one; she still felt sorry for the timbers of the Dutchman's Wreck.

She remembered, far away in childhood, brother Michael hearing her speak to it, and how he had laughed at her and called her a silly. She remembered her shame now, when still the strange feeling remained. How gladly she heard Maddison say beside her: There are tree spirits here, spirits that are lost in the sand. Do they remember the forest where their seeds swelled and split? For a tree lives as a man lives: it is a dumb brother of man: from the sea it came, as he came, to look up into the face of the sun. Everything has its dream: who shall know even the dream of this grain of sand? What dreams will our dust have, when it is loose in the wind again?

The sun had gone down behind Lundy, and the sea was growing grey. He turned away from the wreck and walked towards the Burrows. She followed, buoyantly, and longing to say a thousand things to him, but she had not the gift of tongues. He thought about the wreck as she did! And when the head of the rabbit whose neck he had broken had rolled on the iron, it had been *as though in a caress of forgiveness*. She thought of Rigmarole, the water-spaniel, being found a few days before with feathers on his top-knot after the remains of a hen had been discovered in the orchard, and being thrashed by Uncle Suff, and creeping to lay his head on his master's boot. Uncle Suff had said that dogs and animals only acted from instinct. Then Aunt Edith had come hurrying down the stairs, tears running down her cheeks, to tell them that she had seen Dave killing and eating the chicken, while Rigmarole had only watched him from down wind, where the feathers had floated and lodged on his woolly head! Why did she feel as though her heart had suddenly melted in her breast, and tears come in her eyes? For she was filled with the lovely feeling she always felt on the Burrows at dimmit light, when the body seemed balanced in the harmony of day and night.

He had stopped again, and was waiting for her, as he had waited before. She was beginning to know that habit! His face was so gentle and wondering, the face she had seen in her mind whenever she had thought of him. She stole a glance at him, and saw him as a little boy, much younger than Ben, a small boy who in some strange way was beyond sadness; a dear little boy, who had no one to look after him.

Silently they reached the sandhills and saw again snow in the hollows. The roar of the breakers sank away with backward sight of the sea. The snow purred under their leather soles. For a mile the marram grass bound the dunes, and thereafter were plains whose white expanse was spotted by dark clusters of rushes, whose hardened points, as they hastened through them, stabbed their legs. They disturbed rabbits scratching for herbage in the snow, and around them in the twilight came clicks, followed by the rattle of chains, and then stillness. What rabbits they passed in the gins he took out and killed; for the next day was a Sunday, and the trapper, an earnest member of Bethel, would not visit his gins again until the Monday morning. Until then the rabbits would remain trapped, fresh for the market since they would not die, except those the stoats came upon to eat the eye and side of the face and neck, and those the buzzard hawk 'broke abroad'; and those the crows and magpies battered. Above the southern hills the heavy weight of snow clouds ended in an almost straight line, and in the clear sky the foot and belt of Orion were flashing. There was hope in the stars.

When they came to the high rough cob garden wall, with its ridge of thatch clogged with snow and holed by roosting birds, he said, 'Mary, please be frank with me. I'd much rather stay here with you, but am I in the way?'

'Of course you aren't! Mother wouldn't ask you otherwise.'

'Shall we be able to sit and talk together in the kitchen?'

'I think we'd better be with the others,' she replied after hesitation, thinking of Benjamin doing his homework, and of her mother.

'I see.'

In his mind he saw again her excitement and risen vitality when she was with Howard. She must love Howard. How she had yielded to him when he had picked her up in his strong arms and sat her down in the boat! He followed her through the postern gate in the wall, and along a path leading to the mill-shed, where before the War corn from the Great Field had been ground into flour, for baking in the clome ovens of Wildernesse. The icicled wheel had not revolved for nearly ten years. Ivy grew on wall and roof. They heard the chirp of sleepy birds as they passed. The cypress trees by the stone clapper bridge over the frozen mill-leat swayed dark and sighing in the wind. Beyond was the kitchen garden, with its rows of bean-sticks, and mounds of sea-weed rotting for top-dressing, and glass frames, all white. The sighs of the cypresses passed over the lifeless garden.

Mary's mother was in the kitchen, waiting for the kettle to boil. She stood with one foot on the fender – a woman whose greying hair was arranged without any attempt to hide her fifty years. She was popular in the district, and liked by her friends; equally good at golf or bridge. Her friends were wont to say, after bidding her good-bye at their own places or at Wildernesse, Connie *is* a nice woman, or, Isn't she a *perfect* dear, and, How she finds time for *all* the things she does, we *don't* know. And they would recall how *perfectly* splendid she had been through all her trouble with Charlie Ogilvie – he whose irresponsible and intemperate life had been battered out by summer Atlantic breakers while trying to save the life of a stranger bathing off Aery Point. Greater love hath no man . . . every one had softly quoted it, and so many carriages and motor-cars had come for the funeral service of the man whose acts of behaviour in life had been so assiduously deplored and discussed, that the parish church of St. Sabinus would not hold one half of them. Thousands of flowers had wilted for their sentiments.

Mrs. Ogilvie looked up as they entered, and seeing what she thought to be an uneasy and timid look in the queer young man's eyes, she said, with a forced gaiety, 'Just in time for tea, you two. Have you had a nice walk?'

'Yes,' said Maddison nervously.

'Tell me all about it,' suggested Mrs. Ogilvie. For answer

he pulled the rabbit out of his pocket, and said that his dog had carried it to him. Its broken forelegs hung limp over the edge of the table.

'That's very clever of your dog. He seems to be a most exceptionable beastie. Jean's dogs, now, would have fought over it, and eaten it, certainly not have brought it back like that.'

Through the open door came the sound of a piano.

'You must be cold, being out so long,' went on Mrs. Ogilvie. 'Well, tea won't be long, I dare say you are ready for it. And don't go back to-night, if you would rather stay here. Rather dull for you perhaps . . .'

'Thank you very much,' he said softly.

Taking advantage of a conversation between Mrs. Ogilvie and Mary about a Whist Drive she was organizing on behalf of her political Committee, Maddison slipped away down the passage, drawn by the music. Miss Edith Chychester was sitting by the fire in the hall, enjoying the blaze. Dogs slept around her feet. She did not see him. He wandered over to the suit of armour, and was looking out of the window when the notes of a piano fell again through the quiet and shadowy hall. Some one was playing in the drawing-room, in which he had not yet been. Walking towards the sound, he saw that one door was partly open, and he went through, drawn by the beauty of the music. The invisible player touched the notes in darkness, out of which stole the glimmer and mystery of moonlight in an unearthly waterfall. A Spirit glimmered in the pool, a Spirit of the celestial stars, and then the Spirit fled; the moon's light dimmed and vanished, the music ceased, leaving him standing by the window.

A pallid gloom was cast about wall and ceiling from the snow on the lawn, and he could see the outline of a figure sitting on the stool before the piano. It was smaller than Jean, and sat quite still.

'Play some more, please!' he said.

92

'My fingers are so cold,' replied a voice, calm with a slight drawl, which he recognized. Diana Shelley. 'Just you feel,' and a small hand with chilly nails was put into his palm.

He clasped it, and breathed upon it. 'What were you playing? It was beautiful. You have a marvellous touch.'

'Debussy's *Claire de lune*. Where's Mary?'

'In the kitchen, talking to her mother. Do you remember the goldfinches splashing in the water? I think you must be like them. Give me the other hand.'

His breath made them warm and damp, the blood flowed warmly into the nails by his eager chafing, and she drawled 'Thanks.' And added casually, 'Do you honestly want to hear me play?'

'I should think I did!' he answered eagerly.

'All right,' she said, sitting still on the stool. He dropped her hand, and walked to the window. A mouse was gnawing the wainscot. Under the sash a plaining wind fell into the still air of the room, a voice telling the despair of life in snow, a voice weak and of the ancientness of the unresting sand. Grain grinding grain, grain grinding shell and bone and sapless twig, the voice of the wind plaining that it knew not why it drove them so, even to the end of the world. I am like the wind, he thought, for I have come to the end of the world, and the Khristos leads me on. The thought gave him a strange joy.

The *ric-ric-rac* of minute incisor teeth cutting the wood of the wainscoting ceased. The shadelike player touched a note, and waited. *Ric-ric-rac* again, to the rise and fall of the wind's plaint.

She began to play the Schumann concerto, hearing the orchestral accompaniment in her head as she hummed it. He sat in a deep arm-chair, peaceful in the dim light of the snow. The long quavering hoot of a wood owl came from the dark trees of the garden. Soon the music put strange life into him, so that he could not sit still, but must prowl about the room, feeling a wraith in human form, a wraith of Khristos, all powerful, all embracing. The wraith revisited sights and

93

feelings of the years in London: pale faces stared at him again, as one night they had stared through the window of a shop in the New Cut, watching the joints of horse-flesh being carved for cheap beef sandwiches. Could not eat when children's eyes stared so; they had fought for the food, being starved. Another memory, of an old woman in a pub, bent as a tree, dirty, a London beggar woman defying the law by two boxes of matches held in a hand, her eyes run to pus, her voice a scraping sound; she could neither see nor talk. She held out sixpence, and a glass of whisky was put into her hand. A harlot of eighteen sitting with a stevedore in a corner, nearly drunk, laughed when the old woman could not reach her mouth. A policeman came in, and gently, firmly, with sympathy and humour, led her out of the bar into the streets, and she slouched away into the shadows, she who was once a child denied the sunlight.

Another memory, of a little sparrow-legged boy dragged by his father over London Bridge, and trying to point at the sea-gulls soaring above the parapet. 'Aow, look at them birds!' A clout on the head, tears, dragged another fifty yards. 'Aow, look at 'em now!' A growl of 'Shurrup!' More tears, little feet trotting to keep up with father, and wet eyes raised from pavement to sky, and again, 'Aow, look at 'em naow!' Another clout on the head, a thin arm jerking a wailing bundle of bones and clothes as though it were a puppet. Clatter of little feet on paving stones! He saw again the passionate face of a woman who ran upon the father with an umbrella, and almost struck him. With trembling cries she called him a brute, and looked round for a policeman. How was she to know that the man's digestion was ruined by semi-starvation, that his wife was ill at home, and that after two years unemployment he had heard that morning at the Labour Exchange of a job, to which he was hurrying before the vacant place was filled by one out of the hundreds given hope in the same way.

WINTER

He began to pace more firmly, inspired by the passion in the music. 'Look at 'em naow!' in a thin whining cockney pipe. Through the unthinking, unsoiled mind of childhood had risen the spirit, with which its mind was correlated. How many centuries of summers laying its sights and sounds on the tissue of the human brain had made that faculty, by which man might receive his heritage of the earth, its Khristos? Why did men look on pavements, and children at birds in the sky? Why did blood and sweat drip in agony, where poppies had grown, and corn? Why were metal disks of gold esteemed before the sun-disks of dandelions? Why were larks eaten, when they sang to heaven?

He wandered again in the scarred and rolling Picardy country, where he had been working with others to collect the dead into nations again. The beautiful desolation of rush and willow in the tracts unploughed had given strength to the spirit which had been agonized for so long in a town, where men thought the old thoughts, and the narrow ideas of nationalism had returned among them, so that men reading their newspapers hated others they had never known, and never seen. Only the dead of the lost generation of Europe were magnanimous, they neither envied nor hated; but they were beyond the end of the world!

'My little children,' he thought, striding in a mental agitation towards the snow-lit window, 'you shall not be in darkness much longer!' He felt strong as the earth, the sun, and all the stars as he strode up and down, rapt with the Khristos.

The music stopped. He did not speak. After a few moments a shadow slipped through the doorway. Some time later Mary came into the room, and stood before him, and looked into his eyes which seemed not to see her. He is seeing visions, she thought, and made as if to take his hand. Then in a low voice she said that tea was ready, and he followed her into the hall, his eyes screwed up at the lamplight, as though he would quench it with his mind. During tea he spoke only to give answers, and then in single words. Mary was silent, too; and towards the end of the meal Mrs. Ogilvie noticed the strained look on his face, and the fixed look in his dark eyes, and wondered if he were unwell. Perhaps he had a headache . . . some aspirin?

'I'm all right, thank you, Mrs. Ogilvie.'

'You are not eating anything,' said Miss Chychester. 'Come, let me see you eating, please. My dear birds eat fast enough when I call them by clapping my hands together, and you must take a lesson from them.'

After tea he sat in shadow by the fire, then rising, he went upstairs and brought down his pack. To the astonishment of Mrs. Ogilvie, and to the protests of Jean and Benjamin, he bid them good-bye, saying he must get on with his work.

'Ah well, don't let us hinder if that is the case,' said Mrs. Ogilvie. 'Let's hope your book will be successful, and make your fortune. Money is the problem of all of us to-day, I'm afraid.'

She did not expect any answer to what was a conversational remark, and was therefore surprised when he said, seriously:

'Well, you know, Mrs. Ogilvie, to be quite frank I don't expect to make any money out of it at all.'

'You are too modest about it, perhaps. Well, we shall look forward to seeing the book when it's published. It will be in the libraries, no doubt. What is the subject? Birds, or a novel, perhaps?'

He hesitated. 'Oh, I don't know. It's just, well, a sort of a fantasy, I suppose.'

'Well, come and see us again some time, won't you? Have you no coat? My dear boy – Well, I'm glad I'm not you! Good-bye!'

He thanked her, and after hesitation shook her hand, and opened the door. The bitter cold came in, and he closed it quickly after him, and after the least pause for a last glance of Mary, walked away with his dog in the darkness and the snow.

Chapter 5

On Easter Sunday morning, when mosses made green the lower hillocks and plains around Wildernesse, and the buds of the willow were a soft grey, and the fresh water in the dykes gleamed with the sky, Mary and Jean went early to the parish church of Speering Folliot. The sisters were in charge of the children's Sunday school, which was held before the morning service. A year previously the Vicar had altered the time of the classes from the afternoon, on the suggestion of Mrs. Ogilvie, who knew that many mothers after the cooking and eating of the Sunday beef went to sleep with their husbands, Sunday for the field-worker being a real Day of Rest. Sending children to Sunday school in the afternoon meant an extra labour of washing hands and faces and putting on clean frocks and woollies, for the cottage wife who would send her children into God's House as though it were the school-house was exceptional.

Outside the lych-gate on the grass about thirty clean children were waiting, many of them holding hands. The sisters said good morning to them, and were immediately answered by an assibilate murmur of their mingled names.

'M'ss Mary.'

'M'ss Jean.'

The sun's wind blew from the south, and moved the gilt cock on the tower. Starlings sang up there. Mary said she could hear the mimicked notes of curlew and thrush, of black-poll, gull and kestrel; and Jean, as they were walking under

the lime-trees which made an arch over the sett-stoned path
to the porch, told Mary that if she were to listen carefully,
she would hear them call 'M'ss Mary' and 'M'ss Jean.'

Mary smiled at her sister's fancy, knowing that she had just
invented it. Curious mimic noises, however, were to be heard
in the merry din of the Speering Folliot starlings, including
the whine of puppies, the rumble of cart-wheels, the crack of
whips, the squeal of hungry pigs, and the wheezy coughing
of an old man.

A sundial was above the porch, and the shadow of the
gnomon had cleared the Roman numeral X when Mrs.
Mules, the post-mistress, peering through her window,
observed at the lych-gate the young gennulman who had come
some weeks before with Miss Jean. She watched him walk
up the path, and stare at the lettering above the porch.

'The tower of this Parish being by force of arms pul'd down
in ye late unhappy Civil wars, Anno Dom. 1646, was rebuilt
1696.'

The walls of the porch were hung with various documents
concerned with the life of the village – Rates and Taxes,
Income Assessment, Armorial Bearing and other licences,
printed lists of the Polling register, and notices of the Parish
council. There was a Roll of Honour, bearing the names, in
Old English lettering on illuminated parchment, of those men
who had served in the Great War. About one in eight of the
names, including that of Michael Ogilvie, had a cross beside
it; and below, a larger cross, with the words, *Made the Supreme
Sacrifice.*

On the wood at the angle of the roof Maddison noticed as
he tip-toed into the church the marks of old swallow nests
which had been knocked down. The children sat obediently
in the pews near the pulpit, their backs to him, facing their
teachers. He trod slowly and softly, lest he disturb the classes.

Like its sister Church of St. Brannock, whose grey broach

spire leant among trees to the northwards, the Church of St. Sabinus was old in its association with human endeavour. By the font was a grave slab, engraved with the name of Chychester. There were monuments on the walls, with Latin inscriptions, and effigies of men and women kneeling at prayer with the Chychester coat-armour – the crest a cormorant sable with wings extended, in its beak an eel argent – between them. Some of the mural tablets were surmounted with skulls and crossbones, and infant figures with wings below the decayed leaden letterings, similar to those of Maddison's forebears in Rookhurst Church. There was a more recent monument among them, of Sir Orlando Bassett, who died in 1727, with his two wives and his two crests and his shield of thirty-two quarterings.

In the south wall was a huge affair, containing perhaps more than a ton of material, looking as though some monstrous sea-worm had cast it there. The centre tablet was like a vast black shining beetle, set with dark indiscernible letters, with four smaller beetles around it. Child-faces were set in the sepulchral thing, with expressions of fat horror; and a death's-head, with dragon-skin wings out of its bony mouth; and a black bird, neither crow nor eagle, perched on a casque, among sea-weeds, eels, blazoned shields, all massed like undersea lichen, heavy, sombre, powerful, conceived in the spirit of dreadful darkness expressing the soul of the departed, Sir Incledon Chychester, who, so disliking his two daughters, had told his executors to pull down his mansion after his death, and let the brambles grow over the ruin. During his life he had feared darkness (never realizing it was within him) and at night every window of the house had been lit up. He was the grandfather of Sufford Chychester, and the great-grand-father of Mrs. Ogilvie, who resembled him in features, according to his portrait.

Along the wall was a marble tablet to the memory of the Honble William Pomfret Ogilvie, sixth son of the seventeenth

Earl of Inshewan, who was killed in the hunting field on 11 November 1888, and of his wife Mary, only daughter of John Bassett, esquire, of Wildernesse, who died on 14 November 1888. 'They lived and died together.'

And next to this memorial, which he imagined to be of Mary's grandparents, was a smaller brass plate, with red and black lettering, to the memory of Charles Sholto Pomfret Ogilvie, drowned in an attempt to save life at Aery Point, 7 August 1908, aged 37. 'Thy will be done.' Beside this, a brass tablet to Michael, with the Ogilvie coat-armour, and motto, *Quae moderate, firma*. 'Who dies if England lives?'

He examined the oak bench seats, the timber of which, he remembered, was said to have been grown on the Burrows, and drawn to the site of the church by deer. Many of the bench ends had been mutilated by Cromwell's soldiery; noses struck off by sabres, faces hacked, whole panels smoothed by the strokes of an axe. Others untouched were carved with the scenes of the crucifixion; pincers and nails; hammer and ladder; whipping post and garments; purse and thirty pieces of silver; hands, feet, and heart; the cross with the crown of thorns. On others were the scourge and rod, the sponge and spear, and coat-armour, with the profile of a heavy head, with a long nose – exactly like the profile of Mr. Sufford Chychester.

His examination had brought him near the children. He had been conscious of the glance of both Mary and Jean, but until now he had not looked at them. When Jean caught his eye her eyebrows went up, her mouth opened, and she smiled. 'Hullo, Will! Don't go away. Turn round, Billy Herniman! Now then, John Frankpitt, midear, tell me, Who was it the ravens brought food to?'

John Frankpitt did not know. A hand fluttered eagerly, and its owner answered, 'Plaize Miss Jean, I knaw. 'Twas the prophet Elija.'

'Quite right, Billy.' A picture book apparently was then shown to the ignorant John Frankpitt.

SPRING

Sunlight fired the copper-reds and cobalt-blue and iron-browns of the stained glass windows. Christ the Sower was radiant. The church was filled with the scents of flowers decorating the window ledges, pulpit, font, and choir stalls – primroses, daffodils, narcissi, arum lilies. He went quietly to the door, not to distract the wandering attention of the children, and noticed two boxes on the wall, labelled *Free-will Offerings*, and *Parish News Bulletin Fund*. His dog, who had been sitting patiently on the coco-nut matting in the central aisle, followed him into the sunshine.

Chaffinches sang in the lime-trees, and bees burred over the grassy mounds and daffodils and leaning stones. He walked among the graves, reading the epitaphs, most of which expressed in homely and pathetic verse, a strained joy that the dead had gone to a better land. Many times he wandered back to one stone, cut with the words of the hundred and third psalm, and repeated slowly,

'As for man, his days are as grass; as a flower of the field so he flourisheth:

For the wind passeth over it, and it is gone; and the place thereof shall know it no more.'

Yellow-glistening celandines, with seven, eight, nine, and ten petals, were open in the grass. Sometimes a thin coloured line gleamed in the air, for spiders were throwing out their gossamers. He nearly trod on a slow-worm, lying coiled beside its refuge and winter sleeping cavern at the base of one of the elm-trees – a jam-jar once holding flowers on the mound of a suicide. It was weak and torpid; tenderly he placed it in the sun beside some primroses.

On many of the grave-mounds rested wreaths of marble-chip in the form of flowers and leaves, with stalks and twigs of wire, made in an Exeter factory and sold by the gross to store-masons.

Maddison had been in the churchyard nearly half an

hour when a man in black clothes walked with a quick shamble up the avenue of limes, and prepared to touch his cloth cap several times before he finally took it off, revealing hair close-cropped, and the colour of carrots.

'Good morning, Mules,' said Maddison.

'Bootiful air, sir, bootiful weather. Tes nice to see the sun, zur.'

'Yes.'

'Bootiful air and weather, sir. Be ee looking at the tomb-stones, zur, be ee looking at the tombstones?'

'I be, Mules, I be.'

'Miss Goff likes to see they graves looking tidy, zur, looking tidy. I shall have to fetch along my scythe soon. Daffodils be bootiful, zur, daffodils be bootiful. Miss Goff planted over five hundred bulbs last autumn, zur, over five hundred bulbs. Miss Goff did. Planted them with her own hands. Miss Goff. Miss Goff be very good to poor people's graves, zur.'

'I'm sure she is, Mules.'

'Very fine daffodils, zur. Daffodils. Fine Daffodils.'

'I think I would rather see living flowers than artificial wreaths.'

'That's what the parson doth say, only don't ee go telling I zaid zo, zur. They hartifissal wreaths, zur. His reverence, zur, don't like to see they hartifissal wreaths. On this last month's *Parish News Bulletin*, he wrote he would like to zee the lobster pots and bird-cages removed. His reverence, zur, he called them lobster pots and bird-cages. People didden like it, zur, only plaize don't ee zay I told ee. It bant my business. Not my business at all, zur. It bant my business, so my wife doth tell me.'

Mr. Mules, the sexton, verger, and church-cleaner, also the village postman, was nervously fingering his cap. Maddison thought that the reason of his garrulity was probably due to fear of other people, and of Miss Goff and the parson in particular. Actually he had meant to bid the

gennulman good morning, and to say it was a fine day, and
to pass on. Now he was in a mental agony lest he might have
said too much.

'You won't mention what I did tell ee, will ee, plaize zur?'

'I shan't say a word,' Maddison promised him.

'Thank ee, zur, thank ee very much. Thank ee. His
reverence be very good to me, zur, I'm sure. Thank ee.' He
patted his waistcoat. 'I've got windy pains very bad this
morning, zur.'

'Then don't drink strong tea with your meals. And you
would probably feel very much better if you had those stumps
of teeth in your jaws pulled out.'

'Ah ah, you'm a funny man, zur, a funny man, beggin' your
pardon. I've never had no trouble with my teeth, zur, no
trouble at all, zur, never had a day's toothache, zur.'

He laughed, showing rows of brown stumps, and repeated,
'You'm a funny man, beggin' your pardon, zur. Beggin' your
pardon, midear.' He looked over his shoulder. 'Us musn't
laugh in the churchyard, zur, musn't laugh in God's ground.
Do you think us must, zur?'

'No, we must be either hypocrites or idolators. Can you tell
me who owns that empty cottage over there, just under the
church wall? It's empty, I see.'

'Belongeth to Cousin Billy's widow, zur. Cousin Billy's
widow. Scur cottage. Over there, Scur cottage. Why, be ee
thinking of renting thaccy, zur? Be ee thinking of renting
Scur cottage? Be ee surenuff?'

'I did think of it.'

'It be turrible damp inside, zur. Turrible damp. It bain't
good enough for a gennulman, zur. Beggin' your pardon. I
shouldn't like vor ee to live in Scur cottage.'

'What's the rent?' asked Maddison eagerly.

'I can't say for sure, zur. Cousin Billy's widow might not
like it if I told ee what the rent was. The rent's been rose, I
vancy. They do say though that it used to let vor a pound

a quarter. But don't ee say I said so. Tes Cousin Billy's property, zur. Cousin Billy's widow doth own Scur cottage. Cousin Billy's widow.'

'Well, I'll see Cousin Billy's widow. Where does she live?'

'Tes by the Plough Inn, sir, the Plough Inn.'

'Thanks. Now I want to know something else. Do you knock down swallows' nests every year? In the church porch, I mean.'

'Oh yes, zur. Yes, zur. They be dirty birds. Miss Goff be very particular lady, zur. Very particular. Miss Goff. Particular, zur. Miss Goff. Oop. I got they windy pains bad, you'll excuse me, zur.' He tapped his waistcoat again.

'Get it up by all means, my dear fellow. So Miss Goff has the nests knocked down, does she.'

'Yes, sir, they'm dirty birds. Miss Goff's been very kind to poor old Mules, zur. Very kind lady. I hope to be alive to bury her one day. I should like to see her settled in safe. Miss Goff's been very kind to me, zur.'

At this point in their conversation the children ran out of church, greeting the verger with cries of 'Mules! Ould Daddy Mules!'

'Hurry along homewards, midears. Hurry along. The gentry will be coming soon. Hurry along homewards, midears.'

Maddison thought with irony of the shelter denied to swallows, and the legend of the bird's name. Svala! Svala! as it flew in a darkening sky, crying to a man on whom the bludgeons of lightless minds had fallen. Console! Console!

As the verger went into the church, Maddison said:

'Not with eggs in, Mules?'

'Oh no, zur. I don't let the birds bide there long enough. Miss Goff told me not to let'n bide there. Miss Goff says the swallow be a good bird, zur, and aits up all the vlies. All the flies, that's it. Swallows aits the vlies, zur.'

'I'd like to put a board up to protect women's hats, then they could bide there, couldn't they?'

'Oh no, zur, don't ee do that,' cried Mr. Mules in alarm. 'Miss Goff wouldn't like that, zur. Proper lady, zur. Miss Goff. Proper lady. Miss Goff, zur. Richest lady in the parish, zur.' And putting on his cap and taking it off three times, and smiling all the time, Mr. Mules hurried into the church.

'He seems to see three of everything, your dutiful digger of graves,' murmured Maddison to Jean, meeting her in the porch.

'Where have you been? Why haven't you been over to see us? You'll come to dinner? He must stop, mustn't he, Mary? Aunt Edith will be bucked. She's fallen in love with you. Ron and Pam are home from school, too.'

When the greetings were over Jean went away to see an absent child of her class, who was sick, so she said, and Mary stayed with him by the old stocks beside the porch. Rooks were cawing in the elms above the western wall of the church-yard, and through the lower branches could be seen the plastered end of the empty cottage.

'Mary, will you come and look over that cottage with me? Now?'

She hesitated before saying Yes, and he said:

'But perhaps it would be better on a weekday? Perhaps people –'

'I don't see that it can make any difference being Sunday. Do you?' She looked doubtfully at him.

'*I* don't think it matters a bit: but most people think important what I think unimportant. The thing is, I don't want to get you in any sort of trouble. Let's go up the church tower instead. And look into the rooks' nests. They won't be scandalized!'

'You shall go up if you want to,' said Mary.

'What about Billjohn?'

The spaniel walked slowly to them, over the graves, his stump-tail moving regularly with his forefeet.

'He'll be all right,' said Mary, greeting the dog with affection.

The key was in the door in the wall at the base of the tower. A curtain hid the space wherein depended six ropes with coloured sallies. Here were hung the surplices and veils of the members of the choir. The slow dull tick of the clock came down from above, where the weights hung motionless on steel wires.

The air behind the door was musty, and they climbed in darkness, turning at each upward step upon the narrow stones, worn concave by centuries of nailed boots. A lancet window soon let in light. Darkness again, and upwards, touching the rough cold stone with their fingers, their feet clopping loudly. They paused at another narrow cobwebbed glassy slit, and their whispers drifted up and down. After the fourth slit they had climbed to the belfry, where the ponderous bronze bells, green with the blown salt of the centuries' storms, hung in their oaken cages, with roped wheels motionless and stays upright. Sun-bars like wasps lay on wood and metal, where light came through the southern slats. Maddison climbed over the beams of the cages, and felt in an old swallow's nest on a mildewed joist of the roof above.

'The swallows will be back soon.'

'Yes, how lovely!'

The wind passed with a beautiful soft sound through the belfry. After some minutes, she said, suddenly remembering that it was Easter Sunday:

'We'd better not stay here. They will be starting to ring soon.'

'Plenty of time. I am listening to the wind. What's the lettering on the skirt of the tenor bell?' He knelt on the cage and peered down. *R-e-l-* – it's very hard to decipher – *i-g-i-o-n.* Religion. *D-e-* is that a *v* or an *a* – it's an *a* – Death. Religion, Death, – '

'They'll start soon,' said Mary, patting the whining spaniel with her in the doorway. 'Don't distress your poor boy.'

'There's bags of time,' he replied, happy that she was anxious for him, and more deliberate than before. 'Religion, death, so far. *A-n-d p-l-e-a-s-u-r-e –*'

'It's "Religion, death, and pleasure make me sing." '

'But there's something more,' he replied, hanging head downwards between the skirt of the bell and the cage.

'They are only the impressions of pennies.'

'Yes, I can see where some one had been trying to dig them off.'

'Every choirboy for six hundred years has tried to do that. Come on.'

'No hurry.'

'Bother the boy, he's worse than Benjamin,' she murmured, playfully, springing on to the cage, and sitting against the wheel of the great bell. She was barred like a wasp from her waist up.

'If the guest is to be decapitated, the hostess must also, I suppose.'

'Don't you fall!' he exclaimed. 'And if that wheel revolves you will be flung off.'

'I don't care.'

'Get down! They may start ringing at any moment!'

'I'll get down when you get down!'

'Mary, you are deliberately being a naughty girl! You do what I tell you. Get down!'

As she did not move he put his hands on her ribs, and pretended to shake her. It was a sweet shock to feel the warm flesh of her ribs under the thin silk blouse; she blushed, and he looked steadily at the lovely face whose eyes were turned away from his gaze. 'No, don't,' she whispered, 'the ringers will be coming in soon.'

Immediately he climbed away from her, and jumped off the cage. He waited in the doorway and held out a hand to help her without looking at her. She jumped off the beam by herself.

The circular stairway led up to a door, and when he pushed it open starlings and jackdaws took flight from the embattled stone parapet, and from the wire stays of the flagpole. A dazzle of sunlight extinguished for a few moments the colours of the yellow and grey lichens spread on the stones, and the thick green coin-like leaves of pennywort growing on the dark mould of elm leaves in the corners. Outlines of hearts and of boots, with initials and dates, were cut on the dull lead roof; he saw the letters M.F.O. within the outline of a small naked foot, and was about to take out his knife and remove his shoe when he saw a larger foot near it, with the initials H. de W.

'Howard cut them both, ages ago – it was the year the War broke out, just before he went up to Oxford.'

A faint and momentary feeling of blankness came over him. It departed. He examined other initials and dates, as though intently, thinking, I will go back when we get down, and never come again. Why did I come? Fool, fool, fool. He put back the knife in his pocket, and looked down at the churchyard.

The tower seemed to sway in the wind. Below, the shadows of the tombstones cut across the green mounds. The celandines were like stars in the grass. He imagined himself falling, and the power of his imagination transfixed him like a sword driven into the length of his spine.

Mary saw him shudder, and pulled his sleeve. 'Don't lean over.'

'I am still afraid of height,' he said mournfully. 'I am a coward. Fancy me climbing over a precipice for young peregrine falcons!' He added, nervously and quickly, 'All my philosophy of the world and the human spirit is based upon a conviction that everything I think is right; that my beliefs are the ultimate truth. Well, they told me when I was young that I was deceitful, indolent, and cowardly. I am still everything I was! They must be right, and I am wrong! If you weren't here, I should jump down.'

'It's not cowardice! People tell children stupid things about themselves. It is a question of being used to height. You lift up a kitten that's not used to it, and see how it claws you in its fear! Howard hasn't any fear; he's been climbing since he was a child; but he doesn't know one note of music from another. He gets miserable because he hasn't got a musical ear!'

He said hesitatingly, 'Then do you think I am not all wrong?'

'I have always believed in you,' said Mary, surprised and concerned for his sudden haggard look.

'I wish I had always believed in you,' he replied, with his head turned away, and she felt so happy.

From the tower he could see the white lines of the breakers on the estuary bar. Water gleamed in the creek between the sea-walls, in the dykes, and in plashes on the green plains under the sandhills, where the snow-water still lingered. Below the low heave and shift of thousands of sandy hillocks, the sea was bluer than the sky; and so clear was the air that the cottages of Clovelly could be seen across the far-lying bay, like a trickle of white shell-specks in the long low headland ending at Harty Point.

The Great Field, a flat hedgeless area of tilth, lay beyond the street, divided by landsherds, or narrow grass strips, into scores of elongated and curved fields. Some were green with winter wheat, others with clover in stubble, others a dark brown with recent ploughing. Rich dark furrows, smoothed by the share, gleamed in curved lines. Seagulls, daws, starlings, and rooks walked on the Joseph's-coat of drab colours. More than thirty landlords of the Great Field, more than thirty thousand rats as hated tenants of the holes in the landsherds. The colours of the corn and clover, of plough and fallow, of water and sea and air made him say, 'Lovely England! The Great Field was like that before Doomsday.'

'I am so glad I was born on the Burrows! I love them more

than anything. It would be miserable if we had to give it all up.'

'You mean if all property was taken over by the State for the common good? And human nature relieved of the corrupting influences of possession?'

'I meant rather, if we had to sell it. Mother thinks of Michael having given his life for the Burrows.' A gull cried above them. 'Poor Mother. She loved Michael too much, she told me once.'

'And I don't suppose Michael thought of the Burrows at all when in France, except when poignantly longing to be back home, away from the fear and the misery, and the fatigue of rain and shells and sleeplessness.'

His voice became slower and filled with an impersonal sadness. 'Poor little English Michael, poor little German Michael, each a shovelful of brownish dust and bones lifted from the chalky subsoil of the Hohenzollern Redoubt, and taken, each in a coffin twelve inches wide and six feet long, one to Laventie perhaps, the other to that dreadful forest of black crosses on the white chalk of the Labyrinthe. Many coffins to a lorry-load, they are so light after the years.'

The cadence of his voice brought the tears to her eyes, and she turned away. Immediately he was remorseful for what he thought was his callousness, not knowing that her tears were impersonal. He took her hand and pressed the back of it against his lips.

'O Mary,' he said, 'I was speaking my thoughts, which are often sad, for the truth of things is sad.'

'I know.'

'The truth of things can only become joyful if things are plainly seen by every one.'

'Yes, I know.'

'People who don't see the earth and sea and stars plainly are spiritually corrupt – and spiritual corruption begets physical corruption. That is the real cause of the Great War.'

SPRING

Whenever the rooks' cawing ceased they could hear the high shrill slurs and trills of larks above the Great Field. Gold-finches sang in the orchard of the Vicarage lying under the northern wall of the tower; white hens were in a field behind the orchard, small as orange-pips.

'I want that empty cottage,' he said, pointing to the sloping thatch below.

'I don't see why you shouldn't,' replied Mary, turning her hand now loose in his, and clasping it. 'But it is very damp, I believe. It has been empty since the War. Have you given up the other one?'

'It has given up me. The roof fell in last night.'

His smile gave her encouragement, and she asked why he did not go and live with them at Wildernesse. 'We've got many spare bedrooms, and Mother meant it when she invited you, you know.' He did not reply, and she said, 'I can see the governess cart.'

Along the road below the sea-wall, beyond the marshman's cottage, Mrs. Ogilvie was driving Miss Chychester, while Mr. Chychester with Benjamin and two other children were walking behind.

'They will be here in ten minutes. The ringers have just gone in.'

They lingered in the sunshine, listening to the larks, to the remote pealing of bells borne down the valley of the Taw from Pilton. The footfalls of a man walking the village street were distinct, as was the voice of a woman talking at her cottage door two hundred yards away. He heard the name of Miss Mary, and another woman's voice asking 'Who be'n.' The tower appeared to be creaking; the ropes and wheels were moving under the lead roof. Mary said they had better be going down, and she was stooping to enter the low arched door in the turret when the tremble underfoot increased, and with a dinning crash up the spiral stairway the six bells began to ring the treble-hunt. As they trod slowly down the stone steps a sonorous beat rose and fell through the torrent of sound; the tenor bell by the doorway hurled itself to the top of its swing, where the metal tongue smote its deep mouth. He leant for awhile against the stonework, exhilarated by the immense torrent of sound, imagining the flame and smoke of a barrage.

Six coatless ringers stood at the base of the tower. Ropes ran up through holes in the beam above, to be tugged at the sally, to run down, to be tugged, and released to fly up again. The captain told the changes. Maddison had to push between the wall and the back of one of the ringers, until recently a colt; it was his first Sabbath ring, and the unexpected touch on his shoulder caused him to start, and to hold on to the higher end of his rope, at the downward roll of his bell's wheel, an instant too long, with the result that he was jerked off his feet and pulled up to the beam, to drop again, still clutching the rope. As he was about to be jerked up a second time Maddison leapt and gripped the rope with his right hand, and the extra weight of eleven stone lessened the jerk and the ringer dropped off. Fortunately the bell was next to the treble, and light; for if it had been the tenor, which weighed a ton and a half, the ringer's neck would have been snapt against the beam.

'Upwards!' cried the captain, and in two rounds the five bells were set in stay. The single bell tolled on.

The captain of ringers, a butcher by trade, spoke loudly in his anger, for he had been frightened.

'Corbooger, what be ee doing up to tower on Zunday? You'm no right at all to be up there.'

'Hush!' begged Maddison, thrusting his injured hand into his pocket, and dreading lest people in church might hear, and Mary be blamed, when it was entirely his fault. 'I am so very sorry. Do please go on ringing.'

'Being sorry wouldn't have been much good if my boy Sam had been killed,' shouted the captain. 'Tidden right for you to go up to the tower on Zunday, and you'm a gennulman, and should know better. Us'll see what Miss Goff has to zay to it! And bringing dogs to church, too!' and he kicked the spaniel, who was standing on hind legs, and whining with agitation. It yelped, and Maddison stood still, forcing away a desire to attack the captain.

A hand with work-nobbled knuckles pulled back the curtain, and the verger's cropped head, celluloid collar, purple tie, and black shoulders were thrust through. 'It be all right, Mr. Budd. It be all right. You shouldn't speak so to a gennulman, Mr. Budd. Miss Mary went up the tower with the gennulman, Mr. Budd.'

'Gennulman or no gennulman, the gennulman's got no right up to tower on Zunday,' asserted the captain.

'That be quite all right, Mr. Budd, that be quite all right,' said the soothing voice. 'You'm in God's House, Mr. Budd, and the tower be His, and it be for Him to zay whether the gennulman should go up the tower, and not you, Mr. Budd. Plaize to peal they bells, midear. Plaize to peal they bells. Miss Mary, plaize to come this way, plaize to come this way. This way, zur. Thank ee.'

With relief Maddison, who was breathing fast, saw that the church was empty, except for an old woman being helped into a seat by two young women. With Mary he went through the porch, and into sunlight. The lone bell ceased to toll. He pulled his bleeding hand out of his pocket, turning his back to Mary.

'You've hurt yourself,' she said, at his side. 'Do let me tie it up. O dear, the skin is torn.' He took the handkerchief and tried to tie a rough bandage with his teeth. She waited with fingers ready to help, but he would do it himself.

Outside the Plough Inn, fifty yards down the street, about a dozen boys and young men in blue serge suits were standing against a wall. Every fine Sunday morning they stood there, waiting for five minutes to eleven. Most of the village maidens coming alone down the street never dared to pass the young mechanics, masons, and farmers' sons, and either went by in a band arm-in-arm, or, if they were alone or in couples, waited for the Wildernesse gentry to go by, to follow immediately behind and so escape the cheeky remarks and bold stares and requests to 'come walking.'

The pony and governess car soon appeared at a trot, and three girls walking behind it. Some way farther back walked Mr. Sufford Chychester with a boy and a girl Maddison had not seen before. The old gentleman wore a bowler hat and a grey suit creased down the arms and trousers; the boys wore Eton jackets and trousers, and worked their legs with long strides to keep pace with the old man. When they came nearer he saw that the girl was beautiful, with a mass of fair hair down her back. Mrs. Ogilvie and Miss Chychester were surprised to see Maddison with Mary, but only Miss Chychester showed it. Mrs. Ogilvie observed that he wore no hat, and greeted her with one hand in his trouser pocket, and that he had brought his dog with him. Did he intend to go to church with a dog? He was shaved, and otherwise normal; wearing the same flannel trousers which looked as though they had recently been washed (indeed, they were still damp, but drying rapidly).

He offered to put the pony into its stable for her, but Jean came out of the post-mistress' cottage and led it away.

'Don't you worry, I say. Shall I take your dog and tie him up?' He went with her, afterwards returning to the church, while the spaniel tied to a yellow spoke implored with eyes and shaking stump not to be left.

'I saw Mother's look at old Billjohn, but I'm very glad you've brought him. We'll enter him for the hunt to-morrow. My dear, you must stay this time. It's so damn dull at home. I'm in the choir, wouldn't think it, would you? Cheerio. See you after the service.'

They entered the church. Maddison walked to the bench

farthest back, and sat down. Just behind the members of the choir were assembled. The girls were arranging white veils. There was whispering and giggling among the village maids; one said quickly, 'After you with the glass, Gladys, quick, for gracious goodness sake, 'tis for Miss Mary.'

He pulled a book from his pocket, and began to read. It was *Songs of Experience*, by William Blake. He was reading:

> 'So I turned to the Garden of Love
> Which so many sweet flowers bore,
> And I saw it was filled with graves'

when some one touched him on the shoulder and he saw Mules' head beside him.

'Won't ee sit upalong in front, sir? Nearer his reverence? His reverence, zur? His reverence likes to see his flock upalong in front, zur. Tes the ringers' seat back yurr, sir. Upalong in front, if you plaize, zur. Plaize to follow me, zur.'

He followed, and was shown into a pew near the children. He thought how much better village children were dressed than when he had been a boy. Or was this a faulty retrospect? He wondered if these children hated the village schooling; and looking back on his own schooldays, recalled the fear and repression in the presence of some masters, the fear that was a bending of the spirit: the rowdiness and insolence in the presence of others, the straightening of spirit. For the boys were uninterested in nearly all they were taught; putrid mental food vomited in rowdiness! He wondered how many years would pass before men and women would have common knowledge of the havoc wrought on an immature mind's tissue by forcing into it facts which the mind refused. Nailing the tiny quivering white wings of the child mind to a wall of bricks and mortar, where they withered, and – farewell to a mind that might have soared to the stars when it was grown! The child Shelley had escaped, Shelley had grown to manhood with the beautiful luminousness of his mind's pinions unbroken. That luminousness cast a pale glow on the earth around it, which was kindness, and understanding – a race of Shelleys would not make war, because they would neither distrust nor fear, being trustful and fearless themselves . . . the bells 'coming down' made a riot of sound. The organ began to play.

Mr. Mules, walking awkwardly on the extreme tips of the rubber heels – cut from an old motor tyre – of his Sunday boots, his body bent, his arms held partly out for balance, returned up the aisle to the young gennulman who had so taken his fancy, with a prayer book. Mr. Mules made no sound, and at the touch on his shoulder Maddison started violently, as though from a trance.

'No, thanks,' he muttered.

"Ave ee got one?' whispered Mr. Mules. "Ave ee got a prayer book? 'Ave ee a buke? 'Ave ee surenuff?'

Maddison shook his head impatiently.

'Won't ee have a book, then? A buke? Won't ee have a buke?'

'No, thanks, I said,' said Maddison, frowning. 'I hate prayer books. For God's sake leave me alone.' Then seeing the concern on the other's face, he took it. 'All right, I'll have it. Thanks very much.'

'Thankee. Thankee,' mumbled the verger, retiring on his rubber heels, glancing from roof to floor, from floor to roof again, in his agitation before so many faces.

Astonished to hear music from the third act of Parsifal, Maddison peered to see the organist, and recognized the slight figure of Diana Shelley in a grey toque covering curls tawny as a squirrel. He awaited the service with alertness, pleased at this augur of reality. Wagner's spiritual testimony revived in a Devon church! The vicar appeared out of his vestry, walking slowly forward, his hands clasped in front and his face composed and expressionless. He looks horribly solemn, thought Maddison doubtfully.

SPRING

A very little child came into the church, half running, half skipping, holding the big red hand of her adolescent brother, a farmer's son. The child's nervous smile darted about the church; quickly they entered a pew, and sat down. After them walked a tall woman, with a man's stride and thick figure and big brownish face. She wore a black velvet hat, which gave her a Tudor appearance – she looked like a portrait of Cardinal Wolsey, as she strode to her rented pew. Many eyes watched her, for she was the richest woman in the parish.

The Vicar walked slowly down the aisle, and waited by the font for the organ to cease; but the Parsifal music flowed from the organ for nearly two minutes. Jean grinned, Mary smiled, the Vicar stood pale and composed, the Tudor woman fidgeted in her pew. The Vicar began to pray; and watching his lips, the members of the choir said *Amen* in unison, just as the Parsifal music ceased.

The congregation rose as the organ began to play the air of hymn 135; the choir walked slowly up the aisle, led by the smallest choir-boy carrying a brass cross, and followed by the Vicar, all singing.

After the hymn and prayers the second psalm was announced. With stealthy-careless glance Mary watched Maddison opening the prayer book, and finding the place. The words of the psalm she sung without thought; but Maddison was reading them as though for the first time.

'The kings of the earth stand up, and the rulers take counsel together; against the Lord, and against the Anointed.

Let us break their bonds asunder; and cast away their words from us.

He that dwelleth in heaven shall laugh them to scorn: the Lord shall have them in derision.'

Mary saw him smile ironically, and knowing that she was looking, he glanced deliberately at the Union Jack hanging over the Lady Chapel; but being unable to see this, she wondered why he had smiled. During the reading of the first lesson he frowned good-humouredly at her once or twice, while the Vicar was reading,

'And the Lord spake unto Moses and Aaron in the land of Egypt saying . . .
Your lamb shall be without blemish, a male of the first year: ye shall take it out from the sheep, or from the goats:
And ye shall keep it up until the fourteenth day of the same month: and the whole assembly of the congregation of Israel shall kill it in the evening.
And they shall take of the blood, and strike it on the two side posts on the upper door post of the houses, wherein they shall eat it.'

She saw him open his book of poems, and become absorbed in it.

> 'Turn away no more;
> Why wilt thou turn away?
> The starry floor,
> The watery shore,
> Are given thee till break of day.'

He stood rather wearily during the Te Deum, she thought; and sat down very quickly before the second lesson, which was read from the first chapter of Revelation. After the words –

'I am Alpha and Omega, the first and the last: and, what thou seest, write in a book,'

their eyes met, and he smiled, and slightly nodded his head. She knew he was thinking of *The Star-born*.

The Benedictus, and prayers for the King, Royal Family, Clergy, and People followed; and then Hymn 138:

SPRING

'Christ is risen! Christ is risen!
He hath burst His bonds in twain;
Christ is risen! Christ is risen!
Alleluia! swell the strain!
For our gain He suffer'd loss
By Divine decree;
He hath died upon the Cross
But our God is He'

was sung by the congregation in lusty relief, and roving eyes moved about to catch anything interesting. During the second verse Mr. Chychester left his pew, and went forward to light the altar candles. He returned slowly, avoiding the gaze of others by looking on the coco-nut matting, and quietly re-entered his pew. Jean smiled at Maddison twice during the singing; and he glanced more than a dozen times at Mary, casually, not to reveal to others his interest.

They went down on their knees again for more prayers. One of the congregation, a grocer who came to church for business reasons, sitting with another man just behind Maddison, discussed how he had bought a bag of potatoes cheaply from a man at Heddon Mill; his whispered account breaking off abruptly with the Vicar's voice.

During the next hymn the Vicar disappeared, to reappear in gorgeous vestments of crimson and gold, and read from the Gospel. The Nicene Creed followed. Its plaintive melody appealed to Maddison, and he wanted to sing; but he did not, owing to his ignorance of its whereabouts in the prayer book. Mrs. Ogilvie dropped on her knees during this chant, and Mr. Chychester bowed and crossed himself.

Afterwards the Vicar gave out announcements, standing in front of the choir stalls. He thanked 'all those who had so kindly helped to make our beloved Church look so spring-like.' He asked for gifts of eggs for 'poor old people in the Work-house.' After the announcements, he delivered an address.

He said that nowadays Man searched after God in many ways; but the laws of Nature were unchanged; God was unchanged; the Spiritual World was unchanged. Men were trying all over the country to find Truth, but they were going about it the wrong way. That was why the churches were empty, as they could read for themselves in the newspapers. It was very simple. Christ said, 'Come unto Me.' Where else would one answer that summons, except in church? The Truth had been discovered already; no man need seek the Truth in vain. Christ was their Life. They believed in the Resurrection of the Dead, its comforts, because they were united with all those who had gone before them. There were empty chairs in some cottages after the great winter they had passed through; voices were silent of loved ones, forms no longer seen. Where were they? Rejoicing with them all in church at that moment, knowing of the reunion to come, which Our Blessed Lord had made possible, by His Blessed Sacrifice on the Cross nearly nineteen hundred years before.

At this point in the address Mary saw the spaniel walk up the aisle, with a dragging leash, and after searching and sniffing, enter the pew where Maddison was sitting. Heads moved with curiosity. The least pause in the Vicar's voice, during which *swink-swick-svala! Swink-svala!* was heard somewhere up in the dim cavernous church; and a bird flew over the carved oak screen with its apostolic figures, decapitated in Cromwell's time, and wheeled above the choir stalls. From Africa it had flown, to the green and pleasant land of its birth, the first swallow!

She looked at Maddison, half turned round in his pew, watching with keen bright eyes the sweeping throw of its wing-tips as it rushed into the sunlight at the open door. Benjamin stared too, and Ronnie, until nudged by Mrs. Ogilvie. Then Maddison was walking down the aisle, leading the spaniel by the leash. The sunlight illuminated him before he vanished.

The address continued, so far as the small congregation was concerned, as other addresses or sermons had continued. The voice of the Vicar lost whatever personality it had ever had in a drone, so that the voice should carry without strain. No one was moved in spirit; and few listened. One very old woman – it was the cottage-owning relative of Mr. Mules, referred to as 'Cousin Billy's widow' – followed the address with moving lips; for years she had had a fearful conviction that she was shortly to die; as she had believed that every one in the village was after her money, especially Mr. Mules, whom she called 'Sly Fox' when he came once a week to tend her garden. She believed among other things that the bad weather had been sent by the Lord because of His dislike of two General Elections in Great Britain during the same year.

The labourers' children who had been sent back to church to have them off their mothers' hands thought of sweets, birds'-eggs, toys they would never have, pictures in the Bible they had been shown, Sunday dinner coming after the words and hymns, play in the afternoon, and Jesus on top of a cloud without proper boots.[1] Often they giggled, and wriggled, and stared about, in the unnatural stillness.

The labourers' and farmers' growing daughters thought of clothes and hats, their own and other maids', of sweethearts real and probable and imaginary, of their artificial silk stockings, of the coming dance in the new Club-room, and of Miss Mary and Miss Jean and Miss Diana. Bant they nice! And such smart clothes. Oo, how lovely to be a lady like they!

Mr. Sufford Chychester, among a multitude of semi-formed cogitations, thought of his wife, of his sons, of the coming otter-hunting season, of the gentians that were blooming in his rockery, of the veins on the back of his hand, of the probable length of the address. He did not care very much for

[1] During Sunday School they had been shown a picture of the disciples wearing sandals, and of Jesus suspended above.

Garside's sermons; but he lived in the form of the high-church ritual, and never doubted the literal truth of its every part. Miss Edith Chychester sitting beside her younger brother actively enjoyed every part of the service; she could hear nothing of the address or the lessons. Church on Sunday was a happy change to which she looked forward; she loved the ancientness of the building, and being deaf, she could think her own thoughts without interruption.

Mrs. Ogilvie was thinking of the discomfort of having to listen to the strident nasal bellowing of Mr. Budd singing out of tune and time across the aisle. One really must suppress that man's voice; but how to do it graciously, without hurting his feelings? She listened to fragments of the Vicar's address, as he stood near the pulpit whence extended the iron arm holding the old-fashioned hour glass. As a girl one had had to endure an hour, and frequently more! And again she thought of that young man, coming hatless to church and with a dog, and of his ridiculous and unrestrained staring at a bird. Such a bad example to the children! She forgot him, and listened to what the Vicar was saying – that things which at the time might perhaps appear almost too hard to bear, were ordained for the good of Man by God Himself in His Infinite wisdom – whose infinite Goodness and Grace were once and for all proved by His Blessed Gift of His Only Begotten and Beloved Son Jesus Christ for crucifixion by His Chosen People.

Miss Goff, sitting alone in her rented pew, in front of Mrs. Ogilvie, was ruminating on the pity it was that one's Vicar (he had been the incumbent for two years only) was not a gentleman. Many times Miss Goff had remarked in drawing-rooms that one liked one's Vicar to be a gentleman, and the people liked it too. He was so tactless and obstinate in many things; sometimes he argued almost rudely with her, and once had told her that he was in charge of the parish, and of the affairs of the Church, and not herself. As though one would

interfere with his legitimate work! Miss Goff listened critically
to his pronunciation, as she had listened many times before.
Yes, definitely a cockney tinge in some of his words. He was
common. But why must he advertise the fact by wearing a
celluloid collar? Then looking at Mary Ogilvie's profile, so
grave and sweet, she felt more restful, and wondered where
she had heard the name of Maddison before. She would have
to speak to the Vicar about the rudeness of that man Budd
to one of the Wildernesse guests. It was all part of the dreadful
Socialistic ideas, which were spreading so alarmingly, and must
be religiously checked. But where had she heard the name of
Maddison before?

By the choir stalls the Reverend Aubrey Garside preached
with all the earnestness of a nature devoted to what he believed with almost all his conscious being. This earnestness of
his convictions showed in the lines of his face, in the emphasis
of his manner, in the uses of phrases and terms that came
easily, phrases too worn and old to make impression. His
brain gave out a paraphrase of his assimilated theological
readings. He employed, without consciousness of any tech-
nique, a sort of archaic Eastern imagery to express to unimagi-
native English people the letter of the New Testament. He
said things that raised no speculative thought in his half-
listeners: referring to the Virgin Mary in one sentence, and
mentioning her several children in another: speaking of the
Miraculous and Divine paternity of Jesus of Nazareth, and
then of his royal lineage from King David through his father
Joseph.

Children played and fidgeted. The grown-ups sat still and
patient in the pews. Towards the end of his address the Vicar
saw a mouth open before him in a yawn, giving a glance of a
few remaining teeth. Catching the Vicar's eye Mr. Budd
clapped four large fingers and a thumb over his big brown
moustache and his mouth closed behind them. The Vicar
turned away.

123

A noise of breath and stirring on seats. All were relieved. Many saw plates of beef and potatoes and cabbage with the mind's eye. The Vicar could think no coherent words in prayer afterwards, as with eyes shut he kneeled before the altar. He felt distress that Christ – the Crucified – meant so little to most of them. He thought that all they cared about was making money, eating, drinking, and loving. He felt himself as destined 'to fight as a humble soldier of Christ' to his life's end, and this phrase passing in his mind fortified him to face indifference and misunderstanding and even hatred. And feeling strengthened, he began to pray to God for power to continue his Work.

Out in the Great Field Maddison was striding, in the sun and the wind, his spirit spread out to all the life around him – bird and tree and grass and man. He moved buoyantly, his mind aspiring beyond the lark-song, beyond the heat of the sun, luminous with the thought of Man's liberation through his unfinished work, *The Star-born.*

Chapter 6

THE two men guests, Maddison and Garside, sat opposite to each other at supper that night. The Vicar of St. Sabinus' Church was unmarried, and forty years old. He and Mrs. Ogilvie were supposed to be friends. Their friendship had begun on an unspoken understanding that they had certain tastes in common; but when a few months after his arrival in Devon from a curacy in a northern suburb of London, Mr. Garside had brought Mrs. Ogilvie three volumes on psychology, and had urged her to read them, he discovered that common taste bifurcated at what he called the new literature. Mrs. Ogilvie read very little, except the *Morning Post*, the literature of her various charitable organizations, occasional stories in monthly magazines that found their way into the house, and an occasional novel, of a light and undepressing type, such as a good murder mystery, from one of the lending libraries in Barum.

Recently Mr. Garside had been worrying about himself; for he had moments, of which he was ashamed, when he disliked Mrs. Ogilvie. He found himself, in her company, repeatedly having to repress remarks upon what he, in facetious self-excuse, was wont to call the 'serious side of life.' Thus the previous Sunday evening – for after every Evensong he returned to supper at the manor, with Mr. Chychester and Mrs. Ogilvie and Benjamin – he had pronounced, in Benjamin's absence, the result of his 'little talk' with that disobedient and furtive boy.

'I spoke to him in a friendly fashion, Mrs. Ogilvie, as you requested me to, and my diagnosis, if I may use a term that is perhaps permissible, is that he has a pronounced Oedipus-complex.'

'An Oedipus-complex? Whatever is that?' had asked Mrs. Ogilvie.

'It is one of a series of terms instituted by Professor Freud of Vienna, to describe a pathological state wherein the patient behaves morbidly owing to inhibitions and repressions. It should not trouble a healthy boy; indeed, it is the source of much that is often best in a man.'

'I am afraid that doesn't explain Benjamin, Vicar.'

'Well, you see, Mrs. Ogilvie, the Oedipus-complex is complicated.'

'Oedipus? Whoever or whatever is Oedipus?'

'Well, Oedipus was a Greek who, as you know, of course, er – well, how can I express it now, well, Oedipus, as you know, committed incest with his – er – maternal parent.'

'But how absurd,' had said Mrs. Ogilvie, in her smooth voice, and the clergyman's eyes, which always seemed half-closed behind the convex lenses of his spectacles, had almost closed in a laugh. Not a laugh of mirth, but of embarrassment and a feeling, never quite absent from him at Wildernesse, that perhaps Mrs. Ogilvie did not quite approve of himself. On the question of his early life, and his education, or his lack of education – even now at times he longed to be able to call himself a Keble man – he felt sure and happy, for he had told Mrs. Ogilvie about himself, and she had been like his own spirit reassuring him. There was nothing like a lady – a real lady – he must remember not to pronounce *real* as though it were a fishing reel – 'true' was a safer word. Dreadful thing, to have to worry about such trifles! The young man opposite did not appear to worry about them: what a nice sensitive face he had, cultured and thoughtful.

He looked at Maddison with friendly expectancy across the refectory table, which darkly gleamed with the shine of the branched silver candlesticks. He felt sure that he was intelligent; and he needed only to meet an intelligent man at Wildernesse, he felt, to be fully understood. After all, Our

Lord Himself was silent and ill at ease in certain atmospheres.

Beside Mr. Garside, sitting small and still, was Diana Shelley. Her white face, faintly freckled on the straight brow, was immobile. Every feature was clear-cut, Grecian. She ate her food slowly and slightly. When spoken to, she replied with the least words, with the least movement of lips and eyes. The light blue eyes had the coldness of ice-light, as though strange with sleeplessness, which was the more suggested by the faint red rimming of the lids, and the colour of the lashes. The eyes were both ardent and cold like the sky above snow-peaks. Mr. Garside thought her very beautiful; but affected, posing, conceited; and he was determined never to refer to what he thought was meant to be a snub to himself, and an affront to his church, by her playing of that German music on the organ that morning.

She was tawny-tressed, wearing her hair bobbed; the ends were curly. Mr. Garside thought the pointed and manicured nails of her fragile fingers was an unnatural affectation. He was not the only person who considered Diana Shelley cold and vain.

But Mary! Mary was – was charming. The same manner for every one, rich or poor. She would make an ideal wife for a parish priest – alas, he would never dare to ask her, much less her mother, for permission to pay her attention. Ha yes, a snag there! For the Reverend Aubrey (as sometimes he thought jocularly of himself from the viewpoint of his earlier aspirations) had more than a suspicion that Mrs. Ogilvie's friendship would cease if she knew what he thought of Mary – for Mary was 'county,' and he – well, he was far beneath them really. Also, there was Howard . . .

Roast beef, a pressed tongue, and pie for supper, with potato salad, and pickled onions for whosoever liked pickles, said Mrs. Ogilvie. Unfortunately Mary's green tomato chutney had 'run out.'

'I like pickled onions,' said the Vicar, forcing a light and humorous tone. 'I fear my taste is profoundly vulgar, but I must confess a pickled onion is most tempting.'

He made several attempts to transfix one with his fork.

'They're rather hard,' said Mary, 'The last lot I made went very hard; I can't think why.'

'There should be a pickle spoon,' remarked Mrs. Ogilvie. 'Benjamin, would you fetch it, please.'

'I'll go,' said Mary, half-way to the door before Benjamin had laid down his knife.

'I like pickled onions too,' said Benjamin, and grinned at Maddison.

'You would,' replied Ronnie promptly. 'Awful things.'

'Don't be silly,' said his mother, tolerantly.

A fire was already lit in the drawing-room, for the music after supper. The dogs were shut in the hall; periodically the familiar blowing of Coalie came under the door. Roast beef, a pressed tongue, and rabbit pie for supper! Coalie sometimes groaned in the outer darkness, as in his mind he ate the supper several times over; but he swallowed only the juices in his mouth. But Coalie's god was not his belly; his god was the memory of his dead master, Michael, for whose smell he still sought about the house and the garden on warm, good-scenting days.

The walk and swim that afternoon with Maddison had made the boys hungry. The spaniel sat between them, silent with privilege, his snout upheld, waiting. Portraits were shadowy on the walls. Old brass pestles and mortars, wherein dead Bassetts or their servants had pounded damp saltpetre and sulphur and charcoal into a paste of gunpowder, stood on the tall chimney-piece, with square miniatures painted on ivory. The oak beam overhead was rough-hewn, showing the marks of axe and adze; it had been the timber of a ship. Wooden pins stuck out of it. Wild daffodils leaned out of a bowl on the table, beside clusters of primroses, gathered that afternoon by Mrs. Ogilvie and Aunt Edith.

'Did you see the eclipse of the moon the other evening?' said the Vicar, to Maddison. 'It was most interesting from the Vicarage garden. Actually it did not look like an eclipse – rather a coppery colour over the moon; but the round shadow of the earth was quite – er – notice – er, to be clearly seen. If anyone in England doubted that the earth was round – er – all round, that is, a circle everywhere –'

'A sphere,' suggested Ronnie.

'Exactly,' beamed the Vicar. 'The shadow was absolutely a proof of the earth being spherical.'

'So we all read in the paper,' said Jean. 'But I don't believe it.'

Mr. Garside paused with a fork-load of beef and pickles on the way to his mouth.

'Oh, but surely –'

'I believe,' said Jean solemnly, 'that the earth is round in one sense but not in the other. Endways it is round, but lengthways it is long-drawn, shaped like one of those half-boiled suet puddings we called Spotted Dogs at school. The Americans dwell in the half-boiled part – as Uncle Suff knows. Nothing will shake my belief, for I am dogmatic, and have a closed mind.'

She laughed at Maddison.

'Quite right about the Americans,' remarked Mr. Chychester, whose experience of them was three motor-coach-loads of heavy-jowled, horn-eyed Rotarians, looking on at the annual August meet of the otterhounds at Lynmouth.

'Bravo!' said Mr. Garside, and swallowed his mouthful when it was only half-chewed.

A noisy and a merry meal, for 'the kids' were home for the Easter holidays, Ronnie from a South Coast preparatory school, Pamela from a cheap school in South Devon.

'Mum,' said Pam, hugging herself with delight at being

home, 'a girl at school called me a guttersnipe when I said we cleaned our own boots at home, but I didn't care, so that was sucks to her, wasn't it?'

'A peculiar word, sucks,' remarked Mr. Garside humorously, 'but very expressive. Children are expressive in their vocabulary, aren't they?'

Miss Chychester, who sat next to him, touched his hand and said, 'You are not eating your beef and pickles, Vicar.'

'I am getting on very nicely, thank you, Miss Chychester.'

'What did you say?' asked Miss Chychester.

Jean, who had been staring moodily at the table before her, said suddenly, 'He said, "Sucks to you."'

The old lady was puzzled. 'To me? I do not see any. Where are they?'

Mrs. Ogilvie looked worried. 'Do be quiet, Jean. It's not fair to talk like that to Aunt Edith.'

Jean's answer was to pick up a leg-bone of a rabbit and drop it on Miss Chychester's plate. 'There's one.'

'Jean, please do behave,' said Mrs. Ogilvie.

'I merely gave her a bone to suck to keep her quiet. Here's another one, Aunt Edith!' and Jean picked one half of a skull off the side of Benjamin's plate and dropped it beside the leg-bone.

The three children waited eagerly for more fun. Mr. Chychester ate on, Mary sat still, Maddison moved a crumb on the table, Diana looked bored, Aunt Edith looked puzzled.

'And here's a sphere to float in your pond,' as she dropped pickled onion in the old lady's glass of water.

'Jean, please behave, or leave the table.'

'Hurray, that's what I wanted. I can't stick you people. Mustn't do this, mustn't do that, it's bad form, it's unconventional, it's – except Will. You ought to have heard the Old Jig's indignation because you went up the tower on Easter Sunday morning! I would have remained up there, if I'd been you. I jolly well admired you when you walked out this morning. Wish I'd done the same. Well, cheerio, chaps.'

She went out of the room, slamming the door.

Tears came into her mother's eyes, but did not fall. No one looked at her, except Benjamin, who took furtive glances.

' "Umbered" is the word to describe that moon,' said Maddison softly, looking across at the Vicar. " 'Umbered – discovered by gleam of fire." '

'Ah, yes!'

Mrs. Ogilvie said, as the kitchen door dully banged, and in her normal voice:

'Uncle, may I give you some more tongue?'

'Ha, good tongue,' said Mr. Chychester, holding out his plate to Maddison, who had jumped up to take it. The rest of the feeding went easily.

After the port had gone round, and during the nibbling of biscuits, the dogs were allowed into the dining-room. Coalie did the tricks taught by Michael. First a piece of biscuit was placed on his nose pointing to the ceiling; then Ronnie ordered, Trust! The muzzle remained in that position until the cry of Paid for! when Coalie snapped the biscuit and crunched it up. Then Jock, at a cry of Three cheers for the King! barked thrice, and was rewarded with a biscuit tossed at him. Piece after piece of biscuit rewarded Coalie and Jock and the beggar Billjohn, until Pam noticed Rigmarole the Irish water-spaniel looking on, his curly ropelike tail sweeping, sweeping, sweeping! Poor Rigmarole had learned no dining-room tricks, so he could only sit and watch and hope. No boyish laughter had gone with his training, but the stings of a hazel stick on his back.

'Here, Riggy,' she cried, taking a biscuit out of the box. Maddison watched her. She was a cloud in the shadows beyond the table. She floated in a white frock, tall and slender, her hair free as sunshine. Stroke poor Rigmarole, she was thinking, and then dear Billjohn, who was beating the carpet with his stump. No snarling, no jealousy, Dave was not there, he had gone out with Jean.

The Vicar with his hostess, and Mr. Chychester, went into

the drawing-room, while Mary piled up the tray for Maddison to carry to the kitchen, and Miss Chychester brushed up the crumbs and put them in her box for the bird table. The cloud fell to the carpet, and rolled with spaniel dogs and a brother and a Scots terrier that snarled sturdily in play. A fox's brush was tied to Billjohn's stern by Ronnie, and he was supposed to run and be hunted; but all he would do was to lie down and thump his tail.

Maddison watched them when he had returned from the kitchen: if they could always be happy! Pam with her shy and gentle eyes, that saw no evil anywhere; and Ronnie, with his quick bright movements, his joyousness and health. But children changed; they were changed. Their minds were slain!

He strayed into the hall, where it was dim and quiet. He could hear the murmur of voices in the drawing-room, and the noise of plates being piled in the kitchen down the passage. While he was hesitating about returning to help Mary, he heard a faint scraping hiss, and immediately afterwards the hall was filled with music. He saw a movement in the far corner, as Diana Shelley sat on the floor beside the cabinet gramophone, and put her head inside the open doors, which slightly muffled the sound. After a short while the door of the dining-room was flung open and Ronnie ran out.

'I say, Mr. Maddison, do come and see your spaniel, I say. Don't listen to Diana's muck. She'll ask you to bury your face inside the gramophone in a minute. She tries it on everybody. She's quite harmless.'

'Go away, you little crow,' said Diana, jumping up and stopping the record.

'I say, I like that. Anyway, you're only a crow yourself,' retorted the boy, amiably stroking her hair. She kicked at him, he jumped backwards nimbly, and seeing Billjohn wagging the fox's brush in the doorway, left her to throw his arms round the dog and cry endearments into its ear. This tickled the spaniel, so that it shook its head, and immediately Ronnie made a buzzing noise to tickle it the more. The spaniel growled, while his stump wagged, whereupon the boy put the dog on its back and kneeled over it, growling with bared teeth and pretending to bite its throat. Then seeing that Benjamin was helping himself to more prunes from the sideboard with his fingers, he abandoned the dog to do likewise.

The hall was quiet again.

'Dreadful little beast,' said Diana.

'Put on the record again,' he said eagerly, 'I want to hear it. What is it?'

'César Franck's Symphonic Variations.'

'It's great stuff!'

'Put your head close to the thing, and you'll feel the power of it,' said Diana.

He sat down, and put his head sideways into the hollow, resting his chin and cheek on the cold interior wood. The amplified scratch of the needle was hard like the crackle of light-waves in space; the deep notes of the strings harsh in his ear. He thought of a barrage before the first assault on the Hindenburg Line, which he had watched before dawn from an upland cornfield by St. Leger, of the light and sound of massed cannon that thralled the senses. He took the weight and strength of the barrage, and grew mighty with it, until it was but a seam of sound nicked with flashes, and puny in space and time controlled by the vaster roar of stars. The scratch of the needle was the sound of stars travelling through elemental darkness, and after their age-long travail the Light of Khristos was arising in the void, wan and phantasmal and pure, while Huquol the Shadow was everywhere, Huquol the never-seen, Huquol the all-powerful, yet powerless with the Star-born! Though the little earth fell into dust, and all the suns burnt black, and every star-dwarf of the infinite firmament joined with Huquol, the Light would arise again, and life stir on new worlds, and be raised out of Darkness.

The celestial music ceased, and was renewed; and he withdrew his head to see through his tears Benjamin placing a small oil lamp on the table, and Mr. Chychester regarding him with amusement.

'I can't understand what you can see in that row,' he said. 'It beats me.'

Maddison tried to keep sudden hate out of his voice.

'It's the celestial spirit of man expressed in music, Mr. Chychester.'

'H'm. It sounds a horrible noise to me. I'll have mine in the drawing-room, thanks, my dear,' turning to Mary who was standing beside her uncle with a tray of coffee-cups. After the spiritual exaltation, during which his ideas were reality to him, the remark of Mr. Chychester was a wrench to his mind. He refused coffee with a shake of his head, and looking up, saw that Mary's eyes above him showed the rebuff, although she still smiled. She bore the tray through the drawing-room door, and he stood up, thinking that he had done an avoidable unkindness. And to Mary, who worked for others so hard and so cheerfully! It was no virtue so to do, for it was her nature to think of others before herself. With these thoughts he walked to the window, seeing the evening star, bright with beams over the dark tree-tops. A mountain range of cloud lay above it.

When Mary returned with the tray he beckoned her, while hurrying on his toes towards her. They were alone in the hall. She placed the tray on the table, and he led her by the arm to the window.

'The Night is alive,' he said beside her, 'Come with me to the wreck on the sands. Think of the loneliness of the sea.'

'I wish I could,' she replied, looking at the planet. 'I love her in the evening, but I think I love her best in the morning.'

'Oh yes. She is the White Lady in my book.'

'Do show me that book.'

He shook his head. 'It is not right yet.'

SPRING

'How is your poor hand?'

'All right. Mary, come with me now, and I will tell you about the Star-born, and the Water Spirit, and Wanhope. The ruin of Lydford Castle on Dartmoor is the scene. I passed it in the winter, and made a fire there, and tried to sleep, but it was too cold. The owls were hooting in the ivy.'

Mary said, 'I love owls.'

'Then come out with them. Listen! You can hear the roar of breakers on the North and South Tails of the bar! Salmon will be running up the rivers, and leaping into the star-lit weir-pools! An owl! In the trees – see its dark shape? Come on, Mary! You should have been with me years ago, only I did not know it until now!'

They stood by the window, feeling as one being, inspired by the globe of light that trailed its beams for them, and gleamed in their eyes.

'Keats' Bright star,' he said.

'And Jefferies.'

'And the nativity star of little Jesus.'

The voice of Pam calling eagerly, 'Mary!' and Ronnie bawling, 'Where are you? Oh, there she is. Thinks we can't see her. Silly ass, standing by the window.' He came to them. 'Good lord, I say, Pam, it isn't half bad. Jupiter, of course. No, it isn't. It's Venus.'

Pam stood beside Mary, tall, short-skirted, slender, feet close together. She was waiting to say something, all eagerness, bright eyes, and loosened hair.

'Mary!'

'Yes.'

'Can – can we have some music?'

'Ye-es, I should think so. Unless mother wants to be quiet.'

'You ask her, Mary. Oh do!'

'Songs,' cried Ronnie. 'I'll sing "Sea Fever"! It's in my bag still. I'll go and get it.' He leapt upstairs.

'Come on,' said Pam, skipping away, and returning to pull her sister by the hand.

'Coming?' Mary called back over her shoulder, before disappearing round the wall that led to the lower door of the drawing-room.

The drawing-room was shaped like the letter L, two rooms of the original farm-house having been made into one. The piano was near the lower door, by an open fireplace lined with white tiles, in which stood a basket-grate of iron wrought in a design of four cormorants, each gripping in its beak an eel. The basket stood empty; a vein of rust ran down one of the cormorants, to spread in brown around its webbed feet, with a few flakes of soot. Near the fireplace was a pedestal and white marble statue of a female figure reclining on the moon in its first quarter. Next to the pedestal was a Chinese lacquer cabinet, and beyond it a Chippendale cabinet with glass doors, the shelves within holding china.

Opposite the white-tiled fireplace, at her rose-wood writing table, sat Miss Edith Chychester. Before her was a blotting pad, crossed and recrossed with the faded inversions of her thin handwriting – some of it more than three years old, she was so careful. Neatly beside it lay a yellow ivory paper-cutter; a paper-weight made out of the fuse-cap of a 77 mm. German shell; an eyeglass that her father had worn when hunting, screwed into the brim of his tall hat; a tray with sealing-wax, candle-snuffers, seals, pens. There were photographs on the table; one of Mary sixteen years old, long haired, wearing white blouse with collar and tie, hardly smiling, big eyes looking a little startled (at the photographer's unnatural requests); another of Michael four years old, a brave small figure on a Shetland pony; a miniature of Miss Chychester herself at three years, tiny and pink and good, sitting on a rocking horse, white linen trousers, with frills, to her ankles. This miniature was a favourite of Miss Edith's; to her it was a pretty relic of quaint old-fashioned days.

SPRING

Miss Edith was writing in her diary. She dipped the pen in an inkpot of polished horn shod with a silver shoe held by eight silver clenches, which had belonged to her father, and which bore, on a silver shield, above another shield engraved with the Chychester coat-armour, the inscription,

The Hoof of
The Castaway
A Favourite Hunter
the property of
Rawleigh Chychester Esqr
Queens Bays
He carried his owner well for
three seasons and died 5 September 1847
in consequence of over-exertion on
The Chains, during a severe run with
The Devon and Somerset
Stag Hounds.

Miss Chychester wrote in her diary:

'Sufford's lumbago better. To-day a swallow, the first this year, flew into church dur^g Morn^g Serv^e, so trusting are God's small creatures in His Everlast^g goodness. My nuthatch has returned with a pretty mate; they run up the legs of the tray like mice, and he chooses a tit-bit for her, and she flutters her pretty wings, and away they go. Young Mr. Wm Maddison was taken ill in church this morning.'

Miss Chychester had made a small round stop after the last word of her entry when warm lips touched her cheek, and she turned to see Pamela's hair on the black silk of her upper arm, and Pamela's smiling lips and eyes.

'Darling!' breathed Pam, skipping away. She *had* to kiss some one; there was to be music!

'Yes, dear, if you like,' was Mrs. Ogilvie's reply to her breathless question. 'You don't mind, Vicar?'

'Oh no, no. Not at all,' beamed Mr. Garside. 'We should be rejoicing now,' he added, half to himself.

His glasses glinted; his eyes almost vanished in his expression of affability. He tried to feel affability on all occasions, towards his fellow-creatures; he was often appalled within himself when he found he disliked, even loathed, some of them. Having never lived a full life himself, he had strong convictions of what was sin and what was virtue. One of his habits was to deplore, in his sermons, with all sincerity, what he called the modern young woman. Quite often he saw Jean with his mind's eye when he thought of the modern girl. But he liked children, and most children, in their trusting natural generosity, liked him because he liked them.

'What a big g – child Pam is growing, to be sure!' he said, balking at the word 'girl.' He avoided the word in conversation whenever he remembered it in time, as his pronunciation rhymed with 'curl,' and this, he feared, was incorrect and vulgar. Once only he had dared, in Mrs. Ogilvie's presence, to pronounce it 'gel'; and whenever he thought of that occasion he felt uneasy, and filled with exasperation at the idea of such trivial things being considered important (as he thought).

His remark about being a big child made Pam feel uncomfortable. She remembered her skirt, and the need, which on several recent occasions had been impressed upon her, of covering her knees when she sat down. She turned about, and skipped to the piano, where Mary was turning over an untidy heap of music scores.

'Mary!' she whispered, lest Aunt Edith might hear; then turning in the direction of the group round the fire, hidden by the wall, she made a fierce grimace, hopped on her toes, clawed the air with her fingers, and hissed, 'Sucks and sucks and sucks to you!'

A bump and a bang on the door, and a rattle on the floor. With a vision of himself singing *I must go down to the sea again*, Ronnie did not reason that the door would open easiest when the handle was fully turned. It was an old brass lock; the iron screws holding it to the door were loose and rusty in the wood. Their worn threads had held against many impatient bumps of shoulders; but since Ronnie had become one of the senior boys at his prep. school, he had, literally, and in the slang of preparatory schools, been throwing his weight about.

While he and Pam were searching for the screws on the floor, Mary slipped through the open door, and saw Maddison still standing by the window. She went to him.

'Won't you come in?'

Looking out of the window, he said in a low voice:

' "There were nights in those times over those fields, not darkness, but Night, full of glowing suns and glowing richness of life that sprang up to meet them. The nights are still there; they are everywhere, nothing local in the night; but it is not the Night to me seen through the window."

'Jefferies is dead, but he lives in the night. At least, he lives for me. I must go out . . . these walls and roof shut it away. Mary, come with me.'

She hesitated.

'I can't,' she said. 'Howard's coming, for one thing. But don't think I don't want to go out. Another time I'll come.'

She felt he would not understand, and suffered a little.

'Mother expects you to stay to-night. Your bed is made up.'

How lonely he looked standing there. She was sure he did not have proper food, his face was so thin. He was a poor little boy, with no one to look after him.

'I think I shall walk back to-night.' The spaniel, lying two yards away, chin on paws, sprang up, for 'walk' was the sound he had been awaiting.

'But no roof to Rat's Castle!' exclaimed Mary. 'Of course you can't go. I like talking to you,' she added, with a sort of laugh in her throat.

He said in a changed voice:

'Ronnie, Pam, Jean, Diana, your Mother, Uncle, Aunt, that's seven, eight with yourself, nine with Howard, ten with yourself. And you do the cooking and washing up! Roof or no roof, I'll stay and help you.'

'You counted me twice,' said Mary, feeling happier. 'And Alice Bissett comes in from Burrow Farm to help in the morning.'

'You're twice as important as anyone here, that's why I counted you twice, deliberately.'

'Anyhow, you needn't go if it's only a case of making extra work. Beside, Jean is expecting you to stay for the opening meet of the Wildernesse Rabbit Hounds to-morrow. The Master will be disappointed if you're not there.'

'Who is the Master?'

'Jean!'

'And the hounds?'

'Oh, Dave and Coalie, and Jock, and any other dog that comes along! It's great fun, and we never kill anything. Michael started it when we were all kids.'

Ronnie reappeared, saying, 'I can't find one of the mouldy screws. But the others aren't any good. The threads are rusted away. Are you coming to play, Mary?'

'All right. Come and hear Ronnie sing?'

'Oh rot, I can't sing,' said Ronnie.

'Come and sing "Sea Fever," ' said Maddison.

Aunt Edith, having done her duty by her Diary, had joined the others by the fire, and was hidden round the turn of the room. They were reading, and made no sound. Mary sat on the wide piano stool, and placed Ronnie's song open before her. He began in a sweet tremulant treble. While he sang, he imagined himself on the bridge of a destroyer, going down the Channel without lights, steering by a star through the running tide. Cleared for action against the enemy! Glorious! His voice became firmer.

SPRING

*To the gulls' whay and the whales' whay where the whind's like a
phwetted knife*

he was singing, his eyes fixed on the western window, when a
face moved palely behind the black glass. It smiled. Pamela
yelled, 'Howard! All right, Son, I'll go! I'll go!' She was
already rattling the worn handle. 'All right, I'll go. Let me
go,' cried Ronnie, behind her. The two children rushed out
into the hall. Mary did not turn round.

Maddison sat in the arm-chair behind her, his hand shading
his eyes, studying her. Dark hair, gentle line of cheek, small
head whose beauty would not pass with age. Warm face and
hair of Mary, warm shoulder and round upper arm and
gentle breast shaping through her blouse. A spirit in harmony
with wind and leaf and star, a natural spirit, wild and pure as
a linnet in sunlight. How sweet a thing to love, to be loved
by Mary! With the desire came a sweet ache, a faint terror,
for the darkness beyond mortal love.

Mary was touching a key with one finger, waiting. She would
not turn round. Voices were coming through the hall. She
rose off the stool, lovely with flushed cheeks, gave Maddison a glance, smiling and startled, and slipped through the
door.

He listened to hear how she would greet Howard. He heard
her eager 'I'd almost lost hope of your coming to-night. Why
didn't you come to supper?' and he said, as though to another
being in travail within himself, Go away before it becomes
agony and blackness. Don't go back to the old ways.

He jumped up as they came into the room. Mrs. Ogilvie's
clear voice behind him said, 'Well, Howard, my dear, I was
beginning to think you had given us up altogether,' obviously
pleased to see him, as she went forward.

'Hullo, Aunt Connie,' said Howard, kissing her. 'What have
I been doing with myself? Oh, the usual sort of thing. Never
seem to have time for anything, and yet I seem to get nothing

141

done. How's Jean after her toss last Monday?' He gave a casual glance round the room after he had asked this question, and seemed to lose some of his freshness.

'She's all right, I think, but rather bruised, poor child. Tell me, Howard, what did really happen? It is the hardest thing in the world to get Jean to tell us anything. She is very plucky, you know.'

'I know. In fact, she's sometimes reckless, the way she takes her own line over that rough country. Last Monday, for instance, when hounds –'

After greeting the people round the fire, Howard told them about Jean's mishap, which had occurred during a run with the Stevenstone Foxhounds across a boggy tract called Melbury Moor, when Jean, whose high spirits in the hunting field had made her most popular, had taken a high bank instead of waiting to follow through a gap; and the Buccaneer, taking off from boggy ground, had fallen back. Fortunately Jean was thrown clear, but she had picked herself up, trying to smile, yet only able to walk at a limp, owing to pain. One of the motor-cars following the hunt had taken her home.

Every one in the room looked at Howard's face while he was speaking. He seemed to fill the room with the richness of good humour. Broad shoulders, ruddy face showing the blue of shaven chin and lip, baritone voice, pleasant and easy – their feet felt firmer as they listened to him.

'Diana's here,' said Pam, during a pause, her bright eyes fixed on his face.

'Yes, Mary told me she was coming,' said Howard slowly, looking into the red-brick hearth, where a great brand, of a split ship's timber, was glowing among the coals of lesser wood. He pulled out a gold case, and offered a cigarette to Maddison.

'You've got the Red room this time,' said Pam. 'He's been put in the Patchwork room.'

'Who?'

'Willie. I mean Mr. Maddison.'

'You're living in the cottage by the iron mines, aren't you?' asked Howard, turning to Maddison.

'I was until yesterday, when my roof fell in.'

Mr. Sufford Chychester and the children shouted with instant laughter. When the merriment was over Howard said to Ronnie:

'I'm afraid I barged into your song. What about it?'

His arm rested on Mary's shoulder. She was smiling up at him. Maddison said something about nothing to Pamela as they went back to the piano. Howard sat on the curved stool beside Mary, to turn over for her. There was just enough room for the two of them, sitting close together. Mrs. Ogilvie came and stood behind Howard, while Mary turned back to the beginning of the song. She smiled at Maddison – she had compared him to Howard, and felt sorry for him, so obviously was the comparison to his disadvantage. A little queerness, eccentricity, about him – perhaps it was accounted for by his having had no mother or brothers or sisters. There was no harm in him, one could say that fairly confidently, and perhaps Howard and he, both being out-of-doors young men, might get on together. For herself, she found him rather a bore, with nothing to say, outside the subject of birds, which he seemed to know fairly well.

Returning Mrs. Ogilvie's smile, Maddison felt an acute sense of his detachedness. Suddenly, as Ronnie, having drawn a deep breath, and opened his mouth, was about to sing, *I must go down*, Howard got up and said:

'I say, Aunt Connie! Won't you sit down?'

'No, dear boy,' replied Mrs. Ogilvie, putting her hands on his shoulders affectionately, and pressing him down beside Mary again.

'I wish you'd shut up, Mother!' said Ronnie. 'I can't sing if people keep mucking me.'

'What an expression to use to one's mother, my darling.

However, I promise I won't muck you any more. Oh Mary, before Ronnie begins. What has happened to Diana?'

'I don't know where she went to,' replied Mary.

'Mum,' said Pam, 'I asked her to play the Gollywog and that gorgeous thing Ciccly Buller played at half-term concert, you know, the Sunken Cathedral, and she said – Pam glanced in the direction of the fireside group, and her voice dropped to a whisper. 'She said, Not while that – that – priest is in the house!'

'How very stupid of Diana,' said Mrs. Ogilvie crossly. 'She and Jean think it is fine, I suppose, to use those stupid words and expressions. Besides, it is such bad form to speak like that of anyone. Now Ronnie, darling, the song.'

Ronnie was kicking one of the legs of the stool with his foot.

'Ready, Ron?' asked Mary.

Ronnie would not begin.

'Come on, dear,' said his mother, caressing the back of his head. At school Ronnie had been looking forward to singing his new song so much at home, and this evening he had wasted so much nervous energy in fortifying himself to sing before a stranger, that now he had little desire left for his song.

'We're waiting, dear,' said his mother, when Ronnie did not begin. She thought, with sudden fear, Oh dear, I hope he isn't going to develop a moody nature like Jean's. Head downcast, Ronnie kicked the leg of the stool.

'Ready, Ron?' asked Mary, giving him a smile.

Ronnie squirmed inside as he thought of the disaster he had brought upon himself; he felt it was too late to begin now; he had gone too far. He began to dread he might cry.

'Come on, Ronnie, don't be foolish,' said Mrs. Ogilvie. Ronnie's lips quivered, and he kicked the stool harder.

'Well, perhaps you will sing in a minute,' said Mrs. Ogilvie. 'Pam, dear, sing your pretty little fairy song.'

Pam looked uncertain. She knew what Ron was feeling.

'I don't know where it is.'

Ronnie gave the stool an extra hard hack.

'Ronnie, you are just being silly. Now sing like a good boy,' said his mother, in a conciliatory voice. She believed that Jean's moods of bad behaviour were due, in part, to the leniency of Nan, the children's old nurse, aided by the lax parental attitude of her dead husband. All her hopes were in her remaining son. She patted his shoulder.

'Shut up,' said Ronnie, in desperation. The worst happened; a tear fell.

'Come, Ronnie, do not speak to me like that. And please stop kicking that stool.'

Ronnie's face was puckered.

'Damn you, shut up,' he blubbered, shifting away from her.

'Ronnie, go up to your bedroom,' said Mrs. Ogilvie quietly, as the Vicar, who had been listening with intense interest to what was being said, moved down to them.

Ronnie did not move.

'Orders, Ron,' said Howard, who knew that Mrs. Ogilvie was feeling almost as miserable as her son was. Ronnie's restraint broke entirely. He snatched at the song, ripped it up, and flung down the pieces, and blundered to the door with bowed head, and unable to see for tears. The lock came away in his hand and was thrown violently into the corner; and, flinging back the door, he rushed out. They heard the thuds of his feet as he ran upstairs.

'Poor Ronnie, he did so want to sing his song,' said Mary, softly, to Howard, after Mrs. Ogilvie had gone out of the room, murmuring an apology for Ronnie's bad behaviour.

'It wasn't bad behaviour,' said Maddison, very softly. 'It was natural behaviour.'

The Vicar looked puzzled at this remark.

'Oh come, Mr. Maddison,' he said genially. 'Surely it is not natural to be rude to one's mother?'

He heard Maddison murmur something, and caught the word 'unnatural.'

'But surely that is a contradiction in terms?'

'In the letter, I suppose it is.'

'But tell me, Mr. Maddison; I don't quite follow you, but I want to. How do you define natural?'

Maddison hesitated, pushing his hand rapidly over his hair, and frowning. 'I'm afraid I might hurt your feelings,' he said, with a shy smile.

'Come,' said Mr. Garside quizzically. 'I belong to what to-day is probably the most bitterly criticized profession. I shan't take offence at anything you may say, even if you did walk out of my church this morning.' He added apologetically, 'But perhaps it was the dog?'

'No,' said Maddison, also apologetically, 'I'm afraid it wasn't entirely the dog.'

'Well, then, what was it? Mayn't I know?'

Maddison did not reply for a moment; but overcoming a nervous reluctance, he said, 'Well, I'll put it this way. When the swallow flew in, and out again, I had to follow, for truth is to be found only in the sunlight.'

'Oh!'

There was another pause. Both men seemed to be trying to control and conceal the agitations of their thoughts. Mary and Howard went to the other end of the room. Maddison said, breathing deeply, and touching a black note on the piano, 'When men begin to isolate truth out of its native sunshine, they lose it in many sects and creeds.'

'What has that to do with being rude to one's mother?'

'If you want children to absorb the genius of the earth, then leave them to play in the sunshine, and do not let them come into your church. If you must have them there, then tell them natural, that is, true things of their little brothers of the hedges and fields, the birds and animals and trees and flowers, which are linked to them somewhere behind the sun. But tell them nothing they cannot understand, or in your zeal you will distort Jesus for them when they are grown up.'

146

Mr. Garside was held by the strength that came into the bright and steady eyes that were now looking into his own.

'Have you any experience of teaching small children, I wonder?'

Maddison frowned violently. 'No. That's on another plane altogether.'

'Exactly! There's a theorist all over. Nail him down to facts –'

'Such as a cross!'

' – and he slips away on another plane. And, you know, they seem to like Sunday school. Fortunately in Mary and Jean,' added Mr. Garside, 'Mary especially, but Jean is good – they have ideal teachers.'

'Yes, I suppose you are right,' replied Maddison slowly, his eyes becoming moody.

'But do go on. You interest me very much. I cannot tell you how refreshing it is to meet a young man nowadays who thinks of other things besides cricket or football, and this jazz dancing and flying about on motor-cycles.'

'The growing spirit,' smiled Maddison.

'You agree with such things?' asked Mr. Garside in astonishment.

'I can see that you don't play football, or dance, or own a motor-bike; but to be serious, have you considered the possibilities of the machine? One day they will be the true servants of man; but the old civilization must pass away first, with its old ways of thought, its growths that are ruining men – the growths of industrial nationalism condoned by its organized religions, its newspapers which serve industrialism and not truth, with their negation of nearly everything that is beautiful and of the spirit.'

'Oh come, Mr. Maddison, things are not so bad as that!'

'No, things are fine, aren't they? Let us recall the really splendid work of the Church during the last War, when most of the European Christian bishops preached that their national cause was holy, or if they were even stupider, that God had ordained the War for His special purpose. All filthy blasphemy.'

Mr. Chychester shifted in his chair, and sat still again, as though reading.

'You sound to me very much like a Communist, Mr. Maddison.'

Maddison smiled, a little sadly. 'I was hoping you would not say that, although I feared you would. Why must you label ideas? Why don't you think plain – *plain*.'

'I do, I hope. Surely you aren't a Communist?'

'The ballot is secret,' replied Maddison, 'but even then I will answer your question. I have never yet voted, or made a political speech!'

'Ah ha, a clever evasion. But perhaps you believe in the gospel of Lenin, that murderer, that anti-Christ?'

'Rather anti-priest! The violent mass-reaction against unnatural things! Now we get back to where we started. Lenin dared to be rude to Holy Russia! He is a stupendously great spirit.'

The Vicar began to breathe harder with inward agitation.

'Really, Mr. Maddison, I can't stand here and listen – I – it's appalling, what you are saying! Lenin –!'

'Lenin should be judged by his peers,' said Maddison, with a sort of cold sneer. 'Of course he is a great spirit. He designed a new way for humanity; or rather, slung the old bag of rubbish overboard – all the old mass virtues – those virtues arising out of mass fear, distrust, jealousy, and held together by dividends.'

Mr. Chychester half turned in his chair.

'I've heard that sort of half-baked nonsense before,' he said, and settled down to his book again.

'But I don't understand what you are getting at,' said the Vicar, feeling easier now that he was being supported. 'You must have some reason for what you say. Now let me

148

ask you – since you are frank, and want me to be – Have you any dividends? I don't ask in curiosity, but –'

'I have no dividends.'

'Well, if you owned property, I'm sure you would not talk like that.'

'Exactly! It is because I have nothing that I talk like this. If I had property, I might talk like you. It might be too strong for me; and that is surely what was meant when it was suggested to the young man that he should give all that he had –'

'Yes, I know the modern political trick of quoting Holy Scriptures to support revolutionary theories. But Our Lord is most definite on the subject of combining politics with religion. He said, Render unto Cæsar –'

'A trick? Do you call stating truth a trick? The words of Jesus on that occasion were a retort to dogmatic lawyers trying to make him incriminate himself with the Roman Government – what to-day are called *agents provocateurs* – one of the filthy things our beautiful patriotic civilization is responsible for!'

'I am afraid that subject is beyond me – but I do know that it is both wrong and mischievous – that is, I mean, mischievous – er – the two should not be confused, Mr. Maddison.'

'Why will you insist on my remarks being political?' replied Maddison hastily, to cover the other's confusion at the mispronunciation. 'What I have said is plain truth.'

'Your idea of truth, let us say,' remarked Mr. Garside, shortly.

'Well, the sort of Truth you are supposed to have been celebrating to-day,' replied Maddison softly.

The Vicar responded to his friendly smile, but shook his head as though hopelessly.

'Ah well, Mr. Maddison, perhaps when you are my age you will think as I do.'

'That again will be natural,' said Maddison, smiling. 'For all things that bloom have to decay.'

'Do you suggest that I am in a state of decay?' asked Mr. Garside, beaming through his spectacles.

'Oh no,' replied Maddison, patting his shoulder. 'For some things never bloom at all.'

'Ah ha, I recognize the smart Oxford undergraduate.'

'And my dog –' the spaniel, responding to his master's mood, was standing up with his paws as high as he could get them – 'You recognize a Devon and Somerset staghound? But seriously, you know, padre, the hope of life is in the child.'

He pulled a notebook out of his pocket. 'Listen, this is what I wrote this morning in the Great Field:

'We must free the child, let its mind grow itself like green corn, and all will be well. Putting on the abstract virtues of form, tradition, reverence to an ungrown mind is to produce something unnatural, false, and death-bringing. The swelled and faceless corruption of Ypres was the grave of the old-world ideals! The virtues must develop from within, from the spirit; not from sayings that one's creed is the only true religion, or beliefs that the gilded class of one's nation is the finest product of mankind, that one's flag is the only holy and decent flag. All nations thought that in the Great War. Leave it out of the child's life; let the sun, which tries to get all flags back to one colour, and the wind, that floats all flags, be the ideal of the visible world – the sun that grows the corn and the wildflowers, and the child's mind.'

He stopped, and rubbed his forehead hard, and then went on jerkily, not daring to look at the other man's face.

'And then there's just another little bit.

'Above the sun and the wind is a light that flows as wind, which is a Spirit; but the foundations must be left to grow naturally, or man will never grow in stature with the Khristos.'

Mr. Garside stared at his face, which had become haggard. After awhile he said sympathetically:

'Tell me have you ever seen or heard things as extra manifestations to your thoughts?'

'Only in my own mind.'

'You were in the War, of course?'

'Yes.'

'Were you shell-shocked?'

'No. I wasn't much in action. I was cavalry, or calvary as the footsloggers called us. Whereas it was Calvary chiefly for the Infantry! But why do you ask?'

'I am very interested in psychology, Mr. Maddison.'

Maddison looked at him sharply.

'That needs a preliminary process! Know thyself!'

'Exactly.'

'William Blake was thrashed when a boy for saying that he saw an angel on a tree. Joan of Arc had her voices. So did Socrates and Paul. And Moses, that flat old tyrant. And Dostoievsky the epileptic, who created an idealized modern Christ in *The Idiot*. I say idealized because Jesus himself was probably an irritable – that is, irritated – man. How about them? Were they inspired, or diseased?'

'Undoubtedly they were diseased, with the exception of Moses.'

'Well, damn Moses, anyway. How about Jesus of Nazareth. Was he diseased? He heard and saw things, also, remember!'

'He was divine,' replied Mr. Garside promptly.

'And the others were not divine, in the same, although perhaps lesser, sense?'

'Certainly not. Only Our Lord was divine.'

Maddison said in a hard voice:

'Your conception of Christ is as spurious as your psychological knowledge! In your service this morning there was nothing to wake the spirit so that it could live its life nearer the celestial world – I mean, by way of the imagination. Your ideas are unnatural, and therefore stupid, like the barbarous passage you read out about knocking the little animal's blood on the door-post. You act and speak as though you have never heard or known of Jesus of Nazareth. Of course, you have with your ears, which appear to be of the usual type – inlet and outlet. Otherwise, you haven't yet.'

'Oh come, Mr. Maddison, you must not be so sweeping. Why did you go to church, if you do not agree with religious worship?'

'I thought I might find a friend there.'

'Oh.' The Vicar considered this, then he said, more hopefully, 'Have you read any books on psychology, by any chance?'

Maddison shook his head impatiently.

'I thought not. I will lend you some. I shall be very pleased to do so. Even you might learn something from them.'

They were both absorbed in themselves for a few moments; then looking up, Maddison said, 'Don't take my remarks personally, padre. It is only ideas I hunt.'

'Then you really ought to read –'

'Thank you for offering, but I know already the truth that may exist in them. I don't need to read.'

'Oh! I thought I saw you reading during Morning Service '

'Yes, I was. For companionship, I was reading Blake.'

Mr. Sufford Chychester looked up.

'What, Sexton Blake?' he asked incredulously.

'No, sir. William Blake. A poet. A celestial thinker.'

'Ah, a poet,' muttered the old gentleman, turning over a page of the book, Hawker's *Shooting*, on the reading stand before him.

Mary, sitting on the arm of Howard's chair and watching Maddison's face, smiled: but he would not look at her,

'Oh, look!' cried Miss Chychester, concern in her voice, as she pointed to a wood-louse, crawling on a log in the fire. Maddison saw it instantly, and putting his hand in the flame, calmly picked it off the wood.

'A poet!' repeated Mr. Chychester, leaning back his head and throwing up a glance at the Vicar, whom he thought rather an ass. 'Haven't heard of him. Hullo! where are you?'

'He went out a moment ago, Mr. Chychester.'

'Ha,' said Mr. Chychester, picking up his little pipe, 'I didn't see him go!'

'He will put it in the garden, where it will be happy,' said Miss Chychester, contentedly. 'Well, Vicar, did you enjoy the music? Ronald has a sweet voice, has he not?' She indicated an empty chair beside her. 'Pray make yourself comfortable.'

'H'm,' said Mr. Chychester reflectively. 'It's a rotten age! They'll be stopping otter-hunting next. Oh well, I shall be dead by that time, and so I don't care.'

Chapter 7

On the hall table a tiny lamp, which burned in its steady flame
less than a farthing's-worth of oil in a night of deep winter,
shed a yellow twilight about the bowls of flowers and the tops
of chairs around. Bookcases, the carpet, chests, staircase, were
part of the duskiness beyond the wan white globe of the lamp.
Nothing stirred in the wide and cavernous hall. Listening by
the dog-gates at the bottom of the stairs, Maddison heard a
voice's mumble through the door closed behind him. Then a
tap on a lower panel, and a scratch. The door was quarter
opened, revealing a benevolent spectacled face above black
clothes. The spaniel walked through, and the door was closed
again. It sniffed stocking, heard the enticing whisper of
Walkees? and pranced, panting.

Maddison waited, thinking of his pack in the bedroom, and
wondering where he should go. To the Nightcrow Inn, and
beg a night's lodging from Albert Gammon? Through the wall
he saw the face of Mary: Mary smiling, an apple-bloom of
happiness in her cheeks, smiling up at Howard, his hand – his
big hand – on her shoulder. He could not see Howard with
the mind's sight: he saw only Mary, rising starrily sweet and
remote, out of his spirit's dark pain. Had he but seen her as a
child, solitary and shy of the feelings and intuitions near the
spirit's core, roaming the burrows among the birds and the
flowers in the wind and sun of summer mornings. Why, when
he had known her since childhood, had he never *seen* her until
now; he had sealed his sight with another, and then another:
all the years of wasting life, and Mary never seen till now!
He revisited the Christmas party at Skirr Farm, far away under
the tumuli of the years, when she had stared at him, hearing

154

nothing, seeing nothing, since all her being was given forth in dream. A brighter newer memory, of Mary on the downs above Rookhurst, in the long grass of late summer, and his head was turned away, thinking of that other. Had he but taken her then, bare-kneed, her beauty just out of bud, and drawn her to him, gently, with her loosened hair, and clasping, been as one with her.

Mary's image, starrily sweet and near, filled the shut air of the silent hall. He began to pace around the chair-cumbered space by the hearth, urged to movement by the succeeding mental vision. In its light, which came as a bright yet invisible flash, and started tears in his eyes, he saw Man shackled by ideas that were not of the Spirit of Man: ideas that were of the brain only, not of the spirit which like a White Bird soared over the trackways of the stars. Remembering the wood-louse, he put it on a pot of hyacinths, and then seeing the dull red embers on the dining-room hearth, walked through the open door.

'Brain thought is evil – a sort of glittering scum of darkness,' he said aloud, and stopped, at the sound of a poker banging charred wood.

'I'm umbered,' drawled a voice by the fire, as the sparks flew upwards. Flames broke out of a brand's end, to light half a face, and a hand moving a poker. In the recess of the hearth was a low stool, standing against the stonework; she slid along the stool as far as the back wall, and began to push with the poker-tip the embers into a pyramid. He sat on the stool beside her.

'When I heard the door open I hoped it was Mr. Garside going home,' said Diana.

'I've just been talking to him: he thinks me an idiot,' said Maddison savagely. 'I am an idiot, too, to talk to him.'

'Do you feel squirmy inside?'

'Yes.'

'I know the feeling; when some one talks when I'm trying

to play. So I won't go near them when he's there, or Mr. Chychester, whose idea of good stuff is "The Blue Danube Waltz." '

The reddening embers made faint noises of crackling and tinkling, as though hopeful of new life. Flames rose up, died, were lost in smoke, and flapped again.

'Howard's here.'

'Is that why you came out?'

The spaniel settled under the stool, curled up, and sighed.

'I wanted to go out for a walk,' he said, staring at the embers.

'With Mary?'

He hesitated. 'Yes. Did you hear me asking her by the window.'

'Yes; and I knew she wouldn't go.'

'Why?' he asked, breathing through his mouth, to conceal any sound of breath.

'Because she was expecting Howard.'

He touched the head of one of the fire-dogs with his finger; the iron burned the skin; he deliberately held it there.

'Yes, I thought so.'

Moving a charred knot to one side of the dull red pyramid, Diana said musingly, 'Mary is a faithful friend.'

'Yes. She has been a faithful friend to me,' he said slowly. She was playing the piano – Howard sitting beside her on the curved stool. He watched a pale flame playing above the pyramid; and when the music ceased, he said:

'Will you play to me when Garside has gone? Play that music you played when I was here last. That was noble stuff. I could listen all night to your playing. Will you play it again?'

She shrugged her shoulders. Through the hall and the open door of the dining-room came the tender and plaintive melody of an old Scottish song, a melody simple and true as water flowing in the burns, as the bubble-link and trill of the curlew floating over his young on the mountain side, as the love of a mother for her son. Mary was Scots, dark and true to the earth as her father. In flamy darkness on the opposite wall he could see the portrait of the dead man; he had looked at it intently before supper, seeing Mary in the features.

'That gramophone music was beautiful. Like the creation of light.'

'César Franck's Symphonic Variations?'

'Yes. Is César Franck alive?' He rubbed his head, and said, half to himself, 'I could go to him.'

'He's dead,' replied Diana. 'He died in 1890. No one thought anything of his music. Even men who could write good music themselves.'

He heard Howard singing *Over the Sea to Skye*.

'Even if he were alive, he might not want to see me. He might think, "Who is this fool who clasps my hand and babbles about being my brother when I'm in the middle of trying to orchestrate this blasted new concerto." O Christ, sometimes it is lonely.'

Diana stood the poker against the wall.

'You seem to need friendship.'

He saw himself leaving the house, never to return; leaving Devon. Where to go? Where? Where? And not see the face of Mary. A calm inner voice said, You have felt that frenzy before, and it has passed. It is merely sexual attraction. Eveline Fairfax is nothing to you. And so it will pass with Mary. If only he could be born again out of his old self, the virgin-birth of ancient mystics!

'I'm neither one thing, nor the other,' he groaned.

'What does that mean, Mr. Maddison?'

'I've been bitten by a mosquito, and my blood is infected. A starry mosquito of Khristos, that sucked the blood of Jesus, and ever since has been wandering on the face of the earth, infecting the souls of men. No, before Jesus. The Khristos was before him, and after him. That mosquito arose out of the first steamy swamps of creation; it arose when Light arose, and its wings are God-glimmering.' He ceased wearily, and hid his face in his hands.

'Go on,' said Diana. 'Please.'

'You don't want to hear! I'm only trying to impress you, by quoting my own feeble stuff.'

'I like to hear it. Really. Please quote some more.'

He opened his notebook, held it low over the solitary flame. 'Well, here's a simple biological fact dressed up like a fire-cracker.' He began to read without expression. ' "Man was once one being, and the being became two – man and woman. The spirit seeking its lost part causes the scar – the pre-adam scar – to feel again the travail of the old break. The pain is acute also in animals – our little cousins. It is called falling in love. The more complete the spiritual reunion, the nearer to the Spirit." It sounds to me like nonsense now. The Bible is much better. By God, yes!'

'I thought that was the matter with you!' said Diana, taking up the poker and turning over an ember. He saw Mary in the ember pile, virginal, mystic, shadowy with his hovering love.

'It's the matter with everything!'

'I'm not disagreeing with your paraphrase of the Book of Genesis, Mr. Maddison. No, I oughtn't to have said that; it was cheap. I was trying to impress you, that's all.'

He laughed. 'You've got a mind, Diana.'

'So Howard is always saying, whenever I make a perfectly footling remark. Do you know what the time is?'

'I don't know. I never have a watch. Why?'

'I was –' She hesitated.

'I was merely wondering,' she drawled a moment later, with a cold distinctness, 'whether I should go to bed.'

'I thought you were going to say, "for a walk." I'm going for a walk, before the moon sets. Will you come with me?'

'So I was – and how immodest! However, now you've asked me, I can say, Yes, thank you, Mr. Maddison.'

He took the poker from her, and knocked the pile of embers. 'As far as the sea?'

'Yes.'

'It will take an hour, over the sandhills. Do you still want to come?'

'Yes.'

'I may come back very late.'

'I don't care.'

'What will Mrs. Ogilvie say?' He meant Mary.

'I don't know. And also I don't care. How long is this catechism going on?'

'One question more. Are you any relation to –'

'The famous poet? Yes.'

'You have his beauty of face,' said Maddison.

'So Howard once tried to tell me. But I don't feel flattered; indeed, I feel flattened. Have you seen Shelley's true face?'

He asked what she meant.

'The usual portraits of Shelley aren't true. In Sussex there is a bust of Shelley, done by Leigh Hunt's wife – bulging eyes, curious mouth, and the chin – well, Carlyle, to whom Leigh Hunt left it, said "the fellow looks as though he had swallowed his chin, and didn't like it." '

'Are you speaking the truth?'

'Yes. Wilfrid Meynell, who bought the bust at Browning's sale, told that to a relative. So the family decided not to bid, I expect. Coming?'

She pushed against him, and waited for him to move.

'What is the matter now? Does it matter what Shelley looked like?'

'I was thinking what people said about him when he was alive; and now his face seems to bear it out,' he said.

'The chin was probably due to insufficient nourishment when he was a baby,' said Diana promptly.

'And his ideas due to insufficient mental nourishment when a boy,' he said, speaking his thoughts. 'So much for my ideas!

The psychology of the revolutionary – an incorrigible egotism sealing the consciousness from all good influence, a law unto one's self, accepting mental vapours as reality, believing things held good by the majority to be bad, in actions a disruptive force against things as they are.'

'Father would be pleased to hear you say that. He would say, "You are epitomizing the disease of the age; you are exactly describing the half-baked ideas of my youngest daughter Diana." At the same time, you understand, he has a proper pride in his most distant connection with the famous poet.'

She looked steadily at Maddison's face, and was stirred by its beauty. 'Anyway, you needn't worry,' she said casually. 'Your chin doesn't recede.'

'Thanks to my foster-mother insisting on my having the milk of the "li'l old white spotty cow" of Skirr Farm.'

'You mean Biddy?'

'How did you know?'

'Ah, I know.'

'Did Mary tell you?'

'Yes, years ago. Also about the mutton fat on her hair, and her eyebrows blown off with gunpowder!'

Mary told her! He fell silent.

'What about this walk?'

'Yes-s.'

Thump, thump, thump, went a tail-stump against the leg of the stool.

They went into the hall.

'Don't you wear a coat?' asked Diana, when he had helped her on with hers.

'No. Only this leather jerkin sometimes.' He was listening to laughing words muffled by the wall.

He took such a long time to put on his jerkin and to find his stick that Diana opened the door and went into the lobby. She stood still, waiting. 'Come on, come on, come on,' she muttered to herself. When after a minute she heard no sounds of him she muttered, Damn you then, turned the handle of the front door, and pulled. Smoothly it swung back on its hand-forged iron-hinges, and she walked into starlight.

Her footfalls made no sound on the grassy borders of the path. Half-way to the gate she stopped, watching the open door, which she could just see. Mary was playing one of those wretched dances of Brahms. There was a light fading in one of the bedrooms. After a minute it reappeared in the attic – in the boys' room. She saw Mrs. Ogilvie pass across the window. A natural reason for his disappearance occurred to her, and she waited less impatiently. One minute, two minutes, three minutes, then she heard a footfall on the gravel, and the spaniel racing forward. She thrust hands in the pockets of her short lamb's-wool coat, and walked towards the gate, lightly whistling the air of the fourth movement of the Symphonic Variations.

'Sorry to keep you waiting,' he said, overtaking her. 'I've been talking to Ronnie.'

'I saw Mrs. Ogilvie go to the room with a light.'

'Yes, she said she heard voices, and came to see who it was.'

When the voices and footfalls had passed her bedroom door, Mrs. Ogilvie had been sitting on the side of her bed, holding a letter in her hand. For nearly five minutes, since taking it from its envelope, she had scarcely moved. An untied bundle of letters lay spread beside her on the coverlet. In the open drawer before her was another and larger bundle, with English postage stamps on the envelopes; she rarely untied this bundle. The envelopes of the smaller bundle, which contained twenty letters, were unstamped, except by the red imprint of a rubber stamp, about the size of a pigeon's egg, bearing within its oval a crown, a number, and the words *Passed Field Censor*. On the top of some of the envelopes was written *On Active Service*; and on others, written more hastily, and in pencil, the letters *O.A.S.* only. Each envelope was franked by the signature

M. S. Pomfret Ogilvie. They were letters written from France by her son.

In the same drawer were Michael's first little socks and shoes, with a lock of his fair hair, and those of his toys which in childhood he had thrown behind the big walnut cupboard in the schoolroom. This cupboard had been moved against another wall when Uncle Sufford, bringing some of his own furniture, had come to live in the house, and she had found them, and hidden them away.

Sitting on the edge of the bed, Mrs. Ogilvie did not read. She knew every word of the letter, as she knew all the letters. One glance at the page had been sufficient to unfocus her sight, when conscious thought had forsaken her. Her being seemed to go out of her body. This feeling of being in a void lasted an instant, leaving a woman grieving for her baby – for usually she saw Michael as a baby, when he had needed her most. His first hunger wail, oo-la, oo-la, in the firelit room. In her tears she saw his first smile – a six-weeks smile, that silly Nan declared a wind-pain, as though she had not known her own baby! His first shouts of dad-dad-dad; his first tooth, which had grown from the top jaw, so un-expectedly, when she had been peering at the lower jaw, and gently feeling for the first roughness there. And again she lived through those moments of numbing dread, when, during the packing of a parcel of socks for his men, she had seen the telegraph boy cycling along the road under the inner sea-wall of the marsh; those moments of watching him turn into the drive instead of keeping on to the farm, of taking the telegram, of hiding herself, of praying, before she dared to glance; and crying, in an agony and blackness, to a wraith, Charles! Charles! He is dead, he is dead.

It was Mary who had run to her, and held her and kissed her and said again and again, You've got me, Mummy, you've got me. You'll always have me, poor little Mummy darling; and Jeannie, and Ronnie, and Pam. Words, coming from beyond darkness, wherein she was straying, and searching, and finding nothing, for he was dead.

The apparition of old griefs was fading away when an inter‑rupting voice passed the door. She frowned, recognizing the somewhat soft voice of that young man of Jean's. She sighed, and began collecting the few letters, tying the ribbon round them tenderly, as though it were the baby foot again; and touched them with her cheek in caress, and smiled wanly into her own mirrored eyes. Yes, she was getting old, and how quickly: but that did not matter.

She walked into the passage, and listened. Voices mur‑mured upstairs in the boys' room. She listened; hesitated; and returned for her hand-lamp. She yawned, and felt curious, and went along the carpeted passage, humming notes of no particular tune. She passed Jean's room, and looked in to see if she was there, meaning to 'make it up'; but the room was empty, with breeches hanging to the floor from one chair, muddy leggings flung across the room, drawers left open, her best evening frock worn at the Denys' dance four nights ago still lying over the bed-rail, stockings, skirts, and knicks on the floor, anywhere. Her husband Charles over again! Really, the room was in a dreadful state; hopeless to expect Jean to be tidy. The child's life was disorganized by her disastrous love-affair – one could no longer regard it as calf-love. If only she could meet more young men; but young men were scarce in North Devon.

The stairs to the boys' room – Michael had called it the Crows' Nest, a name still in use among the children – creaked as she climbed. Her shoes tapped on the bare boards. The eight steps ended on a landing, laid with oil-cloth, where an old rocking-horse, a hip bath, a white washstand, an old worm-eaten pony skin, riding boots, a 'cello case, and hat boxes, were piled. There were four attic rooms, and a hair of light lay under the door of the largest, which was the Crows' Nest. Mrs. Ogilvie heard Ronnie's laugh, as she knocked on the door.

163

It was immediately opened, and candle-light leapt into lamp-light, revealing Mr. Maddison tall and smiling of face. Ronnie stood by the bed, Eton coat and waistcoat off, and braces unbuttoned from trousers. Usually he unslung them at night, and unbuttoned in the morning; but to-night every opportunity for lingering was taken.

Had he been alone, Ronnie's mother might have thought little and said nothing of his slowness in obedience – it must have been nearly half an hour since she had ordered him to bed – but now, with a feeling of resentment, she ascribed it to the presence of that young man. In amiable tones Mrs. Ogilvie mentioned that she had heard voices passing her door, and not recognizing Mr. Maddison's, she had come to find out who it was; and she was about to suggest that they should leave Ronnie alone, when he broke in upon her words, saying, G'night Ron, and swiftly closed the door behind him. They heard his shoes clumping down the stairs as he felt his way in the dark.

'You've been rather a long time getting in to bed, Ronnie.'

He made a tremendous effort to see Mum as he had seen her when Mr. – when Willie had been with him; for now she was different to the vision. He saw himself as a lonely and heroic figure, determined to regard her as before. He sobbed, and shuffled over to her, holding up his trousers with one hand, and putting an arm round her, hid his face.

She moved to the bed, guiding him, and sat down, while he fell on his knees before her. His body shook.

'Hush, my darling. Hush!' she soothed him, and he sobbed the more, for now he saw her as a figure noble with the light of her sacrifice and suffering. 'Ronnie, little son, dear little boy, there, there.'

'Mummy . . . sorry . . . Mummy.' Other words were stifled. Soon he became calmer, and flinging his arms round her neck, held her in an embrace of utmost love. She said presently:

'There now, you won't be rude to Mother any more, will you, dear?'

'No, Mum. I promise.'

'There's a dear boy. Tell me what Mr. Maddison said to you, darling.'

Rubbing the tears off his lashes with the back of his hand, Ronnie said, 'Oh, he was' – sniff – 'decent. And he asked me to call him' – sniff – 'Willie.'

'Well, that is nice of him, isn't it. Did he say anything else?'

'He didn't say much,' said Ronnie, hitching up his trousers, and beginning to talk in his prep. school voice, 'because he said he didn't want to say anything that was beyond my development. I quite understand how he felt about that. He said he used to be punished a lot as a boy, and that his father's mind had been dulled by his father, and so on. I quite understand, but it is hard to explain.'

Ronnie felt an absolute aversion from speaking the decent things Mr. – that Willie had said about his Mother and her hopes.

'Oh. Well, my dear, I'm very glad you've done the right thing, and apologized. We'll say no more about it. You can come down if you like.'

But Ronnie was glowing inwardly with the new thoughts. He wanted to be alone, alone with the candle-light, and think about the life his spirit had been wanting to live when he had wanted to sing *Sea Fever*; to look at the stars beyond the window, and to think of the wind going everywhere in the darkness, over sandhill and shore and wave. No, he did not want to go down.

'I think I'll go to bed, I'm rather tired, Mummie.'

'Very well, dear.'

She thought she would wait while he got undressed, as she had done, it seemed, until yesterday. What a pity children had to grow up, she thought.

Ronnie hurried, for the sooner he got into bed, the sooner

he would be alone, when he meant to put on his grey flannel trousers and coat, and sit by the open window, with the sea and the stars.

'Good night, Sonnie.'

'Good night, Mummy darling.' He added: 'I do love you, you know.'

'Do you, Sonnie?'

He hugged her, and was the little son she loved more than anything in the world. When he had released her, she said in her happiness:

'I want to be so proud of you, darling. Promise me you will try and behave finely, always, won't you, Son?'

He promised, thinking of that tall strong decent chap. Like him, yes, always!

'There, boy, I must go now.'

She got up from the bed, tucked in blankets and sheets, arranged the coverlet, and moved to blow out the candle.

'Oh, leave it, please!' he begged, looking at the friendly gleam. 'I shan't want to sleep for a bit. I promise I won't read.' The boy's eyes were not strong; and it was his mother's ambition that he should pass into Dartmouth. 'And I may want to get out soon.'

'Very well, I'll leave it on the wash-stand, where it will be safe.' Owing to the thatched roof, Mrs. Ogilvie was very much afraid of fire. One more embrace, and she took up the lamp, and went out of the room.

As the door closed, he drew up his knees, hugging himself into his thoughts. His books opposite in the bookcase, his fishing rods and boxing gloves and old sabre on the walls, that had belonged to his great-great-grandfather at the battle of Waterloo, his rows of boots and shoes, Kipling's poem *IF* over the chest of drawers, the coving ceiling where shadows played, the barking of a dog chasing a rabbit, coming through the open window, Mum, every one, *his home*, O, lovely, *lovely*!

When Mrs. Ogilvie entered the drawing-room Mary looked

at her mother, knowing at once that she was happy. For a moment she hoped that she had been talking to Willie Maddison (as she always thought of him); but no, Mother would not understand him, and he could not be himself with her. She was curious to know where he had disappeared, but she could not ask an indirect question, and so she said nothing.

Mr. Garside was sitting in the arm-chair, and he jumped up, his shoes thumping on the carpet, when she came in at the lower door. The noise he made heartened him, and he felt more at home. For five minutes he had been depressed in his admiration for Mary. Hopeless, he knew; for obviously Howard – such a fine example of a young English gentleman! – and Mary were made for each other. Yet realizing this, he had, rather shamefully, to admit to himself that he could make but the feeblest attempt to deny his amorous imaginings of Mary as his wife, alone with him, holding his head against her warm secret breast, guarding him. He convinced himself that there was nothing sinful in this; for he was not as other men regarding women; he had ideals; his thoughts of love were pure; occasional dreams, as Freud showed, were not one's real thoughts.

'Your daughter's playing has been giving me the greatest pleasure,' he said affably to Mrs. Ogilvie. 'I can't tell you how nice it is to hear music with a tune in it, after all this terrible modern jazz stuff.'

'What have you been playing, Mary dear?' asked Mrs. Ogilvie, for one never knew quite where one was with the Vicar's spasmodic compliments.

'One of Brahms' Hungarian dances, mother.'

'Oh yes, you play them very well. Has anyone seen Diana?' No one had.

'Jean, I suppose, is somewhere or other?'

No one seemed to know. Mary, although she suspected Jean to be at the farm, said nothing.

'Is Mr. Maddison in here?'

No one had seen him since he had left the room about twenty minutes before.

'But how extraordinary,' murmured Mrs. Ogilvie, moving a chair to its usual place. 'One hardly knows how young people will behave nowadays. Won't you smoke, Howard? Cigarettes over there on that table.'

'No thanks, Aunt Connie,' he replied, in the deep clear voice so admired by Mr. Garside.

While they were speaking the grandfather clock in the hall struck ten, and Mary left the room to fetch Aunt Edith's hot-water bottle.

'I really must regulate that clock,' said Mrs. Ogilvie. 'It's been like that for ever so long.' Howard said he would do it, and left the room, as Mr. Garside anticipated he would. He transferred some of his thoughts to Pam, who with feet turned in to make a level support for the *English Boy's Annual* on her legs, was sitting with bowed head and fingers stopping her ears, engrossed in a story. Mr. Garside thought, with a tinge of melancholy, that they were the most delightful family he knew; but it did not occur to him that he had no other friends.

In the kitchen Howard sat on the table, while Mary leaned her head on her forearm resting against the rack above the bodley, wherein the fire was sunk almost into ash. She was tired: her mind wanted to stray away, with the eager form it beheld. She need not fill Aunt Edith's bottle for a couple of minutes: but what could she say to Howard? What *could* she say? She was unable to say things in a roundabout way, or to lead up to them gently, as some people could, Mother for instance. Poor Howard, still hoping!

'Have you any idea where she went to, Jo?' asked Howard, casually, filling a pipe.

'I'm afraid I haven't, Dags.'

The intimate nicknames were remnants of early comradeship –'Jo' for Jonah, for it was an eight-year-old Mary who, having discovered a great sperm whale on the sands near the Dutchman's Wreck, one morning, ran most of the way home to gasp out the news, looking, her father had said, as though she had been swallowed, and cast forth again; 'Dags' for the 'daggers,' or reeds round the duckponds, wherein Howard had built a secret hut.

'Oh well,' he said, continuing to press tobacco into the bowl. He fumbled for matches, struck one, tried to light the tobacco. 'I think I'll clear off to-night, Jo.'

'Oh no, don't do that, Dags. You're much too much an asset to the cheerability of this house to be allowed to go!'

'Cheerability' was a word coined in their early friendship; a secret word, to be used only on special occasions, and never when others were present.

'I wish I could feel it, Jo.'

Mary stood upright, and took the rubber bed-bottle off its nail. 'She's different from other people. I don't know what to make of her half the time I'm with her, and yet I suppose I know her better than anyone else does.'

'Yes, that's just it,' sighed Howard. 'She is different from every one else.' He stared at the pipe he had packed too tightly, dejected by the vision of what he desired, a vision eternally beyond realization. It was his only love – excluding occasional war-time episodes, which had been half-sorry affairs – which had endured in varying degrees the torment of alternate hope and despair since the outbreak of the Great War, at the age of eighteen, until the present time. Only to Mary had he written and talked of it.

'One day she'll fall in love with some one who'll come along in a moment,' he said moodily; and sliding off the table, rapped the pipe on the stove sharply, so that the bowl snapped off the stem. 'Jo, where is she gone to-night? With Maddison?'

'I don't know,' said Mary, who during the last few minutes had been wondering the same thing.

'By Jove, didn't he just pitch-in to old Garside? A lot of hot-air, of course, but I couldn't help admiring the chap. He seems very sincere, which makes it all the more . . . I suppose that sort of thing would appeal to some women, wouldn't it?'

'He worries rather a lot about things,' murmured Mary, while Howard picked up the bowl, and poked it through the bars of the grate.

'Jo, I rather fancy it's a miserably rotten thing to say, but you know, I don't feel quite easy about him. You know, there was that affair a few years back with Mrs. Fairfax. For God's sake don't think me a prude, but I can't help remembering it.'

Mary slid the heavy kettle along the hob, and tilted the spout down to the rubber funnel of the bottle.

'I ought not to have said that, Jo. I feel a cad.'

'You needn't. I quite understand how you feel.'

'Jo, how long had she been in the room before I came? Did she go out because I'd come, do you think?'

'She didn't come in at all after supper. She played the Franck records to him.'

'But where has he gone to now? . . . Do you think anything was arranged?'

'Oh no, Dags!'

He sat on the table again, in silent dejection, while she filled the copper can.

Mary went away through the flagged passage to the hall, leaving him sitting there. She put down can and bottle on the table, and stood, matchbox in hand, some moments before lighting Aunt Edith's candle. She watched, without fully seeing, the sinking flame melting the wax at the base of the wick, the flame arising in brightness, the steam particles curling out of the copper can. She began slowly to rub her right thigh, where she had bruised herself coming down the spiral staircase of the tower that morning. Her hand stopped, but her fingers still held the cloth of the skirt. A childlike look came over her face, as she stared, unseeing, past the candle. She began to hear the breath in her nostrils. Littleboy,

Littleboy, her thoughts cried; and she became uncertain, and then afraid, for the heavy feeling in her breast.

The fear grew deeper, and changed into a dread of going into the lighted drawing-room, lest they should see. Nor to Howard in the kitchen, for she would not know what to say to him. Mother or Aunt Edith might come out of the door at any moment!

Noiselessly she went upstairs, leaping two and three at a time, over the landing and down the dark corridor, up three steps, and into her room in the gable end. She closed the door quietly, and was alone in the intimate darkness of her bedroom. She was standing in the middle of the room, putting off the delight and pain of beholding him in the belfry, of imagining his eager face and funny way of walking with shoulders held high, when she heard the barking of his spaniel. In two strides she was at the window, and leaning out into the freshening cold air. Night with its luminous dust of stars spread over the earth, and the dark air was filled with a roar faint and even, of waves on the shore beyond the burrows. At the bottom of the sky lay the lights of Appledore, like sparks of embers glittering in the wind.

The barking had stopped. Far to the right, across the unseen sea, the lighthouse of Harty Point flicked, and shone, and went out. At other times, looking out of the window, she had felt herself of the night, a being of thought only, free as the wind in the trees; but that feeling was gone. Nothing in the night now.

A red speck grew in the distance from Harty Point, opening into a remote glare, that decreased, and vanished. Above her a voice began to chant with soft melancholy:

> 'I must go down to the sea again
> To the call of the lonely tide
> To the gulls way, and the whales way,
> That will not be denied.
> And all I ask is a tall ship
> And a star to steer her by . . .'

Looking up, she saw the palest glimmer of uncertain light along the eaves where his window would be. She called up in a whisper:

'Is that you, Son?'

'Hullo, you there, Mary?'

'Yes. Shall I come up?'

'Yes!'

She found him in his sleeping suit, sitting on one leg in the window recess. 'Oh Son, your feet are cold!' She made him wrap his overcoat round him, then sat down beside him. He was the Ronnie who had not been to school, the Ronnie who used to put his arms round her, whom she could hug, and talk secrets with – of the golden plover that would nest in the marsh, of the mullet that would come through the culvert and be land-locked in the Horsey Pit, of bathing, of making driftwood fires and boiling tea, of many lovely things to be done during the holidays. He told her what Mr. M – what Willie had said to him, and what a decent chap he was; and when he, Ronnie, grew up, he was going to be just like him, and walk about with a pack and a stick and a dog, and understand everything.

'Isn't the world lovely, Mary?'

'Lovely, Son.'

She held him warm, and he went on speaking in his young and happy voice, while she listened, a little sadly.

Chapter 8

JEAN OGILVIE, in breeches, Master of the Wildernesse Rabbit
Hounds, was speaking on the lawn before the house. In the
bright sunlight her clothes looked shabby, her face tired.

'Will you take a whip, Will? A whip, poor Will, to whip
your poor boy Biell? What, will poor Will willingly whip poor
boy Biell? Oh, shut up. Isn't this rot, don't you think? I say,
I don't know if Mary knows you've come.'

'I think it's jolly.'

'Do you really? It used to be such fun, but things change
when you grow up. Micky started it – ages ago.'

Out of the front door walked Mr. Sufford Chychester, laden
with a grey, called white, pot hat, a dark blue coat with brass
buttons, white breeches, blue stockings, and heavy black boots
covered with a kind of mildew. It being a hot sun, Mr.
Chychester was about to air his uniform of the Two Rivers
Otter Hunt, in order to evaporate the winter smell of moth-
ball. The annual opening meet at Pilton Bridge in Barum
would take place the following week; an occasion he had been
imagining many times recently. Although seventy-five years
of age, Mr. Chychester was able to walk for many hours,
following the hounds up the pleasant wooded valleys of the
Taw and Torridge. Hunting the otter was his greatest joy in
life. When alone, and not reading his newspaper, Mr.
Chychester was gentle to everything, except slugs, wireworms,
snails, and thistles.

Unsupple and slightly stooping, Mr. Chychester walked to
a zinc cylinder on the lawn, which covered a glass jar the size
and shape of a jampot. He bent down, and picked up the rain
gauge.

173

'Rainfall nil. Wind south,' he exclaimed, throwing up his bearded chin and sniffing the air. 'This will bring my broad beans along. Now the thermometers.'

For more than thirty years Mr. Chychester himself, or by deputy were he absent, had kept records of wind, snow, rain, lightning, and temperature in his place of dwelling; sending information thereof regularly to the Meteorological Office in London. When he was gone, he hoped that Benjamin would continue the records.

He tramped away round the house to the orchard, where his bee-hives stood, and a taller slighter white structure among them, like a bees' summer-house. Here the thermometers were kept.

'A brave old boy,' said Maddison, meditating on Mr. Chychester's retreating back. 'A bit of old black church oak.'

'I wish those fools would come,' said Jean, cracking her whip. 'I'd ride the Buccaneer, but those rabbit holes would break his legs.'

'Where are the others?'

'I left Mary cutting sandwiches in the kitchen with Howard. Are you sure you've had breakfast?'

'All I want. I saw Diana as I came in: she said she had a headache.'

'She says that because she doesn't want to run. She's a lazy little beast.' Jean stared at the grass. 'No, that's not true. Poor kid, she has fits. Only for God's sake don't say I told you! She'd kill herself if she thought people knew.'

'I shall say nothing.'

Jean swished at a bee with her whip. 'I say, I feel rather a beast to have told you that about Diana.'

'But why, Jean? The result of your telling me is that I want to be as nice as possible to the child.'

'It's not a disease: it's what they call functional: she's been like that only the last year or two.'

'Poor little darling, she feels too keenly.'

SPRING

'As soon as I told you, I thought of what I said about Miss Goff, when we had that walk together to the village in the winter: and now I'm doing the same thing!'

'Extending your feeling and understanding to Miss Goff! But you are not the same. Miss Goff's type, and it is fairly common, is that of thought on a low level; and ironically, her way of thinking is the indirect cause of many of the things she so self-righteously deplores.'

'Poor Old Jig; I'm often sorry for her.'

'Jean, I like you,' he said, picking up a pebble and throwing it with all his might over the trees. 'I wish you could be happy.'

'What do you mean?'

'I know how you feel at the present time.'

'What do you mean?'

'I want to be your friend, Jean,' he said shyly.

'What has Mary been telling you?'

'No one has told me anything. But I can see. Jean, talk to me when you feel miserable. It isn't good for people to keep their unhappy thoughts behind their tongues. Having done and felt many things, I can understand many things. And if you feel miserable now, Jean, you won't later on.'

She gave him a full look; and trusted his eyes.

'You mean about Howard?'

'Yes.'

He had not known it was Howard.

A chaffinch flew to a blossomed almond tree, and sang its song to the sky.

'Did you see me last night, when you passed the farm with Diana?'

'No.'

He wondered why his answer had made her seem happier; beauty came into her face, and drew the life into his own. He would have liked to kiss her, but the thought of Mary chilled the impulse.

175

Ronnie and Pam ran out of the house, each with a whip. They laughed and ragged one another, trying to crack the thongs whirling round their heads.

'Mind my ear, curse you Pam, you nearly snicked it off.'

'Then take your beastly ear out of the way of my whip. I thought it was a cabbage leaf.'

'I like that! Why, your ears are like – like – like cabbage leaves also.'

'Ha ha, copy cat. If I couldn't think of anything fresh, I'd boil my head.'

'I shouldn't, it might burst, it's boiled enough already.'

'Oh, feeble ass.'

He chased her, she darted round Maddison, who caught her, she was so fair.

'Hullo, Pam!'

'Hullo!' said Pam, suddenly shy.

'The correct epithet for describing Ronnie's ears is "shell-like." Every novelist likens beautiful ears to shells. Ronnie's ears are like the shells of those giant Japanese shell-fish that are said to trap and devour men.'

'Ha ha, jolly fine joke,' said Ronnie. 'Anyway, your ears aren't any better.' He watched Maddison's eyes, a little unsure of himself, uneasy lest he might have been rude. 'Good old Willie!' he cried.

They asked him where he had got to the previous night; and he said that, on returning with Diana, the night was so lovely that he had returned to the sea, and slept in the bracken of Ferny Hill.

'Oo, I wish we could too!' said Pam. 'Ron! Let's!'

While they were gambolling on the grass he saw Diana strolling from the direction of the kitchen, a figure strange and small in the sunlight, with her red hair and white face. Yet when she came near he saw that the beauty of her features was marred by powder lying unevenly on the cheeks, and nose, and chin. Extraordinary! The sunlight seemed to lack power to give her warmth; perhaps she was suffering. He looked at her with a new, compassionate interest.

'Headache better?' asked Jean, in tones of genuine inquiry; she too saw Diana in a new, compassionate way.

Diana nodded.

'The others ready?'

'Haven't seen them.'

Mrs. Ogilvie came out shortly afterwards, smoking a cigarette, and Miss Chychester in ancient rustling silk behind her, carrying a paper bag much creased and folded. Miss Chychester stopped at the end of the lawn, and waved to them from a distance of ten yards.

'I hope you will enjoy your game, all of you. Mind the sand in your eyes. It blinded an eye of Farmer Bissett's only quite recently.'

Farmer Bissett had lost an eye as a result of a fight for five shillings with a Negro in a boxing booth of Barum Fair in 1896; but he had declared it was done by a sand-storm. In reality the sight had been destroyed by conjunctivitis.

'Now you'll be careful not to let the dogs go near the duck-ponds, won't you? Mr. Maddison, will you keep an eye on the children for me? The birds are laying now, and we've let the shooting, you see.'

Having waved good-bye once, Miss Chychester looked as though she could not quite comprehend why they were still there. She waved her paper bag once more, then remembering her birds would be waiting, hurried away to the bird-table outside the open dining-room window. Tomtits and finches and robins flew after her, the robin scolding with ticking cries because the crumbs were late. Mrs. Ogilvie watched Maddison as he followed the small figure with his eyes, and reading what was in them, said without thinking, 'Isn't she a dear with her birds?'

The unusual intimacy of voice, the gentle look with it, had the effect of making his reply unsteady. 'Ah yes, she has never lost the innocent spirit of the child.'

'Unfortunately we cannot all of us remain as children, Mr. Maddison.'

'His name is "Will," Mother.'

'Very well, it shall be Will. But I prefer Bill.'

'Thank you, Aunt Connie. Do you mind?'

'I like it, dear boy. Won't you hurt your hand holding that whip?'

'Oh no, it's healed already. What I meant about the spirit of the child, Aunt – er, Mrs. –'

'Aunt Missis!' Ronnie and Pam yelled with laughter. 'I say, that's a fine name for Mum.'

'Well, Bill?' said Mrs. Ogilvie, smiling indulgently at the children.

'Well, I meant that – that – it is really practicable to make a heav – to, er, well, it seems to me that birds, such as swallows, are superior to us in many ways, because they don't think, but just accept. No, that's not it – I meant – er –' He faltered to a silence, and saw, with a strained smile, that she was puzzled; a dreadful feeling of hopelessness, of humiliation, twisted him, and he wanted to run away, to yell, to dive into the muddy dyke, anything, to rid himself of the twist.

'Hurray!' cried Ronnie, turning a somersault. 'Mary, I say, Mother's adopted Willie! He's our brother now. Come on, boys, fetch the horns! The famous Wildernesse Rabbit Hounds will now move off to draw the celebrated Ferny Hill covert. They'll probably give tongue to the scent of Willie, where he slept! Very strong scent, no doubt! Yoi-yoi-yoi! Coalie! Jock! Billjohn! Up over, up over!'

'What a boy,' said Mrs. Ogilvie, as she watched her son tenderly. Ronnie went up to Jean, and whispered, and ran away round the house, to set Rigmarole free from his kennel.

The Hunt moved off, cracking whips and winding horns – or making noises out of horns. Howard walked in front with Diana; he spoke in a subdued voice to her, but when they were out of the garden, seemed to have nothing more to say.

178

'Keep by me,' said Jean to Maddison, as they shut the postern gate in the wall.

'Yes,' he agreed.

The Great Plain lay before them, a level tract of turf and moss stretching wide and green in the sunlight, with clumps of darker green rushes and small mossy hillocks breaking its smoothness. Half a mile in front rose the sandhills, irregularly overlaid with grey-green marram grasses. The sky met the uneven line of dunes, and there the land ended.

'I say, wait for us,' cried the voice of Ronnie behind, as he ran after them with the abducted water-spaniel.

They spread out, and at a yell from Jean, started to run forward. Almost at once Coalie thrust his muzzle into a clump of spiky rush, wagging his stump furiously. He gave tongue as a rabbit ran out from the other side, white scut working with every leap. So the hunt began, every dog straining to catch it; Dave the lurcher outpacing spaniels and terrier, and running mute. Ronnie, Pam, Jean, and Maddison hollaed and cracked their whips behind them, Maddison leaping over all the spiky rush-clumps he came to. 'Ride straight, ride straight!' he yelled.

'It's all right for you,' yelled Pam beside him. 'You've got long lanky legs, and don't get stabbed.'

It was harmless sport from the life-view of the rabbits; for the Great Plain, as well as all the Burrows, was tunnelled with buries. The rabbit got into one, and they left it, finding another and losing it again; and going on a few yards, turned a third out of its lair on the dry brittle rush-scriddicks of old years lying scattered under the clump.

'The best hunt I've been to,' panted Maddison to Jean, a quarter of an hour later, as he reached the summit of a hill with her, and saw the sea over a miniature Arabian Desert, calm and disappearing into an infinity of mist. A single collier blacker than its smoke which trailed level and vague behind it, lay in the sky-blue water like a fly logged in the eye of heaven.

See-o-wit! See-o-o-wit!

The wild cries came from the Great Plain behind them, from plovers flinging themselves with soughing wings through the air over their nests, while they watched in wild fear the solitary red-haired figure walking below. The dogs were hidden in the warren of the sandhills.

While watching the sea, he knew that Jean was looking him over, as though she saw him in a new aspect.

'You're not a bad sort,' she said, admiringly. 'Only you take some knowing. How much do you know, I wonder.'

'More than you have ever dreamed of.'

'I believe you are a dark horse.'

'I started to go grey years ago, Jean.'

'It's when you laugh and rag about as you did when we met you on the sands yesterday afternoon, that I like you most. You're very quiet sometimes, and it's then I don't quite understand you.'

'Yes, I know I must be dull company.'

'Oh, I didn't mean *that*.'

'Well, you see,' he tried to explain, 'I see things as the sun sees them – without shadows; whereas most people accept shadows as pleasant to sit in. Am I very obscure?'

He saw she was puzzled; and before she could say anything, ran down the wind-smoothen hill with long plunging strides in the sand, that filled his shoes. The sudden impulse to be alone carried him up the farther slope, and over the crest, into a hollow where the hot ribbed sand was braided by the tracks of beetles leading to the corpse of a rabbit flattened and stiff in the sun. He went through a gap torn by the winter wind in the next ridge, and into a further hollow, in which were spread the grey leaves of a mullein plant whose tap-root went down deep into the sand.

A track of footsteps in the loose sand led round the mullein, and up the slope to the sky. The others were ahead somewhere, and fancying that the track might be Mary's, he followed it, up and down the purring sands, until he reached a long dry slope, ribbed by the last wind, which ended at a broken summit. He stood on the summit, above a cliff hung with loose roots of marram grass, and looked down into an immense valley of sand, lying north and south. Sunlight and silence brimmed the wide empty place. Above the uneven level of the Burrows the white lines of breakers on the estuary bar crinkled in the air arising off the hot sand.

The footsteps led down the long slope, which bore of the winds winnowing innumerable white shells, like beads, and larger grey shells of Roman snails, worn thin and holed by sun and sand and wind of the wilderness. He saw a round leaden bullet that lay on the sand near a rusty shrapnel case, relics of olden artillery practice, and dead men rose up before him, among the litter of skulls and bones and shells. Placidly the wraiths flowed away in air, and he walked on, his body light as sunlight.

A plain lay between the bottom of the slope and the seaward hills, where plants of hawkbit, dove's-foot, crane's-bill, ragwort, plantain, and scorpion grass were starving, each a dwarf, in the dampness of the poor soil. Some grew big, among taller grasses, where white bones lay. A beautiful frail cry came along the level way as he walked, for he passed near the tuft dreamed on by a sandpiper for her nesting place.

At the northern end of the valley he saw a kneeling figure, and rejoiced, knowing it was Mary. She was alone. He whirled the whip round his head, and loped forward, his feet crushing shells into the grasses and mosses; and came on the prints of her toes distinct across the damp sand, and followed them. Beautiful in the morning are thy feet in the wilderness!

They led a wandering course from flower to flower, and on the mossy turf were nearly hidden; but he must walk beside them, and come to her by her own way. A strange fancy obsessed him that by so seeking he would gain his heart's desire; that were he to lift his glance, she would never be his.

An idle idea, but he dreaded to disobey it. He walked slowly, while a desire to look up grew powerfully. He shielded his eyes with his hands, and planted regular steps beside her own.

At last the footmarks pressed sand again, where only the runner roots of the sedge-grass were pushing out green tufts in straight lines. They made a maze like the wire of the Hindenburg Line seen from the air. He walked on quickly, until he came to the edge of a mossy knoll where doe-rabbits had been scratching their own fur to line their nests. There he saw her bare feet and legs, and the lovely colour of her cheeks, and he looked away again.

'Look,' said Mary.

In the palm of her hand was a snail shell filled with bright green moss.

'I found it growing like that,' said Mary.

'I followed your footsteps all the way from the Great Plain.'

'Yes, I saw you tracking me. I mean, following the track. After you waved, I was afraid you were going to look up.'

Her words confused her, and to hide her face she knelt to put the shell on the ground, with the mossy opening uppermost to find the rain. He dropped beside her, and touched with his fingernail grains of sand around a tiny plant with a red leaf, and a white stalklike flower.

'What's the flower, Mary?'

She leaned over him – 'Three-fingered sacrifrage' – and moved back again.

'Mary.'

'Yes.'

'I was afraid to look up too.'

'Yes,' she said, the words catching in soft laughter in her throat.

'I did think we were thinking the same thing.' What had she said now; why was her heart beating so, why did her face burn for almost anything he said. His remark probably meant nothing. She pretended to have found something in the sand.

SPRING

'Mary.'

'Yes.'

'Did you want – did you – I wish you had come out last night.'

The sound of thudding feet disturbed the sunlit silence; it grew louder, and they saw the spaniel, his pink tongue looking as long as his head, charging along their tracks at full speed. He slowed to a trot when he saw his master's face, and smiling as a dog smiles, he trotted into his shadow, and collapsed. Sand roughed his tongue.

'Poor Bill,' said Mary, as the dog got up, scratched a hole to ease his thumping heart, and dropped his body in it, with legs thrust straight out behind him. Flack flack flack, er er (swallow) flack flack flack, went his tongue.

'Yes, I did want to go out, too. But Mother –'

'Oh,' he said, 'I thought it was – I imagined – weren't you waiting for Howard?'

'Yes, I was. You see, he didn't say when he was coming.'

A shadow passed across the knoll where they sat, and over the sand, under a hawk flying to the Great Plain.

He began to hope, and said, for effect, 'I think I ought not to be here. You and Howard – old friends – whereas I, an intruder –'

With wonder he saw her hand move towards him, and take his hand, and clasp it between her hands.

'Ah Mary,' he stammered, 'Dear Mary.'

'Don't you be a silly boy,' she whispered, as though to the captive hand. 'Don't you talk any more about going away,' and gave his hand back to him.

'I wanted to tell you about this place. It's called the Valley of Winds. A village is supposed to lie under here, buried in a great storm centuries ago.'

Ah! He wanted her to go on holding his hand.

'Sometimes I come here, and try and think back into those days, before the coast subsided. Further that way' – she

183

pointed south – 'is another valley, where, on a hot still summer's day, if you lie on the sand, you can hear bells tolling. Or it sounds like bells to me. Poor Bill, how thirsty he is.'

'Yes,' he said, getting up. 'My poor boy want a drink.'

The dog wagged its tail. He took her hand and pulled her to her feet, and hesitated before letting it go again; then touched her cheek. 'O Mary, I have never seen such beautiful country! Listen to the skylarks over the Great Plain. Mary, can I stay at your house?'

'You may,' she laughed. 'Have you only just realized that every one has been asking you to stay?'

They returned along the valley, toward the fresh water lying in the pans beyond.

'Is it true that Howard is going to East Africa?'

'Yes.'

'Would you rather Howard or I stayed?' he asked, feeling sure of himself now they were holding hands.

'Well you, obviously –'

'And I would rather choose you than anyone,' he declared, whirling his thong.

'Obviously I must choose you, because Howard has *got* to go.'

She wanted to laugh, so suddenly had the thong ceased to whirl! It was a shame to tease him.

'Is he coming back?'

'I hope so.'

'You hope so?' he said, letting go her hand.

'Of course I do.'

'Why?'

'Because I like him.'

'I like him too.'

'Now we can both hope together for his return, can't we?' she said, taking his hand.

He dropped one of her shoes farther on, and stopped to pick it up, still holding her hand.

'You haven't altered in the least since you were a little boy,' she said, and beauty grew in her face.

'I can be myself with you,' he answered, with such pathetic gratitude in his voice that the tears almost came into her eyes.

They walked along, holding hands firmly. The dog walked in their blended shadows, thinking of water he had gone by in the past, and not lain in and lapped. Sometimes he flopped on the sand, imagining this water; but the sight of his master growing small before his eyes filled him with anxiety, of which he could rid himself only by following.

Words, glances, sunlit airiness, the Valley of Winds was behind, and they were branching from their old tracks. Everywhere in the sand lay white bones of rabbits, and among them, the skull of a fox from which the lower jaw had fallen. The sand stretched smoothly to the crest where the marram grasses, round and thin, dropped with their pointed tips motionless on their abandoned wind-arcs. Some of the grass bents, having freedom to swing in the last sea-gusts that had driven blindly in and out of the hollows, had scored deep circles about their stems.

He sat down under the crest, she beside him. He smiled in her face, and saying that at last he was himself, balanced in sun and air and earth and sea, began to walk on all fours around her, drawing a rough forefinger. When he had enclosed himself and Mary in the circle he asked her if she knew why he had done it. She shook her head, although she had an idea.

'I am exorcising unhappiness. Creating a new world, with you and me in it only. And the circle is made up of two halves.'

Under her nervousness Mary was aware that the sky was full of the shrill music of invisible larks. She saw a wheatear, white-patched between tail and back, standing on a sandy spur near them, and pointed to it.

'You understand, don't you?' he smiled, boldly watching

her face, to make the colour rise. 'Ah no,' he said, in a changed
voice, hiding his face on her knees. 'I am making you unhappy; as I used to feel at school when the Head Master
asked me a question, trying to search the deceit out of me with
his eyes. Only I used to go white.'

Gently she stroked the head on her knees.

'You can be all yourself with me,' she murmured.

He crept nearer, and laid his head in her lap. She shifted
to give him comfort, and smoothed his hair and forehead,
smiling to herself. Then the spaniel thrust his head under her
arm and licked his ear.

'I didn't do it!' she cried, 'It was your poor thirsty boy!'

They ran down the steep side of the hollow, until the weight
of sliding sand buried their feet, and they sat down, laughing,
while the spaniel, in spite of his thirst, pranced around them.
On again, Maddison pulling her up the next steep slope, pounding into the loose sand. They climbed sideways to the crest,
and walked along a matted ridge, balancing across narrow
infirm sandy walls. Hearing the note of a horn echoing far
behind they turned, and saw Howard with Ronnie and Pam
standing on a cliff above the Valley of Winds half a mile away.
Hi! Pam's high yell floated along the lightly moving airs.

'Don't let's go, Mary!'

'No, don't let's.'

'Besides, we must let Billjohn drink. Humanitarian
principles demand it.'

'And there's no water that way.'

'Come on, then.'

Hand in hand, they ran down into a larger hollow, and to
another, trying to keep direction while walking with the grassy
fringes always against the sky, and stealing delight from each
other's glances.

The loveliness they felt in the sky filled all their being,
brimmed without words, and flowed into things seen as though
by one mind, so quick and plain saw they. A loving thought

for a lark's nest in a tussock, with its four warm eggs; for the cast feather of a gull, poor that it had forever lost the air; for a beetle, fatigued by its journey across the great desert, to be carried to an oasis of cool moss; for plover pinions, linked by frayed bones, the kill of a peregrine falcon.

They came to a plain, grey with the frond-like leaves of the silver-weed, each plant with a pair of leaves 'open-armed to the sun,' he said, feeling that the aspiration of life was one complete Spirit.

A pair of burrow duck flew splashing out of the water as they approached the shallow lake, leaving white feathers float-ing in the ripples. They sat on the sward, while the spaniel walked on, and lay down in the water, and lapped and lapped. The surface wavered with the sky and the yellow-white sand-hills, and the thin gold ripple-shadows moved over the grasses drowned under the clear snow-water. After awhile Mary said she must paddle, and gathering her skirt at her side, she stepped into the water, and moved slowly about, stooping to pick a grass or a shell by her feet, without reason or purpose, except that he was watching. And moving about with a feeling of double happiness, that he and the sun were blessing her, she trod on something sharp, and cried out as she drew up a leg, nearly falling.

'What is it?' he cried, springing up, but she laughed, and said it was nothing; she had only cut herself. He saw the big toe run red, and leapt into the water, to where she stood with lifted leg, and carried her out to the sward. She lay back happily, resting on elbows, watching his intense and anxious face, while he held the foot before him, frowning. 'Some fool broke a bottle there,' he said, and pressed his mouth against the welling cut. He spat violently into the water. 'I'd knock his head off if' – another suck and fierce spit – 'I knew who it was.' Mary began to laugh. 'You're tickling,' she said. 'It's better now, really it is.'

'You lie still. You'm bad, and I be doctoring ee, my maid.'

187

'Thank ee kindly, my d –'. She was going to say 'my dear,' but checked herself. Very gently he put her leg on his coat, and ripping his clean, unfolded handkerchief into strips, bound up the cut. Afterwards he worked her foot into its shoe – a flimsy cloth shoe, with a rope sole.

'Now I can't paddle any more.'

'I shall have to carry you home.'

They both looked at a pipit singing as it glided down the sky, its tail spread and wings downheld, 'fetching song from heaven.'

'It's only a very little cut,' said Mary, protesting. 'I'm so heavy.'

As he did not straighten his back she scrambled on; he shook her higher, his arms for saddle, and set off round the edge of the lake. Neither thought to ask the other where they were going, or why there was need to go anywhere. Nor did the spaniel; he was happy to go wherever his master went. He ran after many rabbits, but kept an eye on him at intervals from various hillocks.

When Maddison had carried her up the further slope of the sandhill enclosing the lake she begged to be put down, saying that he must be tired; for answer he jerked her higher up his back, and staggered down into another hollow, and across it to a broken bank. Here, breathing wild thyme, he set her down.

A wild bee came burring out of the sunshine and settled on her skirt. She put out a finger for it to crawl upon, and lifted it up. It was a large black humble-bee, with a yellow band round its middle.

'Look at me, I'm here,' said Mary. The bee combed the hairs of its head, then burr-rr, was gone.

'I've washed my face and brushed my hair, and off I've flown, I have.'

She was her shy twelve-year-old self again; and undeliberately revealing herself to him. He turned to her, and stroked her cheek with the back of his fingers. Looking at his face without knowing she smiled, Mary thought, with a sudden sweet pain. How beautiful a world if all men were as he!

They wandered on, she by his side. They descended from the sandhills, and came to a plain into which the last of the snow-water had soaked, leaving a grey sediment on the coarse sedge-grass, and a jetsam of rush fragments and rabbit droppings marking the drift of wind and water. A fine piping note came from before them, and another from the way of the sun, and searching the dull green level space around, they saw a small grey bird run a few steps, pause in grave stillness, and run on again. They walked on, silent among the plants of marsh helleborine and yellow wort arising in that ancient bed of the sea, and the faint haunting notes passed them in the still air.

When the sun towered in the south, a cool wind flowed in from the Atlantic, washing them as with water, and leaving a glory about them. Lapwings filled the sky with lament. Mary took two apples from her knapsack, and gave him the better apple, and they sprawled to eat them on a heap of sand, one of many raised in the plain by rabbits. While idly thwacking the mossy sward with his whip handle, to their surprise an owl ran out of a rabbit hole between them, clacking its beak. They watched it flying away to a distant gate, where it perched, and hooted softly. Some time afterwards they got up and wandered on, and drawing nigh the grey weathered gate, rough with cracks and lichen, they saw the dwarf owl still perching. When they were near enough to see its yellow-ringed eyes, it opened its wide beak and bowed, leaving on the top bar a pellet of bones and fur and beetle skins; and flew away quickly, undismayed in the intense clear light.

A cattle shippen with cob walls stood by the gate, and they climbed among the rough-hewn beams, under its dim rafters, saying that they were exploring for swallows' nests, although they knew that the blue birds had returned but yesterday. The

189

years fell away from them, and they were children again as they climbed about their secret lair. One of the tiles of the sloping roof was fallen out of place, and Mary said they must remember that shippen, as a kestrel might want to lay its eggs on the top of the wall inside; the little red mousehawk dared to enter only by a hole in the roof, and never by the dark wide open end. He asked her if she took birds eggs, and she told him she still had her collection, which she must show him when they got home. He thought how he had forgotten his own collection, once so prized and wellbeloved, until now; and the years returned upon him, so that he stood still, while before he had been swinging and stepping from beam to beam.

A sense of foreboding grew in the shadowy place, and he saw into the future, but darkly, and the seeing filled him with regret for Mary, bound to himself, who must tread a desolate way glimpsed in the shadowy secret mind. Yet thought is evil, he cried within himself: the ideal is to be as a flower or a bird, pure creations of earth and light. They did not think: they were poor, save in the beauty of the earth!

'Mary.'

'Yes, Son,' she replied, adding hastily, 'I didn't mean to say that.'

I wish you had, he thought.

The full look of her eyes, dark and untroubled, rested upon him; and his eyes fell before their innocence and trust. He saw then that nothing had changed her since childhood, that her spirit was simple as water, sky, grass, and wandering air, whose product she was. Therein lay the hope of the future, for her mind was the essence of these things stored in the young consciousness.

'Shakespeare, Burns, Keats, were normal men,' he said, 'who would have been harmonious always if other men – the world, that is – had not been sub-normal. A Shakespeare is a natural man, the blossom-mind of man's immense struggle out of darkness towards the Light. Yes, I am right! The ordinary man or woman is denaturalized. The remedy is not to teach Shakespeare to children, but let the spirit of earth, arising naturally for each child, to make him into a Shakespeare! And Shakespeare, you see, is half-way to Christ!'

'But are all children born alike?' she said, timidly.

'Some bear the tragic loading of heredity: but under this heaves the natural impulse towards goodness. I don't mean the Sunday-school goodness, which would mean colourlessness. Goodness, I mean great-mindedness or natural-mindedness, comes at the end of development to all grown naturally. Do you think I am right?'

'It is a little confusing,' said Mary.

'Yes!' he cried, in a voice that startled her by the sudden despair in its feeling, 'I am what Garside would call a paranoic – subject to delusions. O God, I am a self-blown bubble.' He leapt off the beam, which was eight feet above the ground.

'You'll hurt your poor hand!'

'I don't care,' he replied, getting up from the hard hoof-trodden earth, and knocking dried fragments of cowdung off his hands. Then he went outside, climbed over the gate, and waited in the lane. When she came to him he was looking at a mullein plant whose leaves had been eaten to the joints by black and yellow banded caterpillars; it bled with green sap.

'Mary, you are like one of Shakespeare's heroines.'

'You're as bad as Benjamin,' she said, to hide her feelings. 'When he was a small boy he thought he could fly by standing on a ladder, and holding out his arms, and letting himself go. The surprise of Ben when he fell flat on his nose!'

'Where is Ben? I haven't seen him this time.'

'He's gone to spend Easter at Combe with his mother.'

'Oh, I didn't know he had a mother.'

'Yes, she lives there.'

He was curious about Benjamin, but asked no further questions.

'I like Ben. He probably tells lies, and has all the other natural devices of immature intelligence.'

'He doesn't lie to me,' murmured Mary.

'You dear natural child.'

They clasped hands.

'Mary, I want to quote you your epitaph. It is in Rookhurst Church, on one of the flagstones, and is partly of brass and partly of stone, to the memory of William Maddison, who died in 1680. There are two inscriptions, one in English, the other in Latin. It's the English one I love – it just fits you. Shall I say it?'

'Yes, I'd like you to.'

'It's in quaint spelling.' He began to recite it in a slow voice, looking into her eyes:

'Silence (deare shado) wil best thy grave become
And griefe that is not only deep but dumbe
For who'll beleive our vocall tears, but see
The very tongues themselves, here dead in thee
Twelve wellspun lustres sent thee speechless hence
Twice child in age, always in innocence,
To smooth thy Entrance, where true blisse doth raigne
Nature and Grace would have thee born again.'

'Ah! Beautiful!'

'It would suit you best,' said Mary.

'Yes, it is great verse – like Shakespeare's sonnets.'

'Yes.'

They walked along the lane, which was a grassy track bordered by thorns and brambles, with sandy ruts made by the carts fetching seaweed for the fields. Pale green brake-ferns were rising out of the earth, curved like the trunks of elephants. Primroses grew on the banks, with the first blue-bells – the unopened heads saturated with dark blue colour.

He would point to a tall plumy grass, sere and yellow, that winter's wind and snow had not beaten down, rising out of a bramble. Then on again, swinging locked hands, talking and smiling, turning heads together to see, in the same bright glance, the white double-petalled flowers of the stitchwort; the red of campion, that was to be found, said Mary, blooming somewhere in the lane all the year round; the yellow of charlock, which the wild bees were bending for its rich honey prizes; ground ivy, celandine, the thick trumpet leaves of pennywort stored with water; the sun-beloved dandelion, the red marsh orchid with its spotted leaves. All old friends, with the willow wrens and chaffinches, the robins and the thrushes.

Wild flowers are the more beautiful, he thought, seen through the eyes of love, for they mingle and return the thoughts given to them.

Southwards, towards the sun and Wildernesse, the rutted lane left its hedges. They sat down by an ancient blackthorn that, harried in the winds of many years, and overladen with strangling snakes of ivy, lay in the long grass. The ivy was dead, its life blasted out; a thin stream of sap still pulsed in the thorn, which held out in the sun, on one small branch, a few green leaves and brown-wilting flakes of blossom. Lichens red and grey and black covered its dry wooden bones. Mary said the thorn and the ivy were friends from early days; they had been old always, and once a wren had built its nest in the ivy, and another year a chaffinch had moulded its mossy cup in the fork, sitting on its nest and rearing its young although a buzzard had used the thorn as a perch when watching for rabbits.

Many friends of her inner life Mary showed him, in her happiness; and, when the sun was sinking over the sea, the loveliest thing of all – a golden plover flying over the marsh, and pausing high in the air, vibrating its wings while it scarcely moved, then resting in a glide with its wings held downwards as it cried the love-notes of a ravishing sweetness. Other birds flew up to join the singer, and they watched them in silence, sitting on the sea-wall, until the sun spread in fire along the line of sandhills, and then they rose reluctantly to go home.

They returned just as Miss Goff was driving away in her car. She made a gesture of greeting with her hand to Mary, and appeared not to have noticed Maddison. Mrs. Ogilvie met them in the hall, but her face showed nothing of what she was thinking. She remarked to Mary that she had been anxious about her, and that she must not be away so long again without first letting her mother know; and when she had gone away they ceased to be isolated beings, and together set the table in the supper room.

A cloud passed by the open door, checked in its silent glide, and Pamela with loose hair and bright eyes peered at them unseen, and fled silently up the stairs, in a whirl of joy and delight. O, Mary was in love, in love!

Chapter 9

Mary awakened into the summer morning with the sun on her face, and smiled, for the robin was perched on the rail at the foot of her bed. The bird stood still with the perfect tranquillity of its kind. It had nested in the garden; the young birds had wandered away, or been eaten by the several cats that walked in and out of the kitchen. Having become acquainted with these places through the food it had sought and found, the old robin had developed an affection for the faces and forms associated with the food-places, and had no fear of anyone.

She stretched up an arm, as though to clutch the sunlight, and the robin flitted out of the open window. The bedroom glowed like a buttercup. She stroked the wall with her fingers, and lightly felt down the cool smooth surface. You dee-ear! she whispered, imagining him as he had been a fortnight before, with the spots of colour-wash on his hair and face and clothes, intently decorating her room – part of her birthday present. Doors, cupboards, towel-rail, all had been painted a deep old-gold colour. In his zeal he had even painted the loose tarnished nobs of the iron bed. Such a labour! It had been difficult to get him to come down to meals, so engrossed had he been, every brush-stroke being made with care. Dee-ear!

'Dee-ear!' had been Pamela's baby word, which twelve-year-old Mary had imitated ever since; it expressed the tenderest feelings.

She got out of bed, and stood by the window, breathing

deeply, enjoying the rays of the sun on her body. The sun blazed over the hills; under them the estuary lay wide and burnished. The tide seemed level with the green sea-wall. She heard the cuckoo with the cracked voice calling in the orchard, and another cracked voice faintly answering from the direction of the Great Plain. It was just after five o'clock: she must go out: she could not stay under a roof at such a time!

She was dressed in two minutes, and tip-toeing on bare feet down the passage and the stairs, carrying her shoes in her hands. Down in the hall a black head was lifted over the arm of Uncle Suff's leather chair, and gummy eyes watched her. Coalie knew Mary was going out; but although he wanted to go out, Coalie was warm and comfortable on the woollen shawl Miss Chychester was knitting for the Polynesian Missionary Society. Uneasily the old spaniel watched her sitting at the foot of the stairs, by the dog-gates which all the dogs could leap so easily, and putting on her shoes; and with a minor anguish he heard the kitchen door open and her footfalls going away. Coalie groaned, and curled up tight again, head on cyst-sore paws.

Mary went through the rhododendrons bordering the drive to the coach-house, passing under the elms which reared out of the grassy banks. Beyond the trees was the tennis court, a rectangle of plantain, dandelion, daisy, and other plants enclosed by a high fence of wire-netting. Around the rectangle the Buccaneer was ambling solemnly behind Bess, the little fat pony. They were greeting the sun. Bess stopped when she saw Mary, and whinnied; the Buccaneer stopped obediently behind her. 'Buccy! Bess!' she called, passing on; and they resumed their walk on the narrow track worn by their hooves.

Before the coach-house and the loose-boxes, on grass under a spruce fir, were the coops, out of which came whistles, chirps, and clucks. She lifted up the bars of the first coop, and twelve ducklings ran out in twin streams of six each, followed by a hen. They followed her at a rapid tiny waddle, crying *queep-*

queep-queep. The next two coops held chicks, which ran out and scattered like balls of froth on a windy shore. The fourth was the home of little turkeys.

'Nothing for ee,' said Mary, but they ran after her, stopping at the harness-room door, behind which were the bins of corn and bran.

In the kitchen garden she disturbed a pair of wild pigeons which flew up with clattering wings. By one of the rows of peas, near the path, a rat with a red-crusted nose gibbered at her, as it sat up against the weight of the iron gin which held it by its forepaws. She regarded it sadly; and went back along the path to the tool and potting shed, to return with a fork and a mattock.

The rat whined and bared its yellow teeth as she pushed a prong through the chain of the gin to hold it fast, while thrusting with all her strength on the mattock against the spring to open the iron jaws. The rat hopped away, rolling over at every attempt to run. 'You'll get better, my poor boy,' said Mary; and wishing it well, she went along the path. By the cypress trees she remembered the duckling that had been taken by rats a few evenings before.

'They are all poor little things,' she thought, as she walked over the stone footbridge of the dyke.

She must peep into the grey wagtails' nest in the ivy on the mill-house, to see how the nestlings were getting on. The down waved on their new-feathered heads; they half-opened their beaks when she parted the leaves and peered in. She saw the four heads, and went on, happier by the thought of their safety. There had been five eggs in the nest three weeks before, but a cuckoo had substituted her own egg for one of them; and finding this egg, Mary had taken it, and added it to her collection.

The sun shone full on the tall cob wall, and on the peach and cherry and plum trees trained against it. The wall was made of mud and cowdung mixed with stones and slapped on straw, yet it had withstood more than three centuries' rains driven by the south-west gales without check from the Atlantic. The thatch of reed cut from the duckponds had topped it for half a century, and kept its core dry and sound. The wall was four feet thick, and based upon smooth grey stones, some of them weighing a hundredweight, brought from the Pebble Ridge when the original farm-house had been rebuilt for a 'gennulman's house' with parts of the prize-money saved by one John Bassett, esquire – 'a retired cut-throat, in other words,' as Mary's father used to tell the children, to the slight annoyance of his wife.

A wasps' nest was hung near the apex of the arch of the wooden gate, a grey and brittle globe of dry wood pulp which must not be disturbed, for Uncle Suff had watched it being built from the beginning, when a solitary queen had journeyed to and fro between the gate and the potting-shed, taking the paper of *Old Moore's Almanac* which he happened to have left there during the previous winter. Now the nest belonged to Uncle Suff, and no one must so much as strike at a wasp, lest his friend the queen be injured.

Mary unbolted the door, and squeezed through the least space. She took off her shoes; she was on the Burrows at last, the wide and open Burrows where all silly things such as cooking and housework and being proper were left behind. The white tails of a score of rabbits jumped and grew small before her. Oh, the smell of the wild thyme, and the dew sparkling on the grasses by her feet! O swallow, and the blue sky, and the light of morning! Swim in the sea she must – bother, no bathing dress or cap – no matter, no one would see.

She walked slowly backwards when the tower of Speering Church came into view beyond the house and trees, dreaming on what he might be doing. Was he asleep in that damp cottage, or had he gone away? Was he really 'unreliable and undependable,' as Mother said? He would come and go, and they would hear no more of him, except casually from

Mules, or Mr. Garside, or Diana, unless one went to his cottage to find him – and Mother had forbidden Jean and herself to do that, unless they were together, which was practically never nowadays.

Miss Goff had been talking – why couldn't she leave other people alone? And walking across the Great Plain, wending her way through dark-green clumps of spiky rush and low thick bushes of privet, she brooded on him. Somehow the sunlit place seemed less enchanting now; and she realized suddenly, with a feeling of vacancy and slight fear, that one found in the earth only what one put there. The spirit of the Burrows was herself; and all her old self was changed.

'I love Willum,' she said sorrowfully to the air. 'But does Willum love me? Perhaps he loves Diana, who is much cleverer than Mary.' She began to sing in a low sweet voice as she wandered towards the brown-mossy hillocks, over ground springy to the foot with short curled grasses, reindeer moss, and the small round leaves of the marsh pennywort low and numerous on the ground. Flowers of a rare orchid, the marsh helliborine, rose ankle-high in the level place, a tribe of dwarfs, which had made their seeds there century after century. Further on, another flowery tribe was scattered over the plain, each plant with its thin upright stems passing through several tiers of leaves, and bright yellow flowers crowning its life. Then she came to a forest of strange little dark-green bamboo-like stalks with black heads and joints, impoverished descendants of the great prehistoric trees which had made the coal-beds. How are the mighty fallen! Scarcely thicker than a darning needle, they feebly whipped her bare feet as she passed. Farmer Bissett called them 'tidy-pipe,' and declared that horses and cattle grew fat on them: whereas they did not eat them. 'Oh, the darlings,' she cried, walking over a hillock and coming upon a plain pink with innumerable little veined blossoms of the bog pimpernels. When last she had crossed the plain he had been with her, and they had agreed to meet there when the flowers were open: but O, the blossom was sad and fragile underfoot, and soon would fade with the summer.

'I love Willum,' she sang, scarcely louder than the under-voice of a bird. 'I love Willum,' and her heart ached for him. He was growing so worn and haggard, and wasting his energy in declaiming against nearly everything. Perhaps they would both be happy, and talking in low voices, when sitting in the hall after supper, and Uncle Suff or Mother, reading the paper, would say something or other about the coal-miners, or politics, and watching him, she would see agony concealed in his eyes, and he would speak no more, but perhaps go out, and wander about all night. He might return to sleep in the house, or not come in until the middle of the next day, or keep away for days. She understood so well, and longed to help him, but what could she do? Ah, if she could take him away, and look after him properly, and see that he had regular meals, and that he worked regularly, instead of pouring out his nervous life on things that could not be helped – at least, not on the Burrows.

She sat on a knoll bronze-coloured with dying moss, and taking a comb from her pocket, began to unplait her hair, which had not been touched since the night before. A plover flew round her head, in laboured flight, its hoarse and liquid cry sounding like *Why why? Woe, woe, Why?* It flapped round in a circle over the hollow where its young were crouching, its wings soughing, crying forlornly. Other plovers were crying in the distance, black specks flinging about in the sky. She wondered what had disturbed them, for she would not have disturbed any birds herself beyond about a quarter of a mile. Under her hand she scanned the sky, looking for a peregrine falcon ; for while other birds sought cover on the ground when the falcons were aloft, plovers took the air. Nothing there, except a pair of carrion crows flying towards the sun.

She shook her hair loose with her hand, and began to comb

it. Bother! she had forgotten hairpins. She determined to have
it cut when next she went to Barum, although this would
mean a new hat for church – a silly custom, that women must
not enter a church without a hat. Well, it did not matter one
way or another, really; the point was that she had no money
for hats. Hats! Hair! And she had come on to the Burrows
to have a lovely time by herself, and here she was combing
her hair, which was so tangled that the comb would hardly
move through it. Damn that, as Jean would say.

Why? why? woe-woe, Why? the plover called, again and again.
She got up and wandered on, so that the poor bird could be
happy again.

Larks were beginning to rise and sing their second songs of
the day, having fed and rested and sand-bathed after the first
dawn songs; one after another mounted, roused and inspired
by the notes of its neighbours. Mary reached the sandhills,
meaning to go straight to the sea and bathe; but when she had
climbed to the summit she hesitated, and looked back. The
plovers were still flying around in the distant air. Sitting down,
in order to be invisible under the hill-top, she waited and
watched expectantly. After awhile she saw the figure of a man,
and soon afterwards, a dog running before him, as though
hunting rabbits. She slid down the sandhill to be out of sight,
and gathering her hair over her left shoulder, began to plait
it. When this was done she tucked the rope into her blouse,
and sat nervously still, wanting both to run away and hide
and to go and meet him. Then she thought that he might
have seen the plovers disturbed in her direction, and have
guessed or divined – for he seemed to know and to anticipate
things in the strangest manner – it was she.

So Mary ran down towards the south, crouching low by the
hollows between the hillocks, meaning to watch for him from
a hidden place, and then to track him. Should it happen that
he was going to bathe, she would call out to him, and let him
know she was there. He had cheated her out of her swim,

and so she would prevent him having his! Although if he wanted to swim, he would probably swim, naked, whether she was there or not: he did exactly what pleased him when he was with her. As it should be!

Some distance from the sandhill where she had espied him, Mary lay down, behind a hummock. At the moment he was invisible, but he would have to cross the plain in front of her, and then she would see him. While waiting she regarded the flowers of a doll's-house. The leaves of a dandelion were an inch long, the flowers smaller than a threepenny bit. Tinier still were the disks of the hawkbits and the pink flowers of the dove's-foot crane's-bill, and the blue and yellow flowers of the scorpion grass – midget forget-me-not; the delicate blue of the germander speedwell, and the seed of the vernal whitlow grass on its weeny bleached stalk – its white flowers came earliest of all in the spring. Ladies bedstraw with tiny white chains of blossoms, and then yellow bedstraw. Some of the thread-like roots in the sand were exposed by the wind and whitened by the sun; others by a single thread clung to life, low out of the way of wind and the curved teeth of rabbits. The flowers were as fine and as delicate as one of Aunt Edith's mosaic brooches.

How beautiful were the Burrows! – but supposing he did not love –

She blushed, for that he would think she was deliberately lying in wait to meet him. Well, she was! Not exactly, though – it was partly an accident. She kicked her toes into the sand, irritated by her own stupid ways of thought: all bits and scraps of convention. He saw life plain, indeed! The truth was that she loved him, and wanted him to love her – but supposing he did not love – There she was again, her civilized mind like a squirrel raging in a wretched cage.

Mary hid her face in her arms, and lay still, dreading to meet him, longing to meet him. The plovers never ceased to cry over her head, all the while she lay there; and the sun grew hot on her bare legs. At length an ant ran over her hand, and she raised her head, and watched it hurrying on the mat of flowers just under her eyes. It ran with amazing energy, over stalks, blooms, bead-like shells, and gold-crusty lichens, and coming to a pit dug by a rabbit, it attempted to scramble up a cliff, causing a slide of sand grains which must have appeared to it to be as big as the boulders on the Pebble Ridge. As she watched it scrambling out of the pit and hastening on through rootlet and stalk she began to breathe more quickly, while a feeling of fascination spread up her body. She dared not raise herself on her elbows, and look over the top of the hummock; and yet she would miss him if she did not. Now she knew the sensation a rabbit had when, instead of running away miles when pursued by a stoat, it sometimes crouched still, while the dreadful lithe form rippled nearer and nearer, and froze its life in fascination.

She lay with her head on one bent arm for what seemed a very long time, while she became more and more entangled in the thrill and fascination of not moving. At last, with almost a physical wrench she looked up, and saw him at once: he was passing just in front of her, so near that she could see the creases in his shirt sleeves rolled above the elbow, and the knots on his stick. She pressed herself on the sward immediately, her face so close to the sand that she could see the grains being blown by her nostrils each time she breathed. Then she heard above the pounding of her heart a sudden noise of feet and panting, and her ear was being licked by a large sandy pink tongue.

'Hullo, Biell,' she whispered with relief. The spaniel gave two rapid licks of her nose before lying down to ease his heart. She waited for the inevitable, stroking the dog's head, and not looking up. A shadow fell on her legs. It startled her, for she had expected him to appear from the other side. The shadow remained unmoving, but there was no sound. At length she looked up and smiled wanly, and seeing his face, she looked down again, and went on stroking the dog's head. The shadow lay across her legs for a few moments, and then it moved away.

The spaniel watched his master going away from him, and whined, and stood up, glancing at her face and then at the retreating form. He is not pleased with me, she thought dully; and she sat still, there being nothing else to do. Perhaps he had come out to be entirely alone, so that he could live his thoughts in solitude; and the sight of another human being had broken in upon them like a shock. I am a fool, she thought wildly, I am a fool. Both Jean and she were fools – no not Jean: Jean was only a child when she was 'smitten' by Howard, whereas there was no such excuse in her own case – she had deliberately encouraged herself to fall in love, thinking she could serve him and cherish him, as she had wanted to do from the first moment she had seen him, a little boy with whom she had played 'Pirates' at a tea party. She remembered, with shame now acute after all the years, that she had offered to marry him, forgetting that it was 'Pirates' and not 'Kings and Queens.' He had disliked her then; he disliked her now. Friendship, yes – he was lonely, and must have some one sympathetic to talk to: as he had been lonely on the Kentish downs four years before, when she had pitied him, ensnared by the wanton Eveline Fairfax. He had not wanted her then. And now –

She dug her nails into the sand, wondering what she might do. Anything; it did not matter what she did now. Anything, so long as she would not appear to be following him. Go back to the house and do some work – scrub out the kitchen, which had not been done for a fortnight; polish the rusty fender and black-lead the grate; weed her part of the garden, which was nothing but creeping thistles whose roots went down more than two feet into the sandy soil, and always had been there, and always would be there, however hard or deep she hoed and dug. The washing, too – that might be done to-day; a fine washing day it was, oh, a fine washing day.

She would work and work and work, and not be silly any more.

She stole a glance at him, and saw that he was still walking away, not with the swinging stride of five minutes before, but slowly, as though dejected. Ah, she had spoilt the Burrows for him. Dreadful thought, he had known she was lying in wait for him, he had divined her thoughts; and being one who always spoke or acted his mind, he had immediately gone away. Tears are for those who may still hope, she thought, and jumping up, walked towards the sun, back to the house and work.

When she got back, entering by the front gate, she saw Uncle Sufford standing before the porch, blue-coated, hands in white breeches pockets, his knees bent slightly like those of an old resting horse, and puffing thoughtfully at his small black pipe. A red bandanna handkerchief hung out of one breeches pocket. He was wearing his uniform of the otter hunt, with his new grey (called white) pot-hat on his head. This hat had arrived by yesterday afternoon's post, and Mr. Chychester had walked into the village specially to get it; as he had risen early, specially to try it on in the sunshine.

'Well midear,' he said, speaking in broad Devon. ''Tis weest weather coming, I vancy,' and his pipe dropped out of his mouth. 'Damn the thing,' he muttered, in his usual voice. 'The trouble is I've got no teeth,' and laughing gruffly, he flung it into the hydrangeas. 'I'll have to smoke beastly cigarettes in future, I can see that. Egging?' he inquired. 'Rather late, isn't it?'

'I just went for a walk, Uncle Suff.'

Mr. Chychester sniffed the air, and adjusted his new white hat.

'I suppose you didn't see anything of Maddison? I saw him as I was getting up, and thought perhaps he had come to see you younger folk. He ought to come otter-hunting to-day. They're meeting at Kismeldon Bridge.'

Mary tried to look composed, but her eyes were too honest, her cheeks too expressive.

'I did see him,' she murmured. 'I think he's gone to bathe. The new hat looks fine, Uncle Suff,' she added, blowing the loose hairs of her widow's peak free of her reddened face, and staring at the ground.

'Well, I'm glad I'm not him,' said Mr. Chychester, looking at the clouds drifting up in the western sky. 'Hot baths for me – hot as I can get 'em. Oh, by the way, I brought back a letter for you yesterday, and forgot to give it to you. It's on my desk in my room. I'll fetch it directly.'

'Don't bother, Uncle Suff; I'm going in shortly.'

A few moments later he said:

'You ought to bring Maddison otter-hunting,' and saw that he was speaking to the air. H'm. He must be getting deaf. Pity so many fine mornings turned dirty later on. There was enough water in the rivers already, so de Wichehalse had said, and a 'fresh' rose quickly in the Torridge. Queer how the Torridge bitch-otters seemed to have the characteristics of their (probably) native river. They were fast and light – fourteen and fifteen pounds – just as the summer 'freshes' were fast, quickly rising and falling. Whereas the Taw – the 'Gentleman's River,' with its pubs all so handy – was bigger, and slower, to rise and fall, and its bed not so clean and scoured. A dog-otter. H'm, too fanciful – like that young fellow's ideas. Too fanciful altogether. Nice young fellow, though – damned interfering old woman, that Miss Goff. Too much money – thought herself too big. People afraid of her because of her money. Those wealthy middle-class people always too bumptious. Oh well, as long as she didn't want to stop him otter-hunting!

People lapsed from his mind; and with hands clasped under his tail-coat, the old man went to look at his rock garden, where grew many Alpine plants which daily absorbed much of his affection. He peeped into his thermometer stand on the

way, to see if his aerymouse was still there. Ah, there the little
beggar was, with a little tacker cuddled to its breast. It ticked
at him, showing its small red mouth and tiny teeth, peering
with its mouse-like eyes. No accounting for such things. He
carefully shut the slatted door, for morning temperatures were
not taken until nine o'clock.

Having taken her letter, the handwriting of which she
recognized with a leap of hope, and thrust it into her pocket,
Mary had gone into the kitchen. There she examined the
envelope, back and front, and felt the contents, delaying the
sweet act of opening it. 'I'll read ee when I've done my work,'
she whispered, and hid it on the chimney-piece.

She opened all the windows, and lit the three burners of the
American blue-flame oil-stove, a type of heating and cooking
range which had come to stand in many West Country
kitchens that summer. Two full kettles and a flat-iron were
put on to heat, and then she began to sweep the kitchen.
Hurrying out into the garden when this was done, she gathered
in some table linen and underclothing from the line, between
two apple trees, and put the basket on the table. Afterwards
a heavy pail of water was carried in with a mop, and the stone
floor was swabbed, then wiped with a cloth. When the small
kettle boiled she fetched cups and tea-pot, but looking in the
larder, behold, a disaster – a mouse lay drowned in the milk.
Pouring the milk into a bowl for the cats, she flung the mouse
by its tail into the briar-tangled gooseberry bushes outside
the scullery door, and went to the farm to fetch the new milk.

This building, the more wretched half of its thatch covered
with rusting corrugated iron sheets, stood about a quarter of
a mile away. Before the War it had belonged to the Ogilvie
estate. Farmer Bissett, a man with an immense paunch, had
bought it after the War, with part of the money he had received
for the rabbits trapped on the Burrows during the 'submarine
peril' of 1917 and 1918, when rabbits had fetched as much as
half-a-crown apiece. The trapping rights had been let on

a long lease before the War, at a fixed annual rent of eighty pounds; and so Mrs. Ogilvie, much to her secret regret, had not shared in what she, with others, had generally deprecated as 'profiteering.'

Farmer Bissett had one son, twenty-eight years old, who was considered one of the best judges of cattle around Barum. About a year previously Jean had begun to spend a lot of her time at the farm, talking 'horse' with him; then she had gone for rides with him in his car, as he went round buying cattle – actions which had been commented on, much to her mother's annoyance.

Several black pigs stood about, with fowls, on ground trodden smooth and grassless and littered with rusty pots and china shards, before the farm-house. As Mary approached three dogs barked furiously and ran to her with waving tails when they recognized her, the tone of their barking changing at the same time. Jack Bissett came round the corner and shouted at them, and they slunk apart, and then trotted to the door, their anxiety giving way to an easy amiability.

'Good morning,' said Mary. 'Is it too soon for the milk?'

'Not at all. Alice has just finished,' replied the man, who was dressed in a pair of smartly-cut riding breeches and leather leggings. 'You'm about early, aren't you? Jean's still a-bed, I suppose?'

'I expect she is.'

'Are you going to the pony races at Shebberton to-day?'

'I'm not,' replied Mary, resisting a desire to dislike him because he called her sister 'Jean.' 'I don't know if my sister is.'

At this moment old Bissett himself moved into the doorway, completely filling it. 'Good morning, Farmer,' said Mary.

'Good morning, Miss Mary,' chuckled Bissett. 'You'm about earlyish midear. Alice!' he roared over his shoulder 'plaize vor fetch the milk vor the Big House, now to once. Miss Mary be waiting.'

'Aye, aye, you,' sang a voice from the dairy, and iron-shod boots clattered on the stone floor.

Poor Jean, thought Mary, on her way back with the milk, I do hope she won't come to any harm. Her sister's moodiness had lately become acute, and several times a week she would be absent from supper, returning at all hours of the night. Mrs. Ogilvie no longer asked where her daughter had been, for whenever she had done so Jean had usually given her a variation of the same reply, which was to the effect that she, Jean, had no interest in her house or family, and that her life was her own, and no concern of her mother's.

The kitchen was filled to darkness when Mary returned, the air thick and stifling with smuts that poured and spread out of reddish-yellow flames around the kettles. Mary swore, using a word of Jean's she had never used before deliberately – although in childhood she had pronounced various 'obscene' words, unconscious of their meaning, when Michael had first brought them home from school – and dashed through the cloud of smuts to the stove, to turn down the wicks.

She slammed the door leading to the hall, then ran through the kitchen to the fresh air, one glance at her basket of washing telling her that it was ruined. Every cobweb was grimy with the soot from the stove, every plate and cup on the dresser was filthy. She clenched her hands, and was about to cry when she remembered the letter. His letter! – that would be smitched! She ran back into the kitchen and snatched it from the shelf, broke open the envelope, and read:

SCUR COTTAGE,
Midsummer Day

DEAR MARY, –

I've got to clear out of here next Michaelmas: Mules' Cousin-Billy's-Widow has just come round to give me notice. I asked her if there was any reason for it – as you know I pay the rent in advance – and she said that she 'desired me to be clear of her property next Michaelmas Quarter Day,' and gave me a letter saying the same thing. So I went to see Mules in the churchyard and he declared, in whispered multiples of three, that he knew nothing about it. By his fearsome glances at Miss Goff – he was scything the grass under the elms, and she was putting out plants on a grave the other side of the churchyard – I imagined he knew why, but didn't want to say.

I've done a lot of work since I saw you last: The Star-born is two-thirds finished; and the *Express* has printed some of my nature sketches, etc., so I'm all right for money, thank God.

The green corn is beautiful in the Great Field; and I can hear the swallows twittering on the ridge of the barn opposite. Mules continues to poke down the work of the pair trying to build in the porch. I have pleaded with him, but he has his duty to do, I suppose. Oh, I am sad to hear their cries: they are weaker than we are, their joy in life is so keen, they are such bright things, like happy children. If I could but be as a bird and forget there is so much suffering in the world – suffering which need not be, if only we would let the swallows build where they list. Oh, to be a swallow! And you'd try to find sanctuary for your unborn in the porch, and the church-warden would order your cradle walls to be knocked down, and you would cry, and forget quickly, and begin again and again, until in anguish you had to drop your eggs in the grass.

The summer is beautiful over the Great Field; but it has nothing to do with the high internecine finance that owns newspapers, each group to inculcate its 'patriotic' point of view. The summer is beautiful over all countries, and the sweet wind floats all flags: but they are not living things, like the tall grasses in the hedges, and the drooping heads of the reddening sorrel.

One day men will love the swallows, and learn that their wings are a more intense blue than the biblical heaven.

Meanwhile let us hate like hell, and follow the ideals of the respectable millionaire barons, and believe their newspapers, and the Old Man who hates and distrusts and makes virtues of his corrupted mind, so that unborn men shall be involved in agonies unimaginable and unwritable, in the name of patriotism. Let us call the miners' leaders damned swine because they want their men to see a little more of the sun.

One day men will know that the flower of the tree of life is the Christ-state, or Khristos, which was grown in laughter, but blooms among men in sadness.

Meanwhile let us continue with our excellent and sufficient prep-school ideas: and believe that people without our father's incomes are a sub-species, nevertheless superior to all foreigners; excellently stubborn in War defending our easiness of life; but damnably stubborn in Peace when demanding a sufficiency of life. Let us hope that the next generation will not die in vain, for death would surely be vain if the prep-school philosophy and the top-hat disappeared entirely.

Meanwhile I am dead, and seven million others, and Ludendorff has thanked his Junker God in the simple little Church in East Prussia for God's goodness to the Fatherland; and we have thanked the God of our Far Flung Battle Line in St. Paul's for our Victory. And a million sub-species German patriots rot in France, far from the fields they loved the sun in; and the sun does not shine on the dead. And the other day an English Bishop blessed the 17-inch guns of a new warship in the name of Jesus. It is all proper, the guns will only be fired in a just cause! God will be on our side, for how could he ever be on the side of a foreigner?

Good heavens, the fellow's shell-shocked, writing like this! It's all very well, but he's a damned nuisance also. Hot Air, as the Vicar blandly (à la best tradition) remarked to me. Half an hour later, while watching Mules digging up the skull of a former grave-digger he'd known, and hearing him discoursing on it like Hamlet, I thought of a suitable reply.

'Hot Air? Yes, sir. It is the heat of the sun, and the air of the world that is striving to make people natural, and as Christ himself!'

I told Mules, but all he would say was that I was three funny men; and there was One above who knew everything. In fact, three Ones above. I begin to apprehend the type of mind that composed the Trinity.

'Us'v all got to come to it, haven't us, sir? Poor old John Hancock, this be his grave, sir. His grave. Poor old John Hancock. It makes you think, don't it, sir? Us'v all got to go sometime. Wan thing, us'll have so good a place in heaven as they 'igh-class gentry, won't us, zur, me'n you? Us'll all be so good as they in ab'm.' I love my old Muley.

I've got rid of my rather depressed feeling by writing this to you, Mary. Now I'm going on with the Star-born. If I get really going, I shall probably write all night. Sometimes I feel I've got the strength equal to the light of a hundred suns and moons – moonlight for the poetic or inactive side, sunlight for the active.

W. M.

P.S. This is the fourth letter I have written; I tore the others up. I had lunch and a quart of beer to-day at the Plough Inn for a change; I love having my meals with old Muley and his wife, but sometimes Mrs. Mules talks and talks *at* me usually, and I smile and nod and say 'Ye-es,' as though deeply meditating her every remark, not wanting to hurt her feelings. She is an old bore, but very kind.

I am carrying the crust of the whole world to-day – but it is no more obvious than the sun carrying the earth.

P.P.S. I often think of the bog-pimpernels, and of that walk. Have you forgotten. But I must work on the S-b, for the night cometh . . .

Mary had read the letter for the second time when she heard some one coming, and turning round, she saw him walking along by the rhododendrons. She stuffed the letter into her pocket, and feeling that she must not remain standing still, she went to meet him. He seemed taller, the bones of his cheeks more pronounced, two dark sickles under his eyes.

'I had to come,' he said, stopping before her and speaking in such an unhappy voice that she moved a hand towards his arm, and with a light touch led him into the kitchen. Inside, with no one to see, she stopped before the head which was turned away dejectedly from her full pitying eyes.

'What is it, Billy?' Never before had she called him by that name.

He looked at her feet.

'Hungry?'

He shook his head. 'Nothing physical – I've often been hungry, and don't mind that. I came to say good-bye.'

She said nothing, believing that he meant what he said.

'It isn't fair to your mother or yourself for me to remain.'

'If that's all, then you needn't worry any more, my dear. Mother never listens to what people say.'

She had lifted one heaviness from him, at any rate.

As though from a remote part of her life came the thought that it must be getting late – and Uncle Suff wanted his breakfast early, and sandwiches cut for the meet at Kismeldon Bridge.

'Don't worry, Billy.'

'I feel the Star-born is based on illusion. I've been writing all night, and this morning it seemed entirely worthless.'

'Of course it would. You're worn out. You don't know how to look after yourself, that's your trouble.'

He touched her cheek, saying hoarsely, 'Mary!'

They looked towards the passage door together. On her toes Mary moved away from him, saying, 'Uncle Suff will be waiting': and the door opened, and Benjamin came in with long strides – one of his various practices by which he hoped to hasten growth to manhood's voice and stature – and stopped.

'G' morning, Captain Maddison.'

'Hullo, Benjamin,' said Maddison, genially, with an effort.

'I saw you coming,' said Benjamin.

'Did you?'

He began to walk up and down, while Mary, having returned from the larder with frying-pan and two rashers of bacon, pushed a kettle aside and began to fry her uncle's breakfast.

'Ben,' she said, 'will you go and collect the eggs?'

'Right-o,' replied Benjamin, and went out of the door.

'Uncle Suff's having his early because he's going otter-hunting,' said Mary, to Maddison.

'You go hunting, don't you?'

'Sometimes. Not very often now. I'm much too busy.'

'Your wicks want trimming,' he said, going near to the stove and peering at the high yellow points leaping and quivering behind the mica of the chimneys. 'They're wasting oil, that way.'

'Uncle Suff said he saw you about an hour ago.'

'I walked along the sea-wall. I saw you looking out of the window.'

'When? I didn't see you.'

'I was in the orchard,' he said, looking away. 'I hid when I saw you.'

She pondered the hidden significance in the remark, as she shook the sizzling rashers in the pan. Then conscious of him looking at her, she turned and met his gaze. His eyes dropped before hers, and realizing when he had seen her, she became hot with shame.

'You are so beautiful,' he said in a low voice. 'Mary, I – I –'

He did not finish what he was going to say, but began to walk up and down again. Benjamin returned, breathless and slightly flushed.

'I say, Captain Maddison, you are staying this time, aren't you? Make him stay, Mary.'

'Help me lay the table. Mary's in a hurry. Come on, Benjamin! We'll show them how we can work if we want to. Supper things washed up? Good, come on.'

'Lay places for five,' said Mary. 'Aunt Edith has hers in bed.'

When Benjamin had gone with the tray to the breakfast-room he asked if there were time to go otter-hunting.

'Plenty. Uncle Suff is meeting Howard's car at Appledore at nine o'clock. I expect there will be room for you.'

'But you're coming too?'

'Shall I?'

'Yes!'

He asked, with hesitation, if he could have some breakfast first.

'You're hungry!' she said.

'I am a bit.'

'You poor dear, I believe you're starving! Have you had anything since that lunch yesterday at the Plough Inn?'

He shook his head.

'Was it a big lunch?'

'Enough for me.'

'What was it?'

'Bread and cheese.'

'And you've been working all night, too! No wonder you felt depressed this morning. Now just you go and sit down in that chair – mind you don't fall through – while I cook you a nice fried breakfast. Do you like fried bread as well as eggs and bacon?'

'Yes, please.'

He sat down obediently.

You're a poor boy, you are, thought Mary, and was glad the stove was against the wall, for tears were falling from her eyes, and her lips unsteady with smiles.

Chapter 10

AFTER a silent minute in the broken chair:

'You've been blooded, I suppose?' said Maddison to Mary. She shook her head. 'No. I always kept clear.'

'I have,' said Benjamin. 'But not fox or stag. I have been done with otter, badger, rabbit, and rat.'

'With rabbit and rat! Your education has certainly not been neglected. Who did the blooding? Your grandfather, or the Vicar?'

'Jean did the rabbit and I did the rat myself.'

'Then what is it the Vicar does? Oh, I know. Of course, he baptizes you.'

Mary felt a twinge of uneasiness, but she understood what he meant. Benjamin would not.

'Babies are baptized, Captain Maddison,' he replied seriously. 'And the rabbit and rat blooding wasn't really proper. It was only fun.'

'Of course it was. I was only trying to be funny,' said Maddison, ruffling the boy's hair.

Mr. Chychester came into the kitchen, walking warily on his iron-shod boots on the stone floor. He carried a little keg, bound with brass hoops, under one arm.

'Breakfast just coming, Uncle Suff!'

'Ha!' he exclaimed appreciatively, sniffing. 'You coming otter-hunting, Mary?'

'Yes, Uncle Suff.'

'Good girl. You coming also, Maddison?'

'Yes, sir.'

'That's proper. Nothing like otter-hunting, providing the water's right, and you find an otter. They're getting fewer

216

nowadays, I fancy; London ruffians put advertisements in the local papers, asking for skins, and so farmers trap them. They ought to be put in a gin under water themselves, and see how they like it! Brutal things, those gins. You drink beer, I suppose?'

'Aye, aye, sir.'

'That's right. I must put some more in my firkin.'

'Grandpa!' said Benjamin.

'Well, my boy, what do you want?'

'Please may I come otter-hunting?'

'H'm. 'Tisn't holidays, is it?'

'No, but it was midsummer day yesterday.'

'Well, that seems a good reason. A day in the open will do you more good than a day in school, I've no doubt. But I can't give you leave. You'd better ask your Aunt.'

'But she'll say No, grandpa.'

'Well, boy, I can't give you leave.'

'I was ill at half-term, grandpa.'

'Ah!'

'All day in bed, grandpa.'

'H'm!'

'And grandpa, I think the Master nearly gave me a pad last time I was out. I saw him looking at me once or twice as he pulled his moustache, but in the end he gave them to the farmers. Can I say to Aunt Connie that you said I could ask her, Grandpa?'

'I don't want to ask her,' muttered Mr. Chychester testily, as he clumped to the cellar, to put another pint into his firkin.

'I wish I could come,' said Benjamin dolefully. 'Mary, you ask Aunt.'

Mary was warming plates with hot water. 'I'm afraid she'll say No, Ben.'

'Then I'll come without asking.'

'You'll get the stick,' said. Maddison.

'Well, the fact is,' said Benjamin, with a grin, 'I shall get the stick if I do go to school to-day.'

'Ah, now we understand!' said Mary.

'Why are you going to get the stick?'

'For not doing homework, Captain Maddison.'

'Damned nonsense! You poor little bored wretch! Bored at school, bored at church, coming home with your satchel full of potential boredom: you refused to be bored, and probably are too scared to admit it, and get caught out for telling lies. A barefaced liar, I expect you were called.'

'Well, as a matter of fack, that's what I was called,' admitted Benjamin.

'A barefaced liar! Whereas if you were big enough to have whiskers, your master wouldn't have dared to insult you!'

They all laughed. 'I'm not going to school to-day, I'm going otter-hunting. Don't you like otter-hunting, Captain Maddison?'

'Like it? Good God, no. If it were a man-eating lion, it might be different. Indeed, it would be different: you'd see your grandfather throwing away his little barrel of beer, and beating it for John o' Groats.'

Observing the look on Benjamin's face he hastened to add, whilst amiably stroking the boy's long close-cropped head, 'Don't think you're wrong. You're young. It wouldn't be normal for you to think like I do yet. Your god is still pagan. The human consciousness passes through many stages of growth, just as the body does before it is born.' To Mary he said, 'That's what I meant by my apparently disrespectful remark about baptism. I saw you flinch; your eyes are too honest.'

'I didn't really.'

He went close to her and whispered, 'You have given me back my strength. This morning I was in the slough of despond, for seeing all things plainly I had decided to go away and leave you to the happiness which, surely, is in store for you.'

'Then you would have taken it with you,' she whispered, and hurried away with the breakfast tray.

Benjamin had listened hard to hear what was said, but he had heard nothing; for Maddison, making allowance for the sharpness of a boy's curiosity, had turned his back when he had spoken. He saw Mary's red cheeks as she picked up the tray, and guessed that she was 'spoony'; but he was unable to understand why Maddison went into the scullery, and then into the larder, picking up glasses and plates, quite aimlessly. When, however, on returning to the kitchen, Maddison squared up to him, and pretended to punch him round the room, he guessed that he was 'spoony' too. They're safe with me, he thought. They don't know I know, but I won't tell anyone. He felt that he loved Maddison, and how fine it must be to be grown-up; and when Maddison had followed Mary, and he was left alone in the empty kitchen, how lonely and friendless he himself was. No one wanted him, really. He went into the larder, prying round for food, for if he could not go otter-hunting, he had determined to go off by himself somewhere on his bicycle Trusty.

He did not appear again, and the three set off from the house at half-past eight, watched by Mrs. Ogilvie who had come down just as Mary and Mr. Chychester were taking their ground-ash hunting poles from the rack in the hall.

They walked down the drive which lay beyond the 8-barred gate along one side of a meadow of poor mowing grass, sparse and hardly more than fetlock-high.

'It was beautiful meadow-land before the War,' Mary told Maddison. 'But we were forced to let it be ploughed for corn in 1917, and it's never been the same since.'

'Ha, that's another thing we've got up against the Kaiser,' said Mr. Chychester.

By the culvert over the dyke called the Boundary Drain, Mary said, out of earshot of Mr. Chychester, 'Some of my relatives are characters. You heard what Uncle Suff said? Well, my grandmother Chychester – mother's mother – achieved quite a local fame when War was declared, by going on the Instow sands and solemnly pouring away all her eau-de-Cologne.'

'Well, the wife of a Prussian Junker was known to have thrown away her little bar of Sunlight Soap into the Baltic, so it's honours easy.'

They both laughed. They were walking on the narrow road lying under the high green slope of the inner wall of the marsh. A burrow duck flapped out of the dyke in front of them, and agitated feeble whistles from the reeds showed where her brood was supposed to be concealed. The duck waddled over the field, half flying, to try and draw them away from her little ones. They walked on, and she arose and flew round in circles, watching. She ceased as they came near the lime-washed cottage standing beyond the join of inner and outer walls. This was the White House. Tall tree-plants of mallow grew here: the keeper, who suffered from asthma and rheumatism, smoked the leaves in his pipe and drank mallow tea, and rubbed his limbs with their essence when he was bad. The fisherman with long hair, and a hook in place of one hand, stood beside him, by a wind-stunted willow tree.

'Good morning, Pedrick,' said Mr. Chychester.

'Good morning, your honour.'

'Fine weather, Pedrick.'

'Fine weather, your honour.'

'Boat all ready, Luke?'

The man addressed as Luke made a bird-like sound in his throat, and nodded.

'How's the asthma, Pedrick?'

'Oh, 'tis about the same, your honour. But I mustn't grumble.'

Through the sandy banks of the sunken lane they saw the estuary. The fisherman followed them down the shingle to a salmon boat with its bows at the water-line.

'I suppose there will be room for all of us in de Wichehalse's car?' said Mr. Chychester, as Luke hauled up the lug sail. 'He's only expecting me, I fancy.'

The sail flapped and bellied; the boat began to move against the flowing tide, with the slip and slap of wavelets running under it.

'Shall we go for a walk if there isn't room?' said Maddison to Mary, trailing a hand in the water. 'I want to explore the Northam Burrows.'

'Yes. Or we can walk to the pony races at Shebberton if you like. Jean's going, I believe.'

Slowly the boat passed the sandy spur of the Crow, and heeled with the fresher breeze blowing straight up the estuary. They sailed over the frothy String, where the water of the two rivers was leaping and splashing. To the west the dark stony ridge of the Sharshook showed up wet and blue-crusted with mussels.

'You'll be at the slip about six o'clock, Luke?'

Mr. Chychester held up six fingers, then pointed at his watch, and the quay they were sailing to. Luke nodded.

The sail began to flap when they came under the hill of Appledore, and the fisherman got out the sweeps and pulled. As they drew into the sand Mary said she could see the others, and looking between two ketches beached against the quay, Maddison saw three men in uniform, and two women.

'Diana and Gwen are coming,' said Mary.

They walked over the soft sand, to rocks littered with old iron pots, parts of bedsteads, tins, broken plates, boots, bones, fish-heads, and other rubbish chucked out of the windows and doors of the waterside houses.

'Who's the other girl with Diana?' asked Maddison.

'That's Gwen – Howard's sister. I say, I don't expect there will be room for us.'

'Good.'

They climbed the drying stone slip, and joined the waiting group.

Diana looks ill, thought Mary, as they greeted them.

'I've brought two young people,' said Mr. Chychester. 'You'll be able to squeeze 'em in, I expect?'

'I'm afraid I haven't room,' said Howard. 'The spare seat on the floor's already taken.'

Each of the three uniformed men suggested, in almost the same words, that he would stay behind.

'No,' said Diana. 'Mary can go in my place. I'm not keen.'

Howard looked anxious.

'Look here, Diana,' said his sister promptly, 'I'm going to stand out, anyhow, so that's that.'

'No, I really don't want to go,' replied Diana. 'Thanks all the same. Good-bye.' With a faint smile, she walked away, turning round to say, 'Really, I'd much rather not come.'

Mary and William looked at each other, while Mr. Chychester said, 'Well, I'm going to get in, anyway,' and he got in, followed by the spaniel Billjohn, who liked the smell of his stockings. 'Here, you're not coming! Get out, dog!'

'You go,' said Maddison to Mary. 'I shall stay with Billjohn, anyway, there's not room for me.'

'I say, we can't really let Diana go off like that,' exclaimed Howard, and he ran after her. Coming to Diana, he said:

'I say, Diana, do come. I don't believe Maddison and Mary are really keen.'

'I don't want to come, thanks.'

'I say, old thing, it will be rotten without you, really.'

'I've told you I'm not coming, and I meant it. I loathe all sportsmen, anyway. You'd better go back – they're waiting for you.'

'I say, what's bitten you now?'

'A mosquito.'

'No, seriously, old thing –'

'I've told you. A mosquito that sucked the blood of Christ.'

He stared at her white contemptuous face. She was breathing fast. He was alarmed, anguished, and made nervous by the thought of the gaze of others.

'For Christ's sake leave me alone. Go and join the other half-wits, and hunt otters until they stiffen up, and then tear them to bits and cheer with the same old brainless enthusiasm.'

Raising his hat, and trying to look easy, Howard left her, and went back to the car.

'She's not feeling very fit, and would rather stroll back home,' he said; and aside, to Mary, 'I say, Jo, stick by me.'

Unable to refuse him because he was so unhappy, she said, 'All right.'

'I'm so sorry, Maddison, I can't offer you a lift,' said Howard.

'Ask Luke to put you over to the Crow if you want to go back,' said Mary, coming close to him. 'Go and have lunch with Aunt Edith and Mother. There's a cold chicken. I'll be back before supper.'

'I'll be quite happy exploring this place, thanks. I'll see you when you return.'

She got in beside Howard.

'Good-bye!'

'Good-bye!'

The car drove away, and with a sudden anguish he saw it turn the near corner without Mary having waved. Ah! she had turned, and waved just in time. The sunlit quay seemed vacant.

Observing Diana a few yards away, looking in the ship-chandler's window, he decided to walk round the corner, the way the car had gone, and reach the western end of the village by the back-streets. He wanted to be alone with his dreams of Mary. He was about to move away when, stealing a glance at Diana, he saw that she had glanced at him at the same moment. Dreading lest he might hurt her feelings, he walked towards her, meaning to exchange a few remarks and then pass on.

'I'm afraid we've spoiled your morning's enjoyment, haven't we, Diana?'

'No, you haven't. I didn't want to go in the first place.'

'How are you going to get back to Branton?'

'I'm not. We're staying at Westward Ho! Personally, I prefer Appledore. People *live* here. They're a rough lot, but that's why I like them. They've got vitality. Publicans and sinners.'

'You know, Jesus meant that remark, about calling the righteous to repentance, ironically!'

'Of course. A righteous person is the most dreadful bore in existence. It was the righteous who had Jesus killed. Westward Ho! is full of them.'

'So's the whole of Europe.'

'Can you imagine a more filthy idea than that of God deliberately causing His finest product to be murdered in order to redeem a lot of lousy Jews?' said Diana, her face lighting up.

'Merely a piece of primitive tribal darkness,' replied Maddison. 'But don't let's bother about that damned nonsense. It will all have passed away long before you're a grandmother. Poor Garside, he hasn't the faintest glimmer of the historical Jesus.'

'He's a half-wit.'

Four dirty little boys, in rags, with bare feet and legs, padded past them, dragging a box with ropes. They were going to collect driftwood for firing.

'Topping kids,' said Diana. 'But Gwen and Howard would only say that they smell. No, that's untrue. Howard wouldn't have said it; but Gwen would. In fact she did.'

'Lack of imagination! Or perhaps of a sense of smell on our part! Look here, I want to see over that old wooden battleship they're breaking up round the corner. Let's explore.'

'The *Revenge*? Come on, then.'

Walking along the quay, she said, looking at his staff, 'I didn't think you were a sportsman!'

'I'm not. I ceased to be one in 1918. My stick has no notches, if you look.'

She glanced without looking, and said, 'I hate sportsmen.'

'I hate their ideas, because I've outgrown them, I suppose.'

'How did you begin to outgrow them? Seeing a wounded bird's eyes, or something?'

'Well, looking back, I think I first began to doubt on Christmas Day, 1914.'

'That sounds interesting. Do tell me about it.'

'We were in trenches under Messines hill, and had a truce with the Saxon regiment opposite. It started on Christmas Eve, when they were singing carols, and cheering "Hoch der Kaiser!" and we cheered back for the King. Then they lifted a Christmas tree, lit with candles, on their parapet, and shouted for us to come over. We feared a trap; but at last one of us climbed out into no-man's land –'

'That was you, I expect.'

'Well, yes, I did go. A German approached me. It was bright moonlight, and the ground was frozen hard. We approached each other with trembling smiles, and hands fumbling in tunic pockets for gifts for each other. He could speak English. 'I saw you coming,' he said, 'and I've told my comrades not to fire at you, whatever happens. They appear to be afraid of a trap.' I was so moved that I could hardly speak. We shook hands over our barbed wire fence – in those days our barbed wire was a simple fence of five strands. He gave me cigars, and I gave him a tin of bully beef and some chocolate. After awhile other men came out, and we stamped about and swung our arms to keep warm, smoking each other's Christmas tobacco.'

'I wish I had been there,' said Diana, moving nearer to him. 'What happened next?'

'Well, we had to go back to work on our parapet, making them up with sandbags carried out of Ploegsteert wood by fatigue parties, making loop-holes with steel-plates, fetching wooden planks for trench floorboards, and other fatigues. It was quite enjoyable – the mud was gone, except in the bottom of the trench, and we all felt it was a proper Christmas. There was not a shot fired all that night, and when the sun came up we were all walking about without any fear.

'The trenches were about a hundred and fifty yards apart where we were, and we stood about all Christmas Day in the flat turnip field, in which dead cows were lying – most of them riddled with bullets fired by young soldiers – including myself – wanting something to fire at, from both sides during the preceding days and weeks. The ground was bone-hard, but we managed to bury the dead who had been lying out in no-man's land since the October fighting. We marked the shallow graves with crosses made of the wood of ration boxes. I talked with my German friend and asked him what the words "Fur Vaterland und Freiheit," which were written in indelible pencil on their crosses, meant. He said "For Fatherland and Freedom."

'This staggered me, for I had not thought for myself before; I believed, as nearly all English newspapers, priests, and politicians had declared, that it was a righteous war, to save civilization; and that the Germans were all brutes, who raped women and bayoneted babies and old men, and had to be rooted out of Europe like a cancerous growth before the world could be safe. I was very young, you see, not then eighteen. My German friend said that Germany could never be beaten; and I said, Oh no, England can never be beaten. He said Germany could not be beaten, because his country was fighting for the Right. I said, But we are fighting for the Right! How can you be fighting for the Right, also? We smiled at each other. He put his hand in his pocket and pulled out another cigar. "Please smoke it, English comrade."

'The papers called such actions "exchanging gifts," but it was more than an exchange in many cases, such as ours. It was the pouring out of the spikenard oil of the spirit. Later, the Germans sent over a note that their regimental staff was going round the front line at midnight, and their gunners would fire their "automatic pistols" – that was the wording of the note – but they would fire over our heads: and would we please keep under cover, "lest unhappy accidents occur." And at eleven o'clock of that frosty starlit night, the machine guns started their harsh pop-pop-pop which grew loud with sharp cracks as the traversing flight of bullets passed well over the trench, where I stood ice-cold in mud and water to my knees.

'Next day we sent over a note that our heavy artillery – that is, three guns! – was going to bombard their front line, and would they keep clear. Twelve lyddite shells went over, two of them duds, three falling in our trench, one in no-man's land, and six some way behind their front trench.'

Fishermen lounging against the stone wall at the end of the quay looked at the tall 'visitor' who talked so quickly beside the pretty little ginger-headed maid, and stared after him as they passed.

'How did it end?' asked Diana, as they walked by the church with its noisy rookery.

'My German friend and I agreed that there was no real hatred between those who had to fight: that the cold and wet and sleeplessness and hopelessness and the whole bloody business was worse than the old-time slavery, for slaves were not out in the sodden fields in all weathers as we were: we agreed that all the soldiers were miserable and homesick and longing for the war to end, clinging desperately to any rumour that came round about Russian victories and peace – and I was very sorry for the Germans, because they were deluded into thinking the victories were German victories! (whereas it was the British papers that were wrong about the direction of the "Russian Steamroller") – by the springtime. So we agreed – he was not much older than I – that if we could persuade every man of our respective armies to turn round and walk home, the war would be over.

'It seemed so simple, and such plain truth, that surely every one would perceive it at once. But even before I had finished suggesting my simple idea, I knew it was hopeless.

Quite hopeless: the unpatriotic suggestion of a simpleton who was not fit to fight in such a Christian War. Unfortunately my suggestion did not get me kicked out of the Christian band, for which, indeed, I should have been very glad: instead, the German and British staffs both issued orders, about the same time, that any man found fraternizing with the enemy, would be court-martialled, and if found guilty, suffer the death-penalty. At least, it was so in our case; but I believe the Germans didn't have the death-penalty in their army. At least, so I was told.

'Of course, it was quite right in one way; for if you are going to have an army to fight you may as well have one that fights. But that was the end of our Christmas Brotherhood idea.'

He stopped, and stared before him.

'I expect my Saxon friend has been dust many years now: dear dust, that once trembled to wish another man well, part of the beautiful spirit of heaven.'

Diana saw tears in his eyes; but brushing his hand across his lashes, he went on smilingly:

'Well, I was not free from the old set of ideals as yet; I became an officer, and in due course despised all pacifists, conscientious objectors and others we thought of as traitors, and skunks. With others I declared that such people ought to be put up against a wall and shot; in fact, I was just an echoing box, with never a thought of my own in my head all through the War that was not stifled. Being a coward, I died a thousand deaths during the War; in fact, I died altogether, and in December, 1918, coming home to be demobilized as a coal-miner – for I said I was a coal-miner in order to get out quickly – I happened to go into a bookshop at Dover, and saw a copy of Jefferies' *Story of my Heart*.'

'I know it,' said Diana. 'Mary lent it to me last year.'

'Well, I opened it and glanced at it: I read one sentence, and in that moment was changed: all the stored impressions of my boyhood seemed to return, with a mysterious spirit that brought the tears to my eyes many times as I read on. I stood there more than an hour, so rapt was I in the pages, which were a revelation to me of my own self, which had been smothered and overlaid all through the hectic days of the War. Indeed, for some time afterwards, when walking about alone, under the stars or in the sunshine of solitary places, I thought that Jefferies was with me, and of me. I grew and grew in spiritual strength; and I realized that all the world was built up of thought; that the ideals which animated the world, were but thought: mostly mediocre and selfish thought. Change thought, and you change the world.'

They were walking down a long sett-stoned street, narrow between two rows of houses. The door of every cottage was open, showing a clean threshold and passage lined with polished oil-cloth. Many small children played in the street; Maddison touched some of them on the head as he passed, and most of them smiled back at him. Diana walked by his side, stopping when he stopped, and not speaking; but often her lips opened, as though to say something. At the end of the street they saw the estuary and the sandhills, the tide flowing fast, and raising plumes of water over the stems of the leaning fairway buoys. A boat with a black net piled in its stern and three men sitting still in it and one man dipping the sweeps was drifting in the flood as fast as a trotting pony. The Sharshook ridge had vanished.

'The tide comes in fast,' he said.

'Yes.'

She seemed to be fumbling with speech.

'I say.'

He looked at her, waiting.

'I've changed, honestly.'

'Yes, I thought so. Many people in the world to-day are on the verge of the new world-consciousness.'

Again she seemed to be trying to say something.

Again he waited.

'Has Mary changed, do you think?'

He seemed to consider the question profoundly, and to become uncertain. 'I don't think she needed to change.'

Diana seemed to be perplexed by this answer.

'Then the ideal is a man or woman gentle in thought and deed to every one and everything?'

'Yes, I think that is the ideal.'

She said with a nervous laugh, 'Well, then I cannot have changed, because I hate some people. At least, I dislike them, or dislike being with them. Or perhaps, excusing myself still further, a habit of mine, I should say that it is their ideas I hate, because they distress me.'

'I know.'

They walked on, crossing the rusty iron rails coming out of the closed doors of the life-boat house, that led down a concrete slip into the sea. They came to the end of the semicircular village, to low sandy cliffs above a stony beach where wooden hulks rested, and baulks of old timber were tied together and moored by rusty steel cables. Beyond, the sea was lapping the lower timbers of the dismasted wooden battleship *Revenge*, which, with port holes and brown poop and projecting stump of bowsprit, lay like the body of a gigantic cockchafer on the flat Skern mud. Noises of knocking came from the high hull. In one of the sheds on shore an oil engine puffed unevenly, with the intermittent harsh screams of a circular saw. Other hulks inshore were broken-up to the discoloured wash-lines of their bilges, with gulls perching on the tops of their ribs. Maddison and Diana went down a path in the cliff, by a ruinous lime-kiln, and walked about on the shore. In his mind he calculated where the tide would be about six o'clock, when Mary might be expected to arrive back. Until then, it did not matter much what he did or where he went; he would be incomplete until she was with him again.

They watched baulks being sawn for awhile, and then climbed up another path, passing a tablet in a wall, which named the place Bloody Corner, where Hubba the Dane and all his men had been killed by Saxons more than a thousand years before; and they sat down by it, on the grassy fringe of a low cliff, among flowers of yellow birdsfoot trefoil, purple knapweed, and poppies. A cart lumbered down to the shore, tipped its rubbish at the water-line, and rattled back.

'Have you finished "The Star-born" yet?'

'The first half: I can't get on further. Perhaps I shall never finish it.'

'You must finish it.'

'Why, what do you know about it?'

'Nothing; but I know you.'

'You know *me*? What do you know about me?'

'Ah!' said Diana, 'I know you through and through.'

'No, my dear, you do not really. I expect you think of me as far in one direction, as some people do in another. Don't idealize any man, Diana.'

'I shan't – and certainly not you. But I've read a bit, and I know good stuff when I see it; and also, I may tell you, I've read your articles, or sketches, whatever you call them, in the *Express*, – and I know that in time you will be famous. And then people who now say horrid things about you will tell how they knew you in your early days.'

She glanced, without expression, at his coat, frayed at the sleeves and worn through at the elbows, as though by the frequent support of his head on a table; at his thin flannel trousers, at his shoes, which might have been picked off the rubbish dump in front.

'Why do people run me down?' he asked suddenly. 'I have never injured them. Why, I don't even know them. What people? But I won't ask you – I know them already. Their names are immaterial.'

He plucked a grass blade, and snapped it in his fingers.

'Well, I shan't trouble them much longer. I've got to clear out of my cottage in September.'

'I know.'

'Who told you?'

'Mother. But it is common knowledge.'

'I shan't wait until September. I'll go to-morrow.'

'No, you mustn't go.'

The tone of her voice disturbed him, and he sat quiet, looking at the grasses below his feet.

'Please don't go.' A hand touched his knee, and he looked round at her face, which smiled, as though in pain. He became uneasy of what he saw in her eyes, and took her hand while he got to his feet, and pulled her up after him. Gulls were screaming and circling over the rubbish dump below, for the tide was floating away the lighter scraps of offal.

'Let's go for a walk. That is, unless you want to go home. Perhaps I may come with you as far as Westward Ho!? I'm quite free until six o'clock, when I promised to meet Mr. Chychester and Mary at the place where we met you this morning.'

They walked on towards what were apparently the gasworks.

'Let's go round by the shore,' he suggested, wrinkling up his nose.

'You look so funny like that,' she said.

'Ah.'

They walked on in silence, over the rough beach of stones and sea-worn bricks, bottles, cans, kettles, boots, and bony heads of large fish, some stuck in streams of tar. The shore of the bight curved, facing north to the Santon Burrows; southwards lay the flat green tract, set with darker green clumps of spike rush, which was the Northam potwallopers' grazing marsh, and the Westward Ho! golf course. A long low smudge of grey topped the green, where the Pebble Ridge kept back the sea from the marsh. Above the grey line rose the distant promontory of Hartland, and over all the land clouds were moving to fill the morning sky.

'Are you going to the Otter Hunt Ball next month?' asked Diana, as they came near to the sandhills. 'Mary always goes.'

He shook his head. 'I haven't been to a dance for years.'

'I thought you might be taking Mary.'

'I didn't even know there was to be a dance.'

'But if you're staying at Wildernesse, I suppose you will be expected to go as Mary's partner.'

'I can't dance, and I've got no clothes.'

He stopped to examine the hard grey leaf of a low-growing plant of sea-holly.

Diana walked on alone for about twenty yards, and then walked over a sandhill, and disappeared. Maddison lay on his elbow, watching a cormorant paddling in the sea about three hundred yards away. The bird held the slightest interest for him; his sight became diffused, and he lived again and again that moment when, looking up at her window, he had seen Mary standing there, leaning slightly forward, with parted lips to greet the summer morning. Ah, not to greet *him*! Only to the morning was her beauty given! A thousand centuries had shaped that form, a thousand centuries of sunlight pouring down on the green earth, passing through and charging with mystic power every leaf and stone and blade of corn; everything calmly perceived by the living senses of Man had helped to shape that virgin loveliness, whose being was a spirit: a spirit of light in which, could he mingle and lose himself, were of more intense brightness than sunlight!

He saw the face of Mary regarding him – the eyes of Mary open as the sky, without a thought to harm any living thing; filled with the spirit of the green earth rising pure from the founts of life, as pure as the feeling in the golden plover flying over its nest in the hollow. A strange and shaking thought! He felt that he must never return, but wander for ever solitary in the sandhills, with the spirit dwelling gently in that mortal flesh, the complement and guardian of his own. The years of repining fell away from him as a rind, before the gaze and mystic sweetness of those eyes.

Unable to sit still, he sprang up and strode through the loose sand of the beach, quickened by the thoughts that brought tears to his eyes. He stopped again, and sat down by the skull of a bullock, whitened by sun and polished by the sand-blast of gales. Using the skull as a support to his note-book, he wrote rapidly:

'When my eyes saw Mary plain, I saw the White Bird that hovers over the oneness of life, the phœnix that flies through heaven, and flaming Sirius, and all the roaring suns of the night, whose wings are the beautiful shining Truth of Khristos. To be able to feel this would make the poor nihilist glad there is life. Little one, how can I but love thee for ever, for thou art sunrise and evestar, and a song in the wilderness of the heart.'

The sands and the sea lost their colour, which soundlessly moved away behind him; cold spots hit his face and struck through his trousers. The sudden rain squall hissed on the water; loose sand spread thin before the wind shaking the marram grasses. He hastened back to where Diana stood, as though lost, and looking for him.

'There's a sort of cave in the sand up there. Run, quick, or you'll be soaked.'

He took her hand and they ran to the cavity he had noticed, about fifty yards away in the weather-cut bank of sand ending the beach. The hollow was slight, and made by dry sand falling from under the roots of the grasses which yet bound a damp and matted roof. In a few moments he had made the hollow large enough to shelter her completely, and ordering her to get in, he continued to extend the cave along one side. Diana did not obey him, but stood in the rain.

'I don't care for a skit of rain.'

'Get in, quick.'

When she did not move he sprang up, and catching her up in his arms, set her down in the hollow.

'You little child, you. I don't suppose your clothes weigh a pound altogether.'

'Come in yourself, you big child, you.'

He pushed himself in backwards, beside her.

'Ow, sand all down my neck, you demobilised coal-miner.'

'Here, put on my coat.'

She pulled him back as he was starting to push himself out again.

'You're much more likely to get pneumonia than I am. I shan't let you be silly. Ow, keep still: more sand.'

'Very well then, you must have my coat with an arm inside it.'

He unbuttoned his coat, stretching it like a loose wing round the back of her childlike body, then laying his arm for a scarf on her neck and shoulders.

'It won't last long,' he said.

Steadily the rain pitted the sand before his shoes. If I lived for ever, and went all over the world, and saw every woman, I should never find one sweeter than Mary, he thought; and extended the coat farther round Diana, for she was shivering.

A small hand reached up and held his own hanging loosely over her shoulder.

'My turn now to warm your hand,' said Diana.

'I don't worry about being cold.'

'That's because you don't know how to look after yourself.'

'It isn't; it's because I'm not cold.'

His hand was released.

'Snub number three; I'm going,' said Diana, hiding her face as she tried to get up.

'Hush, my child,' he said. 'You are too valuable to be allowed to catch cold. Let Brother William warm you, please.'

She struggled fiercely for a moment, and then lay unresisting against him.

'You're just laughing at me.'

235

'I'm not really, Diana.'

She began to breathe fast; then held her breath and was rigidly silent; and burst into tears.

'Diana! My dear child – you poor little dear –'

He stared at the drifting grey skits of rain over the white and broken waves, remembering what Jean had told him about her frail nervous health. She was weeping because of him: an innocent without guile, who had taken his words for inner confidences, held his ordinary manner to be rare and particular: he had seduced her spiritually!

'Diana, I have injured you.'

'You're not to feel like that!' she said vehemently. 'I am a damned little fool, who has no right to make you feel unhappy.'

'You don't make me feel unhappy, my dear. I only wish I could make you feel happy.' And he thought, If it were a hundred years hence, she would not need to be unhappy.

'Don't worry about me, I'm all right. I suppose,' she added slowly, 'you and Mary – are fond of each other –'

'Yes, Diana.'

She took his hand and kissed it, then nursed it against her cheek.

'You dear child,' he said, kissing her head. 'Don't worry because of me. I'm all right.'

'You don't hate me?'

'Hate you? I think you are most lovable.'

She turned and smiled at him, then laid her cheek on his hand again.

'Mary wouldn't mind. Ow! More sand down my neck! Don't bother. I love your hands, Billy. You don't mind if I call you Billy? Dear hands, that gave the poor Saxon soldier presents on Christmas Eve.'

'A tin of bully beef! Part of the trench was paved with unopened tins of the stuff!'

'I don't care what you say, I shall love you for doing it, for ever and ever.'

A three-masted Norwegian timber boat, with a pink and grey hull, moved out of the sandy edge of the cavern, sailing up by wind and tide.

'Hullo, ship!' said Diana, nursing his hand, and caressing it. 'I'm here with Mr. Maddison. I'm not frightened of him any more.'

'Were you ever frightened of me?' he asked in surprise.

'Well, not exactly frightened in the ordinary sense; but you rather awed me sometimes. Silly of me, wasn't it?' as she kissed his hand. 'Billy, will you marry Mary, do you think?'

'I don't know, Diana. I don't suppose she will have me.'

'I do. Why, she's always loved you, you silly!'

'Has she? How do you know?'

'Ah, I know everything.'

'Did she tell you?'

'Not in words. But her eyes told me; I don't see how anyone could fail to observe it. Didn't you know?'

'I wasn't certain. Once I thought she liked Howard.'

'Oh no, Howard likes someone quite different. He will go to Kenya soon, and forget all about her, probably on the boat.'

They sat there for more than an hour, while the rain fell in heavy grey skits towards the north-east, and, at last, the damp roof fell on their backs. Diana, having decided that Westward Ho! was too far, said she would walk with him to Appledore, and have a hot bath in an hotel, and then something to eat. Would he be her guest for lunch? No, she must be his guest. Very well then, she would insist on paying for herself if he did not see the propriety of allowing her to pay, after her behaviour, for her 'gentleman-friend.' Cold hand in cold hand, and laughing, they ran and walked the way they had come, past the gasworks where they made wry faces, past the ship-breaker's beach, over the rusty rails, now drowned all but four yards, of the lifeboat house, and along the narrow street to the Prince of Wales Hotel.

Chapter 11

FROM the Victorian horsehair-covered arm-chair, which
having been made to the manly ideal of a stiff and upright
back, had resisted all his efforts to sit with natural ease,
Maddison watched the afternoon away in rain. The tide
filled the Pool, the buoys settled upright, then swung about
to lean with the westward ebb; the foamy String leaped with
jets of water, brown Sharshook ridge appeared and grew
larger. His trousered legs, stretched out towards a blazing
coal fire, had ceased to steam; the room was papered red,
and decorated with two pictures of almost identical composi-
tion, colour, and light, entitled respectively, *Sunrise in the
Highlands* and *Sunset in the Highlands*; he dozed, and thought
of his pleasant life. Behind the chair the mahogany table was
covered with a wrinkled cloth, on which were plates and egg-
shells, two white cups and a large black teapot with a chipped
spout, jars of jam and marmalade, half a loaf cut askew and
the remains of a pound of butter, much jabbed by a knife.

'Feeling all right, Diana?'

'Quite all right, thank you, my dear. Aren't your feet too
near the fire?'

'My socks will burst into flames any minute. But I'm quite
happy.'

They sat, each in a chair, on either side of the blazing coal
fire. How she had played! The keys of the piano had been
stiff, but it had been tuned recently; surely never before had
it been awakened with the true force and feeling of the Schumann Concerto. Some of the fishermen and sailors had come
out of the bar, to listen outside the door. Then some Welsh
miners on holiday had knocked at the door, and offered to sing,

and started to sing without waiting for an answer, so great their enthusiasm. Song after song they had sung in their ardent voices, while Diana got more and more bored. Towards closing time they departed for the bar, and sang there; and after closing time, being denied re-entrance to the parlour by the landlord, an old sea-captain, they had gone outside and sung in the rain. Diana would not play again, but sat in the chair, leaning forward with chin on hands, staring into the fire.

A knock on the door.

'Come in.'

The voice of the landlord's daughter, behind the door opened a few inches, said the lady's clothes were now dry. Diana got up, and shuffled to the door in the borrowed slippers. She had come down from her bath wearing the slippers and a borrowed overcoat buttoned round her neck and pinned down to the skirts trailing to the floor.

'I shan't be long, Billy.'

'I'll be here.'

He looked at the clock on the mantelpiece. Four o'clock.

On the mantelpiece beside the clock stood two glasses, empty of hot rum and sugar. He had ordered these on arriving, meaning one for Diana; and then deemed it wiser to drink them both himself. Another knock on the door.

'There's a lady and gentleman wanting tea, sir. Would you mind them coming in with you?'

'Not a bit!'

A moment later Jean's clear voice said outside, 'Thanks most awfully. I'm afraid I'm very wet. Give her yours too, Jack.'

A man's voice in the passage replied, 'Aw, I don't worry about a little bit of wet. In here?'

'That's right,' said the landlord's daughter.

He came in, followed by Jean.

'Hullo, Jean! Did you get very wet at the pony races?'

239

'Good God! It's William. Whatever are you doing here?'

'Oh, just warming myself.'

'All alone?'

'No, Diana's with me. She's upstairs at present.'

Jean stared at the other chair, and turned to the man with her.

'I say, do you know each other? Mr. Bissett – Mr. Maddison.'

'Pleased to meet you,' said Jean's friend, so 'Pleased to meet you,' said Maddison, as they shook hands. 'Sit in my chair. I'm warm.'

'That's quite all right,' said Bissett, and the landlord's daughter asked what was wanted for tea.

'Eggs,' said Bissett, looking over the table. 'Have you got any ham with it? You'll have ham, too, Jean? What about the others?' He looked for guidance to Jean.

'Jack's inviting you to have tea, Will.'

'I don't think I could eat any more, thanks.'

'Come on, Mr. Maddison, another feed won't make any difference.'

'Don't ee deny your stummick, midear,' said Jean, imitating Farmer Bissett.

'Ha, you've got the poor old dad proper, Jean. You'll join us, Mr. Maddison, please? That's right. Four plates of ham, eight eggs, bread and butter, cake, jam, scald cream, none of your separated stuff, and tea for the lot. Make it strong.'

The table was relaid when Diana came in, quietly, showing no surprise at seeing the others.

'Good afternoon, Miss Shelley,' said Jack Bissett, 'please will you join us in a cup of tea?'

'Thank you. Did your pony win anything at the races?'

''Twas too mucky, Miss Shelley, and they de-cided to postpone the events.'

They sat down to the meal. Maddison was soon talking

and laughing at a great rate; while Diana, sitting beside him, scarcely smiled or spoke. However, Jean did not fail to notice that she was alert to every word and action of Maddison's; and wondering if there was anything between them she imagined Howard's face, and began to hope again; and hoping, and imagining thereby, her vivacious manner died away, and she became silent.

'Aw, ait y'r 'am up, 'twill do ee good,' urged her companion.

'It's damned hot in here,' exclaimed Jean, springing up to open the window wide, because she wanted to get away from him. 'Thank God, it's stopped raining.'

Jack Bissett ate his two eggs and plate of ham; and, when convinced that Jean had really abandoned it, her share as well.

'It's all the same price,' he said, eating without falter; yet wondering how much that chap Maddison really knew. They said in the village that he was always a-studying, with his light going half the night. They said something 'bout a married woman, so 'twas said: but that wasn't no odds: and he wasn't the only one by a long chalk.

Lighting a cigarette, he took long stealthy glances at him through the smoke, wondering what he might be doing there with Miss Shelley, when he was supposed to be courting Miss Mary to Wildernesse. A quiet bit of fun, perhaps; you never knew – often the quietest was the worst. Well, what was the odds if he was? Nice young fellow, too: no swank about him. And glancing at Jean lolling in the arm-chair, he felt jealousy, over a woman, for the first time in his life: he was first there, he could be certain of that: and he would see that he was the only one, too. He looked at Maddison again, becoming more interested in him, and more puzzled; but Maddison, without a glance at his face, knew exactly what Bissett had been thinking.

The grassy sandhills across the estuary were greener, the lighthouse became white; soon the sun was shining everywhere. Immediately the fire lost its attraction. The Welsh miners

strolled down the street again, passing the window, exalted
with singing. A few seconds after they'd gone a voice grumbled, 'Horrible fellows,' and the sodden grey hat and bearded
face and blue-coated body of Mr. Chychester moved past the
window, followed by Mary.

'They are at least moved to sing,' said Maddison, getting
up in rage. 'Unlike that mechanical noise in Speering Church.
My God, the wonder is they can sing at all, shut up more
than half the day in a filthy mine.'

'You're right, Mr. Maddison,' said Jack Bissett, and stared
as though the thought had suddenly revealed something new
to him.

'I like Welsh miners,' said Jean.

'Now then,' whispered Bissett, in an intimate aside, 'don't
you go liking one of they singing chaps, Jean.'

'Oh, shut up,' replied Jean curtly. 'Are you going, Willie?'

'Yes. Coming, Diana? See you later, Jean? Good-bye, Jack
Bissett. Thanks for your food and company.'

'You'm quite welcome, sir.'

Maddison and Diana paid their bill in equal shares, and
went out into the sunshine. Patches of the sett-stones of the
street were already dry. White clouds drifting over threw down
rapid shadows on the sea, broken grey with waves and stained
a dull brown by the flood water; the wind blowing up the
estuary was filled with the noise of waves on the rocks. Several
salmon boats with dark nets piled in their sterns were grounded
along the Sharshook, their crews walking on the gravelly
ridge waiting for the tide to fall lower before they could shoot
their drafts. Mary and Mr. Chychester had already gone round
the corner, towards the slip and the lifeboat house, near which,
they had been told, Luke was dredging for mussels, whilst
waiting for their return at six o'clock.

Imagining them waiting for Luke, Maddison hastened
along the long narrow street, Diana stepping silently by his
side. At the end of the double row of houses the sea and the

sky opened wide again. Diana put her arm in his, and led him over the grassy space before the coastguard's, hiding the slip immediately behind it, where, she thought, the others would be waiting.

'I'm going back now. Good-bye. It has been beautiful.'

'I've enjoyed it immensely. Good-bye, Diana. See you again some time?'

'Yes, Billy, we are friends, aren't we?'

'Yes,' he said, wanting to hurry away to Mary, but hiding this desire. 'Friendship isn't the right word. I know – amity. It is a word that holds everything. 'Diana Shelley – sweet amity,' he said.

'You dear,' she replied, caressing the words. 'See me sometimes, won't you? You come so near me, nearer than anyone before. Promise to treat me as a friend, Billy? There now, go to your Mary, my dear.'

He was moved by her gentleness, and stood still before her, staring at the grass as though drawing power and virtue from the cool green blades. With a touch on his sleeve and a backward smile over her shoulder, and a slight wave of her hand, both slight and typical of her outward self, Diana Shelley left him. Maddison could see the west wind as a living thing as it rushed over the grass, brightening every blade into a vivid green. Lines of white were breaking on the north and south tails of the bar; the air over the marsh and the Pebble Ridge was thick with shining mist. Now to see Mary! A village maiden of fifteen, with ragged skirt and bare brown legs, thrilled to the gaze of his eyes as he strode towards the sun; she turned and looked after him, and waited, without knowing why, and walked on again, beauty in her face.

Mr. Chychester and Mary were standing at the edge of the water on the sand beyond the concrete slip, watching a fisherman leaning back against a rope over his shoulder, walking slowly and heavily. The feet of his rubber thigh boots, mended with red patches, sank with each laborious step into the loose wet sand. Eighty yards from the shore a salmon boat was being strongly rowed in a horse-shoe by two men, while a third kneeled by the seine and paid it out over the stern, throwing the head-rope of corks free of the net. Maddison jumped off the slip, and ran to Mary, while his dog, who all the afternoon had been lying as though dead before the parlour fire, pranced around him, barking. Mary turned round, showing a flushed and smiling face.

'Hullo!'

'You are very wet,' he said, looking at the drooping brim of her grey felt hat, the shrinking lines of her coat and skirt, her sodden shoes.

'We don't bother about a little rain,' remarked Mr. Chychester cheerfully.

The boat reached the shore a hundred yards farther down, and the men jumped out, and began to haul on the rope. Maddison went to help the solitary fisherman. The tide had carried the head-line of bobbing corks into the shape of a loop. Pulling on the dripping rope of coconut-fibre was like pulling against the weight of the earth, yet it gave a little after each strain. Broad back and shoulders, thick brown neck above woollen slop, stoically the fisherman tugged, never speaking. Maddison felt the rope straighten and stiffen behind him, and turning his head, received more smiles from Mary.

After a long time, it seemed, the corks were drawn into shallow water, and laying the rope over his shoulder, the man began to plod towards the boat.

'Aren't you going home to change those wet things?' asked Maddison.

'We're waiting for Luke.'

'Where is he?'

'Down there.' She pointed to a solitary figure in a boat about a quarter of a mile away. 'He's getting mussels.'

'I'd like to get some muscles,' said Maddison, feeling his thin arms. 'The army was fine for its physical exercise – in England. Thinking is a disease.'

'Quite right,' said Mr. Chychester.

'If you want physical work, there's plenty of digging to be done in the garden. You'd better stay awhile with us, and get on with it,' suggested Mary.

'That's settled!'

They walked after the fisherman, followed by Mr. Chychester; all three were curious to see what might be in the net. More hauling, of head and lead-bound sinker line together. The loop of floating corks and the weight of the net diminished together. None of the four men spoke, but watched the water by the corks. They had not taken a fish for five days. Two pulled at the head-ropes, two at the heel. Seaweed growing on stones was drawn in, with green crabs, and a battered pail half filled with concrete – which made the oldest man, who owned boat and net, swear as he flung it on the mud behind.

As they tugged slowly, hand before hand, leaning back with wet and ragged trouser-ends sinking into the watery sand, something flapped and splashed in the purse of the net. The skipper's son pulled too quickly at his end of the head-rope, and was checked; the last corks slid in the shallows, the mouth of the purse reached the wavelet line and he dashed forward, heaving out a fish by the gills. How it threshed the sand with its tail! A noble fish, streamlined and tapered, as though hammered and wrought by many waves from a bar of frosty silver. The lad ran to the boat, and pulled out a thole-pin, and running to the fish, thumped the base of its skull, so that the sand-slapping ceased, and the lovely water-thing lay still and flat among crushed crabs and its own curd and fallen scales glinting in the sand.

Without pause two of the men began to shake and pile the net into an ordered heap.

'Thirty pounds, should you think?' asked Mr. Chychester.

The owner of the boat gave the fish a glance.

'A score and eight – maybe a score, eight and a half.'

'Ah, I thought it was something near thirty pounds. Have you had a good season so far?'

'They'm very scarce this season. One or two running this fresh, maybe.'

Mr. Chychester considered this; then he said, 'Well, we're killing the otters for you.'

'It bain't artters, it be rod-and-line men us don't vancy much,' replied the fisherman. 'Us has to pay five pounds licence money, from twelve noon on Monday to twelve noon on Saturday, and they rod-and-line boogers pays two pounds, and may fish all the week, and a month before us, and a month after the net season finishes. Tidden right, and us be poor men earning our living, with wives and childer to keep. 'Tis the gentry makes the laws to suit themselves.'

The lad and another man returned with the boat, which they towed by the bows to the net. He dropped the fish into the well of the boat, by the rusty bailing can where the bilge slopped over it.

'Ah,' said Mr. Chychester, moving away. 'Well, I'm afraid I don't know much about it.'

When they were out of earshot he said, 'When those fellows aren't grumbling, they're poaching. If they had their way, there wouldn't be a fish left to reach the spawning beds at the heads of the rivers.'

'How long does the salmon-fishing last?' asked Maddison.

'From May to September, is it?' Mr. Chychester referred to Mary.

'Yes; it ends about Barum Fair. Have you ever been to the Fair?' she asked Maddison, shy of speaking his name.

'No.'

'It's great fun. You must come with us this year.'

'I may not be here. I've got to leave the cottage at the end of September.'

'You'll be all right.'

They walked on, coming to mud pitted and scored with deep bootmarks, and a small creek. The *Revenge*, water pouring out of a hole in her hulk, rose like a cliff before them.

'Hi, what are we walking this way for?' asked Mr. Chychester, as they began to flounder. 'This isn't the way home, unless we're going to swim down to the confounded fellow.'

They stopped and looked at each other.

'I was following you, Uncle Suff!'

'And I was following you!'

'And I was following both of you,' smiled Maddison, while Mr. Chychester threw back his head and roared with laughter, considering the situation most humorous. Mary laughed with him.

'Well, what are we to do about it now?' asked Mr. Chychester, looking to Maddison for guidance.

'Shall I shout for Luke?'

'Ah, that's an idea.'

So Maddison shouted, making such a noise that the saws and hammers on the towering broken deck of the wooden battleship ceased, and the heads and shoulders of five men appeared against the sky. One of the men realized at once the object of the shouting, and shouted and waved his arms as well.

Two of his mates imitated him; and they saw Luke stand up in his boat, and fling up an arm. Soon the sail arose, and the boat came up the estuary.

The curved brown ridge of the Sharshook was high and wide when they got aboard, but the rocky bed to the far shore was not yet uncovered. With bellied sail almost at right angles to the keel, the boat rode against the tide, smacking the wavelets with its lightly plunging bows and scattering spray. Mr. Chychester and Luke sat by the tiller; Mary and Maddison crouched, with knees touching, by the iron handle of the centre-board. Every time the bows plunged and smacked up the water they bowed their heads, welcoming the pattering of drops, when they exchanged secret glances. Near the Instow sands they had to shift, while the helm was put over and the sheet tightened for the run up the Taw. They sat side by side on the gunwale while the heeling boat scurried over the wind-fretted water, and Mr. Chychester, who was no waterman, rigidly and conscientiously steered the nose of the boat to the exact post on the shingle tongue of the Crow which Luke had pointed to. Here they got out, choosing to walk the longer way around the shady shore rather than cross the muddy glasswort-green flats of the Bight.

'Well, thank you, Luke. I'll see you this evening. Good day to you.'

'Good-bye, Luke.'

The man croaked at them.

'What a strange-looking creature!' murmured Maddison, moving slowly with Mary over the sand, behind the slow labouring figure of Mr. Chychester; and glancing back, to see again Luke's long narrow face and sombre eyes, the hanks of his long straight hair falling over his narrow forehead and yellow cheeks and hiding his ear-holes. He stood upright in the boat, his leather arm with its bright steel hook hanging by his side, and holding in his hand the mussel-fishing tool called a clum – a sort of bent fork with nine prongs curved like walrus tusks, and lashed to a bamboo pole thrice the height of himself.

'An ominous figure,' he said, turning round again, and seeing Luke staring after him. 'A sort of Old Man of the estuary; a decrepit and local Neptune, with a monstrous fish-hook for hand. I shouldn't be surprised to see him one day look up out of the sea at twilight, beside those black tattered hurdles of the old salmon weir, with his clum and his hook, seaweed on his head, and a cormorant perching on his shoulders; and then quietly sinking under again.'

'He was frozen on an ice-floe when whaling, losing his ears and an arm, and becoming deaf and dumb,' said Mary.

A linnet flew after a thistle-seed before them, lit on the sand, flew up after the rolling silky sphere, fluttered, settled, and taking its dainty, flew away twittering. She looked to see if he had seen it, but no, he was staring straight before him, and so strangely, as though his imagination had called up some dark vision from air or sea. What darkness had come upon him now? His spirit was like a thistle-seed on the sands of the world, that needed a fair and pleasant wind to buoy it to its destiny. Her fingers touched his swinging hand beside her, fluttered, lit, and settled in his clasp. She stole a sidelong glance at him: he was shivering, his eyes strangely staring. His footsteps grew slower, and stopped. She saw tears hanging on his lashes.

'Sometimes I feel that Shelley is very near,' he said, and fixed his gaze on the sand. He rubbed his head wearily. 'I am ill – or tired.'

She clasped his hand between her own, and said anxiously, 'You are probably faint with want of food and sleep.'

'Food!' he cried, alert again, 'I'm full up – Diana and I had bags of eggs and cream and cake and jam in Appledore; and then Jack Bissett came in with Jean, and stood us a high-tea of ham and more eggs! Don't you worry about me, my maid!' He put his arm on her shoulder and drew her to him, holding his face level with her own. 'Mary!' he said hoarsely; then sprang violently away, cursing 'Hell and the Devil,' for Mr. Chychester, a hundred yards ahead of them, had turned round to see if they were following. Ha! He turned round again, and plodded on. H'm. And all the rest of the way home, around the muddy Bight, where the green upright horns of the glasswort made innumerable tiny angles with their shadows, and old footmarks smoothed by former tides glinted with the sky; over the loose shingle to the White House; along the road under the sea-wall and up the drive to the porch, and into the hall and up the stairs to the bathroom – the old sportsman never looked back. In the bathroom he swore, for there was no hot water for his tub, and for an hour he had been imagining himself lying back in water almost unbearably hot.

Mary heard him swearing, for she had come in almost immediately after him, and gone at once to her bedroom, which adjoined the bath-room. She did not want to see anyone. After he had sprung away, agony in his face, Maddison had behaved as though she had not been there; had taken his own line to the sea-wall, walking rapidly, and had disappeared into the sandhills. In the sunken lane below the White House she had met him again, lying beside a patch of bird's-foot trefoil; he had said that he was not going home with her, but if when she had changed her clothes, and had had tea, she wanted to see him, he would be by the Fox Hide; and without giving her a glance he had climbed the sea-wall, and disappeared.

'Confound the women! Damnation seize the house and all its ways!' she heard Uncle Suff's retreating mutter down the passage, as she threw off her damp clothes. She felt sorry for Uncle Suff; but she made the least possible noise, lest he remember her and suggest she should light the kitchen fire. She would not even wait for tea: Mother was there, and she would give him tea. Quickly she dressed, and crept down the servants' stairs to the kitchen, which to her relief was empty. She cut two large slices of plum cake, put a piece in each pocket, and went through the scullery into the orchard.

The goldfinches were piping among the lichen-shaggy boughs of the apple trees as she walked down the mossy path. Three young birds sat on a branch before her, the fledgling down waving like faery lichen on their soft feathers. Under the tree stood a cat, swishing its tail and champing its teeth as it stared up at them. 'Go away, Binky, you beast,' cried Mary, and picked it up in her arms. The cat began to purr. 'Now I suppose you want some milk,' she said, and stopped in the long wet grass. 'Why should I always be giving you milk? If I take you outside the orchard you'll go and kill young rabbits for your kittens: if I leave you here, you'll kill the young gold-finches. Well, if they die, they die, I can't help it.' She carried the cat halfway between the birds and the rabbits, and dropped it near the rubbish pit, where it might find rats and mice.

Her heart beat faster as she came to the walnut tree in the corner of the high cob wall. This corner had been called the Fox Hide ever since Michael, climbing the tree one morning, had seen a fox lying on the reed thatch of the wall. Mary began to climb the tree, but stopped when she reached the bough she would have to crawl along, and waited for the tremble of her knees and the feeling of weakness to pass. Someone might be knocking at the roots of the tree, so loudly was her heart beating in her ears.

The bough, smoothed by many toecaps and knees and fingers, rose in a slight incline until it was above the thatched wall, and then dipped in a curve like an elephant's trunk. Creeping along the branch, she saw him lying in the sun, beyond the shadow of the tree. To the lowest part of the branch, fourteen feet above the ground, was tied a length of rope, and she was swinging down on this when she felt her feet gripped, and, as she let herself down hand under hand, her knees, and then her thighs were encircled in his arms, and she was carried into the sunlight, and laid down on the grass beside him and released. He caressed her burning cheeks, and laughed, and touching a hawkbit between them said:

'I love these flowers of the sun's own image. You can almost see them drinking the sun. Lovely little pagans.'

She smiled down at the brilliant yellow disk.

'There's a carrion crow's nest in that walnut tree. Empty. I looked in it when I climbed over this morning.'

'I know. Benjamin had the eggs. A good thing, in a way, for Uncle Suff would have shot the young birds if they'd been reared.'

'You've been very quick, Mary dear. Have you had any tea?'

She shook her head. 'I've got some cake.'

'Then eat it. You must be hungry.'

She smiled, remembering her own concern for him that morning.

'You have a piece?'

'No thanks.' He was bending over the hawkbit. 'Mary!'

'What?'

'Are you doing anything this evening?'

She shook her head, pointing at her mouthful of cake.

'Come for a walk?'

She nodded.

'Let's get away from here, before anyone comes.'

He pulled her to her feet, and they walked down the meadow of poor grass, beautiful with wildflowers, hawkbit and yellow rattle, knapweed, poppy, scabious, charlock, viper's bugloss, and a strange thistle which she told him had been identified as a Russian thistle, whose seed had probably been carried by one of the Baltic timber ships which used to sail up to the port of Barum.

'When they ploughed this field in 1917, they probably ploughed deep, and turned up seeds which had been lying under the tide-silt, before the wall was built. At least, that's Uncle Suff's theory.'

By a culvert over the Boundary Drain they stopped, watching the dragon-flies patrolling the dyke and the green starwort waving in the clear flow of the fresh water. They were leaning over the parapet, heads together, watching the delicate glow of light in the eyes of an emerald dragon-fly as it rested on the lichened stonework, when a gate clattered behind them. Looking up together, they saw Benjamin remounting his bicycle two hundred yards away.

'This is where we abruptly disappear over the sea-wall,' said Maddison, taking her hand and leading her over the road. 'Pretend we haven't seen him.' They scrambled up the grassy slope of the wall, and were immediately looking down on the harp-shaped tract of marshland reclaimed from saltings when Mary's great-grandfather had built the sea-wall.

'Hi!' came a shrill shout. From the top of the wall they saw Benjamin standing on the pedals of his zigzagging bicycle, as he laboured to speed up Trusty.

'Poor Benjamin!'

'We can't disappoint him.'

The eager boy put on his brakes so hard when he reached them that he skidded and nearly rolled into the dyke.

'Been to school, Ben?'

He shook his head, grinning.

'I've been on Halsinger Down. It didn't half rain. I got in a linhay. Lovely! I found a nest of young sparrowhawks near the old limekiln. I say, is Aunt Connie home?'

'Yes. Ben, you'd better go home at once, and change your clothes. They must be sopping!'

'I don't care.'

He looked an uncared-for boy altogether, thought Mary, with his yellow and black school cap shrunken on his round head, his sodden collar, his worn and undersized jacket, his bony knees and wrists torn by brambles.

Benjamin hesitated, and stammered, 'Can't I – I say – may I – Can't I come with you?'

'Yes, if you like,' said Mary. 'But we're not going anywhere special.'

The boy glanced quickly at Maddison, who was looking away over the duckponds. He hesitated, and said:

'On second thoughts I don't think I'll come. I must go now, I think. Good-bye.'

'See you later,' said Maddison.

'Oh yes, rather, thank you. Good!' Benjamin jumped on his creaking machine and pedalled away with all his strength, hoping they would notice how he could make Trusty fly. By the drive gate he turned round to see if they were watching;

they waved; and Maddison put his hands on Mary's ribs and ran her down the inner slope.

'At last,' he said, 'we're alone with the sky.' A few yards further on, 'And the cause of anguish to the birds.'

Three golden plovers had arisen out of the flat rushy tract, and flew around lamely, as though but part of their life-power controlled their wings: which indeed was so, the other part going from them to their young hiding still in the tussocks below.

'The urge that now weakens the flight of those birds is selfless pure god-like benevolence,' he said. 'They have no other god; for there is no other god. When in spring the male bird utters his ravishing wild notes, which must be even more beautiful to their spirits than to ours, it is the same emotion freed of earthly concentration, and changed into song.'

He thought for a few moments, then said, 'The latest theory among some naturalists – a horrid word! – is that birds sing and so claim, as by challenge, their feeding grounds; but that is no more than an empty snail-shell, and probably came from some young writer striving to be original. The fundamental fault, I think, is in considering all wild things as lower, that is inferior, living creatures; whereas many are higher than man, and all are pure. There is no devil, in the moral sense, among wild birds and animals: no meanness, either. There are the closest links between the spirits of men and birds; and the source of their god is the same: it is derived from the age-long care and regard of their young. Pity is an incipient instinct in man, made by generations of mothers regarding their babes. Am I preaching to you, and boring you, Mary?'

'No, Billy.'

'Your voice is in harmony with the low sweet cries of that sorrowful bird, standing on the green knoll, by the water,' he said, pointing to a lone plover; and turning to look into her face.

'We can cross only by the wooden foot-bridge,' she replied

hurriedly. 'Let's get over before the keeper sees us. The shooting is let, and Mother is anxious that there shan't be any complaints. Could you call Billjohn to heel? The keeper is very strict about dogs.'

He harshly called the spaniel to heel. They walked on silently, until she asked him what was the matter.

'The golden plover is the Shelley among birds; so let us drive Shelley out of England, and shoot the golden plover. That's the right-minded way.'

They crossed the narrow plank-bridge, he leading.

'Don't talk like that,' said Mary, appearing silently by his side, and plucking his sleeve. 'I can't bear to hear you so bitter. And don't think me without understanding – I do understand, really I do, as I told you that time on the hill below Cæsar's Camp in Kent.'

When he did not answer a blank feeling came over her. They crossed the tract of brackish fen, and came to grassy land, where cattle were lying in the lush grass, chewing the cud. They reached the dyke under the outer sea-wall, still without speaking, and crossed over, and walked along the sea-wall. The estuary was half empty, the black weed-tattered hurdles of the ruined salmon weir visible in the sand that silted them.

'Useless and rotten,' he said, 'like me and my ideas.'

'What is the matter?' she asked, in a low voice, as if suffering.

'I was remembering what you told me below Cæsar's Camp.'

'I don't remember exactly what I said.'

'I do. You told me all about God, giving me a summary of Bernard Shaw's gospel of creative evolution which he got from Lamarck, and which you had probably been reading. Then you told me about the wounded poet you nursed, who was afterwards killed, and you ended up by giving me, for some reason or other, your theory that while the mother bears the child, the father with his dream fashions its spirit.'

She said nervously, 'I was very young then, remember.'

'You must have been, or you would not have spoken so intimately with a waster you knew was the secret lover of another man's wife.'

Mary went red at his sneering words, and then white. They walked on again, the spaniel following at his heels, and she behind the dog. The wind made a sibilance in the long green grasses growing on the top of the wall; their feet scattered the pollen of the plumy seed-heads, and broke the swaying wheel-webs of spiders laden with the crushed silk-bound bodies of many butterflies, beetles, bees, and grasshoppers.

Two salmon-boats were resting between drafts on the sand-bank across the sea-channel, and by the near shore the long-haired figure of Luke was kneeling in a boat, working his clum in the mussel-clusters on the sunken rocks. Here the wall turned north, the bend in the harp, following the grey mud-slopes of the pill by which the sea went up to Speering Folliot.

Just below the wall, on the sett-stones at the line of ordinary tides, stood a small cabin, or hut, made by Luke, of odd bits of timber found floating in the sea, or left by the tides along the wall. Lumps of rock lay on the corrugated iron roof, which was also held down by a chain. The sunlight was put out as they passed it, and turning round, they saw grey rain rushing towards them. 'Quick into the hut!'

A narrow seat, made of a single plank nailed to low wooden stumps driven between sett-stones, stretched across the hut, which would have held four men sitting in comfort – the crew of a salmon-boat. They had to stoop to enter. The rain lashed the sett-stones before their feet; sea-broken turf and stretches of gravelly stones, the estuary, and the distant land and hills, were all hid by the swishing skirts of the rain. Wind buffeted the little shelter, and hissed in the chinks of the roof. They watched the storm, delighting in the violence of air and water, while the spaniel curled up on the pile of faded slops and old trousers and oilskins behind them.

'I love a storm.'

'I love a storm too. Don't you love lightning?'

'Lightning and thunder, yes! The giants talking. I am coherent, and understand the world then.'

The violent gusts and the misty flapping sheets passed, the rain fell with a more regular slant, and they saw the estuary again. He took her hand, and saw the colour in her cheeks, wondering if it were the colour made by the storm. He stroked her cheek, her eyes were downcast: how still she was sitting! He ceased, and turned away. She looked at him with uplifting lashes, and to the wild spray blown off the wave-tops, and then to her hand lying in his clasp. Again he touched her cheek, she looked up and smiled, and he pressed her hand against his cheek. 'Dear Mary,' he whispered, stroking her forehead and smoothing her eyebrow. 'Dear Mary, there is a swallow on your brow: the swallow that flew round a broken brow, long ago in another land. Oh, Mary, if all women were like you, that brow would not have bled.'

She sat still, in a sweet unreality which continued when he got up and wandered into the rain, picking up sea-weed, to drop it again, and picking up stones, to throw them violently into a pool, and returning to the hut where she sat, never having moved, as he had left her. A heavy sweet pain obsessed her, and a blankness for all she saw, save the dim form that was beside her, kissing her cheek and stroking her hair.

A kingfisher flew along the shore of the estuary, and perched on a stick in the sand where the stream flowed into the river. They watched it, cheek to cheek. It flew beyond the side of the hut, and when it was gone he framed the lovely vivid face in his hands, and murmured that she was the lovelier one, with the swallow of heaven on her brow; and bowed his head on her lap, while her hand strayed in his hair. She moved to every change of her restless little boy – 'Funny little boy, aren't you?' she said, her eyes tender, her hair darkly ruffled; and he pressed his head against her breast, while all the past dreads and fears of the spirit, like dark birds, took flight before the gentle falcon of her love. There was nothing mortal beyond the highest mortal peak whereon she had sat since the beginning of her life, awaiting him.

'If I lived for ever, and went all over the earth, I should never meet a woman sweeter than Mary,' he whispered. 'Go away, Bill, damn you, don't lick!' He pushed the spaniel over, and it settled on the heaps of coats again. 'Oh, Mary, forgive me being unkind to you just now. I was longing for this moment so much.'

The rain was blown away up the estuary, and swift sunlight brought brightness and colour to the grass and stones before the hut. The faded heads of the sea-thrift trembled on their stalks rising from the saltings. He asked her to tell him if she loved him, and she would not reply; he asked her again, and she said that she did not know. 'Yes, you must know,' he pleaded, and she said he knew already. 'Well, do you like me?' he asked, and she nodded. 'When did you first begin to like me, then?' She whispered that it was after he had talked with the Vicar on Easter Sunday night, when she had wanted to take care of him.

'You seemed to be so all alone, and a poor boy altogether.'

His long arms held her closer, and he leaned down his head, and touched the sunburned neck with his cheek, as though seeking shelter. He murmured to her in a voice rapturous and sad, and with a rough movement unfastened her blouse, so that the first soft swelling of the breasts showed white below the sunburn. 'Oh, my Mary,' he said, kissing her, while she clasped his head, and looked with wonder past the faded flowers of the spring. He asked if she had loved anyone before, and she shook her head, and he asked her if she had ever kissed a man, and again she shook her head. 'But have you never imagined yourself in love?' he said, looking up, and with her cheek nestling against his she whispered, 'No.'

My virgin Mary, he thought, while his eyes filled with tears

258

and he went away from her again. How sweet a thing it is to be pure! And with desolation in his heart he fell to thinking of Eveline Fairfax, and of the things he had said in love to her, and now might be saying to Mary. Never again could he be as Mary, natural and pure, as God meant a maid to be. He strayed down to the shore, and looking at the sky, felt no remorse for having known love before; only regret. All the acts of men, that priesthood called sin, rose before him; but no human action could seem sordid under the blue space around the world. I regret nothing, he said to himself.

The hills across the estuary had grown green again, and larks were singing over the marsh of Horsey Island. Sandpipers trilled at the lapsing tide-line under the mud-slopes, where arose the sounds of water and stones of the stream. Beautiful country that grew Mary, he thought, looking at the dark hills of Exmoor far away under a sun-rift in the sky, and the vivid green splashes of light which were distant grassy fields between darker trees and hedge-banks.

'Mary,' he called, running back to her, where she sat, like a child, in the little cabin. 'It is lovely now. Come with me, my dearest one.'

Bird's-foot trefoil – red and yellow 'lady's slippers' – grew on the wall, every one tenderly thought on because of Mary. Flowers of flax dreamed in the long grass, with heaven's blue in their petals. A pair of swans drifted down the estuary, proud and faithful unto death. Swifts cut the air within a few inches of his head, sighs of black which had travelled over half the curving earth for love. Somewhere over the marsh a wood-lark began to sing sip, sip, sip, down the scale: they must stop, and listen to the wildly sweet notes of the singer who seemed of all birds the most homeless, for the singer was rarely seen, only its wandering voice that knew not why it sang. Round Mary's head a bumblebee flew humming, alighted and crawled, and burred away again.

'Your little friend of the lake come to wish you happiness,' he said, and stared at the grass. 'Poor Mary.'

'Not poor when I'm with ee,' she whispered, touching his hand.

'Mary.'

'Yes, my dear?'

'Do you love me?'

'In my own way I do,' she murmured.

'Only in your own way? Don't you love me as a woman loves a man?'

'I'm not certain.'

'What?' he exclaimed, and she laughed, his face was so startled. 'Mary, don't you love me?'

'How can I tell, when I have never been in love?' she said, with a laugh deep in her throat. He held her, and peered at her face. 'You're blushing, Mary! Now answer me, Would you give up everything for a man?'

'It depends.'

'On what?'

'On who the man was.'

'Me!'

'I might, if that man would give up everything for me. Ah no, don't ee look so worried, my dear. I won't tease ee! You shall always be yourself, you shall.'

'Perhaps I shall only be myself when I am dead.'

'Now I've made you sad by my stupid remark.' She held his arm, and looked at him, to give fortitude with her eyes.

'Your stupid remark? It is I who am stupid, and selfish. What am I doing now, but pestering you with my questions? You are in harmony with life; I am a reactionary, in harmony with an imaginary life. I shall make you miserable, and anything that makes you miserable is blasphemous.'

'You don't make me miserable, silly.'

'I have a daemon, Mary – as the old poets used to say: and when I work, I dissolve the daemon out of myself, and am free to be happy. I was wonderfully happy, writing the first part of *The Star-born*.'

'You must show me that book.'

'It would be like showing the sun a candle-flame.'

He jumped over a slate slab athwart the path, mortared upright in a stone wall to prevent sheep straying, and then lifted her over, kissing her. A friendly voice shouted, 'I'll tell your Ma!' and looking over the mud, they saw a sailor standing, with razor and lathered face, on one of the three moored ketches aground on the bed of the creek.

'Same to you, mate!' shouted Maddison; and waving his hand, walked along the path beside an amused Mary.

'You are so friendly to everyone,' she said, holding his hand. 'Who, or what, is the Star-born, Billy?'

'A sprite – the spirit of a little boy.'

'How strange!' she murmured.

'What is strange?'

'I – I wonder if he is like mine? I was thinking of mine when you first came along the sea-wall, during the winter. Do you remember?

'I remember.'

He told her about the Star-born, and at the end of the marsh, where the two walls ended by a sea-swilled dyke of brackish water dipping into a pool known as the Horsey Pit, they sat on the wall of a culvert, and he begged her to tell him of her sprite. She nestled her face in his jacket, and would say only that it was an imaginary, vague thing – she was shy of the word 'baby' – that she had seemed to have known ever since she was little.

'It never had any form: it was just a fancy, a little thing that I thought of sometimes when looking out of my window on a starry night. I was its –' She stopped.

'Go on.'

'Its mother,' she said, hiding her face against him. He stared at the dark water of the pit below the culvert. 'I knew him as "Littleboy" – I expect you'll think me sentimental!'

'It almost makes me believe in religious supernatural beliefs,' he said seriously. 'Your Littleboy is the same as my Star-born, except that you have a mother's delight in him, and I, as a sort of poet, have an artist's delight in having created a being real to myself – a father's delight, one might almost say.'

'What happened to your little boy?'

'He is sent to earth as a Christ, and is of course misunderstood, and goes away again. He has one friend with him, a spirit called Wanhope, who is Thomas Hardy. It is just a fantasy. You fit in, exactly, with his sky-mother, who sometimes sees him – she lives in the morning star.'

A trout jumped in the pit, and fell back with a splash. They watched the ripples away in silence, and he said, turning away his face:

'I used to think I was a Christ.'

All her love and pity came into her eyes.

'Yes,' he said, with a deep sigh, 'I used to think of nothing else, except of the message I should receive one day: day and night, I thought of nothing else, straining against civilization as something that was deathly. Every motor-bus that fouled the sunshine with its exhaust smoke I tried to heave over and break up with my mind, and grow the trees and the grass in the midst of the dreadful traffic and buildings of London. That was before I went to France, and worked as a labourer under the War Graves Commission. I nearly died in London.'

He sighed deeply again, and went on slowly:

'It was after I left Eveline Fairfax. I used to get drunk, or rather sick with drinking too much filthy whisky on an empty stomach; sometimes I went to the gallery of the Opera House at Covent Garden with my cousin Phillip, afterwards walking through the night, or dozing on the Embankment, with Jefferies' *Story of my Heart* in one pocket, and Blake's *Songs of Innocence* in the other.'

'Hadn't you any money?'

'Very little, or none. But I didn't think or care about money.'

They stared at the water flowing under the culvert into the Horsey Pit, whereon the moon's wraith glimmered.

'I only know that I ceaselessly suffered, until one day I fell down in a sort of fit, and struggled back to life lying in the Adelphi gardens with a crowd round me, asking for my Father, and begging my cousin Phillip, who happened to be with me at the time, not to leave me, so vast was my fear. Then I went into a sort of deep sleep, and woke up feeling very sick in Charing Cross hospital. The doctor asked me if I had had syphilis, or took drugs, and I said no, so he said it was nerve exhaustion and strain coming after the strain of War, and bad ways of living. So I went away to France, and worked all day digging, and regained my health, and began to laugh at things – being free, gloriously free, for the first time since I was a boy, I should think. Now I do not suffer, but only browse in a sort of retrospection, for the cup has passed from me – the cup I held in my trembling hands in those days I had but one thought – that I was the Light-bringer for this age, to lighten the darkness fallen on men.'

He began to walk to and fro on the culvert.

'Yes,' he said, as though to himself, 'finished and dead are those days, and often I wonder at myself, for I saw things then that I shall never see again. I saw God in those days.' He sighed. 'Or thought I did – a poor human soul in darkness and in light, in a garden, pierced with thorns, and crying to the sky.'

'Come to me,' said Mary, taking him, while the spaniel leapt up too. Her tears mingled with his own and fell to the rainy ground, part of the immense sea.

Chapter 12

Twilight was dissolving field and wall and water when they wandered homewards, tranquil as though balanced in the dusk, and free as the stars shining in the dyke. Regretfully they saw the walls of the house glimmering under its thatch darker than the sky. A light moved in the white glimmer, and faded, and became brighter in another space. Through the window they saw Mrs. Ogilvie's face as she set the lamp on the hall table and turned up the wick.

'Well,' she said, when they went in, blinking, 'we've all been wondering where you were, Mary. Good evening, Bill. Have you had supper, Mary? I'm afraid we've finished long ago.' She made a slight noise, something like a laugh, but certainly nothing of mirth or joy in it – a sort of comment of passive disapproval of her daughter's lateness. 'Well, we've left some for you. You'll stay to supper, won't you?' speaking to Maddison.

On most occasions when she called him 'Bill,' it was with reluctance, for only at rare moments was she able to feel entirely at ease when talking to him, or speaking in his presence.

She went away to the sitting-room, where Mr. Chychester was engrossed with his favourite literature, which he brought back with him whenever he went otter-hunting; booklets which contained the innumerable and marvellously varied adventures of two heroic characters called Sexton Blake, detective, and his young assistant, price 3d. each booklet.

They went into the dining-room. 'I'll soon fetch you a plate,' said Mary quickly, for only a place for herself had been set. 'Mother didn't expect you back.'

He followed her into the kitchen, where, in the light of a candle stuck in a bottle, they saw Benjamin standing by the window, in an unhappy attitude. With a burnt match he was picking the shells of wasps and flies, and the wings of moths, out of the old spider webs that cluttered the frame, and cremating them in the candle flame, while taking a melancholy pleasure in thinking of last year's happy summer, so long ago and gone for ever, when perhaps he had heard the very same poor little insects happily humming. His face was tear-stained.

While they were eating supper he came in to say good night, going out immediately, sobbing, to his bed in the attic beside the water-tanks. Later on Mary told Maddison what had happened. Poor Ben, she said: when he got home Aunt Edith saw him, and was much concerned for his damp clothes, and went off to fetch a spoon and the bottle of cod-liver oil. Ben hates cod-liver oil, and so he went away and hid, and Aunt Edith went looking for him, finally running him to earth in the clothes-basket. He refused to have it, and swore at Aunt Edith, and Mother heard him swearing. She told him he had now begun to add impertinence to his other vices, because he said he didn't consider it swearing if the person you were swearing at couldn't hear you. So she ordered Ben to go to bed, and he refused, saying that bed bored him, and he was bored enough at school already: so Mother said she would write to his master, and get him to punish him, as Uncle Suff won't; and later, apparently, she heard a cat howling, and going upstairs, she discovered Ben chasing one of the cats, and throwing a cushion at it, with a most dreadful look on his face. Mother said she would report him to the Society for the Prevention of Cruelty to Animals if she didn't think his mind wasn't quite right: she is quite in a state about it, and says she is going to have him examined, and that she won't have him living here any longer.

Maddison ate no more food; he sat silent at the table. At length he said:

'Ben was taking it out of the cat.'

'Yes, Mother said it was howling with terror.'

'I meant,' he said, 'that he was literally taking nervous strength out of the cat, because it had been taken out of him. It was a natural and unconscious way of restoring his own harmony.'

'I never thought of that,' said Mary slowly.

Later, to Mrs. Ogilvie, Maddison said, 'I say, I am really sorry you are unhappy about Ben. Will you let me deal with him? I promise I will adjust everything in a satisfactory manner.'

Mrs. Ogilvie understood that way of speaking. 'Well!' she hesitated. 'If you promise not to, to – how can I say it – well, to side with him against – er – I'm afraid I'm rather stupid to-night – well, don't let him think he is a martyr! And just one thing: don't talk to him about religion. Ronnie once asked me about something he had heard you say, and it worried him excessively. You may have been quite right: but on the other hand, you may have been quite wrong. You will forgive my plain speaking, won't you?'

'I like you for it,' he replied.

Mrs. Ogilvie made her small tittering laugh – nervousness – again, and he went away to help Mary wash up in the scullery. To Ben, who had returned to the kitchen and was carving his initials for posterity on the kitchen table leg with his knife, he said, in a confidential voice:

'Ben, I'm your friend. As a friend, I advise you to go and have a good sleep, and come bathing with me before breakfast to-morrow.'

Ben sobbed. Maddison patted his shoulders, and said he'd be sleeping in the Crow's Nest next door to him that night, and would wake him in the morning.

'I – I – I didn't mean to – hurt the cat,' sobbed Benjamin.

'I know that.'

'Aunt Connie – Aunt Connie – says, says she is going to report me.'

'She won't, any more than she will report Uncle Suff for doing the same thing to an otter to-day.'

'I – I-I-I didn't mean to – the cat sleeps on my bed most nights.'

'It is probably on your bed now, having forgotten all about your murderous mood, which was natural in the circumstances. I've had them when I was younger. People who don't understand would call you vicious; I think you are a good fellow. But clean your teeth.'

He held out his hand, and Benjamin gripped it as hard as he could, as he knew (from the *English Boy's Annual*) that all manly men when shaking hands always made their friends wince: and having also learned (from his Aunt Constance) that manly men or boys did not cry, he hoped that the hand-grip would make up for the tears. With this hope he went upstairs, returning a moment afterwards and saying hurriedly, 'I say, if you want to go anywhere quickly at any time, please use Trus – my bicycle. The handlebars and saddle will want raising, and Grandpa borrowed the spanner for unscrewing the nuts of the lawn-mower, so I expect it will be in the potting shed. Good night Mary, Good night Captain Mad – I mean, Willie.'

Feeling extraordinarily elated and clean, and somehow bigger, Benjamin went up to his room, where he scrubbed his hands and nails, and brushed his teeth so vigorously that the gums bled, and he was nearly sick with the mouthful of lather of the yellow washing soap. He fell asleep quickly, and awakened with instant remembrance of the promised swim; but to his disappointment he heard water running into the tanks, and looking out of the window, saw the Burrows hid in rain. He got back into bed again, and acted, with accumulating dread and depression, the ordeal that awaited him when he went back to school. After breakfast he left the house at his usual time, with his lunch in his pocket and his satchel strapped on to the top tube of his bicycle, and rode away in sunshine.

When he had gone Jean, who was in an innocently hilarious mood, invited Maddison to go with her and talk while she groomed the Buccaneer; and this being finished, she suggested that he should hack into the village with her, on a horse she would borrow from Jack Bissett, and fetch the newspapers and post. He explained that he had promised to dig in the garden under Uncle Sufford's direction, so she rode away alone, and he went to find Mr. Chychester in the tool and potting shed, on the doors of which were nailed several otter-paws, mummified and hairless – reminder of many good days' hunting. The old gentleman, however, was in his room, entering up the nine o'clock temperature, indoor and outdoor, the direction and approximate velocity of the wind, and the rainfall since seven o'clock of the previous evening.

This room was filled with most of his personal belongings which he had brought with him from Heanton Court, his old home. Thick dust lay everywhere – on the chimney-piece with oddments of old china and glass; a clock set within the open jaws of a tiger-skull shot by him in India; seals and rings; a small bottle of water which he had filled as a youth at the Taw-head on Dartmoor; a set of small ear-tools, which had belonged to his grandfather; a china trayful of seventeen acorns which he had taken from the crop of a shot wood-pigeon, meaning to plant them one day. A fire-screen was fixed to the chimney-piece by a brass arm, a silken shield worked by his sister with the coat-armour of the Heanton branch of the Chychesters, with sixty-four quarterings – undoubtedly Miss Edith's masterpiece. Mr. Chychester sat at his desk, the temperature book, with its neat columns of figures, open before him.

The window was closed; indeed, it was rarely opened. Spider-webs sealed the edges of the frame.

Mr. Chychester looked up when Maddison entered, and said he wouldn't be a moment.

'May I look at your books, sir?'

'Hey? Oh yes, by all means. You won't find them highbrow, I expect.'

The air of the room was old and faded, like many of the books on the shelves that hid an entire wall to the ceiling; the Badminton library was there, and other works on shooting, fishing, hunting, conchology, ornithology, heraldry; the first editions of all the works of Richard Jefferies, including the brown-covered three volumes of Bevis, which his three boys had read, and loved, and never entirely forgotten. The third volume leaned in a space where a modern book had been extracted, lest the children should get hold of it – a book that he had bought only because it had a local interest, containing descriptions of the Burrows – *The Journal of a Disappointed Man*, that Mr. Chychester, considering bestial, had burned – thereby entirely preserving the pre-twentieth-century atmosphere of his room.

'Shall I open the window for you, Mr. Chychester?'

'H'm, no thanks. The proper place for fresh air is outside,' replied the old man, resenting what he considered to be an interference. Maddison was a bit too much inclined that way!

Dust lay on the books; on the stack of water-colours (he had taken to gardening and sketching after his wife's death) in a corner; on the frames of the copies of Gainsborough's portraits of his bewigged and red-coated grandfather and his plume-hatted grandmother; the copper engravings of Heanton Court from the *Gentleman's Magazine*; the horned skulls of Indian animals; the gun cabinet with the guns he would never sell, and the collection of daggers, kukris, swords, krises, sabres, and other weapons. The room was the secret delight of Benjamin, who had explored every nook and drawer of it during the absences of his grandfather. Likewise Benjamin had read many of the entries in the volumes comprising Mr. Chychester's diaries, which were piled on the top book-shelf, with the boxes of butterflies, shells, paints, and other relics of outgrown hobbies.

The entries of the diaries were all impersonal, for Mr. Chychester was quite incapable of expressing his feelings in writing; deeming them, indeed, intimate and personal as his body, as something never to be revealed. Storms, good hunting days, guests, births, deaths, and latterly gardening items and crosses denoting successful solutions of cross-word puzzles, such were the records of his life. Yet in these bare pages his only grandson had educed facts of great interest to himself; that his father Fiennes Chychester had married a wife called Maude in December 1902, after the Boer War; that in August 1908 he had left his wife, and informed his father that he would never go back to her. In February 1909 'Fiennes writes that he had a boy, born at 11.30 p.m. the day before yesterday.'

This boy, Benjamin knew, was himself. In August 1914, his father had gone to France with the British Expeditionary Force; and in September 1914 his grandfather had seen his solicitors to suggest that Maude should divorce Fiennes, there being no possible chance of child *en ventre sa mère*, a phrase which Benjamin's education had enabled him promptly to understand. Then the death of his father in October 1914, and the death of his two uncles, whom he had never seen, in March and June 1915; and the illuminating entry, 'After five centuries direct succession to Heanton must end. Bends-sinister out of fashion.'

Thus Benjamin knew all the circumstances of his existence, and realizing that his father had not loved his married wife, but his own mother instead, and that his mother loved his father, he was satisfied; it was romantic to be illegitimate; there was no difference from other boys, and nobody knew.

The entries in Mr. Chychester's diary of the last few days

of June and the month of July were frequently concerned with the garden, and Maddison.

28 June. Maddison here. Skinned old overgrown strawberry beds and scythed all thistles and nettles. Full moon. Maddison slept out.

29 June. Maddison trenched old strawberry beds and cut lawn.

30 June. Three loads of sea-weed from Crow. Maddison trenching two spits deep for asparagus bed, Connie's suggestion. Hot day.

1 July. Church. Garside to supper. Benjamin has apparently being playing truant all last week. Connie suggests training ship for merchant service. Benjamin agreed, if it could be considered he had already left school already, but C. won't have him on her hands.

2 July. Dug four rows 2nd early tetties. Maddison still here. We dutch-hoed and sifted paths and part of drive.

3 July. Otter-hunting at Umberleigh. Blank day. Maddison and Mary came out.

4 July. Fine weather continues. Maddison still here, and working in garden. Good worker. Benjamin decided to remain at school, and to farm afterwards. Fly in carrots. Connie wants him sent to boarding-school. Hurt my toe falling over cat.

5 July. Hot weather continues. With Otter-hounds at Portsmouth Arms. Killed a bitch $15\frac{1}{2}$ lbs., after $2\frac{1}{2}$ hours hunt. I got the rudder. Maddison and Mary out, but got lost.

6 July. Barum with Maddison and Mary. Left my rudder at Rowe's. Maddison ordered new clothes at tailors for Otter Hunt dance. Very hot day. New moon. Maddison and I and Benjamin made bonfire of old moots at night, and scared Connie.

7 July. Took Maddison to see the great sea-stocks in Santon cliffs. Hottest day.

8 July. Weather still hot. Church in morning with Edith, Connie, Maddison, and Benjamin, and Maddison and Mary in evening. Garside to supper. Maddison talked all evening and went away with him, still talking. Stung by wasp in garden. Must put screws in my hunting boots to-morrow, as nails fall out.

9 July. Destroyed my wasps nest. Benjamin's Prize Day. Very hot. Benjamin no prizes – a proper Chychester.

10 July. Read in the *Morning Post* that a first edition of 'Pickwick Papers' sold in New York for nearly £1,000, so on Maddison's advice sent mine off to Sotheby's. No break in weather likely for several days. Saw heron standing by my lily pond early this morning. Maddison slept out with Benjamin.

11 July. With Otter Hounds at Pilton Bridge. A touch now and again, but did not find. Water low. Had tea with Maddison and Mary at Crook's.

12 July. We all took tea on Santon Sands. More and more trippers every year.

13 July. Maddison and I began to clean and repair the cider-press to-day. Hot weather continues.

14 July. Went fishing with Maddison and Mary in Horsey Pit after land-locked mullet. Waste of time.

15 July. Church with Edith, Connie, Benjamin and Jean. Maddison and Mary with me to Evensong.

16 July – 21 July. Joint week with Culmstock and Cheriton. Connie came out first day, with Maddison, who got lost after awhile. Items for week: Water too low for proper sport. A Culmstock hound died of adder bite. Very hot in the Torridge valley. Total for 6 hunting days 2 dogs and 1 bitch to Culmstock, one dog to Cheriton. Culmstock now lead in the season by a leash, but we shall beat them yet.

22 July. Church in morning with Connie, Benjamin, and Jean. Evensong with Mary and Maddison.

23 July. Sultry weather. Shot three cats.

24 July. Cousin Leicester sent a dozen of port to-day. Sotheby returned my 'Pickwick Papers' as useless, as the leaves were clipped when bound. Well, one less for the Americans, I suppose.

25 July. Hottest day so far. Sparrows gaping on lawn. My bird-bath a proper oasis. Edith departed to stay with Cousin Augusta for a week.

26 July. Hotter than yesterday. Ronnie came home in afternoon, three days early owing to outbreak of measles in school.

A few hours after Mr. Chychester had written the last entry, Maddison was walking on Santon sands with his dog. Westwards the level swell of the sea vanished in mist a few yards from the shore, where small and regular lines of waves succeeded one another; eastwards the sun towered over the sandhills, an earth-smiting dandelion. The shore was strewn with shells, paired and broken apart; and the night ebb had drawn slight lines on the sand below each.

He walked barefoot, with rapid strides avoiding the sharp edges. The dark ribs of the wreck loomed out of the white fog of morning, like a skeleton of some extinct race of giants, buried east and west, awaiting resurrection after the last sunrise. Gulls beside it watched the spaniel trotting forward ahead of the man, and ran with lifted wings towards the sea, and after many steps paddled off the sand and took the air with slow and graceful wings.

He felt himself to be of the morning light – the intangible and unseen morning, the spirit of light in a myriad self-happy objects. Only light was harmonious: to be an object was to struggle against another object, to be of the thing called the world. Jesus' end of the world meant the end of the Old Adam, not the end of the planet. Graves in the churchyard lying towards the east, towards the sunrise, awaiting the coming of Jesus at the end of the planet: Jesus of Nazareth, a Jew, who was put to death as a dangerous revolutionary! The awareness of light was the beginning of the new world, the new Adam; when consciousness had completely changed, then the *parthenogenesis* – the virgin, or un-physical rebirth, as a spiritual butterfly from the Adam-caterpillar. What blind bat had rendered *parthenogenesis* as conception without spermatozoa, thus denying natural laws, the Spirit's own handiwork! Poor Garside, how shocked he had been: unaware that the human truth was more beautiful than idolatry. Maddison's thoughts gave way to a vision of Mary's face, as he walked slowly round the wreck, imagining her coming to him there.

A dog ran out of the mist, and another dog; and then the shapes of two boys. He frowned, for he had been greeting her at that very place: Mary walking slowly among the shells and the stones, slowly towards him, smiling and looking down with flushed cheeks and looking up again; and smiling, and saying gently, Hullo. Poor Mary, so shy and gentle with her robin and her bee and . . . The boys were looking at him, awaiting recognition.

'G'morn – oh, hullo!' said Ronnie, shyly.

'You're about early. When did you get home, Ronnie?'

'Just before supper last night.'

'He hoped to see you last night,' explained Benjamin.

'Shut up, you fool, I didn't,' said Ronnie.

'I meant to see you,' replied Maddison, 'but I went for a walk, and couldn't get back in time, so I slept on Ferny Hill. I've made a shelter there.'

'How ripping,' cried Ronnie. 'I shall make a shelter there too.'

'I've got one already in one of the privet brakes,' said Benjamin. 'Only Aunt Connie won't let me sleep out any more.'

'Perhaps she will if Willie is with us,' suggested Ronnie. 'I say, you are coming back to breakfast, aren't you?'

'Oh yes.'

'Hurray!'

'How about a bathe before breakfast? Look! I saw a bass leaping this side of the wave. Come on!'

Ronnie made as if to speak, and stopped.

'Too cold?'

'Rather not, Mr. Maddison.'

'Don't call me Mister. I'm only a boy like you, except that I appeared on the earth before you did, and will go into it sooner.'

The spaniel Billjohn, who had stood stiffly, with vibrating tail-stump, during the inspecting sniffs of the Wildernesse dogs, was now returning the compliment to each in turn. This being done, he followed them to a particular rib of the wreck; and a thoughtful ceremony of liberty, fraternity, and equality having been performed, the sand was scratched by vigorous kicks of hind feet, and the dogs trotted to the master-group, to await direction.

A commotion of small waves suddenly jumped and splashed around the wreck, and tumbled over each other like many white-breasted spaniel puppies running forward. The boys walked backwards on the sand before the hissing rush of the water. Maddison thrust his stick into the sand above the froth line, and hung his coat on it.

'Aren't you chaps bathing?' he asked, when they stood still.

'Well, the fact is,' said Benjamin, 'we didn't expect to see you here, and so we came without bathing costumes.'

'Bathing *suits*,' Ronnie corrected him, with a self-assured air. 'Only board-school boys say *costumes*.'

'Oh, shut up,' replied Benjamin, with a furtive glance at Maddison.

'Bathing starko is much more pleasant,' murmured Maddison. 'Then you needn't bother about either bathing suits or bathing costumes.' They still hesitated, and he paused with fingers on the knot of the string holding up his trousers. 'I'll go away if you like, and bathe over there.'

'Rather not,' said Ronnie, taking off his coat. Maddison stepped out of his trousers, and with long leaping strides ran towards the sea.

'Decent chap,' said Benjamin. 'Can't he run, too.'

'Rather!'

When Ronnie stood naked he said, 'I love the sun. I wish I could go brown all over, like Willie is.'

'Look, my forearms are brown. Wait for us.'

'Damn well buck up then.'

'All right, curse you.'

'What beastly long toenails you've got. No wonder they've come through your gym shoes.'

They ran to the sea with shrill cries to the dogs. Over the film of the last spent wave, over a secondary wavelet forming line after a ninth wave's crash, and into water clear and green above the yellow meshes of the shadow-net of ripples on the sand. They swam a few quick violent strokes, then standing up they laughed and chattered, knuckling the water out of their eyes, and splashing each other.

'All right?' shouted Maddison, swimming beyond their depth.

'Rather!'

The mist grew thin in the rays of the rising sun, and the shadowy roar of the breakers out on the estuary bar spread with the widening day. Wading out after twenty minutes swimming Maddison saw Ronnie practising surface dives, and the thinner Benjamin standing, with a greenish white face, in shallow water. His teeth chattered.

'Out you both come,' Maddison shouted.

'I feel sick,' mumbled Benjamin.

'Then be sick.'

Benjamin gazed for awhile at the water, groaned, and said, 'I think I'm better now. I say, don't tell Mary. I'm not supposed to bathe on an empty stomach.'

Mary was standing by the second wreck, scattered and broken above the line of ordinary tides, where the great sea of a past winter had made a breach in the sandhills. They waved to each other. Maddison turned and shouted again to

Ronnie, telling him to come in, and then ran to his clothes. Shirt and trousers and coat were flung on in a minute, and picking up shoes and stick, he set off at a lope towards the place where Mary had disappeared.

Westerly winds and spring tides had worn a wide way in the breach by the second wreck, and strewn the pan with clinkers from steamships, tins, bits of wood, bottles, feathers, and pink empty cases of sun-baked crabs. Part of the ship's deck lay buried, bristling with rusty iron bolts – a treacherous place for bare feet. Farther in was the battered iron life-boat of a French ship, lying on its side, half filled with sand, jagged holes as of shell-fire in its bows. Near it lay a glass globe the size of a grape-fruit, drifted in by the wind after years of bobbing in the sea, a float of a submarine net.

A ring-plover ran over the stones and sand before him, piping short faint notes to its young crouching near the iron boat, speckled and still as stones. Hurrying with short steps over the strewn place he came unexpectedly on Mary, lying behind the life-boat, her brown legs bare to the knee. She turned on an elbow, smiling and looking up into his face. Hullo, she said, in a voice scarcely audible, and he knelt down and lay beside her, taking her in his arms, and kissing her.

'O Mary, I have missed you so.'

'You are a wet poor boy, aren't you?' she said, kissing him, and combing his sea-tangled hair with the fingers of her free hand. 'Wish I had bathed with ee.'

'I left my bathing suit in the hall.'

'I brought it with me, in case I met ee!'

'You think of everything! Where are the boys: I say, can't we dodge them?'

They elbowed themselves to the bows of the boat, to peer at the boys dressing by the Dutchman's Wreck. His eye caught a glint, small as a spider's eye glinting in a hole in a wall, from the distant house on the sloping lower fields of Down End. Mary saw it at the same time.

'I expect that is Miss Goff's telescope catching the sun,' she said.

'Oh, that's Miss Goff's house, is it? I wondered who had put up that wooden fence, instead of a stone ditched wall which would have harmonized with the old walls of the district. Here, let's clear off. I don't want her to see me.'

'Poof, who cares for Miss Goff.'

'I say, let's go now, for the boys will be sure to find us.'

'You are coming to the dance to-night, aren't you?'

'Of course I am. A little doubtful of my reliability, Mary?'

'No, of course not, my dear. Now come along, and I'll make ee a nice omelette for breakfast.'

At eleven o'clock they returned to the sands, carrying a basket of luncheon and tea, while Ronnie carried a kettle of water. The spring tide (the moon would be full that evening) had erased the morning footmarks in the loose sand above its earlier binding mark, and left a strand smooth and cool to bare feet parched by walking across the burning sand of the desert, among marram grasses rustled by a swooning wind.

The basket was hidden in a rib-shadow of the second wreck; and while Ronnie and Maddison undressed in the sandhills, by the summery flowers of the sea-rocket, she hid in the fo'c'sle of the wreck, to walk out in a red bathing dress, changed into a smiling sea-maiden.

Although he had bathed with her many times he had not ceased to marvel that she was formed in an exquisite mould, every limb and feature balanced: he took a swift covert glance, and felt that the life and beauty were beyond him. She was not responsible for the lovely curves, for the lovely texture of skin; she wore her beauty as a plant wore it blossom, as a bird sang its song. He might lose the living beauty, never possess in love her whom her mother called Mary, but the thoughts of her were eternally his. Something was created for him; he held the spirit that shaped her maiden body, that lustred her eyes, that gave the teeth their whiteness, and the lips their sun-sweet smile. He walked behind her, but she waited and took his hand and ran with him to the sea, where her little brother was already splashing. He was glad of the exertion, to vent the passionate feelings that surged at her touch.

After the bathe he ran along the sands with his sea-maiden, and the sun dried the salt on their limbs, and deepened the golden-brown of their skin. In the afternoon they bathed again, and strolled towards Aery Point, while little brother lit a fire on the wreck and pretended that he was Robinson Crusoe. They walked by the margin of the sea: the sun was a silver flower, the flower of all beauty, shining on the wet sand whence a long wave had drawn back after its green curl and fall. A million silver flies seemed to be dancing among the ripples as it receded, to rise again to the celestial flower on the sand, and cover it with a silver swarm. Another wave glided up, bestrewn with white and flickering birds, and lapsed, and the swarm clustered anew about the blinding flower.

A thistle-seed rolled in from the sea, from the distant head-land, sometimes touching the water, but bounding on, so light and airy its glistening wheel. It rolled on the wet sand, and passed them. It has come so far, the darling, with its lovely tiny little wheel-like motion, said Mary.

The sun was an immense thistle-seed rolling over the blue sea of the sky, and her footsteps in the wet sand glittered where the light was held and reflected. He followed in her footsteps, treading in the silver prints shed by a glistening water-wraith. A dark blue line of mirage wavered on the flat expanse before them; the white lines on the distant bar were crinkled by the glassy flames of air. A gull cried as though insane, afloat on the blue water. They heard the puffs of the Bideford train three miles away, out of sight behind the sandhills; and voices behind them spoke with such distinctness that they turned together. A white speck and a smaller black speck stood far behind by the wreck, shifting and melting in the mirage.

'Good-bye,' they heard Ronnie's voice, as though from a

few yards away, and the white speck grew in movement with the thuds of hooves.

'It's Diana,' said Mary, 'on Shahzada.'

The galloping grey Arab stallion seemed to rush over the sand, spurning the low infirm line of the mirage. Soon they saw the red of its wide nostrils, and the black brow-band across its broad forehead. At a light pull on its mouth it threw up its head and slowed instantly in a spray of sand, and danced sedately to them, the wasted power of each controlled step passing down its long tail, and rippling away into the air. Diana spoke to it, and it stood still in its strength, regarding them with its large brown eyes. The groom following stopped a hundred yards away, and walked his horse into the sea.

'Hullo, Mary,' said Diana, 'I've just come from your place. Here you are blessed by the sun, and there they've got the sun-blinds down, playing bridge.'

'Who?'

'Our mothers, with Old Jig and Mrs. Hole.'

Maddison stood by the Arab's head, patting its neck.

'Beautiful creature,' he said.

'Try him,' said Diana, lifting her leg over the animal's head and sliding to the sand.

He passed his hand down the Arab's neck, and along its withers. The stallion stood motionless, and he swung into the saddle, crossing the stirrups on the pommel. A touch with a bare heel, and Shahzada glided away at the gallop.

'He rides like an Arab, with his long skinny legs and feet,' said Diana.

'He was a cavalryman.'

'Anyone less like a soldier, and a cavalryman, I can't imagine.'

'He got the Military Cross in the War.'

'Do you take me for one of the local half-wits?' asked Diana. 'I don't like soldiers. "Chinless" said the other day, "I say, toppin' pony you've got, Miss Shelley, what? I'd like 'im for polo." "The other ponies wouldn't have many brains left when he'd finished with them," I told "Chinless," and then he started to get fresh. Perff! You're going to the dance to-night, I suppose?'

'Yes; are you?'

'I don't know,' replied Diana, with a toneless distinctness of voice. 'Though I've been all right this summer, so far.'

Mary knew her friend's nervous dread of fainting fits – as Mrs. Shelley insisted on calling her daughter's disability, in dread of a more ominous word – in public.

'Is he going?' She indicated the centaur with her head.

'Yes, we're all going over by boat, if it's a fine night. You look jolly well, you know, Diana.'

'I'm all right!' said Diana, with sudden gayness.

They watched Maddison cantering in semicircles, aiding the Arab to change its feet; and bringing it back at an African triple-canter.

'He's the loveliest beast I've ever seen!' he exclaimed, dismounting beside them. 'He isn't an ordinary beast – he might have come out of a ninth wave during a gale. Where did you get 'im?'

'His sire came from Scawen Blunt's in Sussex. Well, you two, good-bye. See you to-night.'

Mounting astride quickly, she galloped away, passing the groom whose horse whinnied and galloped after the Arab.

'She is looking better,' said Maddison. 'Is she better?'

'Yes, I think she is,' replied Mary, puzzled to know exactly what he was referring to.

'I didn't tell you Diana told me her dreads and fears, did I? We had a long talk in the Appledore inn that day. People say a lot of things about the new generation to-day, how the War has unsettled young people, such as young men turning Socialists, and disowning their Tory fathers, et cetera, but how many realize what is really happening? A new consciousness is about to develop in the human race, at least among the white part of it, and the yellow and brown too, probably. Here and there in individuals the change has begun, in the frailest, least settled part of the mind. The old bees have swarmed and flown: the hive is agitated, for the new queen has not yet appeared. But the queen is coming!'

He added, 'of course the drones aren't affected by the spirit of the hive!'

She nodded.

'Well, those frail tissues, newly evolved, are easily deranged; their vibrations being broken, as it were, in contact with the lower, older, vibrations. Hence mental distress, and the functional disorders of that dear child who, finding some one to whom she could talk, esteems him with love.'

Mary gave him a full glance; she breathed deeply, and looked down at the hand she had taken.

'I kissed her, Mary.'

She would not look at him.

'To thaw from the fiery icicle any Maddison-spectre of love. Reality *such* a disillusion!'

'You dear!' said Mary, giving him a full glance of her eyes; her emotion quelling a faint uneasiness. The 'fiery icicle' in love with him . . . it was natural. She was reassured when, after taking a swift glance around the vacant sands, he clasped her and kissed her face and neck and lips.

'Not as I want to kiss you, understand,' he said roughly. 'Oh, to hell with civilization,' pushing himself away from her; and running to the sea, plunged into a wave.

The kettle was boiling when they returned, and they had tea with Robinson Crusoe. A low haze was overspreading the sky, and the sea became grey-green, with an oily swell moving beyond the jostling white wavelets of the incoming tide; the air over the Burrows as they walked back came in breathless puffs. Sound of the sea was shut out by the crests of the hillocks, with their green porcupine-like grasses; the shrill songs of innumerable larks pierced the heavy heat of the late afternoon.

They ran down a slope into the Valley of Wind, lying north and south in a vast glare and shimmer of sand which seemed unending. Bones and skulls of rabbits and small shells lay white, as though incandescent, in the steep loose slope they toiled up, their feet sinking in at every laboured step; the desert heat rang in their ears. On the crest a cooler wind washed about their faces; and the sudden open scene of flat wide river-land and the hills rising on either side into distance and the sky gave an illusion of relief. They descended to the hillocks, where the moss was loose and dry and brittle, and tall stalks of mulleins, with grey flannel-like leaves, held their yellow torches to the sky. They passed a fox's earth, with its tunnels smelling rank as drying hops. A low forest of ragwort grew further on, each plant stripped of its leaves by black-and-tan-banded caterpillars. Near the low yellow forest stood an elderberry tree, half its boughs like bones among its green leaves, a cripple of the Atlantic winds. It held a large nest roofed with thorny twigs. A late brood of five young magpies crouched warm and flat under the touch of their hands, for all three must feel in the nest. Wheatears flitted with their young in the dry plains; and in the dyke they surprised a sedate blackish bird with a red mark on its beak, a moorhen paddling with her second family of seven tiny chicks.

When they left these things behind and returned to the house they saw Mrs. Ogilvie and Mr. Chychester gazing at the sky, and Mrs. Ogilvie said she was wondering if it would not be advisable to hire a car for the dance that night, and so to prevent the risk of being drenched whilst crossing in the boat. What did they think? If the weather did not break, the crossing by moonlight would be delightful; but by road the journey was twenty-three miles to Appledore – which was little more than a mile away as the crow flew. That was one of the disadvantages of having to live so far away from anywhere. Was his own home so isolated? she asked Maddison: for apart from the annoying rumours about him, of late she had been seriously concerning herself about how far the thing 'had gone' with her daughter Mary; whether he had any expectations, and if so, what they were. Were Virginia Goff to be believed, he was not at all a desirable young man, having been a co-respondent in a divorce case, and a drunkard; but since Mrs. Fairfax, the person mentioned in the case, had, according to a letter from her sister Maude Pamment, but recently divorced Major Fairfax, Virginia's warnings were obviously based on mere gossip. She meant well, no doubt, but good intentions were not sufficient; and she did not suppose that Miss Goff's scandalous remarks were confined only to herself – probably she had told everybody she had met. Some of her information, she knew, was acquired from boarding-house keepers in Santon: her information about Jean had come from a certain Mrs. Tisard, a stupid and tiresome person.

Yet having disposed, in her own mind, of Miss Goff's inter-ference, an uneasiness remained with Mrs. Ogilvie. Mrs. Shelley had spoken to her about Maddison's visit with Diana to the Prince of Wales inn, where apparently he had engaged a private room and remained there for several hours during the rain; an indiscreet thing to do, although probably done as an act of kindliness: nevertheless, one that had annoyed Mrs. Shelley, who had heard of it through Miss Goff.

'Bill, what do you think?' asked Mrs. Ogilvie affably. 'I'm sure you won't want to spoil your nice new clothes! Is it going to keep fine, or not? Remember, we shall have to walk from the Sharshook on coming back, as the tide will be low.'

Being somewhat unexpectedly appealed to for an opinion, Maddison stared into the stillness of the sky, with a harder frown than the glare demanded, as though endeavouring to justify her apparent belief in his powers as a weather prophet. Whenever Mrs. Ogilvie addressed him as 'Bill' he felt grati-tude and strained to please her.

'What time does the dance end?' he said.

'About two, I suppose.'

'Well, it won't rain for twelve hours.'

'That's what Uncle Suff said –'

'Do let's go by boat, then we can return by moonlight!'

'Very well, we'll go by boat,' exclaimed Mrs. Ogilvie, relieved that she would be saved several pounds by not having to hire.

At a quarter-past eight o'clock they met Luke by the White House, and boarded the boat – Mrs. Ogilvie, Mr. Sufford Chychester, Jean, Mary, and the girls 'partners,' a young sailor called Stukeley who had arrived that evening in a semi-decayed cycle-car, and Maddison.

The water ebbed with the colour of the sky. As they passed the shingle tongue of the Crow the pallid rim of the moon appeared over the hills of the mainland, and the tide shook with its feathery gleam. Westwards the uneven line of the sandhills glowed with a blinding light. With regular creak and knock of the sweeps increasing in the thole-pins the boat was pulled across the ocean-turning ebb, and into the wide Pool. The vast glory of the sun sinking to his deathbed in the Atlantic made Maddison turn to Mary and say in a low voice, Why are we going to a damned dance, when we might be walking by the wreck? He turned his face to the glittering water, and did not speak again until the boat was alongside the slip in Appledore.

'Well, here we are,' exclaimed Mrs. Ogilvie with her peculiar laugh-like sound, as with a composed face she prepared to be handed out of the boat. She disliked the way the fishermen and sailors and their women on the quay were staring, and regretted that she had not hired a car, as she had intended to do. Why had she asked Maddison's advice in the matter at all? With relief she saw that Mules and his wife were standing there – they had gone for a pleasure row in a boat with friends, and were about to return. Both the smiling faces of the grave-digger and his wife were a-bob, as they prepared to greet the Wildernesse gentry.

''Ullo midear,' said Mules, plucking at his cap, and grinning at Maddison who poked him in the ribs, and said, 'Brown boots, Mules? You'm very smart, midear. What be ut, grave-diggers' outing?' Several fishermen laughed.

'Aw haw, you'm a funny man, zur. Be ee going to the dance, zur? Be ee, surenuff? That's right – you'm getting on fine midear, getting on fine. Won't forget poor old Mules, will ee? Aw haw, you'm a funny man,' and patted him affectionately on the shoulder.

'Good evening, ma'm. Good evening, sir. Good evenin', Miss Mary. Miss Jean,' he said, in an unconscious imitation of the Vicar's dignified manner.

'Hullo, Muley,' said Jean, in her clear voice. Mrs. Ogilvie felt easier, and bidding several people good evening, including Mules and Mrs. Mules, whose faces were now positively shining, walked through the group with her uncle. As they followed the four young people up the steep narrow street, she remembered how she had walked that same way with Michael, when taking him with Mary to a Christmas children's party at The Ridge. Then, she thought, she had not known what it was to be nervous of a few fishermen on the quay. Ah well, one could not remain young for ever. She thought of the coming night, and hoped she would not have to cut in with Virginia, as she was a somewhat difficult partner to play bridge with, and could not be persuaded from holding inquests.

Mr. Chychester had never learned to play bridge, and thought it a beastly game; he intended to have a good supper, and hoped there would be champagne that was champagne, not that beastly gooseberry wine they called champagne nowadays.

They heard the voice of Maddison almost continuously in front, and the laughter of the others; and they walked up the hill in silence, having nothing to say.

Chapter 13

SITTING in semi-darkness near the top of the stairs, beside a stuffed bittern in a glass case, Maddison turned to the girl beside him, and said again, with more desperation in his voice:

'Mary, I want to ask you something, but I don't know how to say it.'

'Just say it,' she said quietly. She sat very still, her face pale, her eyes large. For more than an hour they had been sitting there, and he had been talking, except when other men and women, chatting amiably, had sought the stairs for sitting-out after each dance. During these intervals he had spoken hardly at all. She knew that he was suffering, and she suffered for him.

'I can't,' he groaned, turning tragic eyes upon her. 'I don't feel in the least as I ought to feel. Even if I did, I shouldn't care what your answer was.' He looked so funny with the paper cracker-cap on his head, a relic of supper of which he was unconscious.

'O God, why did I come to this place, among men who crash through fences and think themselves the salt of the earth? Let them go out and hunt the darkness in their own minds, and tear up, not foxes, but foolishness. They bring up their sons to be blooded on the face: Christ, hasn't enough blood flowed on the face of the earth already?' He stopped and said, 'Why am I talking like this to you, and spoiling your evening, just because some scowl-browed idiot tells me I'm half-baked?'

'You're not spoiling my evening, Billy.'

'You say that because you have a high sense of duty, like that of a dog, or an army officer of the best type, which I

287

wasn't. An army officer! The human spirit deserves a higher employment than being patriotic; to be dutiful to wider, higher things. The best patriots in Europe are hounds; they don't think; and the best hounds, as that fellow said at supper, are always blooded up to the eyes.'

She waited.

'But the world is thought – mediocre and selfish thought. How can mediocre thought understand high thinking? All prophets are bound to be hated; that's why the old Jewish prophets could foretell the certain destruction of the complete Messiah.'

'Eventually men follow high thinking, and things gradually change for the better.'

'Yes, I suppose that is so,' he said wearily, leaning his head on his hands. 'Yes, things are getting better. Human beings concentrate and reflect in themselves the ideas and ideals of the mass: and the remedy for all unhappiness – anciently called sin – is in the freeing of the imagination. But wasn't this expounded about nineteen centuries ago? – heaven knows what idolatry has come out of it – and there is no truth in an idol. Nothing is true where the sky is shut away: unless it is remembered. Didn't you *feel* truth in the sunlight to-day? It poured down from the celestial spirit; it was all around us in the sunlight.' A minute later he looked round. 'What, you still there, like a moorhen?'

Mary's frock, which she had adapted from one sent her by her cousin Muriel Lorayne, was black with a red flower. 'Well, moorhens are the best kind. I'm not a moorhen – I'm a bird of passage. A peregrine falcon – or a cuckoo who tries to fly like a hawk. No, a phœnix – it has no real existence. And you're a dove – a turtle-dove. The Phœnix and the Turtle! You're too good for me, heaps too good, my sweet Mary.'

She smiled, but her eyes showed that she was not happy for him.

'You have beautiful eyes,' he said. 'There are deep shadows

in them. Do you know what I wrote in my notebook about you the other day? Shall I tell you?'

'Yes,' she said huskily, and cleared her throat.

The syncopation of the piano and banjos, the rich wails of a saxophone, and the noises of voices and feet ceased in the distance. They heard the voices louder, with clapping. The dance-music began again.

'This is what I wrote,' he said, and his voice dropped.

'When I think of those men, of many nations, who laid down their lives for their brothers, and of the spirit of love which dwelled during five summers in the waste places of the earth, how can I regard the feelings of personal love in my own heart? The hair of my Mary is dark, and her eyes are shadowed deep, but the despair of the lost generation was darker, and the water in the shell-holes that drowned them was deeper. How may I rest against her heart which beats so gently, when the heart of the world is troubled, when its breast may be beaten again by the iron of the guns of the lightless people? I am weary, but how can I rest, having seen the Light?'

She took his hand, and clasped it on her lap.

'Don't worry, Billy dear.'

'Mary,' he said, 'I wish I could be serene – that is the ideal. But so many things grind round one, like the sea on the Pebble Ridge. Mary, if – Oh, I can't say it.'

'Go on,' she said.

'Look here,' he said desperately. 'Let's clear off, and go by the sea. It's full moon. O God, summer is nearly over!'

The tum-tum-tum of the music, and the susurration of feet ceased; there was desultory clapping, and many voices coming nearer.

'Oh, blast,' he groaned. 'Look here, I'll go – or people will begin to wonder – no, I'll stop here, pretending I'm a waiter, on guard to see that no one robs the bedrooms.' He glanced at his programme, which was of white pasteboard printed in blue with a blue cat's head embossed on the front, and *Taw and Torridge Otter Hounds.*

Several young men and women, in couples talking vivaciously about subjects that did not interest them, walked up the stairs; each man said, as he stopped, 'How about this?' and each girl replied promptly, 'Yes, rather!' and smiled. Each man with an identical quick movement spread his coat-tails – either blue of the hunt uniform or ordinary black – and sat down on a stair.

'What number was that, I wonder,' said Maddison. His hand touched Mary's, and they remained close together, as though examining the programme, but really seeing nothing. My darling, he whispered. She stroked the fingers holding the hinged pasteboard. Don't ee worry, my dear, she breathed by his ear, Mary's beside ee.

'Ha!' he said, in a voice curiously unlike his own, and like any one of the young men below. 'That must have been number eleven. A foxtrot, "Burning Kisses." By Jove, I've cut four dances, one of Jean's, one of yours, and one with Salmon Pink Dress, apparently, and one with a Miss Hibbert. The next is with Diana.'

When the band began again, they rose with the others on the stairs below them. 'Now you go and enjoy yourself,' she said, whisking the green paper-cap from his head, and folding it swiftly, hid it with her gloves.

By the ballroom door many girls and a few young men were standing, awaiting their partners for the dance. Maddison saw Mary's mother talking to Diana among them: she was smoking a cigarette, having come from the card room after a rubber. Mrs. Ogilvie was happy: she had known the house and most of the older people there since childhood: she had watched their babies growing up – most of them to lead happy, useful lives. Ah, there was Tony Leaver, poor silly young man! but there, it was no use regretting *that*: if all one heard was true, it was a good thing after all that Jean had not responded.

'You're a fine fellow, you are,' said Jean's voice beside her. 'Where were you for my dance? Ah, well, I'll forgive you, William my lad. But don't forget fourteen. Hullo, Mother!' She held out her bare arms to a man, transferring her smile to him automatically as they glided into the stirring mass.

'Well, Bill, how do you like our dissipations?' said Mrs. Ogilvie, turning to Maddison, as contentedly she puffed at her cigarette. She smoked seldom.

'Very much, Aunt Connie. How's the bridge?'

'Oh, I'm well up, I think. Just had a grand slam!' More contented puffs.

Maddison looked at Mary as though he would not be seeing her again for a very long time, as she moved into Howard's arms.

'By Jove, I'd almost forgotten Diana's dance!'

'Run along,' smiled Mrs. Ogilvie. He looked almost distinguished!

Maddison saw Diana in a black frock standing by the wall. She did not appear to see him approaching her, but gave him a slight smile, and opening her arms, started to glide backwards with him.

'I'm sorry I cut your dance, Diana.'

'That's all right: I didn't expect you to appear.'

'I've been talking a lot of damned introversial nonsense to Mary, and worrying the poor child. Sorry, did I hurt your foot?'

'It was my fault,' she replied. 'I think you'd be a dancer with practice.'

'Lots of practice.'

'You said it.'

'This tune is old-fashioned, surely? It's got part of "There's a Long Long Trail A-winding" in it, which we used to sing in the War. What is it, a modern adaption, "The Worm's a Long Time Turning"?'

'Something like that.'

A few bars from *Tristan* shone out of the noise, which then relapsed into a bombilation of wails, brassy clatter, and piano frolicking on the treble notes.

'Filthy row, isn't it? Are you staying with the Ogilvies?'

'Yes, we came over by boat.'

A young man with a white face, and wearing a monocle that increased his air of superciliousness, glided past them at twice the rate of any other couple, with what appeared to be most intricate steps.

'I'm so sorry, Diana; I haven't quite got the time yet.'

'You're all right, I tell you.'

From the walls the heads of dead otters snarled fixedly upon the dancers: these trophies alternated with the long tapered tails, called rudders, of the slain water-beasts, tied with dark blue ribbon.

'I'm glad I'm dancing with you,' said Diana.

'Yes,' he said.

'Because you're the first man among this crowd of half-wits who hasn't remarked to me, "Isn't the band topping," ' said Diana. 'Don't use your arm as a pump handle,' she added, as they worked their way round and round the floor. Maddison felt that he was the clumsiest dancer in the room, but when he observed a strange tall bearded figure of a man ambling patiently with his elderly partner, and noticed his big feet and thick-soled shoes, he forgot to think about his own steps, and his dancing immediately became more flexible.

'You're coming on fine,' said Diana.

'Who is that extraordinary-looking man with a beard?' he asked.

'Over there? Oh, that's Lord Edward Rawleigh. He's supposed to be a great student of Eastern religions and an authority on fleas.'

'Fleas did you say, or peas?'

'Fleas. Father shot a honey-buzzard the other day, and

Lord Edward came hurrying over, and to his delight, discovered an entirely new bug on it.'

'I like his face,' said Maddison.

'He's a dear. Major Shakerley calls him Jay See behind his back.'

'Jay See?'

'Yes – J.C., for Jesus Christ.'

A short elderly man moved beside them, piloting a beautiful young girl wearing white. Her face was demurely radiant; she had just 'come out.' Her partner was almost bald, his head being deeply wrinkled from chin to shiny pate; he lacked eyebrows, but had a moustache like an eyebrow; a monocle was screwed into one eye, and his face was pock-marked. He held the young girl as though diffidently, while inspecting other women with oblique glances over her shoulder.

'Who is that?' asked Maddison, when others had moved between them.

'Major Shakerley.'

Maddison was unable to read the name of the girl which was thinly scrawled against the twelfth dance, and 'silver shoes,' the hasty note for identification added to the illegible name, did not help him to find her, since nearly all the women appeared to be wearing silver shoes. So he followed Mr. Chychester to the bar, which was in Howard's smoking-room.

Here several men stood in varying attitudes of gracefulness, holding glasses. By a table stood a small man with an alert and disciplined face, which was, like nearly every male face in the house, deeply tanned by the sun. He was the huntsman, and answered to the name of Jim.

'Yes,' said a man to Mr. Chychester, as though he had been carrying on a conversation with him, 'I shot that honey-buzzard quite by chance: I mean, I thought it was a common buzzard. Buzzards are getting too numerous. Left alone too much during the War. Now, would you believe it, whenever

I go into Chapel Wood the blessed birds start screaming at
me, at *me*, as though they owned the blessed place! It's just
the same with most of these working chaps in the towns – what
was good enough for their fathers isn't good enough for them,
no blessed fear! They want more, and then more; and they
aren't craftsmen, as they were in the old days, taking a pride
in their jobs. They're getting above themselves, like the
buzzards, as though they own the blessed earth!'

'Ah!' said Mr. Chychester. 'Well, Bill, your health!' he said,
turning to Maddison, and swallowing half his tumbler of
whisky and soda.

A big man in a red coat and a broad, very red face with
toughened purplish features and a shock of white hair was
standing beside them: he was talking to Major Shakerley
about the opening meet of the Staghounds n Exmoor, the
following week. He said that no doubt the place would swarm
with trippers out of char-à-bancs. His contention was that
free education had ruined England.

'Hullo, Maddison! Glad you could come!'

Howard de Wychehalse came into the room. He came for
a drink to put him in form, as he said to himself, for his dance
with Diana. He had proposed to her thrice during the summer,
and he still hoped in the belief that she must love him. Having
had no experience of women outside the magazine stories he
had read, and being unconscious that such stories had influenced
if not entirely formed his comprehension of women, he clung
to a desperate idea that Diana would one day give a little
choking cry, murmur 'My dear, my dear,' and hide her head
on his shoulder. His sister had advised him to give her time,
saying that she was mentally and physically backward,
although a genius as far as music was concerned – genius being,
she had explained, a strange thing that no one could possibly
understand or account for. Having been a full-bosomed
young woman herself from the age of twelve years, Miss de
Wychehalse was confirmed in her theory of Diana's backward-

ness by her slight boyish figure. 'She's a child still, old man; don't rush her; give her time.'

He had chosen this dance – Diana had allotted him one in the first half, and one in the second, and to his misery he had noticed that during at least one dance she had been unpartnered – because of the title and tune of the fox-trot. It was a tune he had been playing over and over again on the gramophone during the past fortnight, in his room alone, and it obsessed him; a fox-trot called, he hoped prophetically, *There's Yes! Yes! in your eyes!*

Outwardly, tall and broad in his blue uniform tail-coat, tanned of face, his cuffs, collar, and shirt-front very white and shiny, Howard looked splendidly self-assured, as though life for him was a matter only of wearing the right clothes, drinking the right wines with the right food, thinking the right things, behaving in the right way before women and in public, and assuming to all people not of one's class the right manner of affability and condescension scrupulously concealed; but under his rind of good form his natural self was cramped and suffering.

'I say, do you know Mr. Shelley? This is Maddison.'

'Hullo, Howard,' exclaimed Mr. Shelley. 'How d'you do, Maddison. Have a drink.'

'I won't just now, thanks very much.'

'I was just telling Chychester what a brother of mine told me about some of those mining fellows. He happened to be in a mining town, I forget where it was, anyway it doesn't matter. I don't know what he was doing there, but that doesn't matter anyway. Anyway, he was passing a fish-shop, if you understand, and saw a miner buying fish, for his tea, I suppose. Anyway, this mining fellow pointed to a fish, a decent-sized fish it was, a peal, although I believe they call 'em sewin in Wales. Very well. "What's that," he said. "Salmon," said the fishmonger chap, or sewin he may have said. Anyway it doesn't matter. Well, as I was saying, this mining fellow said, "How much?" "Half a crown a pound." "How

295

much does all of it weigh?" "Six pounds," replied the fish monger. "I'll have the lot," said the mining chap, and he took away the whole blessed fish!'

"And they're supposed to be starving," drawled Major Shakerley, turning, and nodding to Howard.

'Starving – my foot,' replied Mr. Shelley pleasantly. 'That's just part of the agitators' propaganda. If the miners had any sense they'd kick 'em all out, the whole blessed lot of 'em, unions and all. Those fellows are only out for themselves, and the miners haven't the sense to see it,' said Mr. Shelley. 'Well, my brother went back to the shop when the fellow had gone, and he asked the fishmonger what the chap wanted with such a fish. "Oh, he'll cut a slice or two off, and fry it in the pan, and chuck the rest away in the dustbin," said the fishmonger. Now I don't know what you think, but I call it immoral,' said Mr. Shelley.

'Exactly!' said Howard.

Mr. Shelley looked at Maddison, merely out of politeness, and was therefore surprised when that young fellow replied:

'And the train-loads of cheaper fish that are sometimes diverted from the big markets by the big fishing companies, and rotted into manure, in order to keep the market prices up, is that immoral too? Or is it moral because it's good business, to assure dividends?'

'Well, it's a waste of good fish of course, but unavoidable, like many other things in life. The market would be glutted otherwise, I suppose, wouldn't it, and more unemployment made. All these things are dependent on one another, like the veins and arteries in our bodies.'

'I say, won't you have a drink,' said Howard to Maddison.

'Yes, I'll have some soda-water, please.'

'Good Lord, is it as bad as that?' remarked Mr. Shelley. Maddison liked his kindly eyes and face; as he had been prepared to like him when he had read in a local paper how Mr. Shelley, alone in his parish council, had pleaded against his village applying for the rights and status of a town, as it was one of the oldest in England, and famous in the Middle Ages for its barley grown on the Great Field, which still remained as it was described in Doomsday. Why not drink? the room might almost be the mess ante-room again!

'I'll have some whisky, I think.'

'Good man.'

The huntsman half filled a glass, and Maddison drank it neat.

'It's a rotten bad business, anyway, putting down fish for fertilizing purposes,' said Mr. Shelley, musingly. 'It's the phosphorus that's valuable; but basic slag seems to be the coming thing.'

He began to pick his teeth with a pin; then he went on musingly:

'Used to be chucked away until recently! You'd hardly believe it, would you? It's no good in a chalk country, I'm told. In my opinion, there's nothing like lime; but all our kilns are disused and falling into ruin. Our forefathers used to get the chalk from France, but that's all finished, unfortunately. The beggars charge so much for transport nowadays, owing to the high wages demanded, that it simply isn't possible, more's the pity.'

'Ah!' said Maddison, holding out his glass for more whisky. He drank it neat again.

'I think the whole fabric of civilization is wrong,' he said. 'It's based on what is called healthy competition; but it should be called filthy competition. It doesn't give human nature a chance. It blossoms, or rather breaks out, into a periodical pox, and young men perish for honour, freedom, and glory, and their name liveth for evermore – evermore being until those that loved them die.'

He finished his whisky and asked for some more.

'Cheerio, young fellar,' said Mr. Shelley, amiably pouring his whisky and soda down his throat, without appearing to swallow.

'Oh, war's a tragedy; no one in his senses will deny that.

But it's deep in human nature, I'm afraid. Look at the natural scheme of life; everything either hunting or being hunted. As for flesh-eating birds or mammals, they're usually the strongest. A peregrine falcon is about the only bird that could fly direct from, say, Lundy to New York. Howard here can tell you about falcons.'

'By Jove, yes,' said Howard. ' "Survival of the fittest," every time. I agree with Maddison that war is tragedy; but it has always been and always will be.'

'But it is exactly that attitude multiplied five hundred million times that makes it inevitable,' said Maddison desperately, and a silence followed.

'I dunno,' said Mr. Shelley. 'I was in the blessed trenches, and I found it stimulating to be under fire. I think the mud-and-blood attitude is overdone, personally. It's the reaction to war-weariness. These pacifist cranks and anti-hunting humanitarians are at the back of it. You can't argue with such people. I was in the trenches, and I didn't feel any fear, I must confess. In fact, I felt stimulated, as I said. I don't believe a hunted animal feels any fear, either. Why, last year a bitch-otter with grown cubs was turned out of the holt below Chapel Wood, and two cubs killed; and what happened? She was back in the same holt this year, with cubs! The pate and rudder are in the ballroom, at this moment! Mark you, I wouldn't go so far as to say that it answers the question of whether an animal likes being hunted, but it might possibly answer the question, "Does an animal *mind* being hunted"?'

'Ah,' said Mr. Chychester, who was looked at.

'Ah ha!' said Maddison, waving his empty glass. 'I watched the stimulated French peasants with their children slouching away from their shattered villages in the Somme country in March 1918; and when I returned there in 1921, they were back again. Mark you, I wouldn't go so far as to say that it answers the question of whether they liked war, but it might possibly answer the question, "Do they *mind* war"?'

'Well done,' said Mr. Shelley. 'But whereas an animal doesn't know what death is, a man does – that makes all the difference, in my opinion. A hunted animal merely runs away because it wants to resume its natural conditions. That's the worst of sentimentality: it endows the animal world with human ways of thought.'

'And if a bloody great boa-constrictor suddenly came into the room, and we all cleared off, it would be because we wanted to resume *our* natural conditions!' laughed Maddison, holding out his glass for more whisky.

Mr. Shelley laughed. 'Well, talking about natural conditions, I've got to be dancing with my wife now, so I'll say au revoir.'

'So must I,' said Howard, adjusting his white tie with a nervous movement, and pulling on a white kid glove. They went away with Mr. Chychester.

'Nice young fellow that,' said Mr. Shelley. 'But his ideas are half-baked, like those of a lot of young people to-day.'

'Ah, the world isn't what it was,' replied Mr. Chychester. 'In my young days they didn't bother their heads about all these things.'

'England's played out, that's the trouble, Chychester. It's only history repeating itself; the Roman Empire before its fall. The age is like this blessed music.'

'Horrible stuff. There'll never be anything to beat the "Blue Danube" waltz.'

In the smoking-room Maddison, remembering old days in the war, happy and hectic 'guest nights' in the mess with friends long vanished, was drinking another glass of whisky and soda.

'Of course,' said Major Shakerley, sidling up to him, and looking at him obliquely through his monocle, 'Shelley didn't get properly under fire. He was in the trenches for a few weeks only, in the spring of '16, when it was quiet. Then being over fifty, they gave him a town-major's job at railhead somewhere.

I think if he'd been through, say, the Somme or Third Ypres, in the infantry, he'd whistle a different tune about being stimulated.'

'Perhaps he has forgotten all but the rum. Well, good health!'

'Good health! He's a good fellow, old Shelley.'

'Rather! But I've generally noticed that it's the fireside heroes who are the fire-eaters; the others have had their guts burnt out by real fire.'

He heard again in the flare-pallid rainy darkness the cries of thousands of wounded men abandoned in the shell-crater morass off the St. Julien road after an attack; abandoned because to step off the duckboard track was to be sucked into the mud, and drowned.

'To hear old men talk now, out of their dark minds, is to see little children charred and broken and blasted by the iron of their ideals! Christ! Think of the colossal light of a barrage, generated by those ideals! And after the attack, "I am the Resurrection and the Life" sniffs the padre, with a sad and serious face, when he ought to say, "I am the corruption and the blight." Christ!'

'Sh-sh-shsh!'

Major Shakerley jerked his monocled face warningly in the direction of the door, through which the tall thin stooping man with sharp features and a brown beard had wandered.

'Lord Edward may hear you.'

'So may Lord Jesus Christ also,' said Maddison ironically. The tall bearded man wandered out again.

'I say, that was a pretty rotten remark for you to make,' said Major Shakerley. 'Damn it all, my dear fellow, you needn't say it to his face.'

'Oh, I wasn't referring to anyone in the flesh,' replied Maddison ironically. 'Good health!'

Major Shakerley got out his case from his hip pocket, carefully selected an oval cigarette, and tapped it leisurely on the jewelled monogram. Then lighting it, he spun the match away, inhaled deeply, removed the cigarette, glanced sideways, and said:

'You talk like a Bolshy.'

Maddison laughed.

'I've never seen one, so I can't agree or disagree, my dear Sir. But I expect I'm about as Bolshy as Shelley was.'

This reply seemed to mystify Major Shakerley, for he frowned, and let fall his monocle again.

'I meant the poet Shelley, not this Shelley.'

'The poet Shelley a Bolshy, what? The author of – well, whatever it was – he wrote a lot of poetry – *If Winter Comes*, was one, wasn't it – anyway, don't you let Shelley hear you say that, that's all I'll say, my young friend. He's very proud of that ancestor of his.'

'So I've heard. About his great-grandfather's fifteenth cousin, wasn't he? Said great-grandfather taking considerable care while Shelley was alive, to prevent the connection leaking out. So I'm told by the family. By the way, do you know what the word 'Bolsheviki' means?'

'Sort of scallywag, I should imagine. A sansculotte – no ass to his trousers – as they were called in the French Revolution.'

'It means, The Majority, as opposed to Mensheviki, which means, The Minority.'

'You're writing a book, aren't you, so young de Wychehalse said.'

'Yes.'

'Ah! That explains it! I begin to see light! All you writin' fellows have got bees in your bonnets – futurists, aren't you? Like that fellow Epstein, who flings a lump of clay against a wall, pulls it endways, gives it a twist with his toes, and calls it Art.'

'You've been reading *Punch*,' said Maddison, 'whose regular contributors, like Jehovah, groan for six days a week while trying to think out ideas for the seventh. Except that their ideas must not be too original, too witty, too erudite, too thoughtful, for the great public that brings in such a splendid profit from advertisements.'

'I say,' said Major Shakerley. 'Is there anything you do approve of in this England of ours? Apparently you're agin Huntin', agin the Church and the State, agin all things that most of us consider the decent thing, in fact, you remind me of the fellow who said that he wasn't out of step, but the rest of the battalion were.' And screwing firmly the glass into his eye, while he held his mouth wide open, Major Shakerley walked away. 'Well, I'm off to have a rubber of bridge.'

Maddison swallowed the rest of his whisky, and shuddered as he finished.

'Hot night, sir. I fancy there's some thunder about,' said the huntsman behind the table as Maddison put down his tumbler. 'May I give you another whisky and soda, sir?'

'No, thanks! I hate the stuff.'

'I can't say I care much for it myself, sir. A cup of hot tea is what I fancy, sir. Heat drives out heat, so they say.'

'Why don't you go and get a cup of tea, if you're thirsty? I'll look after the drinks for you.'

'Thank you very much, sir, but I won't just now, thanking you all the same. I'll wait.'

'Shall I go and get you one? It won't be the least trouble.'

'Very kind of you, sir; but I only meant my remark in a general sort of way. I've been much thirstier in Delville Wood, sir, when the water in the petrol cans was half petrol, and half chloride of lime.'

'Ah! I remember the taste. And the red dust of Ginchy rising in the summer heat, during the bombardment!'

The names recalled others to his mind – Fricourt, Montauban, Contalmaison, Schwaben redoubt, the Wonderwork; and the powerful wraith of that summer of 1916, gone for ever and ever, entered into him, and drove out the present.

He bore the wide and shattered country, every broken wood
and trench and sunken lane, the broad straggling belts of rusty
wire smashed in the chalky loam, everything that his senses
had apprehended, the sun and the sky by day and the flickering roaring horizons by night, the columns of enslaved soldiers
and the stench of bodies freed by death, claimed by the sun
for other purposes. He walked through the door like a man
in a trance, and up and down the hall several times, and his
thought came back to the present, to the world of living men
who cared only for themselves, their own interests, and the
maintaining of things as they were. Birds, hunted animals,
poor men – they had no feeling for them, except perhaps sometimes when they were before their eyes; but no feeling in
imagination. How then could they be expected to agree that
their children must not grow up like them?

As he thought of a world inhabited by men with imagina-
tions grown naturally from childhood his mind became
radiant with a light in which all the old world of sorrow and
darkness was melted as metal, and poured into the new mould
of his ecstatic spirit. In that world a Jesus would not be a
man of sorrow, acquainted with grief – or a man of rage and
despair lashing the selfish money-grubbers with a whip: a
Shelley would not be stuck against a wall with mud-balls by
his fellow Etonians: a Ramsay Macdonald not be persecuted
by politically-hired roughs and kicked out of a golf-club
because he cried out against the slaughter of innocent millions:
landlords would not see their slum property or their foul coal
mines without weeping: the Bolsheviks would know what a
mighty man was the Jesus they mocked, or what they thought
was Jesus, out of the mouths of priests who said, God ordains
your sufferings and sores, poor Russian people. Yes, my way
is the true way! he thought, and felt the power returning to
him. The Star-born!

The tall thin bearded man moved in the hall towards him;
hands in pockets of his antiquated dress suit, the uncreased

trousers of which ended a conspicuous distance above his big shoes. He stopped, and leaned his head sideways, looking down at Maddison from his superior height.

'I heard what you said just now,' he said, 'and I want to know you. I liked your face immediately I saw you, and thought you had – er – that rare *something*.'

Maddison looked up at his face, and half closed his eyes as he scrutinized his features.

'I suppose physically we are alike,' he said. 'You've got the small head, and arrowy look. Francis Thompson had it, and Burns, and J. M. Synge and Masefield, judging by their photographs. Shelley too – if one disregards that wretched libel supposed to have been done by Mrs. Leigh Hunt.'

The other man nodded, as he swayed backwards and forwards, hinged it seemed, from the bony fists thrust down into his trousers pockets.

'Yes,' he said, in a soft high-pitched voice, 'yes. Where do you live?'

'Speering Folliot. My name's Maddison.'

The other man nodded as he swayed.

'Mine's Edward Rawleigh. We must foregather sometime. Yes.'

He seemed to sink into a reverie. 'People see – you *see*.'

An elderly woman wearing a diamond tiara came up behind him, and poked him in the back with her fan.

'Come, Edward,' she said, in a decided voice, 'you are supposed to be dancing with me,' and together they went away into the ballroom. Maddison leant against the door, watching for Mary, and examining the faces of the dancers.

The fortunate young people lived outward, not inward, lives; their contentedness was not blighted by the new world-consciousness; everything in their lives they accepted, without thought, as good and proper things. Of one strapping and cheery maiden, his partner in the sixth dance, he had asked why she went otter-hunting; the question had surprised her, and she had drawn back her curly-bobbed head to give him a quick glance, and she had answered, 'Oh, one does, you know. And if he had asked her why she did not go badger-digging, she would have made an identical movement of her curly-bobbed head, and answered, 'Oh, one does not, you know.' They were charming baa-lambs, with no consciousness of the pastures of the mind; and the elderly ewes, their mothers, stamped their feet at anything that was not grass, tree, fence, or the shepherd Tory Member of Parliament. Ah! There she was, his grave and beautiful and innocent Mary.

He went back into the bar, where a little fat man with head and face a shining pink, save for a huge grey moustache, like the wings of a seagull, was standing talking to Jim.

'Why, it's Maddison,' he cried, flipping up first one wing of his moustache, then the other, and rolling towards him like a small barrel, with hands outstretched. 'Have a drink, ol' boy, do.'

He pushed a glass of whisky and soda into his hand.

'My God, Bungy, I'm glad to see you!' cried Maddison. 'I saw you last at Le Cateau! Christ! They were the days!'

'Drink up, Maddison, old boy. I saw you on the stairs, and nearly came up to fetch you: but I know, old boy, I know! Here's good luck to you, old boy! Nor forgetting the twenty-third cavalry! The finest regiment on God's earth, old boy, but those days are gone; those days are – gone.'

They drank.

'What are you doing down here, old boy?'

'Oh, just living here, Bungy.'

'So am I, old boy, so am I. And a jolly fine place it is, too.'

He gulped down his whisky, and asked for another.

'There's no romance left to-day, old boy,' he exclaimed. 'No standing by for "gaps" in the next war. Remember Monchy? The Hindenburg Line? They were the days! But now they're going to mech-mech-mechanalyse the poor old calvary, and put 'em in tanks. Fancy riding in an iron dust-bin, ol' boy!'

305

He looked pathetically into Maddison's eyes, and shook him by the hand for nearly a minute.

'Well, chances and changes, ol' boy, chances and changes. I've had my day. I ended up a captain in the dear old twenty-third, and I began as a boy in India in '75. I'm not a public school man, you know. You won't find in me the gesture of a gentleman. No, ol' boy, I had to fight my own way up, through the quartermaster's stores. A clean crime-sheet all the way. And here I am, ol' boy, in this beautiful old place, talking to dear old Maddison. By Jove, it's good to see your old face again! Have a drink, ol' boy, and keep me company.'

'I won't, thanks very much, Bungy,' said Maddison, not knowing what to say further to him. Yet Bungy had been one of his best friends in the regiment.

Other men came into the room, and greeted Bungy, and Maddison slipped away.

Dancing the next dance with Jean, he collided with the young man with the pale face who, after drawling, 'Sorry old thing,' to Jean, glided on as swiftly as ever with his partner. 'Silly ass,' said Jean, and told Maddison about him.

Apparently the young man had recently come into a considerable fortune, amassed by his grandfather in the business of curing bacon, and the fortune was rapidly disappearing. The only exercise he took was on wheels, or in artificial light. Owing to a supposed delicate constitution he had never been to any school or university, but had been conserved until he came of age by the care of governesses and tutors.

'Poor devil,' said Maddison, looking at the supercilious face.

'He will be before long, if he goes on in the same way,' replied Jean.

'He rented some shooting last year at Millmouth, and had what he called deer-stalking parties in the woods, going after the tame fallow deer with rifles and revolvers. When this bored him, he shot at the nesting cormorants and gulls from the edge of the cliffs. Of course nobody living round about was with him – they were his new London friends. He rents a grouse moor and deer forest in Scotland, a villa on the Riviera, a place in Sussex, a house on the Lido, a flat in London, and a suite of rooms at the Savoy. Besides his racing cars and aeroplanes, he bought an old battleship in order to blow it up in Bideford Bay.'

'What fun!'

'He wasn't allowed to do it. Have you seen what he's brought with him to-night? Every one's talking about them. Tidd'n modest like vor bwoy an' maiden to go rumpsin about zo, be ut, Wull? He won't dance with anyone else: damned good job too. I believe he only came here to try and make me jealous.'

This was an entirely new Jean speaking; he felt uneasy with her. Perhaps the champagne at supper had magnified a trait hitherto hidden.

'Why should he do that, Jean?'

'Oh, he's always playing the fool.'

She added, with a scornful air induced by the recollection of her own sympathetic pity for him on past occasions, 'Tony Leaver was always hanging round, and giving me cameras, saddles, and other presents, the idiot!' She gave a self-contemptuous shrug. 'I don't think anyone's worth caring a damn about. *I* don't care a damn about anyone. I wish I were a man: wouldn't I just have some fun with the girls!'

Poor Jean! He could see how her eyes were roving for Howard. Poor supercilious young man, with his mask to life!

The fat little man with the grey moustache wings bumped into them, fell down, got up, and apologized with a desperate politeness that caused a minor congestion behind them. Seeing this, he apologized the more profusely to all the assorted old boys, explaining to each and all that his polo knee, confound it, had given way. Then seizing his smiling partner, he bobbed on again, the dome of his head reflecting the electric lights above as he whirled around.

'That old "Bungy-pon-Truckles, all vlesh and no knuckles."
There's too much in the little barrel to-night, the naughty old
man. 'Tis a proper high-go-glee party to-night, bant it?'

'Old Bungy was one of my best friends in the regiment. Do
you know him?'

'Know Bungy? Every one knows Bungy. He's a dear. He
takes poor boys from the slums of Bristol camping on the
Burrows every August, paying for them himself; and he hasn't
got much money.'

Dear simple little Bungy's 'gesture of a gentleman'! How
many like him were gone in the soil of France: British,
American, French, German, Belgian! Dead in honour!

Tears came into his eyes, but fortunately Jean, whose own
eyes were slightly bloodshot, did not appear to notice. She
observed, however, his preoccupation for the rest of the dance,
and when they were sitting out she asked him if he were fed-up
with the dance. Oh no, he replied instantly, and she wondered
if her sister were responsible. He was thinking, I'm just a
sentimentalist, after all: a mere sentimental reactionary.
When that red-faced fool says that free education was ruining
England, I feel like hitting him over the head with a bottle:
and yet I hate education. Then I loathe those war memorials
with their false symbols: and now 'dead in honour' moves
me to tears. Christ! I'm a humbug! Christ! I wish I could
be normal!

'Well, thanks very much,' said Jean. The band had begun
for the fifteenth dance.

'Thank you,' he said, bowing.

'Shut up, you ass,' and giving him a smile, she moved into
the noisy throng of bare arms and necks and frocks and stiff
white shirts.

'Well, Diana,' he said during the next dance, 'I've been
talking to your father.'

'This is rather sudden,' she replied. 'I thought from the look
of things you would have been talking with Mrs. Ogilvie.'

'I like your father.'

'Snubbed again. Serves me right. No, no, no, don't be a silly! You are not to take the least notice of me. I'm glad you like daddy. He's a good sort.'

'He told me about the buzzards screaming at him, and –'

' "As though the woods belonged to the blessed birds"? Well, since we've been here only from fourteen hundred, I expect the buzzards have got as good a right to them as we have. I love to watch them soaring, high up in the sky over the valley. So does daddy, really. What else did he say?'

'Oh, he talked about lime-kilns, and what his brother said to the fishmonger.'

'Oh yes, he's always telling that story. He thinks it has solved the Coal Problem. One day he will send it to the local paper, and it will appear in the propaganda column under the heading "Political Buzzings," by "The Bee." And he'll read it over several times, and think he's done his bit to save England from going to the dogs.'

He danced the ultimate dance with Mary. Holding her close during the gallop to *John Peel* at the end, while hunting horns were blown and wild whoops and yoi-overs filled the room, he begged her to change her shoes quickly, and leave with him before the others. The card-players stood in the gallery, and looked down with tired amusement on the sliding and prancing mass below. Major Shakerley, beside Mrs. Ogilvie, had fixed his monocle specially for the sight. 'Bungy,' who had gallantly but rashly 'stayed the course,' as he had put it, fell over, and caused a small commotion around his procumbent form. He closed his eyes and murmured easily, as though he were in the sergeants' mess, 'I'm popped'; but when helped to his feet he was heard to complain, in a different, haughtier voice, about a polo knee.

In the hall Maddison waited for Mary, looking anxiously at the stairs. A long loose hand touched him on the shoulder, and a head bent down like an eagle on a pinnacle, and a gentle voice said, 'Don't worry your young head too much about ephemera, my dear; remember the mind-forged manacles,' and was gone before he could think words of gratitude.

The crowd of animated girls and young men, and the faded chaperones were delighted by a scene that occurred about two minutes later. A smiling man with a pleasant American accent went up to the white-faced monocled young man – whom they all despised, because, in an age when money was so scarce, he had so much money and was wasting it – and said affably but audibly:

'I heard the remark you made about my wife during supper, young man. I don't know who you are, and I don't care, but when next you go to a dance, just take that pebble out of your eye and throw it away among the bushes. It will be safer for you,' and buttoning up his coat, he went away.

'What is it he said, Tony?' asked the girl with Mr. Leaver.

'Oh, he's just an American boor.'

'Just a what, Tony?'

'An American boor, I said.'

'A what?'

'A boo-oo-oor!' exclaimed Mr. Leaver loudly, yawning behind three fingers. He drew a deep breath, and let it out again inaudibly. 'Good night, Jean,' he said, between his teeth as she passed, wrapped in her blue cloak.

'Good night, Tony,' said Jean, steadying her own breathing, that she might say calmly:

'Good night, Howard. It's been ripping. Thanks so much, Aunt Lucy. Oh, there's mother and the others. Cheerio everybody.'

'We must wait for Mary. Has anyone seen Mary? And where is Captain Maddison?'

'I rather fancy they left about three minutes ago, Mrs Ogilvie,' said Mr. Stukeley.

'Oh, I expect they will be waiting for us on the quay. Good

night, Lucy, my dear. It has been splendid. Your decorations were really charming. Good night, Howard. Come and see us soon. Good night. Good night!'

They stepped on to gravel, and were amidst the slam of doors, voices, gear changing, yellow lamps of pre-war motor-cars, blinding sweep of light from modern cars departing, and a high round silver moon over the black foliage of trees.

'It's too bad of Mary to leave us like this,' said Mrs. Ogilvie to Mr. Chychester, as they walked on the grassy border of the drive. 'The whole thing is wretchedly humiliating. I would never have brought him here if I had known he was going to behave so stupidly. Did you hear what Miss Goff said to Lucy, and to Mrs. Pinker and Mrs. King? The whole of North Devon will have heard by to-morrow.'

'H'm,' said Mr. Chychester, 'I shouldn't worry about it, my dear. No one bothers about what interfering old spinsters say. Those middle-class people fancy themselves too much alto-gether. Besides, what business of hers is it who you bring to a dance?'

'It's the children I'm thinking about,' said Mrs. Ogilvie. 'It isn't fair to them. After all, we've allowed him to make his home with us – although we know nothing about him, really, and in spite of all those wretched rumours I begin to think that Miss Goff is right after all; Mary is much too good to be allowed to spoil herself.'

'I shouldn't bother my head about 'em,' said Mr. Chyches-ter. 'If you believe all that people say, you'd never have anything left to believe in.'

They walked down the drive in silence. Mr. Chychester was rehearsing in his mind the annihilation of slugs and snails in his rock-garden, which he intended to lime when he got back, by lantern-light. He imagined the long brown black-blotched slugs curling up, and the green bubbling of the snails, with much satisfaction: they had eaten his solitary rare Alpine dwarf rose, and would have to pay for it.

Chapter 14

Moonlight was streaming on the water, and glistening in points on the wet stones of the Sharshook; the grey space before them was filled with the noises of water swiftly, as though stealthily, moving up the estuary; their shadows were grey on the grey ridge, and discernible only when they moved. Five lights burned in windows of the village a quarter of a mile away. Sometimes a diffused ray of light whisked above the Ridge trees on the hill, swept round, and vanished.

A voice came from a long low black shape crossing the straight track of tarnished silver below them. Sweeps knocked and creaked, blades dipped and flickered, and the boat moved into greyness lit by occasional glints. A shadow stood still below them. A hoarse voice in the now invisible boat said from over the water, 'Ease up a bit'; another voice said, 'The toff's standing by, father,' and the hoarse voice replied, 'Corbooger, tidden no odds if God a'Mighty were standing by. Ease up, I tell ee.'

'It's unlawful to let the seine drift,' whispered Mary. 'Perhaps they think we're water-bailiffs?'

'They'd be in a boat. One night they rammed the water-bailiffs' boat, and sank it. That's old Jimmy Chugg. I'll have a game with him in a minute.'

They walked down the Sharshook, their feet crunching on the gravel. Suddenly before them a disk floated as still and round, but brighter, than the low moon. The water in the pit was dark and still.

'It's like a water-lily,' whispered Mary.

'They will hear us here,' he whispered, leading her on.

The moon's image slid forward into blackness, and shone

before them in pit after pit, where gravel had been dug. They watched the flashes of the Lundy lighthouses over the sea, which lay mysterious and immense in the still summer night. She walked beside him, feeling a dream of her real self. He startled her by the bitter intensity of his voice:

'Oh, I am a fool! Why did I speak to those men like that? I knew all the while they would never understand. Why did I go at all? Years ago I knew I could not be myself among insensitive people.'

She did not know what to say.

'Your mother does not like me. How can she like me? What have I ever done that is likeable? She has been kind to me: I have struggled hundreds of times to get straight with her, but every time I speak she wonders what the devil I am driving at; so I pull back into my shell like a snail whose horns have been touched with lime, and writhe in my own ineffectuality. No, don't touch me, for God's sake. I must get straight with you first.'

She looked at him, longing, as she had been longing all the evening, to comfort him. His suffering, and the things he suffered for, were more real to her than to him; and she suffered the more, as always, that she could not release him. She was beginning to believe that it was not in her power to help him; he did not seem to need her.

'Mary, I want to ask you something. I think you must know what it is. But I am poor, and soon I shall be kicked out of the cottage. So how can I say to you – no, I can't say it.'

He groaned, savagely disordering his hair.

'You won't always be poor if you work,' she faltered. 'Only – can't you work regularly, and not in those long bursts? I'm sure you could, if you – had – me – to look after you.'

'Would you?' he faltered. 'Oh, Mary, would you marry me, supposing I asked you?'

'Didn't you know I would, Billy?'

'I thought you might,' he replied. 'What a horrible proposal this must be! But I haven't yet proposed. Mary, please will you marry me?'

'Yes, Billy.'

'Thank you very much,' he said, smoothing his hair. 'I think we ought to be getting back now, don't you?'

They returned beside the flooded gravel pits, to where the fishermen were hauling on their net.

'Let's see what luck they've had,' he said. 'Mary, I wish I could have the dance all over again! Oh, dear, I'm just beginning to enjoy it.'

The fishermen hauled in silence. The tide had carried their net up the river, and added its weight to the meshes. After a quarter of an hour's hauling they drew in the empty seine.

'Tes oudering over,' said a voice below them. Beside the moon, ringed with spectral colours, were accumulating peaks and precipices of clouds. 'Tes a master storm makin' up, a' reckon.'

'We'd better be going,' said Maddison. 'I suppose we can walk to the Crow? Is that water over there, or moonlight?' They looked towards the shingle tongue half a mile distant.

'Let's ask them. I say,' he called out, assuming a different voice, 'please can you tell me if it's safe to walk to the Crow now?'

'If you don't mind getting wet.'

'Oh Lord! How wet?' he said, imagining himself carrying Mary.

'Corbooger, don't ee try to walk it!' cried the hoarse voice. 'Tes the spring, and the flow travels vaster'n a dog can ait witpot. You'll be drownded, surenuff, if you try to walk to the Neck.'

'My God!' said Maddison in his own voice. 'Then us won't ait no more witpot!'

They all laughed, without ceasing to shake and pile the net. Sometimes a heel crushed a crab.

'Ave ee lost your way, then?'

'Yes.'

'Tes strange time vor traipsing 'bout,' said the hoarse voice. 'I've knowed young men and maids avore go mazed i' th' head under th' moon. Be ee London visitors?'

'Noomye! Us'v been tu a proper high-go-glee party.'

'Tes gentry,' loudly whispered a voice. 'Tes gentry to Wildernesse.'

'Be ee wanting to go vor to the Crow, zur?'

'Yes, please. No hurry.'

'Can ee wait while us shoots a couple more drafts? Us'll be packing up then. Tes aisy nuff getting to Craw, but twull be turrible hard pulling back against the tide.'

'You'll take us then?'

'What's it worth?'

'What do you want?'

'Aw, us won't quarrel 'bout that. Ten bob?'

'Ten bob! That's a month's rent!'

'Aw, bain't the young leddy's life worth a dog's licence? I know you gennulmen got plenty o' money.'

'I haven't got any on me. Very well, I'll pay you ten bob if you'll trust me. I shall have to earn it first by writing an article on salmon-fishing in a Devon estuary by night.'

He knew that the ordinary charge for ferrying by day was a shilling a head.

There was whispering in the boat. 'Tes 'e, I tell ee, father! I knaws'n by his voice. Tes Mr. Madd'zn.'

'Be ee Mr. Madd'zn?' asked the hoarse voice, 'what used to board with John Mules the gravedigger to Speering Folly?'

'I be, Jimmy Chugg.'

'Corbooger, why didn't ee say so? I thought 'twere a visitor from London. Us'll take ee for naught, midear, and the young leddy with ee.'

'Thanks, but I'd rather pay you.'

'Gitoom! I won't take naught for it! Be ould Biell with ee?'

'No, he's at home.'

'Proper ould dog. My childer do love'n. 'A used tu visit us reg'lar when you was boarding to John Mules.'

The net was piled in the stern, and after a couple of minutes' wait the boat was shoved into the gliding grey water, away from the dark upright figure leaning back with the rope wound round its middle. They watched the boat swiftly travelling up the estuary, dropping its regulation two hundred yards of net behind it. The tide was now flowing at the pace of a walking man.

'I don't believe the tide has cut us off yet,' said Maddison, staring in the direction of the Crow. 'It was a ruse to get ten bob out of us. No, that's a mean thought.'

'It comes in frightfully sudden and fast. Listen!'

A subdued but insistent noise was arising from the insubstantial expanse before them. At first they could not decide whether or not it was the tide, for from the whole ridge about them came innumerable trickling sounds. The moonlight faded, and with the growing shade the noise increased and was plainly that of water pouring into pools and around rocks. It grew louder every moment.

'It's lucky we didn't try and cross,' said Mary, holding his arm tight. 'It would be hard going on those rocks, even in moonlight. I've watched the tide coming in there by day. It pours in terribly fast!'

'We must get a boat,' he said. 'And we'll call it the "Pinta." We'll go exploring up the rivers, camping out, when we're married.'

'I'll cook for ee, my dear.'

'I'll make the fire. We'll always see the stars. O Mary, sweet moorhen, we'll go walking with packs on our backs, and sleeping on haystacks, and in barns! We'll tramp across Europe!'

'I've always wanted to do that.'

'We'll go to Rookhurst, and build a boat, and make a hut →rebuild the one on Heron Plume's Island, that Jack and I made. We'll wave at the Normans as we pass their house, but we won't stop. Mrs. Norman will come out, and say how pleased she is to see me, and how glad she is I am at last making good.'

'I don't like her, Billy! When I stayed there as a child, she used to say how untidy I was, and had no gloves to go to church in. I liked him, though.'

'A chocolate-box artist. Calls Hardy a pessimist, having heard somebody else saying it one night at the Chelsea Arts Ball.'

'Don't bother about other people. They're quite happy. I shan't let you waste yourself any more. You're mine, my darling.'

'I shan't ever worry now I'm with ee, my swallow-brow. Old Clippety-Clop. Old Moorhen. Mary Lœtitia Ogilvie, spinster, of this parish, to William Beare Maddison, bachelor, also of this parish. Old Garside beaming. He's a good sort – extraordinary how men are all the same, except for the barnacles of illusions that bore into them. Do you know, there's a sort of barnacle that bores into a male crab, destroying its reproductive organs, and then the crab grows like a female, even laying eggs; and the parasite stays there, clinging like a bean under its tail, protected by the crab, who cherishes it as though it were its own. No more crabs if that illusion-offspring became general!'

'You must write a book about birds.'

'I will. No more illusions for. me – I shall become an observer of the human scene. I must cultivate a slow, quiet way of speaking, and an urbane manner. I shall grow fat.'

'You funny little boy,' she said, and he kissed her, while she smoothed his hair. 'You'll never do that. I like your second name, Beare.'

'It means "Wood." Every eldest son was called "Beare." After the Rookhurst Forest, I suppose: it's cut down now, all those lovely beeches. They're covered with foxgloves in

317

summer. Good heavens, it's summer now! How can it be summer, if the rooks are not in the forest, and Jack and I are not in the crowstarver's spinney in the Big Wheatfield?'

'You are just the same Willie Maddison,' she said, framing his face with her hands. 'The same sweet little boy with the sad wondering eyes: only you were horrid to me, weren't you, my darling? There was Mary, waiting all the time to be your friend, and you didn't want her. Perhaps you don't want her now, really.'

'I always wanted you – only I didn't see you, because others were in the way, and I couldn't see through them. If only I had seen you first! I say, shall we keep our engagement secret?'

'Yes. It's nothing to do with anyone else, is it?'

'Shall we tell Jean?'

Mary considered this: Jean could not keep things to herself.

'No, let's keep it for just ourselves! There's plenty of time later on to tell people.'

'Ages. We shan't want to get married for a year or two, shall us?'

'Two years would be nice.' She snuggled in his arms. 'Hark at the water now, William Beare!'

'It's like a torrent, Mary Lœtitia.'

A harsh cry came from the sky.

'What was that?'

'It was too prolonged for a heron. No gulls about to-night, surely.'

'It may be one of the divers. What a ghastly cry! The fishermen used to say there was a thing here called The Crake, which used to cry in the night when someone was going to be drowned. A Captain Charles Hook was drowned off here once: that's where the name Sharshook came from, they say.'

'It was like the scream of a man bayoneted in the stomach.'

'Don't!'

'My dear, I'm sorry. I'm going to forget the War. "Drive your plough over the bones of the dead," said Blake. Well, I'm not even going to plough.' He added, 'And I suppose I shan't sow or reap. Reap what? I want to have a healthy mind in a healthy body!'

'Gitoom!' she replied, 'you've got both already.'

'And I've got you, too.'

He embraced her.

'Mary!'

'What?'

'Two years, Mary?'

She laughed, blushing. 'I'll see. Oh, Billy –'

He wanted to tell her about Eveline Fairfax.

'Mary, do you realize about her? I'd better tell you now; or shall I wait until our wedding night? Then you might leave me, as Angel Clare left Tessy Durbeyfield.'

'Now what must I do? Leave ee? Very well.'

She walked out of his embrace, and stood an arm's length away.

'Now I'll come back to ee.' Shyly she put her arms round him: 'Now I'm back again to ee.'

They walked about on the gravel ridge, talking of the happiness that was now spread before their lives. Again he declared that he had been foolish to rant: in tranquillity he identified himself with Miss Goff: he and she were two human beings who ranted about others, and were identical except that her bonnet contained different stinging bees from his own.

'She does such a lot of good. From my cottage window I can see her working in the churchyard, while the children run about with their small pairs of shears, cutting the grass and, when her back is turned, creeping up behind each other, and biting them in the back with the points as they bend down. Day after day in the spring she was there, among her roses and primulas and pansies and wallflowers and sweetwilliams. She does it for the sake of beauty. If ever an old man or woman is sick or in trouble, she is there to offer her help. That is her true self then; her bees are not active.'

319

'I wish they weren't quite so active sometimes.'

'Well, they drove her as a moral duty to society to Mules' Cousin Billy's Widow, to have an immoral good-for-nothing young man kicked out of her cottage. "Miss Goff's very fond of Miss Mary," sniggered Mules in triplicate, to cheer me up, as he dipped a rabbit's ribs in a cup of tea and then picked them apart, one by one, to suck between his gums. "Very good family, Miss Mary. Very good family, Miss Mary. That's as true as I'm sitting here, Miss Goff said so, only don't you please say I told ee. You won't forget the poor old gravedigger when you'm high-up, wull ee, midear? Poor Mules, zur, poor old gravedigger, tes hard work breaking the ground, zur. Wan thing, us'll have so good a place in heaven as they 'igh-class gentry, won't us, midear?" '

They kissed.

'You imitate him jolly well!'

'Ah, I am myself now, because my bees are not active!'

They heard the curlews crying down the estuary.

'Mary,' he said, looking at her with the strange childlike gentleness that had always moved her.

'Yes, dear one?'

'Sometimes I feel I shan't live very much longer. If I do die, will you put on my stone that epitaph I quoted to you, to another William Maddison? It's on the church wall at Rookhurst.'

'You're not going to die, silly,' she replied, fondly. 'I'm going to look after ee.'

She squeezed his hand, and saw with a stir of faint sadness that she could not move the mood from him.

He began quoting softly.

> 'Silence (deare Shado) will best thy grave become
> and griefe that is not only deep but dumbe
> For who'll beleive our vocall teares, but see
> The very tongues themselves, here dead in thee

Twelve welspunn lustres sent thee speechlesse hence
Twice child in age, always in innocence
to smooth thy Entrance, where true blisse doth raigne,
Nature and Grace would have thee borne againe.'

'It's strange and beautiful,' said Mary. 'But what are the
"twelve welspunn lustres"? '

'I used to think they were candles for the twelve apostles.
Actually, of course, they weren't "lustres" at all. Paul, who
came after Jesus' death, was the only one who had glimmer-
ings: then he was illuminated. I tried to get far deeper into
life than that in *The Star-born*, and of course I failed.'

He began to talk about *The Star-born*: it must be finished,
and sent off to a publisher. Then he must begin his War
novel, which was to be so true a transcript from reality that
it would be in spirit the story of every soldier in every army
in the Great War.

'I shall put your mother in it, and Michael, and when she
reads it she will see me as I am, and be glad that I am to be her
son-in-law. And I shall write about my father, whom I think
about often, with love and understanding. After that, a new
fairy-tale book for children; following that, a book on village
life. Then I want to rewrite the life of Jesus. Oh, lustres – how
I gabble on! A lustre is five years. So he was sixty when he
died.'

The rattle of stones rolled in the swift tide in the direction
of the Crow had diminished; the tide flowed wider in the Neck
Gut by the far shore, and was spreading in to the Sharshook
by the shallow gulfs and pools among the flat rocks. They
heard the noises of its stealthy advances, and soon the sound
of falling water, for the tide setting in hard not only slanted
the fairway buoys, but ran up them and flung over the stems
in plumes that glistened in the moon. The shape of a boat
rode past the ridge at the speed of a trotting horse, and another
following it; they had come from the sandy spit called the

South Tail at the estuary mouth nearly two miles distant, in under quarter of an hour.

'Zaip out the fore-boat, I tell ee,' cried the hoarse voice near them. 'Tes litter all auver.' There followed the scrape of a bailing-can, and the swish of water on wood.

'They're preparing the boat for the high-class gentry and me,' said Maddison. 'Come on, my beauty. Shall I carry you down?' Without waiting for an answer he picked her up and staggered down to the boat.

'Beggin' your pardon, zur,' said the hoarse voice, 'but if you'll excuse me, you're carrying a better load home than us will.'

'No luck?'

'A couple of dirty old rough fish – bass.' He pronounced it 'base.' 'You'm welcome to them, zur. I owe you somerthing for curing my l'il boy of nimpingangs.'

'Oh, stop your rattle, Jimmy!'

'He was always a nervous li'l chap, but tes a brave boy you've made of'n now. T'other day 'a wanted to put his finger vor the vire, to show 'a wadden frightened, 'a did!'

'Tes true!' said the youth.

They swung into the tide, and glided up the estuary. Five minutes later they jumped from the bow of the boat on to the Crow sands, and with the two fish set off for the White House.

'What have you been doing now?' she asked. 'What are nimpingangs?'

'Poof! I know more about your own country than you do,' he replied.

'That doesn't answer my question, Billy.'

'Oh, that was nothing, really. The little tacker had festered hands, and was terrified of going to a doctor; and as I didn't like the look of them, I treated him myself.'

'But how?'

'Well, it was no trouble to get him to let me cut away the

dead skin with scissors, for he was a friend of mine already.
You know the boy, don't you? Paddy Chugg.'

'Yes. He has a beautiful face, rather pale.'

'That's because he sleeps with too many blankets on his bed
at night, and always with the window shut. Since I cured his
hands, his mother is half inclined to believe me when I tell
her that colds are caused by germs living in stuffy air, and
not by cold fresh air.'

'But didn't he yell when you used the scissors? He is a very
timid little boy.'

'Only because everything tends to make him timid. I had
to dissolve that rind away first, by telling him that I used to cry
when I was a little boy, and indeed, often cried now. Then I
looked at his hands, and said I would take the pain away if
he liked, without hurting him. But he could please himself.
After hesitation, he said he would. So I sterilized scissors and
a needle in a spirit flame, and went to work very carefully.
To his surprise it didn't hurt. I knew that, and told them all –
it was in his cottage, with half a dozen kids looking on – "You
know, this boy is brave! He bears pain better than many men
I've seen." Meanwhile I opened the iodine bottle. "Now be
prepared to hop!" I said, as I dipped the brush in the iodine
bottle. "It won't hurt, but it will sting!" He held his hand
still, and I put a tiny touch on one of the raw places. "Hop!"
I said, "Hop it away!" He laughed, and said, "Gitoom, I don't
trouble," the centre of an admiring group of children. So I
dipped the brush on, and he winced. "That must sting frightfully?" I said. "I don't trouble!" he announced to the crowd.
"Well, hold out the other hand, to make it even: then each
pain will drive out the other." "Aow!" he cried, laughing, and
hopped about, while the children laughed. "Aw, tidden
nowt!" he boasted. There was no repression of natural feelings
of fear and dread, you see; and I told the children that to
be afraid was natural, and that it was the stupidest thing in
the world to pretend not to be afraid. Hence these fish.'

They walked with the moon in their faces, towards the curve of the Bight. Birds piped and trilled on the mud-flats, over which the sea was spreading. They turned north along the shore with the moon over their left shoulders; and walked on, with the black mass of the beached hospital ship looming bigger and blacker as they approached it. The hull was shored upright with props, and held by chains stretched over their heads and secured to rusty anchors half-buried in the low sandy cliff. The moon shone on the gilt knight-heads, and illumined the dewy letters of NYMPHEN on its bows. They heard coughing inside the hulk, for Luke was the caretaker of the cholera ship, which had not received a case for more than thirty years.

'They say it is going to be sold soon,' said Mary.

'I know. Let's buy it! And live in it! The magpies have their nests in trees, the fox has his earth, and we'll have the old ship! I'll grow potatoes and cabbages over there – plenty of seaweed handy – and catch fish; we'll make the place as snug as a badger's earth.'

'Will it be very expensive, do you think?'

'I shouldn't think so. I was looking over it the other day: it's only fit for firewood. They say in Speering that the chap who bought the 'Revenge' is the only likely man to buy it, and he won't give more than thirty pounds. I'll finish "Star-born," and get an advance in royalties, perhaps. I'll start to-morrow morning, and finish it in a week!'

Mary smiled at his enthusiasm; she found pleasure in his changefulness, remembering how, when he was leaving after his first visit in the winter, he had declared his indifference to what money that very book might earn. While she had understood how he had felt on that occasion, yet she preferred this way of regarding it – apart from what the money would mean to them both. It seemed more natural, somehow.

So they agreed to keep the betrothal a secret, and on Mary's suggestion nothing was to be done about making enquiries about the *Nymphen* until *The Star-born* was finished and accepted and an advance paid.

'I wish I hadn't had that filthy whisky to drink. Horrible muck! Or talked like a fool to that amazing half-wit, Shakerley.'

'Bother Major Shakerley: he's an old cynic. I wish you'd forget about silly people, and not waste yourself on thinking about them. There, I've been lecturing you, dear,' she said, her voice deepening in her throat as she fondled his free arm.

The air by the house seemed thicker, as though the light shining through the open hall door were heating the drive. Moonlight swept down a precipice in the mountainous clouds, and seven silver swans rode in the old, uneven glass of one of the bedroom windows. Its pallid glance cooled the air, and again the night was dim and close. They went in.

Mrs. Ogilvie sat by the table, her face worn and lined with fatigue. She wore an overcoat; a cat was asleep on her lap. She was checking figures written in a book with a black cover, on which was a printed label *Slum Cripples and Orphans Society*, of which she had been a local secretary for more than a decade. It was her ambition to collect one hundred pounds in one year; she had never exceeded eighty-three.

The cat jumped off her lap as they entered the hall. Mrs. Ogilvie continued to tot up a column, although her concentration had vanished the instant she had heard them walking down the drive. With her pen she touched figure after figure, while her lips moved, twenty-five, twenty-six, twenty-seven, twen – meaningless figures. In a moment she would look up. The cat was mewing plaintively, and arching itself against Maddison. Twenty-seven, twenty-eight, twenty, thirty. She closed the book.

'You're working very late, Aunt Connie,' said Maddison.

She felt better. 'I was just passing away the time until you returned. Now that you are here, I can go to bed.'

Maddison glanced at Mary. 'I say, I'm awfully sorry. You

look very tired. I had no idea you would be waiting up. We've been enjoying ourselves, watching the salmon-fishing. Haven't we, Mary? Look, we've got two fine bass for breakfast.'

He held up the fish, an act that caused a frenzied mewing from the cat, but no effect whatsoever on Mrs. Ogilvie.

'It seems a strange time to go fishing,' she said. 'Mary, do please put that animal outside, and stop its noise.'

'Don't bother, I'll take the fish in the pantry,' said Maddison. 'I'll clean them while I'm about it. I say, Aunt Connie, don't wait up any longer, please.'

There was silence until he had reached the end of the flagged passage.

'Really, Mary,' said Mrs. Ogilvie, removing her spectacles, 'I should have thought you would have known better than to have behaved like this. We had not the faintest idea where you were.'

'We told Gerry Stukeley, Mother.'

'Oh yes, we knew you had gone on; but why did you go? What will people say? It will only confirm what they are saying already.'

Mary looked at her mother unhappily, for she was really upset. She did not know what to say, so she went to her mother, to put her arm on her shoulders, but her mother moved away.

'It's all very well, my girl: but you can't escape so easily as that, you don't realize quite what has happened. He hasn't the least idea of decency, or how to behave as a gentleman. However, I thought I could rely on your good sense. You will be the talk of the neighbourhood. As though it weren't bad enough already to have one daughter's name bandied about.'

'I'm sorry, Mother,' said Mary.

'What is the use of being sorry? Why be sorry? It isn't for myself I am concerned. I don't matter in the least. It's you that matters, if only you could see it.'

'But, Mother, we've only been watching the fishermen, as we've done many times before.'

'That isn't anything; of course you are old enough to look after yourself in that respect. According to Major Shakerley, Bill has been saying the most disgraceful things; if he had been drinking there might perhaps have been some excuse. He is hopeless, as I suspected from the very first time he came into the house.'

'He did have a little to drink,' faltered Mary, 'but only because he was lonely. Mother dear, you're tired out. I'm to blame, darling: there now, go to bed, and don't worry. Bill said nothing wrong, I'm sure; Major Shakerley is an old silly. Please don't worry any more, Mother.'

'Worry? How can I help worrying? Do you think I can help worrying when I hear my daughter's name linked to that of a man who openly sneers at everything that is good and decent? A man who says the most blasphemous things against our gentle Saviour? And then crowns it by a joke in the worst possible taste about Lord Edward!'

'Oh, I'm sure he never did,' cried Mary piteously.

'There, you don't know, you see! Miss Goff saw Lord Edward speak to him in the hall afterwards: I hope he told him plainly what he thought of him! And you tell me not to worry! I have worried enough in the past over your father, and it isn't fair that at my time of life I should – O –'

'Hush!' said Mary, smiling wanly. 'You really are tired, my dear. Bother other people. What right have they to judge things they don't understand, and so to distress you? Darling Mum, don't cry. Darling, really, I'm not a little girl, and I know goodness from badness, and I promise you that you needn't worry.'

She picked up the account book of the *Slum Cripples and Orphans Society*, and glanced at the pencilled total. 'Seventy-nine pounds! Six pounds more than last year! We're coming on, Mother!'

Maddison came down the passage, two cats running at his heels and mewing, their tails held up with twitching tips. Behind them walked the spaniel Billjohn, yawning. Maddison looked uncertainly from Mary to her mother: the darkness of the arched doorway flickered; and paused; and trembled with another flicker.

'I say,' he cried, striding forward. 'A thunderstorm's coming up. Look! It's beautiful! It's over Dartmoor, I should say. Oh, I do hope it passes over here!'

Mrs. Ogilvie was afraid of lightning. She said:

'Mary, you had better not sleep in the verandah if there's going to be a thunderstorm.'

For the past three weeks, during the hot weather, Mary had been sleeping on the lawn, near the verandah, where her camp-bed and sleeping-bag – her brother Michael's 'flea-bag' – were kept during the day.

'I shall be all right,' said Mary.

Mrs. Ogilvie walked to the door, to close it, but Maddison ran past her, and pushed it into its frame.

'Don't you bother, Aunt Connie, I'll see that all the lower windows are closed. Aunt Connie, please don't blame Mary for getting back so late. It was entirely my suggestion.'

'I am not concerned with whose fault it is,' replied Mrs. Ogilvie, glancing at the clock. 'Mary, are you coming to bed?' She lit her candle, and went up the stairs.

'Good night, Aunt Connie,' he called out, but she did not answer. Maddison and Mary looked at each other, and at the flickers through the windows.

'Poor dear, she's worried,' he said, and fell into a reverie of sadness, for he saw her as one worn by life. 'I saw her hands trembling. It would be best for me to go, Mary.'

The sky trembled with light. He went to the table, and turned down the lamp. They watched the lightning through the window.

'I'll go back and change,' he said, 'and go back straight away. In this beautiful light!'

'Would you?' she murmured, feeling everything to be unreal. He walked up and down the hall, and returned silently by her side.

'Good night, Mary dear.'

'Good night, my only dear.' He held her head to his shoulder, while smoothing her hair with his cheek; but he was watching for the flashes through the window. 'I'll write to you.'

'Won't you be coming here sometimes?'

'Not for awhile, I think, dearest. I'll finish *The Star-born* first, and get it typed, and then let your mother read it. Yes! When she's read it, she'll see me as I am. I'll dedicate it to her! Good-bye, moorhen!'

'Good-bye, dear one. "Twice child in age, always in innocence." Mary believes in ee, so don't feel lonely.'

'I might be going to fly the Atlantic the way we talk,' he laughed. 'Please thank your mother for having me this evening, won't you? No, I'll write. She'll think I mean to be sarcastic, perhaps, if you deliver that message in the morning, and my plate empty at breakfast. I'll compose a nice bread-and-butter letter. I've just remembered there are such things.'

'Well then, forget them immediately! Although Mother thinks they're proper. So they are, if sincere. Well, dear, I think I'll go to bed now – not that I want to, understand, but Mother won't sleep until she hears I've passed her door. Good night, darling.'

'Good night. Oh, Mary, I do love you so.'

She saw tears in his eyes as he turned away and leapt up the stairs. She followed slowly, to her room in the gable, where she undressed as in a dream. Wishing to prolong the lovely heavy pain in her heart, she leaned out of the window, watching the sky; the southern horizon was grumbling at the flickering of light. She judged the storm to be nearer than Dartmoor, probably over Torrington. How strangely still was the air: lying as though dead around the house: not a sound. She turned away, thinking of one face, and how it had grown eager at the coming of the storm; he was like Shelley, who had loved fire and wind and water, and had seen them as wild Spirits of the universe. 'The child's faculty of make-believe raised to the nth power' . . . was it no more than that? . . . were there not actually Spirits in all the things and forces of the universe? Yes, she felt sure of it; and the sweet pain became heavier in her heart.

In the verandah, lying in the camel's-hair sleeping-bag on the canvas bed, she watched the lightning travelling nearer and nearer, running down the sky in jagged purple and greenish flashes, and counted the seconds to determine how far away they were. The flickers were so frequent and continuous that she was unable to tell which were the rumbles due to each, and thinking about the dance, and the unreal walk back and the scene with her mother, she fell asleep.

Without realizing she had been asleep she listened to the rush of wind in the trees, and stared dazedly at the unseen roof of the verandah; the darkness split, and the place was filled with a violet haziness, and lit by a bluish flash. Raising herself on her elbow, she waited for the crash; it came instantly, with rain blurring the glass into water. Incessant flashes lit the garden; she could see through the open door the red flowers of the sweetwilliams in the bed at the edge of the lawn, and the glittering slant of rain. The veins zig-zagged in the sky, amidst a lilac haze, while the trees stood out of the night as though turned to stone by the thunder. She heard singing; and then in a great flash and its crackle and instant shock she saw him crossing the lawn: he glimmered as though phosphorescent, strangely fish-like, and the rain dissolved sight of him.

Chapter 15

THE flame of the oil lamp on the table of Scur Cottage was smitching, but none of the three men sitting round the hearth noticed it. Two of them were leaning forward, staring into the fire, which had been kindled against the chilly September night; the third, shorter and heavier than either of the Maddison cousins, and with red hair, sat apart, upright in his chair, biting his nails and giving small grunts as of contempt. His face, scarred by an aeroplane crash, was flushed and arrogant: he had been drinking rapidly in the Plough Inn, and had returned a minute since, to try and persuade the other two to go and drink with him.

By the closed door lay the spaniel, nose on paws and pointing at the draught which was drawn under the crack. Sometimes it groaned.

'Go on,' said Phillip Maddison, quietly to his cousin.

'Well, what started the row was Benjamin's wireless set. Benjamin and Ronnie and Pam and I had got the aerial up, but we'd forgotten to connect the earth: it was dark when we got home from church, and we couldn't see the wires properly. The set merely howled and vibrated – oscillated, I think is the correct term. Ben was disappointed, for it was his birthday present: but we persevered, trying to get the German station, to hear the Cologne bells. At last old Chychester came out and said, "I shouldn't worry; they're only rotten German bells."

' "Well, they're rung to the same rotten God," I said, for I was already overcharged with the stagnant atmosphere of the old people. I must tell you that before this, during supper, Ronnie caused a sensation by asking me, innocently before them all, "But where do kittens come from before they come out of the mother's body?" Mrs. Ogilvie looked angry, and old Chychester became very much occupied by what he was eating. You see, I had found out, quite by chance, the somewhat amazing fact that Ronnie was ignorant, innocent as Mrs. Ogilvie would say, of the facts of human birth: so I told him that the mother and child are one until it is strong enough to start its own life. I remembered the misery I had felt when I learned it at school, after a forcible catechism from two boys in the lavatory; but I didn't say anything of the father's share in his child, as Pamela was there, and I didn't quite know what to say.'

'What happened when Ronnie asked the question at supper?'

'I said that no one knew: that they grew naturally just as a dandelion grows out of a brown seed, and the yellow flower grows out of the top of a long stalk, and seeds out of the flower, and young plants out of the seeds, unless something eats them. So it went round and round, like winter after spring, and then summer and autumn; just as the earth goes round and round the sun, and the sun round and round the stars; and beyond the stars, no one knew. Mrs. Ogilvie changed the subject by saying, if all had finished eating, would they pass up the plates?'

'Oh.'

'You make *me* go round and round,' interrupted the man with the red hair, in a rough, scoffing voice. 'Why don't you come out and have some beer, instead of talking all that bosh?'

'Oh, shut up, Warbeck,' said Phillip Maddison.

'I shan't shut up! Intolerable insolence, telling me to shut up!' said Warbeck, glowering. 'And who is Old Chychester? Is he a bishop? Old London, Old Birmingham, Old Canterbury, Old Bogside, we know them intimately – but who the hell is Old Chychester?'

'A fierce old man with many guns and daggers and heads and paws of little animals, and a charming smile,' replied Maddison.

Warbeck grunted, and continued to bite his nails with quick nervous movements. 'Well, did you hear the rotten German bells that were rung to God, and not by any chance for the radio?' he inquired sarcastically.

Maddison hesitated, then resumed his account to his cousin.

'Well, as you know, Phillip, I get agitated: I stammered feebly something about my remarks being blasphemous – against the devil: an attempt at irony which fell flat. "Such facetiousness is in the worst possible taste," said Mrs. Ogilvie. However, I still tried to get straight with her by explaining what I meant. I said that my remark about the bells being rung to a rotten God wasn't blasphemous, as all people make God in their own image: but the remark about the rotten bells was blasphemous, because it added its drop in the ocean of human un-understanding and hate, the immense darkness of men's minds; like those blasphemous stories in the *English Boys' Annual*.'

'What did she say to that?'

'She would hear nothing further, and went out of the room. She came back, while I was feeling bloody awful, and said that my conduct since I had been in the house had been unbearable, and that I was the rudest man she knew.'

'Well, aren't you?' asked Julian Warbeck heavily. 'If anyone said that to me, I should take it as a compliment. But I can imagine you pleading with every idiot you come across. I can see that you still cling to the outworn philosophy of pity and tolerance towards all men. Really, Maddison, it's – it's – oh, you're like old Phillip here, always trying to see the other fellow's point of view! It makes me sick to listen to you.'

'Then go out and be sick, for God's sake,' said Phillip sharply.

Warbeck glowered at him, and grunted with disdain.

'Don't take any notice of that beery hedgehog,' said Phillip to his cousin.

'You *are* a couple of drivellers,' scoffed Warbeck. 'Honestly, it's awful bosh you're saying, Maddison. You're like your dog here, whining your way through life.'

A hollow groan had come from the spaniel. Warbeck rose violently, and opened the door, saying, as the dog crept out, 'He who desires, and acts not, breeds pestilence. Then may your master learn from you, shaggy beast of rubbish heaps and dustbins. Well, Maddison' – rubbing his hands and smiling. 'Well, your story is getting interesting. It develops into Victorian melodrama of the most moral kind. The young lover branded as a blasphemer – splendid! What about the lady in the case? Is she in the throes of a struggle, choosing between God and Mammon? Or should I say, God and Mamma? You being God? Your own God? Or has Mamma already won, judging by your somewhat melancholy and unshaven demeanour?'

'Let's go for a walk,' said Phillip. 'Julian's impossible when he's half tight.'

Outside the cottage he said, 'I say, I'm awfully sorry, old man, about it all. Would you like us to clear off now? I wouldn't have brought Julian if I had known he was going to behave like this.'

'That's what Mrs. Ogilvie said about me,' replied Maddison. 'After the way I behaved at the Otter Hunt Ball. Please don't go.'

By the stream, he said, 'I gave her the first half of *The Star-born* to read: all my hopes were in it.'

'What did she say?'

'She was quite frank: If she hadn't known me, she wouldn't have bothered to read it.'

Phillip sighed.

' "It's all very well to babble about pretty little birds and flowers," she said to me once, "but life is quite a different matter." '

'But Mary! She will stand by you! You should have seen the glance she gave you when we met them crossing the Great Field this morning. Old chap, it was the most beautiful thing I have ever seen in any woman's face, except my own mother's.'

'When was that, Phil?'

'It was when you were looking at the man carrying the blazing grass on his fork, lighting the row of couch-grass. All her spirit came into her eyes: I didn't need to be told anything in words.'

At their feet the water of the stream murmured by the stones, and the leaves of the graveyard elms sighed down in the darkness.

'I don't know,' said Maddison, suddenly bitter. 'When I asked her if she'd stand by me, she didn't answer. She just stood by the table, very pale, looking at me. Then she said something that made me realize how she must have been miserable on my account. She said, "You say about the English what you hate Uncle Suff and Mother saying about the Germans." I felt so hopeless at this, that I started to go, but she came after me, and, oh, Phillip – *You* understand, don't you? the whole world seems apathetic! And now, Mary . . .'

Phillip gripped his hand. 'I understand, old chap.'

'Her mother said she wouldn't have me in the house any more: and there was nothing to stay for. I saw Mary for a moment again, and said that our engagement had better be broken.'

'What did she say?'

'She just cried, and said she would never be enough for me '

'And then?'

'I said the truth was I was not good enough for her. So I would release her. She said nothing, so I went away.'

They returned to Scur Cottage. There was one room downstairs, with lime-washed walls, containing a table, wooden chairs, a pitcher of water, a sack for the dog's bed, and a grandfather clock with a worm-riddled case. Two cloam ovens were built into the walls within the open hearth, in which hung a rusty lapping crook from the bar set across the chimney above the clovel beam. The walls were bare except for one picture, at which Julian was frowning. When they entered he strode violently to the table, seized the smoking lamp, and held it up like a torch to examine the picture dramatically.

'Good God!' he was repeating to himself. 'Good God!'

They took no heed of him.

'Is this,' he demanded, after another inspection, 'the source of your inspiration, may I ask? Queen Victoria with birds' feathers in her hair handing metal-bound Bible to an Indian, also partly clad in the property of our little brothers, while he kneels with an expressionless and servile face, and two gentlemen, with moist eyes, gaze silently in the background, and the Prince Consort stares with manly stare into space. Where did you get it from, Maddison? In God's name, where did you get it from?'

'Oh, it's just part of my scheme for decorating my home,' replied Maddison curtly.

'Bravo!' cried Warbeck, laughing, and rubbing his hands together. 'Answered like an Englishman!'

'It's not original,' said Maddison. 'It's what my late hostess said to me when I said something once about the stuffed birds in her house.'

There were steps outside on the sett-stoned drang, and a hesitating knock on the door.

'Come in,' shouted Warbeck, opening the door. Mr. Garside stood there.

'Oh, I didn't know you had guests,' he said apologetically. 'I'll come again some other time.'

'Come in, Vicar,' said Maddison. 'I have two friends here, who are on a walking tour. This is Phillip Maddison, my cousin, and that fellow waving the lamp is Julian Warbeck. Warbeck is a critic of beer and art: he is just commenting on my landlord's masterpiece, *The Bible*.'

336

'How do you do?' said the Vicar. 'Yes, that's a very Victorian picture, isn't it?'

' "This is the Secret of England's Greatness, England's Glory" (vide *Memoirs of the late Prince Consort*, by the Reverend J. H. Wilson),' quoted Warbeck solemnly. 'When I read my nightly chapter of the Bible I shall ponder with renewed interest the Secret of England's Greatness, England's Glory. Now I know why we decimated the Red Indian in North America, and subjugated India and Egypt, and wiped out the Zulus in South Africa! The Secret of England's Greatness! So that trousers should be worn in the tropics, and the Bible be read in a top-hat! Personal gain was just bluff: the Bible was the real secret of our being there! And why all the natives with inferiority-complexes love and revere us – the Bible! Isn't that so, Vicar?'

'That's certainly one way of regarding it, I suppose,' remarked Mr. Garside genially.

'There is only one way of regarding it in England,' intoned Warbeck, waving the lamp above his head. 'And that is – it is God's Word! As a right-thinking Englishman, I will listen to no other point of view! Christ, I'm getting tight!'

'Mind that lamp!' cried Phillip. 'Put it on the table, and turn the wick down.'

'God's Chosen People!' grumbled Warbeck jovially. 'They must have been, for they said so themselves, didn't they, Vicar? An authentic inspiration! He chose them, of course, when the earth was flat, before it became round for the purpose of the sun never setting on the British Empire!'

'Well, you can't unmake history, Mr. Warbeck,' said Garside, almost apologetically. 'And the British Empire may yet become the instrument for World Peace – out of evil cometh good.'

'And out of the pitcher cometh beer,' replied Warbeck, filling his pot, and gulping it down.

'Warbeck is one of the poets of the Sussex ale-horde,' said Phillip to the Vicar. 'He'll quote Swinburne next.'

'I think Mr. Warbeck is most amusing,' replied Mr. Garside, trying to feel at ease. 'I perceive that he takes me for a sort of music-hall curate: well, I can assure you that six months' acquaintance with Captain Maddison –'

'Friendship, padre!'

'Thank you. Of course. Friendship. Yes, six months' friendship has given me a wider insight into the ways of modern thought. Please continue, Mr. Warbeck: I assure you I find your art criticism good entertainment.'

Warbeck grunted, not quite liking the turning of what he thought was sarcasm upon himself.

'What I came round for,' said Garside a few moments later, 'was to find out if it is true that you are going away.'

Maddison nodded.

'I'm sorry,' said Garside simply. 'You will be going with your friends, perhaps? A walking tour will be the very best thing for you.'

'Yes, do come,' said Phillip. 'We've only got a week left, and then I've got to go back to London.'

Maddison did not answer.

'Well, we'll see. We're spending a couple of days at least in the village – I want to explore the Burrows.'

'They're very beautiful, aren't they?' said Garside. 'I'm told that every kind of English wildflower is to be found growing there somewhere. Your cousin is a great man for the Burrows, and he should show you round.' He stopped.

'Sparing my feelings, padre?' smiled Maddison. 'I'll –'

'Not at all!' the Vicar hastened to say.

'Not sparing them? All right, I'm not serious. Yes, I'll show you the Burrows, Phil, if you like.'

The Vicar appeared to be on the point of saying something; he hesitated; and looked expectantly at Warbeck, who had grunted. He seemed perplexed. At last he said:

'There's just one thing, Maddison. I really came round to tell you about this. May I speak before your friends? I mean to say – it's perhaps a private matter – yes, forgive me mentioning it at all. Another time, perhaps, would be better. Forgive my foolishness –'

'The holy man wants to get rid of us,' said Warbeck. 'Well, the beer at the Plough Inn is good enough for me. Come on, Phillip.'

He pulled open the door, and shouted, 'Curse you, why do you go creeping about?'

'I'm sure I'm very sorry, sir,' said a humble voice. 'I be very sorry. My wife sent me to say that supper be ready now, if you please, sir. Don't want vor to put it back, zur, or 'twill spoil, my wife doth say. 'Twill spoil, surenuff. The supper. Zupper. 'Twill be zamzawed if my wife has to put it back. Tes homerletts, gennulmen. Do ee like homerletts? Tés homerletts, surenuff. Aw, tes his reverence standing there. You'll excuse me, sir, I didden see ee standing there. Tes dark. Dark. Tes dark in yurr.' Mr. Mules, plucking at his cap, shuffled away.

'You two go along with him,' said Maddison. 'I'll come in a minute.' They went out, leaving him with the Vicar.

'An extraordinary man, Warbeck,' remarked Garside. 'He must be the man Miss Goff calls the German. She saw him going up the church tower this afternoon with your cousin.'

'I knew him slightly years ago in Folkestone. He was one of the several young men, including myself, in love with Mrs. Fairfax – I've told you about that, haven't I?'

'Oh! Really? That makes him the more interesting. Of course, I remember now: he is the Swinburne enthusiast, isn't he?'

'He was.'

'Your cousin Phillip, I like his face. Let me see, wasn't he also one of the admirers of Mrs. Fairfax?'

'Yes.'

The Vicar thought for a few moments, then he said, 'It is a pity that old affair occurred, for it gives a basis of actuality for Miss Goff's attacks; I mean, if you began an action for defamation of character.'

'I shouldn't do that.'

'I was thinking of it only as an act of self-protection, Maddison,' the other man replied, with concern on his face. 'The fact is, as I came in to tell you, Miss Goff has been to her solicitors this afternoon to see if you cannot be prosecuted under the Blasphemy laws. I did all I could to persuade her not to do anything so extreme, but she would not listen to me. She thinks, I believe, that I am inclined to agree with you; anyway, she does not approve of me.'

'Poor old chap, so your friendship with me has got you into trouble, has it? Well, I do hope it will adjust itself when I have gone away.'

'Of course, I don't know that anything will materialize,' said the priest. 'But I suggested to Miss Goff, and to Mrs. King who was with her, that they should wait until I had seen you, when I might persuade you to leave, and the matter could be dropped. But Miss Goff was most emphatic that you should be prosecuted. My dear boy, I feel it extremely. Please do not worry. Miss Goff and those others are incapable of understanding you, that is the real trouble. Oh, another thing she said was, that it was most indecent for a grown man to bathe naked with small boys, as apparently she had seen you once or twice through her telescope.'

'I have never injured her!' cried Maddison. 'I have never even spoken to her, or of her, to anyone. The only thing I know about her personally is that once she smiled at me. Why does she betray that smile? That was actual, and human; the other ideas do not exist.'

Mr. Garside smiled.

'Philosophically, perhaps they do not; and they will not one day, when our ideas become wider, and we are indeed a Christian league of nations. But to-day they do, and are very real; your own experience is a proof of it. You are still too much in the clouds, if I may say so, my dear boy.'

'But – but blasphemy! Surely there will be some evidence

required? I haven't made any public speeches, or published anything: mere hearsay surely isn't sufficient to prosecute a man on?'

'It is Benjamin,' said the Vicar. 'He has been repeating what you said, apparently, to some of the boys at school. He has left, as you know, and is shortly going to the training ship *Victory*; apparently he has been seeing his old school friends in his new uniform, and there was a fight with one of them, and he was rather severely knocked about. The Head Master saw it, and stopped it, and the cause of it came out in the enquiry. He told Mrs. King, and she told Miss Goff. They have been questioning him before me; he was very much frightened, poor boy.'

'Damned swine!' cried Maddison. 'Where is Benjamin? I'll –' He began to walk about the room, ruffling his hair.

'It shows that one should be careful what one says before the little ones,' said Garside. 'It is indeed unfortunate. You see, many of the people who say the same things, only in a different spirit, are Communists: there is a Communist Sunday School not very far from here, where the children are taught the most blasphemous things. For instance' – he took out a newspaper clipping from his pocket-book – 'this is one of their hymns:

"The whole world at last is beginning to see
The blight of the world is Jesus.
Like sunshine at noonday, free thought has shown me
The blight of the world is Jesus.
Keep off the blight, or blighted you'll be,
Blighted for life by credulity.
Once I believed, but now I can see
The blight of the world is Jesus."

It is dreadful to think of – to contemplate those innocent minds being assailed by that cancerous vileness. Jesus, the gentlest man with little children, in an age when child life was thought nothing of! Miss Goff called the authors of such things devil's vampires, and although the term is perhaps rather more protest than sense, I must say I agree with her on that point.'

'Jesus died in agony,' said Maddison, pausing in his wandering round the room. 'Agony,' he repeated, beginning to walk round the room again. 'Agony! The blasphemer! Those so keen on the letter of religion are bound to be anti-Christ, and such teaching as that is only the reaction against the letter. The letter, the intellect, the earth-brain working, all hostile to the spirit of Christ. However, Jesus of Nazareth was not always the Christ, the Star-born – did he not turn over the money-lenders' tables in the rage of his zeal? If Jesus was human, and of course he was – blast all idolatry! – then there is hope for us who are human, for we can become Christs while we live on the earth. That is all Jesus meant. If the Christian dogma obscures, or does not always emphasize that vital and natural and predominating fact, then it is damned as an unjust steward!'

Mr. Garside smiled uneasily. 'Well, I don't want to argue; I will only say that men are not yet like Christ, and until then, we will continue to be imperfect. Here is some more of this Sunday School catechism:

' "A little child shall lead them. Lead whom? Why, the capitalists to slaughter.

' "What child? Why, the child of the worker.

' "Did Jesus come to earth from heaven? No.

' "Was his mother a virgin? No.

' "Is the story about him true? No.

' "Who was his father? Joseph, in the ordinary way." '

'That's all right,' said Maddison, 'only it should be left out of the child's life. And will be, when the old ideas, of which that is a counter-irritant, have gone.'

'Here is some more,' said the Vicar, determined not to be

drawn into an argument. 'Now, I must say, I agree partly
with this. It made Miss Goff positively rabid as she read it to
me. By the way, do you know a Major Shakerley?'

'Yes.'

'He apparently repeated what you said to him somewhere
or other.'

'I knew he would. At least, not what I said: he would
repeat his preconceived opinions, backed up with quotations
taken from their context: and passing through his mind, they
would emerge with its quality. Repetition is quite worthless
as such; it serves only to reveal the quality of the speaker's
mind. Still, it doesn't matter about that. Go on with what
you were going to read to me.'

'Here it is:

' "What is a patriot? A soldier, a sailor, a policeman, a boy
scout, a girl guide. Never you become one of them. Soldiers
are trained to murder men of their own class. We were made
to murder poor peaceful Germans we had no grudge against;
and they were made to murder poor peaceful Englishmen in
the same way." '

'That's true, from the Christ point of view,' said Maddison.

'Within limitations, I agree.'

'Oh, don't ever agree with me, for God's sake!' cried
Maddison. 'I should burst into tears if anyone ever did that!'

The Vicar saw he was overwrought, and said sincerely:

'You must be patient with me, Maddison. Remember, I
am trying to be always quite frank with you. You asked me
to do that.'

'I'm sorry, please forgive me,' replied Maddison, seeming
to glide beside him, eager remorse in all of his swift supple
attitude, and holding out his hand.

'Of course, of course! My dear boy, it is I who should –'

They shook hands, smiling affectionately at each other.

'This is what I was going to read,' continued the Vicar.

343

' "Thou shalt not be a patriot, for a patriot is an international blackguard.

' "Thou shalt teach revolution, for revolution means the abolition of the present political system, and the end of capitalism."

'Then there follow some things about "man-made sex-laws" and the promotion of free-love, which seems to me more poisonous to the young than any anti-capitalist teaching.'

'Free love? "Consider the birds: their beautiful springtime excitement of love: the fidelity of the mated pair: the sweet free friendship all through the year until the coming again of Proserpine. Their minds are free as air and sunshine until the rapture of the apple blossom!" I'm quoting my own stuff: forgive me.'

The Vicar regarded him with a smile.

'Maddison,' he said, 'God knows, sometimes you make me feel I am not worthy to fasten the latchet of your shoe; but I do appreciate you for what you are, honestly I do. Really, I mean it. And if I may say so, in my – yes, my love for you – in my love for you, it seems such a pity that you have wasted yourself – for waste I feel it to be, most strongly – wasted yourself on, shall we say, a political aspect of things? For it is that, just as Miss Goff says! I feel you should concentrate on – how can I say it now? – on more positive things. You are a poet; and it is entirely through you that my eyes have been opened to the significance of poetry. Well then, may I give you back, in gratitude, some advice?'

Maddison knew what was coming, but tried to look expectant.

'Do not dissipate your energies; shake the dust of the material world out of your ideas, and concentrate on your art. I know you can write nobly, and most impressively, on birds, and their – their beautiful free lives in the sunshine.'

'I have come to that conclusion, too. In fact, I came to it years ago. You see, I am quite hopeless!'

'No, you must not depreciate yourself so; you are always doing it.'

'Ah!' said Maddison, beginning to wander again. 'If only I had come to Devon a year later! Now, I have laid a frost on all my hopes.'

The Vicar followed him with his eyes, stirred by the beauty of his sad face.

'No, no, you must not think like that, Maddison. Who knows? you might return in a year's time, and find all your friends still waiting for you. One at least I can answer for.'

'Thanks, padre.'

They shook hands.

'Now I expect you will be wanting to go to supper. I'll walk with you as far as Mules' cottage, if I may.'

On the way to the cottage Maddison said:

'I say, I'd like to tell you something in confidence.'

'Please do. I shall honour your trust, I assure you.'

'Mary and I – we were engaged to be married. Secretly. But it's ended now.'

'Oh!' said the Vicar, stopping still, and his eyes opening wide. 'Oh dear me! My dear boy, my heart aches for you both. You must both be feeling dreadfully unhappy. Oh dear, I had no idea it was like that!'

'I said some horribly unkind things to her,' muttered Maddison.

'That was because you were unhappy. Her mother would of course be against . . . But she will wait for you! I know she will! I have the deepest respect and admiration for Mary. Of course, it is natural you two should esteem each other. Of course. I should have known it.'

'We promised to marry each other, last August. On the night of the thunderstorm! All that fire and light! I felt as exalted as Shelley in his cloud.'

'I will respect your confidence. And I will say this: Don't worry, Maddison! Perhaps after all it is for the best – you

know, I feel trials *are* sent to try us; at least, we are puri-
fied by experience. Perhaps if you go away for a year . . .
anything might happen – you might be famous by then! But
whatever happens, I shall always think of you as a great friend.
I liked you from the moment I saw you: there was something different in your face, a sort of innocence. Dear boy,
I hope things will turn out all right. I do, most sincerely!'

'Thank you,' said Maddison, and once again they shook
hands.

As he stood on the threshold of Mules' cottage he said shyly,
'I say, I'm going to read part of *The Star-born* to-night to the
others. Would you like to hear any of it too? I mean, I don't
want to bore you with it; you must leave as soon as you get
tired of it. Please promise that?'

'I should be most delighted, really I should. What time shall
I come round?'

'In about an hour's time? Well, cheerio until then. I say!'

Garside came back. 'It probably isn't very good,' said
Maddison. 'It's a sort of fantasy, about an owl and the spirit
of a boy, and other spirits.'

'I should very much like to hear it.'

'But don't expect too much,' begged Maddison. 'It bored
one reader.'

'Who was that? Oh, I shouldn't have asked.'

'She was honest about it, anyhow.'

'Well – at nine o'clock, at your cottage! Good-bye.'

After supper the three men went to the Plough Inn to drink
beer. Warbeck was in his element in a public-house, Phillip
told his cousin; he existed on a small allowance from his
father, and had done no work since he had left the Army four
years before. He still lived and had his being in the hectic
atmosphere of the war years; he had gone straight from school
and an abbreviated course at Sandhurst into the Army, being
seconded to the Royal Flying Corps. To anyone curious,
among his ephemeral bar-acquaintances, about his record

Warbeck would say, with a sort of scoffing frankness, that an unknown hand had held out a drink to him as he entered the squadron mess for the first time, and it had seemed a not unpleasant omen, and one which he had acted upon ever since. Father, he would say, was not a rich man, but he had enough for both of them: and so he, Warbeck, was quite content to observe life until such time as he became mature. Until that state was attained, he did not intend to waste his poetic impressions on juvenilia.

As a fact, Julian Warbeck was almost an outcast; some people called him a blackguard, others were sorry for him, declaring that his conduct was the result of having been shot down in France. When drunk he often had a terrible jeering manner, said Phillip, and wore one down like coarse sandpaper. When sober, he was an interesting and amusing companion, with a marvellous memory for books and poetry; he remembered all he read, and could recite Swinburne and other poets for hours; but he worked very seldom, and nearly all his verse was an imitation, as he admitted, of various manners and periods. He had made a translation of Catullus, but had never tried to get it published.

Warbeck drank half a gallon of beer between half-past eight and nine o'clock, and appeared only to cease talking when he was swallowing. Judging by the guffaws of laughter from the men standing clubbed about him, he was in his best form. The cousins watched him from a settle, half listening to the noise around them; each was preoccupied with his own thoughts. When the church clock struck the hour they got up, and asked Warbeck if he were coming; his ruddy scarred face and broad shoulders appeared in the gap made by the labourers, and he replied, with eyebrows raised to their utmost with anxious courtesy, that he would come immediately.

'Some beer, I think, is indicated. Er, landlord, could you let me have some beer to take away, please?'

The landlord said he had some Bass, and held out a small

black bottle; but Warbeck replied that he was not yet furnishing a doll's house, and would prefer a pitcher of his oldest ale. The landlord asked how much ale he would be wanting; and Warbeck told him to fill the largest pitcher he had. 'Twas two-gallon, the largest, the landlord replied; and a mild sensation was caused by Warbeck's answer, heard by every man listening in the hushed room, that if he had no larger one, then it would have to do for the time being: and in the belief that it was a poor heart that never rejoiced, he would call round again just before ten o'clock, which he understood was the closing-time in that Puritan-ridden country. With four china mugs, and his pitcher of ale, Warbeck left the Plough Inn, content with the evening so far.

In the cottage, seated round the fire, with pots of beer at hand, the three men talked for awhile; and a remark of Warbeck's, followed by a question, made Maddison say:

'My immediate task is to co-ordinate the spirit of Christ with that of Lenin – the two philosophies are related, and the complement of each other. Both show a way of life that is reasonable and natural.'

Warbeck gave a snort of impatience, but Maddison silenced him with a look that reminded Phillip of the glance of a peregrine falcon. 'I know that Lenin himself thought all God-seeking an illusion, a contemplation of the idle and tender part of the mind; but he was almost entirely an active man, and saw all evil as made directly or indirectly by man; and that as man has made evil, so man can make good. Had the old rulers of Russia really been Christians – instead of a mere Bible class – I exclude the parasites and cynics, of course, and refer only to the sincere church-supporters – then there would have been no Great War, no slums, very little tuberculosis, practically no drink-rot or venereal disease caused by unhappy people seeking refuge in their instincts, and no Lenin as a keen flame of heaven to purify mankind. Lenin, the young genius with his immense zest for art and beauty, would have seen

348

Jesus of Nazareth plain, as one who had developed his will deeper into the spirit of the wide and universal sky.'

'You mean Lenin couldn't, or wouldn't, see Jesus plain because of the priests?' asked Phillip.

'Yes.'

'I think so too. Have you read all Lenin's works?'

'None. I know him by intuition.'

'You know him by intuition!' said Warbeck, frowning heavily. 'You know Lenin by intuition! You're talking bosh, utter bosh, Maddison! It *is* bosh! What I can't see is why you bother about either Jesus or Lenin. They are both colossal bores. Well, I'm going to have some more beer.'

'I didn't quite follow your remark about venereal disease,' said Phillip. 'Don't you think –'

'By God, Phillip,' interrupted Warbeck, emerging from his beer-pot with jovial ruddy face, 'you give me a pain. You'll be standing outside the local clinic soon, giving away tracts. "Trust not in precaution, young man: be saved by a co-ordination of Lenin and Jesus." I never heard such infernal nonsense in my life before. Well, Maddison, you are a fellow!' he scoffed. 'Get some beer into you, and drop all that infernal nonsense. Co-ordination! Poom!' He covered his nose and mouth with the pot.

'This fellow's thoughts, like the beer he absorbs, are always gravitating towards the lowest level,' said Phillip calmly, to his cousin. 'That is bad. It will be Swinburne by the yard after the next two pints. That is worse. However, we've got a two-pints time-space before that. What was I saying? Oh, don't you think venereal disease will remain so long as human nature remains?'

'No, for when children are allowed to grow naturally, and unrepressed, they won't be over-imaginative or precociously desirous about sex, as I was, for instance, and young men will be natural. Harlotry isn't natural; it's the inherited fruit of repression.'

A minor explosion, accompanied by a shower of beer, came from Warbeck, who spilled more beer from his pot as he shook with laughter.

'Oh God,' he groaned, 'you talk like one of the extension lecturers of the Salvation Army. Why, you poor fish, if the world became as you would like it, there would be no more great poetry. Have some more beer, for God's sake.' He heaved up the pitcher, and slopped it into their half-empty mugs. 'Here's to life as it is, say I, and damnation to the bourgeoisie, the proletariat, and all poetasters.'

'Give him his beer, and he's happy,' said Phillip.

'By God, you're right!' roared Warbeck. 'Now you're beginning to talk sense. Well, Maddison, well! Here's success to you: may you soon have a mother-in-law, and all the female adoration you need to bolster up the philosophy that all men are as toadstools! Toadstools! By God, you can look at me with your great big luminous eyes, but you're all wrong, Maddison: you're all wrong!' he said harshly, as though striving against some thought. 'You're unnatural: you've built up everything on a fixed idea: and now it's beginning to stick in your guts, you don't like it! Oh damn, I'm getting drunk. Well, here's luck to you.'

'Luck!' said Maddison, drinking. Warbeck drained his pot, and after a frowning stare at the floor, said to him, 'You're like Francis Thompson, an aloof moth of a man. No, you're not a moth: you're an owl, a bird of twilight and darkness. Oh, come, you're not such a bad fellow, Maddison. You take all my jibes and cuts without ruffling a feather. You're all right! You're a good fellow!'

Warbeck began to stride about the room, and to recite from the *Sister Songs* in a sonorous voice.

After a dozen lines he lifted the pitcher, splashed the liquid into his mug, and poured it down his throat.

'By God, Maddison, if you ever write anything *half* as good as that, you will be a great man. Oh, it's great stuff.

AUTUMN

'Forlorn, and faint, and stark,
I had endured through watches of the dark
The abashless inquisition of each star,
Yea, was the outcast mark
Of all those heavenly passers' scrutiny."

'I care nothing,' he said, clenching his hands, 'for anyone or anything. Only poetry matters. Poetry! One day I will write verse that will shake men like thunder. I am a great poet, by God I am! The Star-born! The Star-born!' he glowered at Maddison, sibilating the words with contempt. 'Here you are, bleating about your piffling little fairy story, daring to stand there and think you are a great poet: you who wormed your way into the heart of Eveline Fairfax, with your great soulful stare! Pah! The Star-born! The Still-born! By God, it's insufferable, your insolence!'

'Less sibilation, for God's sake: you send a shower of beer with every "s," ' said Maddison wearily; for he had been rehearsing in his mind the reading of his book all the afternoon, dreading the criticism of Warbeck, and he was nervously fatigued. 'You're right about it being still-born. Have some more beer?'

'Well, yes,' said Warbeck jovially, lifting the pitcher. 'It's the best thing I've heard you say so far. Come, Maddison, old boy, admit you're a humbug, like a man: say it's all nonsense that you believe what you do. Well, I drink your health, sense or nonsense!'

They drank. Warbeck was now smiling. 'You're a good chap, Maddison. I believe you're a great man! Only I don't understand you!' he cried, frowning again, and his voice becoming rough. 'I've understood every man I met before; but you baffle me! You upset me: I can't believe in myself when I listen to your incredible bosh. It is bosh, Maddison: it *is* bosh! Isn't it? I'm all right, I *know* I am all right; by God, Maddison, I know I'm sane: and if you are right, then

351

I'm all wrong! You don't believe in Jesus Christ, do you?
No, you mustn't. Swinburne is right, I *know* he is right.

"Thou hast conquered, O pale Galilean, the world has grown
grey from thy breath.
Thou hast conquered, O pale Galilean, but thy dead shall
go down to thee dead!"

Yes, that's the stuff: not this Star-born nonsense. I could write
such stuff if I wanted to, but I don't want to. No, Maddison,
you don't get over me, by God you don't.'

'That's all right,' said Maddison, understanding the inner
agony that had manifested itself in the other's false contempt.
'I'm not going to read it, anyway.'

Warbeck clenched his hands again, lowered his chin on his
chest, and wept. Hearing Garside's double rap on the door,
Maddison went to let him in.

'I'm not late, I hope?' he asked. 'By the way, if you want any
more logs, I've got a lot in the Vicarage garden, by the churchyard wall. They were lopped from the elms this spring, when
Miss Goff decided they were dangerous. Some are already
sawn and split: I shall be pleased to let you have all you want.'

'Thanks, I'll get some now.'

All four men went to fetch an armful of sticks, which they
carried into the single lower room of the cottage, and flung
in the wide hearth beside the fire. To Maddison's surprise
and Warbeck's approval the Vicar accepted a pint of beer. He
sipped it, while Warbeck recited the chorus from *Atalanta in
Calydon*. The verse seemed to bewilder the Vicar; but his eyes
continued to show their interest. He was enjoying himself.

At half-past nine on that September evening Maddison,
after much hesitation and encouragement, began to read *The
Star-born*.

'It begins with a sort of prologue,' he said quickly and
tonelessly, with a glance at Warbeck. 'It is called "The House
in the Forest."'

'We are all attention,' said Warbeck gravely; and glancing at the picture on the wall, he added: 'No doubt we shall be not amused; but then I think you are a genius!'

When he had finished reading the Introduction, Maddison did not dare to look at their faces. 'To me it seems dreadfully bad. Just what Warbeck said it was.'

He waited fearfully to hear Warbeck's scoffing voice.

'It's good,' said Phillip quietly.

'Yes, it is,' the Vicar said; 'I am fascinated, and want to hear more. I think I know who is the Star-born,' he added, taking a sip of his beer. 'What do you think, Mr. Warbeck?'

'It's either utter bosh, or else it's very good. I can't decide on such a fragment,' remarked Warbeck.

'Julian will be able to tell us if the book becomes a classic, perhaps?' suggested Phillip.

'Classic!'

'The Barrie touch,' said the Vicar.

'Barrie!' snorted Warbeck. 'Barrie! Why don't you say John Oxenham or Beatrice Chase? Barrie! If I thought it was anything like Barrie, I would beg him to burn it as bosh immediately. No, seriously, Maddison ' – his voice became low and courteous, and his eyebrows lifted to their movable limit – 'I like it much. Fortunately your style is simple and Anglo-Saxon, for if it were full of Latinisms I should lose even more of the syllables, for you read in such a soft voice and slur your words, while all the time the Vicar was breathing in my ear as though he were hanging head-downwards from the ceiling. I must go out for a moment: please don't go on until I come back. I'll be only a minute.'

'I must go out too,' said Phillip.

'So must I,' said Maddison.

'The Vicar will not need to,' said Warbeck. 'He can remain here, and watch his beer evaporating. I beg your pardon!' he hastened to exclaim, without thinking, for he had stumbled into the dog lying on the sack. 'Damn you, shaggy beast; take up your bed and scratch elsewhere.'

'Don't rag Garside too much,' said Maddison to Warbeck, outside. 'He's a good fellow.'

'If he takes my nonsense seriously, he's a damned fool,' retorted Warbeck. 'By God, Maddison, I am enjoying this evening.'

He entered the cottage rubbing his hands; Mules was standing there, crook-backed, blinking at the Vicar, and turning his cap in his nobbly fingers. 'You'll excuse me coming over, zur, please; you'll excuse me coming over, but my wife sent me to know if you'll be wanting bedrooms to slape in to-night. Tes nearly ten o'clock, and my wife hath aired one bed. Aired the bed, my wife hath. If you'll please say if you'll be needing the bed my wife 'ath haired. Tes a bit lumpy like, and it goeth down one end, but tes a very comfortable bed, warm and comfortable. 'Twas my father's, and his father's avore'n; tes what to-day they call wan of these yurr antic beds, but my wife won't sell'n; tes an old bed like, and very comfortable, especially if you don't mind lying crossways, crossways, lying crossways. Oh ha ah! hur ha! you'm a funny man, Mr. Maddison, I see ee laughing at old Mules, old rough gravedigging chap he be, poor old Mules.'

Mr. Mules shifted about on his heels as he spoke, and jerked his cap in his hands and ended up by sniggering, and bending almost double, as though half scared of his mirth, which he would hide with his elbows. His vacant light-blue eyes looked anywhere, but never at any face.

'Have some beer, Mules, have some beer, some beer,' said Warbeck, putting a mug in one of his hands.

'Thank ee, sir, thank ee. Here's your very good health, zur, your very good health indeed, zur.'

'Mules,' said Warbeck, 'finish that quickly, and go and fetch some more beer.'

He turned to Phillip.

Got any money on you, old boy?' he said, almost obsequiously. 'I shall be hearing from Father to-morrow, and then I'll settle up.' He finished his pint, and filled up his pot, and the other pots.

Phillip gave Mules some money.

'You'd better get the pitcher filled up,' he said, 'and keep the change.'

'Thank ee kindly, zur, thank ee kindly,' said Mules, backing towards the door. 'What sort of beer would you be wanting? What sort of beer would you be wanting?'

'In his previous incarnation Mules was a gramophone record,' said Warbeck, 'condemned to repeat the same tune over and over again till he was worn out and melted down, and he has inherited from that his habit of vain repetition.'

'Haha! you'm a funny man, a funny man, zur,' said Mules, looking coy, and suddenly waving his pot in the Vicar's face. 'I'm sure, your reverence, I drink your very good health, zur, your very good health, your reverence. I didden mean no rudeness, zur, drinking before I spoke your very good health, zur. Does ee good, zur, does ee good, a li'l drop of ale, does ee good, it does that, your reverence: proper stuff, proper, proper stuff. Don't I wish my poor old vather were yurr to taste it! It makes me feel fine inside, it does that, gennulmen. Fine like. Inside. Inside. Inside me, like.'

'Some day Mules will ring a different change on his sentences, and then his wife will trisect him with the carving knife, and the jury will bring in a verdict against her of trigamy,' said Warbeck, taking up his pot. 'O God, my pot is empty, my pot is empty. Empty. My pot. Empty. Never mind, I'll drink yours.'

He picked up Garside's pot and drained it in three big gulps. 'This, I think, is the life, Vicar!' he said blandly, smacking his lips. 'Now if the amiable Mules will go and get the jug filled, we can settle down for the night.'

'What about the bed, zur, about the bed, if you please? The

bed? The bed my wife bin airing? Haha! she don't know poor old Mules bin drinking your health, zur, drinking your health. Does ee good, proper stuff, proper; tes nice to meet with such company once in a way, begging your pardon, gennulmen.'

'What about these beds?' asked Maddison. 'Do you want them, or don't you want them?'

'I don't,' said Phillip. 'We'll only be disturbing them if we go back late. It looks like a night of it. I'm quite happy.'

'Spoken like an Englishman,' said Warbeck, 'Bed is for the old: beer for the young. Beer and poetry, that's the stuff of youth. Come on, Maddison, drink up; you aren't half a chap, you can't drink.' He began to recite Swinburne.

When Mules had brought back the pitcher, and departed, Maddison began to read again. Assured of a sympathetic audience, he read with more vivacity; and living the fantasy of the spirits of air and water and star, he induced in the listeners a likeness to himself, and held them in wonder and absorption. The fire sank down, and was silently made up by Phillip, and sank down again; midnight rolled from the church tower unheard. When he stopped at the end of the first half, called *Beyond the End of the World*, Warbeck was breathing heavily, his heavy chin sunken on his woollen cardigan, his under-lip thrust out aggressively. Maddison waited, knowing that Garside and his cousin were staring at him, and dreading to meet their eyes. Then Warbeck got up, and filled a pot with beer, and put it into Maddison's hand, and looked down upon the averted head, silently, gently.

Maddison asked if he should continue, and they said yes; and the cadent voice flowed on, while the sense of time and space and the room and its objects became unreal; and when it was finished the fire was out, the lamp had sunk and was dim, and the beer was brackish, flat, undesirable.

Chapter 16

Yᴏᴜ'ʀᴇ another Shelley,' said Warbeck at last.

'You're more than Shelley,' he repeated, throwing out the name between his teeth as though he would charge the very air with all that the name meant for him. 'My friend, I am drunk, but drunk or sober, I tell you that you are a genius.'

Watching Maddison, the Vicar was profoundly impressed by the strange smouldering light of his eyes, which in the past had so disturbed and inspired him. Maddison was absolute in spiritual strength!

' "The Star-born" is nothing,' said Maddison musingly. 'One day I shall write a story of a pony taken from the moor into a coal-mine; and the story shall be of a linnet also taken into a mine, in a cage, to die if there is fire-damp. And though my bird perishes, yet it will be immortal, and live back millions of years into the forests before the earth's crust sank and the trees became coal: and forward into the future, when the coal-mines are all fallen in, and for power men shall dip their hands into the sun, and harness the sea: and men are pure in spirit as a linnet, and their sympathies as wide as the earth.'

He pushed back his chair with a scrape on the cold lime-ash floor, and going to the door, opened it and looked up into the sky. They stood by him in silence. The stars which had shone over the Great Field when they had come home from the inn were gone down beyond the lower seaward line of the Burrows. A murmur came to them out of the darkness, a murmur faint and changing, that died away and was with the stars silent, and rose again, filling the night with a faint roar.

'The breakers on the bar,' he said. 'The salmon-boats will be riding home now.'

357

'The stars and the water have watched the rising of the soul of a Man,' said Warbeck, and turning away, he went back to the table, and began to write.

Maddison shook the manuscript pages of *The Star-born* together, and put them in his pack; and taking an earthenware pitcher of water from the window-seat, he set its glazed lip to his mouth, and drank, between breaths, for nearly a minute. When he put it down his dog got up off the sack, yawned and stretched itself, shook its coat, and walking over to the pitcher, peered in at the unlappable level of the water. It whined, thinking of its unattainable desire.

'It must be nearly dawn,' said Garside, yawning. 'Well, I must thank you with all my heart for doing me the honour of inviting me to hear your wonderful work. How you thought of it all, I can't imagine.'

'Oh, shut up,' said Maddison. 'It's quite simple. I can trace it all back to my childhood: all has been a protest against unnatural ideas. Come on, Bill.'

The spaniel was not in the room.

'He went out just now,' said Phillip. 'I say, Willie, you're not going?'

Maddison was shouldering his pack.

'Yes, I am,' he replied. 'Good-bye.'

He held out his hand to Garside.

'Oh, rot, Willie, you can't go like this,' cried Warbeck, looking up from the verse he was writing. 'You can't go. Don't let him go, Phillip.'

'Apart from other things, by going now I shall escape the inevitable reaction of Julian,' said Maddison, smiling. 'Seriously, Julian, this is the moment to say good-bye. I have actually achieved your friendship! Good-bye, everyone.'

Warbeck gripped him by the arm.

'I won't let you go, you fool. I *can't* let you go like this. Oh, God, you're the only man I care about. Maddison, for God's sake believe me. Listen, this is bloody rotten, I know, but this is how I feel. Honestly. Do you mind if I read it?' he asked, beginning to nibble at a finger-nail.

'Please do.'

'It's called "A Man."'

> Clothed on with silence, but with eyes that burn
> With all the hidden glow of sunsets seen
> Yet able well their struggling word to screen
> However much the prisoned thoughts may yearn
> For spaces wide and Heaven's breath aeterne;
> Yet with the golden pen that erst has been
> Handheld by poets olden and serene
> Whose aching souls upon his page return.

> Such is my friend; and when his thought's duresse
> Is broken on some shining Devon hill
> I see the living poesy Shelley caught
> – But see, alas! the ageless deep distress
> That slew those mighty masters as they wrought
> Their offerings to the world from good – and ill.

> For W. M.'

'Thank you, Julian,' said Maddison, taking his hand; and Warbeck wrenched it away, shaking with sobs.

'Good-bye,' said Maddison, tears running down his cheeks, and without them fully realizing how it had happened, he was gone.

Already, as he was crossing the Great Field, the stars seemed more remote, their beams shortened and steady; the avalanche of darkness as moving away from the world. He felt as immense as the firmament, and filled with a vast impersonal joy. Eos phoros the Morning Star, bright witness to the visions of men, would soon be bringing the dawn over Dunkery Beacon, and he must see it from the hills. He walked swiftly, with long strides, crossing the eastern corner of the Great Field to the road that led to the modern houses of Santon, and, rising thence above the sea-sloping fields of Down End, turned through the rock inland to Cryde, past the sands of the bay.

He followed the road for a quarter of a mile, and vaulting over a gate, crossed a field of stubble, while the first shrill music of a lark dropped in the dimming night. Now Shelley was in the wind and the grasses of the hedge with him, and Jefferies free of the world's negation, and Blake, and Thompson, and Jesus of Nazareth, and his shoulders were wide as the hills, and his spirit strong as the sea, for they said as they moved beside him, We are with you evermore, for you are of us! And he strode faster, with open mouth to draw down the skin of his face, until the hindering tears had run from his eyes.

The songs of larks began to fall as rain in the lessening darkness, as he pushed through a thorn hedge and dropped into a sunken lane, and climbed the steep bank into a higher field. Brambles of wild rose hooked his coat and scratched his hands and ankles, but he hardly felt them. A pair of horses snorted somewhere near him, and their grey shapes fled away with thudding hooves. Soon he had crossed the field, and was pulling himself up another steep bank by the branches of an ash-tree, which had been half-cut and laid along the hedge.

He ran along the headland of a field near Lobb Farm, leaping over the withering plants of musk thistles and cracking the stems of hemlock fallen with old summer weight out of the bank. Through another hedge he broke, heedless of the stabs of the little gnarled wind-savage blackthorns that hardly yielded before him. He must reach the highest point of the down before sunrise!

By a broken gate that flapped to his weight on a rotting post of a planted ship's rib, he stopped, and looked up. The inert heaviness was gone from the night; the darkness was a-stir, lightless light was moving everywhere over the fields, passing through and charging with its mystic power every branch and stone and leaf of clover. The sky seemed to deepen and to glow with a translucent blue that was an illimitable and perpetual joyousness and safety for all life. He breathed deeply, and with the outward breath released himself into the light, wan and pure, of all-knowing. He felt himself of the everlasting life and light of the world.

A tree stood beside him, a pollard oak whose flank had been opened and smoothed with an axe, to make swinging way for the gate. An iron staple was driven deep into its old wound, which had long since healed. He put his arms round the trunk, and pressing his cheek on the hard ridges of the bark, felt the presence of a gentle spirit within the sappy bole. Dear tree, he thought with a sudden and tranquil sadness, we shall never see each other again; and he opened the gate and went up a lane no wider than a cart, whose rocky surface was deeply grooved by the iron of labouring feet of the centuries. At a bend in the lane he looked back, and sent a last thought to his unknown friend.

The rusty-edged leaves of the thorn hedge above the sunken lane began to rustle and the wind to touch his face. He reached the top of the lane, which ended at another gate, and clambering over, was in a stony field on whose poor grass sheep were feeding.

The dawn! The higher ground of the next field grew darker, and the sky just above the hill-line glowed with pale yellow, making the distant trees of Windwhistle Spinney black and distinct. Above the primrose bar light from under the earth's rim flowed to the starry zenith, with a startling loveliness and water-likeness. The sun was remote; yonder was the light of the world, while he, an aspiring mortal, stood in the dusky field and looked at the Morning Star, raptured to the lips. Mother of Keats' spirit, of the world-free Shelley, the broken-winged bird that was Thompson, of Jefferies who was a leaf and a feather and the sea – the Morning Star walked in her whiteness up the sky, the Mother of Life who had led the mighty beams to run with laughter over the heavens, and now was soon to wither, and her spirit to flow back into the sunlight.

The wind blew cold on the hill, and when he turned and faced the west the sky before him was dark and terrible, for clouds were travelling over the Atlantic. The western darkness seemed without life, until out of the darkness invisible things cried harshly, as though insanely, seeming to mock the Morning Star which had shrunk and lost its brimming lustre. They were gulls from the headland, coming inland to seek food in the fields. Then down the hedge a whiteness floated silently, and fell fluttering on a lark that had just dropped from its song to the morning. The owl flew away with the lark in its talons, and glided to earth beyond the farther hedge.

A change came over him immediately.

'That is reality; not my way,' he thought, and the feeling of greatness and joy went from him.

He asked himself why he was walking in the field; and what would he see when he reached the end of the down he had been making for so quickly. Only the heathery slope down to the cliffs and the sea. He had walked there many times before, and knew what was to be seen in clear air – the Welsh coast to the north, Lundy and the Atlantic to the west, and Dartmoor to the south; he knew every flower, bird, fern, grass, rock, animal, bush; and the vain and empty sky over all.

He looked over the Burrows, which lay spectral and flat below the hill. He thought of them sleeping there so tranquilly – the normal human life. He saw Mary's head on the pillow, and as he brooded on the sweet vision a piercing anguish arose in his heart. The power which had gone forth into the sky was now directed to Mary, and made her smile, and open her eyes, and put forth her warm arms and draw down his head and cherish it on her breast. He sat down on a cold stone, and wept, having no hope.

Afterwards he reproached himself for being weak, and walked on, waiting for the sun. The air was now faintly roaring again; a grey mist of spray becoming visible over the Pebble Ridge across the estuary, and a white thin smear of waves in the wide sea-mouth of the rivers. The lights of earth and heaven were equal.

He came to the end of the down, to ground unbroken by plough or mattock, and rough with fern and bramble; and the sun came up, spreading its first pale gold on the rimed grasses, and laying long shadows behind the furze. In a brighter and more open air he began to hope again as he looked at the scene of those happy summer days now ended. The land dropped away below his feet – the estuary and the Branton pill were filled with shining sea; the Great Field, shorn of its Joseph's-coat of summer corn-colours, lay sere and autumnal; the heave and waste of the sand-hills, with their yellowing grasses; the level sands bending round Aery Point, the sea wrinkled like an elephant's hide, but shining; the long blue length of land that stretched into that sea, anciently called Hercules Promontory.

A low sweep of the hand and forearm covered the entire visible land and sea. With such a gesture of the mind he would sweep away all the world of men, and replace it with his own vision – the incommunicable vision he used to call the White Bird. He shielded his eyes, and looked at the ring of trees enclosing a minute smudge which was the thatched roof of Wildernesse, three miles away as the falcon glided. Mary would be dressed now: perhaps leaving her work, and wandering forth to look for mushrooms. Perhaps she was at that moment looking at the hills, wondering if he were there, and thinking of him; but he could not go to seek her, for so he had promised her mother.

He remained on the hills at noon, sometimes lying on his back and dozing, or gazing at the sky through the shutter of his hands. There was no wind; the sea and the sky shared a deep blue; the earth was warm and calm with the mellow autumn sun. He thought of the cider that he and Uncle

Sufford were to make; now was the cider-sun, and dry apple-picking time: and Mary, in her old school gym. suit, might be gathering apples – but he was not with her in the lichen-shaggy boughs, while the appledranes ate the sweetest apples hollow. Appledrane, appledrone, beautiful childlike descriptive word of simple men – the wasps droning round the hollow apples, in the warm, mellow, cider-sparkling autumn air. Bideford Bay was horizoned with mist; a collier was passing through a burnished shield on the sea. England, so beautiful, so inexpressibly beautiful!

Gossamer gleamed in the fields of stubble, in shining paths under the sun; and through the air came the sad-sweet song of a wood-lark, singing unseen from clod or ditched stone wall. The bird was little and drab, it mattered not where or what it was; there was genius in the song, a hymn to the life-giving sun, to the light.

In the afternoon he walked down Sky Lane leading over the hill to the Burrows, by which farmers of olden time had brought their corn from the inland valleys to be winnowed by the wind in the sand-hills. When last he had walked there, on Easter Sunday morning, the bines of the bryony had been pushing with spring fervour their long green slow-worm-like heads through blackthorn and bramble; the way was joyful with the wings of linnets and finches. Now the fruit of the bryony trailed in strings of withering red and yellow berries and all song was silent along that ancient sunken sled-track. Near the Santon road he stopped, and looked back in farewell. Faintly over the sloping fields came the slow-falling song of the solitary wood-lark. Lovely little immortal, he could hear God in its throat-strings.

He walked to the sea, where the lines of waves rearing to fall were burnished by the southern sun, and the foam carried the shattered sparkle up the wet sands. As he was walking over the crest of a sand-hill, after a swim in the sea, he saw figures on Ferny Hill; and sinking down on a mat of wild thyme, beside mullein stalks grey and dry, he watched what appeared to be a hawking party. Mr. Chychester was there, with Mrs. Ogilvie, Howard, Pamela, Ronnie, and other people, including what was apparently a keeper standing apart from them. Two black specks were aloft, peregrine falcons at their pitches, waiting on for partridges to be put up by the spaniels working through the bracken. A magpie flew up. He saw the black and white flicker of wings before it sloped to earth again, when one of the black specks fell and swooped up, to hang still at its pitch.

His heart thudded as he decided to go straight to them, and ask Mary to come with him, as a falcon, espying its mate, cut the air unswerving and heedless of any bird that flew! While he hesitated a dog flushed the magpie again: the other falcon stooped: he heard the thud of the smitten bird, and saw the burst of feathers hang in the still air. Poor magpie! And thinking of Mrs. Ogilvie, he went away unseen.

He crossed the marsh, and walked by the sea-wall. The long summer grasses were yellow and drooping, the thistle cardoons broken and flossy with seed, the sorrel spires dry and brown. In the clayey spaces between the stones leading down to the saltings the leaves of the sea-beet were reddening to drink more of the sun. The tide was creeping over the saltings, shaking the wildered blooms of the Michaelmas daisies, and pouring into the channers and locked pools in the sodden turf.

By the harp-bend of the wall, where the pill merged into the wide estuary, he stood and watched a ketch riding up on the flood. Its sails hung slack; the metallic thuds of its engine, fouling the air, were echoed flatly from over the marsh and the estuary. It turned into the pill, stuck on a sand-bank, and began to swing round with the flood. He listened to the good-humoured chaff of the three men on deck, accompanied by the usual meaningless bloodies, while they waited for the tide to 'rise' them. A mongrel dog sat contentedly on a hatch and watched the water.

With regret he saw the ship float free, and move away, while the long-tailed mongrel dog ran up and down the deck barking with joy as it met again the familiar smells lying stagnant between the walls of the pill. He remembered his own dog, which had slipped away when he had left the cottage, tormented by its own vision and desire; and he thought to return to the village and look for Billjohn, but an unaccountable reluctance overcame the thought. He must see the sun sink away into the sea, as he had watched it rising. O sun, mighty life-giver, he thought, the tears started by his inner strength: let man try to crucify thee, and he will learn who is God! And even as thou must tread the sky, so must I tread the way, narrow and dark, to the shining truth that is the light of Khristos.

The excitation of this thought, and its consequent calm, did not endure beyond a lapse of a few minutes; and his longing for the love and tenderness of Mary increased as the sun went down. With strange sense of foreboding he saw the blinding haze dissolving the Burrows shrink into the line of the sand-hills. He stood on the wall until the sun had set, and only the afterglow remained; and then he went into Luke's hut, as though to find refuge from an indefinable dread.

There Diana Shelley found him some time later, eating an apple: she had seen him from Mary's bedroom window, and making an excuse to leave immediately afterwards, she had hurried along the wall.

She was startled to see him there, and her face went white; she did not dare to speak for awhile, owing to the beating of her heart.

'Hullo!'

'Hullo! Would you like an apple?'

'No, thank you. Yes, I will. Oh, don't bother.'

'It's no bother. I've got many more in my pack. They're rather sharp, but nice and crisp.'

She stooped and entered the hut, and sat down.

'Where did you get them?'

'The farmer at Lobb gave them to me. I found one of his ewes on its back in the spring, and put it on its feet, and he remembered.'

She took a bite of her apple, spat it out, and threw the apple away.

'Next time, leave the ewe on its back!'

She squirmed when he remained silent, as though he had not heard; then stole a glance at him, and saw his sadness.

'Billy, are you really going?'

'Yes.'

She looked at her finger-nails, and asked him why he was going.

'Are you afraid of Miss Goff?'

'No, of course I'm not.'

'Then why don't you go for her? I assure you, as a friend, there's a lot of people on your side. Also, I think you owe it to Mary.'

'What can I do then?'

'Well, you've got good grounds for issuing a writ for slander and defamation of character. For one thing, she said you've been a co-respondent in a divorce case, specifying Mrs. Fairfax. Well, you haven't. Also, she said you were a drunkard: you're not. I can prove she said both things, for I was there when she said them. If you got your solicitors to write to her, she'd get in a fearful panic, and drop her senseless attitude in a moment, like Johnson's hot potato. Or was it soup? I know I'm right; she's really a very timid woman.'

'She loves flowers,' murmured Maddison, his head thrust between his knees. 'And while I am here, she will not be able to absorb much spiritual essence from them, for I, spectre-like, will come between. Why should I continue to make people unhappy?'

'Why should she make you unhappy?'

'I don't think she has. The cause of all the trouble is myself.'

'But, Billy,' she said, 'I don't understand you. Your attitude doesn't seem reasonable. It doesn't seem fair, either, to Mary – or even to me, or your other friends.'

'Perhaps I am stupid this evening,' he said slowly. 'I think the real me went down with the sun. With Shelley, perhaps – the sun-treader.'

'But why is it all your fault?'

'Not fault; I said I was the cause. I have been bitten by that mosquito I told you about: I thought after the dance that Mary would inoculate me against it. Well, she didn't. I agree with everything that everyone says about me, with this reservation: that I could put their case against me very much more clearly and concisely than they have done, and probably much less crudely. I agree with Mrs. Ogilvie when she says that Mary would not be happy with anyone like myself: she called it the independability of the artistic temperament. Apparently she knows all about it; she had a cousin, or someone, who tried to paint, and ran through a fortune, and died of drink or G.P.I. in Paris – her first sweetheart, I think she said.'

'Well, for him the fire was probably better than the frying-pan,' said Diana. 'But I don't see what that's got to do with you. Or her. It's Mary's affair.'

He watched a heron flying up the estuary to the duckponds.

'Billy.'

'What?'

'Do you think that if you married Mary, you would be unhappy?'

'She might be.'

When the heron had flown out of sight he said, 'I shall never marry anyone, so what does it matter? No, I am not good enough for Mary. She would be unhappy away from the Burrows, and her Sunday-school classes, and her robin and Aunt Edith and Uncle Suff and her mother – all her flock.' His voice became desperate and sad. 'What does she care that

Jesus has been idolized and lost: that the Gospels are made up
of collected fragments of unknown date and origin; that lofty
experiences of the soul are taught as outward physical facts;
that we have no copies of the Christian Scriptures that were
made before the fourth century; and that nothing of the original writings or memoranda is known to exist. She can't see
why anyone should ever get upset about it. She just can't
understand.'

She believes in you, Billy.'

'Oh, really?'

'You know she does, Billy. Don't you?'

He appeared to be watching a flock of swallows flying over
the water, twittering as they played.

'They'll be going away soon,' said Diana. 'O, I wish I could
turn into a swallow, and fly away for ever.'

'It would be lovely to fly south with the swallows,' he
said, turning to her; and she saw the eager look in his face
that she had imagined in a hundred passions in solitude.
'Then we could all go together – Mary and Diana, and
Pamela, and Benjamin – poor Ben, his aunt said he would
grow up just like me – he wanted to come with me yesterday
evening. My one poor little disciple. I the teacher! Appalling
thought – reminds me of school.'

'Dear Billy,' she said, with tremulous lips, as she took his
hand, and began to stroke one of his fingers, 'I can't bear to
see you so unhappy.'

She moved closer to him.

'I'm all right.'

'Billy,' she whispered, 'don't you really love Mary?'

He did not answer.

'Billy.'

'What?'

'Do you remember that day in Appledore, and our cave in
the rain?'

'Yes.'

'I've thought of that day ever since,' she said unsteadily. 'Billy, I can't bear the thought of you going away.'

'I expect Mary can.'

Diana leaned forward, and began to pick off the candle-droppings on the lintel of the low roof. She went on picking the wax with quick nervous movements until, overcome by emotion, she turned and looked at him with a bleak smile. He looked at her until with a stifled gasp she sidled to him and put an arm round his neck.

'Billy! Don't be so unkind to me, for Christ's sake. You're kind to those who do you harm, and beastly to your friends.'

He pulled her across his knees, and held her in his arms.

'Billy darling, I would make you happy, I know I would. Aren't we alike? I feel all the things in music you do. I knew years ago, when I saw you looking at the goldfinches, that I was a true companion for you. Billy darling, I can't keep on any more, I can't, I can't!'

She wound her arms round his neck and closed her eyes, seeking with her lips for his mouth.

He kissed her, trying not to reveal his inner desolation. How slight and thin she was!

'You do love me, just a little bit, don't you, boy darling?'

'Yes,' he said, saying farewell in spirit to Mary, as he stared at the water which was lapping the support posts of the hut.

'Ah, I saw your look! You don't really! It's Mary! I know you love Mary,' she cried, twisting away to hide her face in her hands. 'Mary loves you – Mary who – and I – I am a false friend –'

In his relief he drew her to him tenderly, while feeling as though he were a separate consciousness, very clear and calm, watching himself. He bent down to kiss her mouth.

'No don't, don't!'

The separate being regarded himself with a shade of disgust, that he could feel resentment against her for withdrawing. He said, 'Well, supposing I don't let you go?'

She became calmer.

'O God, what must you think of me! Let me go! I'm a silly little neurotic fool.'

She shifted on the seat, leaving a space of a yard between them. How beautiful she was: the chaste profile, the red lips, the straight nose, and forehead. What an artificiality was man's conscience, he thought; a convenience of civilization. How happy Mary, Diana, and he would be, if from the beginning they had behaved naturally, as they desired. All things in their season! Free love! Under the open sky it was no more than a bee passing from flower to flower with pollen. Thwartings, torments, imaginative spicings – it was the devil. Ah, but Mary was the one he loved, Mary he wanted: to lose himself in that flesh's agony of rapture.

'We shall get wet if we stay here any longer,' he said.

She glanced at him timidly, as though reluctantly, and saw with relief that he was not looking at her ; and quickly straightening her frock, she rose to go.

She swung round the post, getting one foot wet, and scrambled up the stones of the wall, followed by Maddison. He walked with her along the road to the toll-gate, and by the dyke, branching across the Great Field by the right-of-way, and stopping by the Santon road. They said good-bye quietly, shaking hands, and after a mutual hesitation and silence, bade each other good-bye again, and went their different ways in the dusk. He hastened back along the path through the stubble, poignantly longing to see Mary once more before he left, and to feel, perhaps for the last time, her hands clasping his head to her breast.

For more than an hour after arriving at Wildernesse he waited in the garden; and only when he saw Mrs. Ogilvie going up the stairs did he dare to walk across the gravel drive and knock on the front door.

Chapter 17

Mrs. ogilvie, who had been sitting for the past hour and a
half before the fire in the hall of Wildernesse, put down her
work, and looked at the clock, which told the time at a quarter-
past ten.

'Ronnie, my dear, it is past your bed-time.'

'Oh, Mother!'

All the evening Mrs. Ogilvie had been mending the socks
and stockings of her son, who was returning to his preparatory
school on the morrow. A basket full of these articles, the
temporary abode of a happy cat, was beside her chair.

'Come along, my dear.'

'Can't I stay up until half-past?'

'My dear, you've had an extra hour and a quarter already.
You'll be very tired in the morning, and we have to go off
early.'

'Oh, Mother, can't I?'

'Come along, my dear: we'll all be going in a minute.'

Ronnie, who had been sitting on a stool very quietly during
the last half-hour, with Mr. Chychester between himself and
his mother, reading a book called *Every Boy's Own Wireless Set*,
got up heavily, and moved slowly across the room. He gave
a sniff, and pouted as he tossed the book on the table. His
mother pretended not to notice, but as he went up the stairs
she asked in her calm voice if he were not going to say good
night to his uncle.

'Hey?' exclaimed Mr. Chychester, looking up from *The
Affair of the Air Bomb Neutralizer*, one of the innumerable adventures of Sexton Blake the detective, the third he had read that
evening: he had acquired a fresh store of these booklets the

372

day before, on his return from the last meet of the otter-hunting season.

'Oh, off to bed? Good night to ye.'

'Good night, Uncle Suff.'

At the turn of the stairs Ronnie stopped. 'Mother.'

'Yes, dear?'

'If Willie comes, ask him to come up and say good night, won't you?'

'Very well, dear.'

Ten minutes later, as she was tucking him up he said, having covertly wiped his eyes on the sheet, 'There's something been puzzling me, but perhaps you can answer.'

'I'll try, dear, but I don't know everything, any more than anyone else does. What is it?'

'Willie said that real Christians were people who were like Jesus Christ, but how can they be, when no one can work miracles to-day?'

'It's absurd, talking to children like that,' protested Mrs. Ogilvie to the air. 'It's very wrong of him to say such things, anyhow, my dear. Don't you bother your head about him. It's a very wicked thing to do.'

'Why, Mother? He didn't say it to me, but to Mary. Also, I understand most of what he says.'

'Well, it isn't really worth discussing, dear. You'll understand why when you grow up. No decent man behaves and talks as he does. But there, you will understand everything in the proper time. What you've got to do now is to work hard, so that you will be able to go to Dartmouth.'

She pointed to the sword hanging on the wall.

'That belonged to your great-great-grandfather, who was at Trafalgar. Think how splendid it will be when your great-great-grandson has yours hanging on that self-same wall, and your son's too, and grandson's also, perhaps. Mother knows how you will feel when you are grown-up, you see; and there-fore think how annoyed she is when an outsider, who cares

373

nothing for tradition or his country, comes along and upsets her little boy.'

Ronnie thought this rather 'wet,' but he pretended to be impressed.

'But, Mother, what has Willie done that is so awful? Surely I've a right to know, being his friend?'

'I think the most broad-minded way of putting it is that he was injured in the War, dear. Even then, it is very thoughtless of him to distress others, but he sees only his own point of view. Do not take any notice of what he has said to you. Kiss Mother, Sonnie: I want you to be a fine man, and be a success in life. You're the only man I've got left.'

As she was going out, after bidding him good night, he called out, 'Mother.'

'Yes, boy?'

'Would you be very upset if I didn't pass into Dartmouth?'

Mrs. Ogilvie said ingenuously, 'But why shouldn't you? You've got plenty of ability, and if you set your heart on a thing, I'm sure you'll get through.'

'Oh, I didn't mean it in that way exactly. Willie said –'

'I wish you'd try and forget what he said.'

'Oh, all right.'

'Very well – what did he say? We may as well settle it once and for all.'

'He said, "If every one thought as I think, there could be no more war, but if they continue to think me wrong, there will always be war." '

'Well, it seems the conceited sort of thing he would say.'

'But, Mother, supposing nobody anywhere wanted to be a sailor or a soldier, wouldn't they be unable – I mean, wouldn't people all – that is, wouldn't it –'

Mrs. Ogilvie waited deliberately. 'I don't quite understand exactly what that means, dear,' she said gently.

'Well, it's hard to explain, Mother, but if you ask Willie he'll be able to explain it.'

'He might: and he might not. I do know one thing, however, and that perhaps he would consider old-fashioned; and that is if every one thought as he did, nobody would ever do anything, and very soon every one would be starving, and no trade done, or food to be eaten. It is very easy to talk, but a very different thing to do what you talk about. Now dear, I think we'd better not bother about this any more. Of course, you needn't be a sailor unless you want to, darling. You shall choose entirely for yourself; but I won't have you, or anyone else, made miserable by any foolish nonsense. Good night, my darling: don't forget your prayers: there is One above who loves you, and He will always tell you what is right, if only you listen. But there, Mother mustn't get "pi," must she?'

He clung to her neck so hard that he hurt her, but she did not complain. She waited for nearly two minutes, smoothing his hair, while he sobbed – the usual holiday last-night tears, she said to herself. When he was calmer she said, sitting on the bed, straightening the sheet, 'Now you go to sleep, and forget all that silly nonsense – for it is nonsense.'

She tucked him in, arranged his trousers over the chair-back, kissed him, and went away with the lamp, feeling satisfied that it was a passing phase. As she was closing the door he called again:

'Mother.'

'Yes, Ronnie?'

'Here.'

She returned beside the bed.

'Well, what is it now, dear?'

He sniffed.

'Mother.'

'Yes, dear?'

'Ask Willie to come and say good night to me if he comes back, won't you?'

'Very well.'

She closed the door quietly, and went downstairs, to find Maddison standing by the fire, his pack on his back. Mr. Chychester stood beside him, warming his hands behind his back.

'Ha, here's Connie,' he said genially. 'Maddison's off apparently, and has come in to say good-bye.'

Mrs. Ogilvie barely glanced at Maddison, but in the glance she thought she saw fear in his eyes, and felt revulsion at the sight.

'This is rather unexpected,' she said evenly. 'I thought you said good-bye to us on Sunday.'

'I was just passing, and thought I would look in, Aunt Connie.'

'Please don't call me Aunt Connie. I'm sorry to be so explicit, but I doubt if you will understand even then. Uncle, shall I get your hot water?'

'Let me get it,' said Maddison, going forward.

'No, thank you.'

'Well, I'm going to bed,' said Mr. Chychester, with a friendly yawn. 'Cold water will suit me for some time yet, I hope. Well, good-bye, Maddison!'

They shook hands, and the old gentleman took his unlighted candle and quickly shuffled up the stairs, stopping beyond the turn to fumble in his pocket for matches. Maddison heard the dry whistle of the first few bars of *The Blue Danube Waltz* while he struck a match and paused for the wick to light. Then his door closed.

'Why have you come back?' asked Mrs. Ogilvie, looking at Maddison. 'Have you no sense of honour, that you must force your way into a house where there is not a man strong enough to throw you out.'

'Please, Mrs. Ogilvie, don't speak like that. I came to apologize for all the trouble I have caused you.'

'Well, that is something. But I hope you realize that what I said on Sunday night, I meant?'

'Yes, Mrs. Ogilvie.'

'I will not have my girls compromised, when they are just starting in life. My boy, too; it is a wicked thing to upset him with ideas he is too young to understand, and so to laugh at them. If you weren't so utterly selfish you would see how you have upset the whole family.'

'But I have never said anything that is not of the truth,' said Maddison, with a desperate appealing look.

'I think you must be utterly incapable of knowing truth, Mr. Maddison.'

'Please don't call me Mr. Maddison,' he begged.

'Do see sense,' said Mrs. Ogilvie, ameliorating at his tone. 'What is your position? Do you think it honourable to make love to a girl under the circumstances, to put it quite frankly? Can you support a wife? If not, it is dishonourable to make love to her; but I am glad to think there has been no nonsense of that sort. If I thought there had been, I tell you frankly I should have put a stop to your coming here long ago.'

He made no reply to her indirect question, and she felt relief.

'Good-bye, Mrs. Ogilvie,' he said, breaking the pause. 'Thank you for being kind to me – for you have been most kind – considering you never liked me.'

'Well, we needn't go into that,' replied Mrs. Ogilvie. 'What I have done, such as it is, I have done for the best. Well, I sincerely hope, wherever you go, that you, well, that you find happiness. It will rest entirely with yourself. Good-bye.'

She held out her hand.

'May I say good-bye to Mary?' he asked; and hastened to shake her hand, accepting its finality, lest he embarrass her.

'Mary is not very well; she has gone to bed.'

'Is anything the matter?' he asked, with an immediate concern that hardened her heart.

'Just a chill. I will tell her in the morning that you came to say good-bye.'

'Couldn't you tell her to-night?' he said, falteringly

'Is there any special reason why I should tell her to-night?'

i am going to cross over to Appledore at midnight, in a salmon-boat, when they go home on the running tide. My spaniel is in the village, somewhere, and he may follow me here; and if he does, would you mind keeping him locked up, or he may try to follow me to the Sharshook when I've crossed.'

'Locked up? Then you are thinking of returning?' asked Mrs. Ogilvie incredulously.

'Oh no. I am really going this time,' he smiled. 'To London.'

'By train? There are no trains from Appledore, surely?'

'I shall walk.'

'Oh!'

'Perhaps if Mary doesn't want him, Mr. Chychester would like him, as a present. He is a good dog. I shall never come back here, so –'

She saw him shiver, staring mournfully at nothing on the floor.

'Very well, I'll tell her.'

'Thank you.'

Jean came along the passage from the kitchen.

'I thought it was your voice, Will.'

Jean,' said Mrs. Ogilvie, 'Mr. Maddison is just going –'

"Mr. Maddison," ' he said in a whisper. 'So formal. Oh dear, why are you so cold with me? I have never hurt any-one: everything I have said is symbolic.'

'Don't take any notice of Mother,' said Jean brightly. 'Be-sides, it should be Captain Maddison, M.C.'

'Did *you* get the Military Cross?' asked Mrs. Ogilvie.

'Yes, it came up with the rations.'

'Oh!'

'A soldier's joke, Mrs. Ogilvie!'

'Well. Captain Maddison –'

'Oh, not so formal. I wouldn't mind being horsewhipped, or going to prison –'

A glowing log fell out of the hearth: he picked it up calmly, grasping the flaming end, and dropped it in the middle of the embers. Sheer bravado, thought Mrs. Ogilvie, and said:

Very well, as you wish. And in my turn, I will ask you not to be more than five minutes with Jean. It is already after half-past ten, and we have ,to be up early in the morning, as Ronnie is going back to school. Will you give me your promise?'

'I promise you, Mrs. Ogilvie.'

'Good night,' she said, and held out her hand once more. He shook it, smiled, hesitated, his lips trembled; and fearing he was going to be so absurd as to kiss her, Mrs. Ogilvie went into the kitchen, closing both doors behind her.

'Are you going, really?' asked Jean.

'Yes, really. Jean, does Mary love me?'

'Of course she does. I say, slip up and see her; why don't you? Up the stairs. Mother's gone to heat her water, there's no fire in the kitchen.'

He hesitated, his eyes brightening. 'No,' he said. 'Your mother trusts me. I must go now. Good-bye, Jean.'

'Good-bye, my dear. I say, I must tell you. Old Jig came this morning, and Diana was here. Something that Mother said – she was sticking up for you – made Old Jig say, "Well, the looker-on sees most of the game, so I've always heard." "It depends on the size of the key-hole," said Diana, and Old Jig looked simply furious.'

'And without imagination understands none of the game,' Maddison said softly. 'Jean, don't worry about Howard. You are going to be happy one day with some one quite different to either Howard or Jack. Do believe me, Jean.'

'And what about you?' asked Jean.

'I'm all right,' he said, staring before him.

'You look it,' replied Jean, moved intensely by his expression. 'You poor lonely darling, you're unhappy.'

The feeling in her voice made the tears brim in his eyes.
'Mother doesn't understand. Don't worry about her.'

'Good-bye,' he said, and went to the door. 'Good-bye,
Jean.'

She went to him in the porch, and as he was pulling open
the door she put her arms round him, saying again, 'Mother
doesn't understand. Don't worry about her. She's getting old,
and doesn't know anything. Dear William. Dear William.'

She hugged him, and kissed him passionately.

'I'll come with you,' she breathed, stroking his face; and
eeling him motionless in her arms, she drew away, and burst
into tears.

He put his arms around her shoulders, and held her close,
while his tears dropped on her head.

'Dear Jean,' he said, 'Dear Jean,' and clasped the head
bowed on his breast. Presently she said, when her weeping was
over:

'Forget what I said, my dear. Really I'm not fit to come
near you!'

'In that case, I'm not fit to come near you, for I have done
what you've done.'

She whispered, 'How do you know? You mean Jack?'

'I guessed, dear Jean,' he said tenderly; 'and I understood
so well. Do take care of yourself, please. Promise?'

'Don't you worry; I shan't get into trouble, I know too much
for that. Besides, I've finished with that sort of thing. You
don't believe me, I suppose?'

'I do believe you.'

Jean moved out of his arms, in order to blow her nose.
Afterwards she said, leaning against the wall beside him:

'Do you remember our walk in the snow, ages ago, it seems
. . . Well, I started to tell you something, if you remember.'

'Yes, I remember. You grew suddenly shy, and hit your

leg with your whip, and ran away, and fell over. I remember everything.'

'Shall I tell you what I was going to say?'

'Yes.'

'I know you won't think it silly – I don't suppose you'd think anything silly that anyone could do on this earth. Well, I was walking there one day with Jack, and there were some steers standing in a corner of the marsh. They looked so – well, you know how they look – that I spat at one's eye. Then Jack and I had a spitting match, seeing who could spit the farthest. I won, because I had a sort of cold, and if you curl up your tongue you can spit much farther – like slinging a ball with a lacrosse racket. My dear, I spat a terrific way, and it hung on the eyelash of one beast. We laughed at its clumsy bowing, as it tried to get rid of it. And then suddenly, I thought of the steers being driven along the road to Barum, to the slaughter-house, dribbling all over the asphalt road, making an awful meaningless scribble after they had run past. I thought of those dumb beasts having no will in the matter – terrified of the smell of blood, of the utter awfulness of killing them. And yet, I had spat at one, and made it miserable, because it couldn't see properly. It looked at me, and I felt the look go right through me. Of course I tried to get it off, and was nearly stabbed for my pains, while Jack laughed. I hate him, the beast. William, you do understand, don't you?'

'Yes, yes,' he whispered, beside her in the darkness.

'And ever since, whenever I've been beastly to mother, or anyone else, and God knows I've tried not to be, I've thought of that unknowing stare of the poor wretched animal, and the feeling goes right through me. My God, William, the times I've wept my eyes out, and no one known a damned thing about it! Ah well, here I am, trying to cadge sympathy, I suppose. Do you think me silly?'

'I think you beautiful. Jean, listen to me. I must go almost at once – I promised, and your mother doesn't think I can keep a promise. Listen, Jean. That feeling that went right through you is the most precious feeling you've had. It is the feeling Jesus had, and many men before and since Jesus. Shelley was one. Nothing else matters.'

Jean said slowly, 'I understand.'

Breaking the silence again she said, feeling a sort of awe, 'I understand you now.'

Then she said, musingly, 'And the things they've said about you! I've said them, too. O God!' and the tears ran down her hot cheeks. She felt hands on her head, and a kiss between them, and heard him saying, 'I love you all. Good-bye,' and then the stars showed through the open door. Come back again soon, she wanted to say, but he was gone. She leaned against the wall, her head bent, shaking with sobs.

A minute or two later she was calmer, and going into the kitchen, she met her mother coming to find her. Jean turned away her face, not wanting her mother to see.

'Come to bed, dear,' said Mrs. Ogilvie. 'You must be tired.'

'Just coming.' replied Jean.

Mrs. Ogilvie waited a moment, and then said quietly, 'Has he gone?'

Jean nodded.

Presently she said, casually, 'He sent his love to you.'

'Oh.'

'He meant it!' said Jean.

'I don't doubt it,' replied Mrs. Ogilvie. 'But there are degrees of love.'

'Yes, there are,' said Jean significantly. 'And some of us aren't capable of knowing all of them.' Then perceiving her mother's face to be so tired and worn-looking, she said, 'I didn't mean it nastily. Dear Mother, I understand you through and through,' and she began to sob again.

'Hush! my darling,' her mother soothed her, holding her

head on her shoulder. 'There, my dearest, Mother loves you, and always will. Hush! Jeannie.'

She wondered what was on Jeannie's mind now: had she taken a fancy to that impossible young man, transferring from Howard? Hopeless to try and understand the complications of the unhappy business. Well, he was gone now – at least, it was to be hoped that he had really gone this time.

And to Mrs. Ogilvie came a twinge of pity for his plight – he was so palpably the victim of circumstances. His upbringing produced his ideas; that wasn't his fault: and yet, in spite of those horrible ideas, he was not a bad young man. What was he doing at that moment? Striding along in the night, probably not thinking where he was going, animated entirely by his queer ideas: taking no thought of where or how he would sleep or eat, his 'poor boy' trotting beside him. He was rather a 'poor boy' himself. Well, it was impossible from the beginning – she ought to have obeyed her intuition, and let him go on his way when he started off in that abrupt manner. He was young – the young soon forgot and outgrew their violent early attachments. Especially the slack-twisted sort.

Jean had stopped crying; with wide eyes gazing at nothing over her mother's shoulder, she was waiting for her mother to cease embracing her. The candle flame wavered on the kitchen table beside her. Suddenly it flung about, and the feeble wall and ceiling shadows danced. She saw the passage door open, and her sister standing there. How dark and beautiful her eyes looked in her pale face. She is in pain, thought Jean, and so beautiful.

'Hullo!' said Jean. She sat on the table. 'What do you want, I wonder?'

'O Mary, you naughty girl,' said Mrs. Ogilvie. 'I thought you were safe in bed, I was just going to bring you up a hot-water bottle.'

'I came to get one for you,' the gentle voice replied. 'It's you who wants looking after, isn't it, Jean? We can look after ourselves, can't we, Jean?'

'Rather,' said Jean, strangely moved by the quiet voice.

Mrs. Ogilvie looked at her eldest daughter timidly, dreading sarcasm in her reply; but no, Mary was incapable of anything hurtful or mean. Thank God for my dear daughter, she thought; and was about to deliver the message about the spaniel, as she had promised: but better not reopen the subject to-night. She said:

'Now we must all go to bed. It's late enough already; and perhaps after a good night's rest we'll all be feeling better.'

'I'd like a glass of whisky,' said Jean. By G –, by gosh, I should! Not serious, Mother: don't get the wind up. Merely talking to relieve my feelings – recommended by all the best doctors nowadays. Also, I know you've got the key safely hidden.' She lapsed into a wide-eyed contemplation of nothing.

Mrs. Ogilvie found the bottle of methylated spirit, and poured some in the iron cup of the Primus stove. She lit it, and had gone to find the small kettle, when she heard the noise of the pump in the scullery. Mary was already filling the kettle for her mother.

When the vaporizer was heated, Mrs. Ogilvie worked the little plunger vigorously; the jet of oil spurted, and hissed into flame.

'It works well, doesn't it?' she said, with a cheerfulness not entirely forced. 'Mary dear, how clever you are with the things. I don't know what we should do without you.'

Jean opened her mouth to say that it was not Mary who had cleaned and adjusted the stove; but catching a glance of warning from her sister, said nothing.

They all watched the iron vaporizer turning a dull red.

'Splendid little things,' said Mrs. Ogilvie. She shivered. 'It's cold in here. Go to bed, you two. I'll bring the bottle up in a few minutes. Now, my dears!'

Mary looked at her mother, unable to speak for a moment.

'I'll wait,' she whispered.

'Sleep with me?' suggested Jean. 'Then Mother can have the bottle. Remember the bolster Nan used to put between us, because we used to kick each other so?'

Mary smiled with her lips, and nodded.

'Isn't your bed the bigger of the two?' asked Mrs. Ogilvie cheerfully.

'No, Jean's is bigger. Also, mine sags in the middle.'

'Of course. We really must get you a new bed. Did I tell you the good news? Mr. Lamprey tells me Greenacliff has let very well, on a long repairing lease, and so we shall be able to do more things shortly, I hope.' Greenacliff was a property recently bequeathed to Mrs. Ogilvie by an aunt.

'It was the springiest bed in the nursery, that's why it sags so, for every one used to jump on it,' said Mary, her eyes fixed far away.

Jean went into the passage, and returned again immediately, looking for a box of matches.

'What do you want, dear?' inquired her mother.

'Just a book.'

She went out again, and came back with one of the leather-bound volumes of poetry out of Miss Chychester's bookcase in the drawing-room – a series which had never been read, and rarely looked at. Jean sat on the table with her back to her mother, and read in the book. She turned over pages, reading fragments here and there, and after awhile she shut the book, and stared at the floor.

The kettle began to chirp, to rumble, to sing like a bird far away; the harsh hiss of the stove altered its interior sounds every few seconds. The water might have been giving out a faint reminiscence of the sounds it had heard during its wandering over the earth – so thought Jean, who had been reading Shelley's *Cloud*.

When it boiled Mary lifted the kettle and poured. The bottle gobbled the water, puffing out steam. When the tap was screwed in Mrs. Ogilvie kissed her daughters good night, murmuring to Mary as she embraced her that she was a dear good girl.

'Now sleep well, my dears, and don't worry. A short while, and you'll see things differently – and don't think Mother is so unsympathetic as she may appear.'

'Aren't you coming up now?' asked Jean, seeing that her mother was not leaving the kitchen with them.

'I've just got one small job to do, and then I shall be following, in about a minute. Oh! Before I forget it. Howard isn't going away until after the New Year; they're all going to Switzerland for the winter sports, for three weeks or a month. I think it might be managed that you two join the party, if you'd like it.'

'Oh, splendid, Mum!' said Jean, her face lighting up immediately. Mary went back to her mother, and kissed her, and murmured, 'Dear little mother, aren't you? Don't worry any more . . . you poor . . . dear.' The last words were almost inaudible; she turned quickly away, following Jean along the flagged passage, feeling her way with her fingers, tears hindering her sight.

Left alone in the kitchen, Mrs. Ogilvie went to the yard door, and opened it. The autumn night was silent as the moon, except for the hollow roar of the breakers on the estuary bar. She listened, but there was no other sound, not even a leaf dropping in the windless air. She closed the door, and turned the rusty key, and pushed home the rusty bolt. Then she went into the scullery, and bolted that door. Usually these doors were never secured at night.

She picked up the book that Jean had been looking at. *Shelley's Poems*! Well, it was a good symptom; it showed the superficial character of the whole affair; she remembered passing through that stage herself – a sort of mental measles. She listened; then took from a corner of the kitchen the holly stick she had noticed there when she had come down to fetch

Jean. His initials were cut on it. What a thing to carry about with one, she thought, as she went through the hall to turn the great key in the front door. If he did by any chance come back, she thought, he would surely not have the effrontery to knock them up: but one never knew in these cases. And yet, she felt rather ashamed of her caution. Mary would know in the morning why she had done it. Should she unlock the doors?

Putting the book back in its proper place, she went upstairs quietly, carrying the staff. She reassured herself that she was right in her action as she went along to the schoolroom, candle in hand; and hearing the sound of a drawer shutting at the end of the passage leading to the gable room, she blew out the light, slipped into the schoolroom, and stood motionless beyond the half-open door. She heard Mary pass on her way to Jean's room; and waiting until the door was closed, she saw her way by moonlight to the walnut cupboard, and pushed the staff behind it. No, no, she thought: not there! and pulled it out again, and stood it within the cupboard among the disused hockey sticks and lacrosse rackets. Then feeling that things were already better, she went into her own room, finding the hot-water bottle inside her bed, where her feet would lie. Dear thoughtful Mary, she remembered everything, even that Mum's feet got so cold!

Mary had put the bottle inside her mother's bed a few minutes before, and gone down the passage to her room, meaning to wash there, and undress in Jean's room. She was feeling for the candlestick when the darkness on either side was scored by a bright streak, that slowed in a rain of fire, and vanished. A meteor and its reflection in the mirror! She moved to the window, and stood there looking at the sky. She knew that it was the season for shooting stars; that they were but fragments of ruined planets igniting when they entered the air around the earth; and yet she was filled with an indescribable dread. Perhaps he had seen it, and was making it an omen of their ruined love. Ah no, not ruined: things would come all right later on; it *couldn't* be the end. Oh, why could not people have left them alone?

The autumnal air was heavy and so still; the stars burned dully, shorn by the moon of their flashing. She imagined the moonlit sea ebbing in silence past the island by Luke's hut, pouring steadily from the gravel pits of the Sharshook, lapping the bows of the salmon-boats idle at their moorings. The tide would be low at midnight – the lowest spring tide of the year, then racing in, throwing its plumes of water over the fairway buoys – the Great Fair Tide. Barum Fair would begin to-morrow. He had a few more days before quarter-day: perhaps he would remain in his cottage until then, and would go to the Fair, as they had arranged. He was sure to be there, as he loved being among crowds of people, and watching them, and sharing their happiness. Oh, all her misery had been needless: he would never leave her. Perhaps at that moment he was with Phillip – the most likely person he would be with. Phillip, whom he liked so much. Phillip, who was to be the best man! She clasped her hands under her chin, pressing her elbows into her breast, and began to feel happier.

Having washed, and hastily brushed her teeth, Mary went out of the room, pyjamas in one hand, and hairbrush in the other. By the half-open schoolroom door she smelt the smouldering of a candle wick, and saw the silhouette of her mother's head and shoulders against the moonlit window. Mother hiding, and against that background! She was reluctant to call out good night after the embrace downstairs, and Mother didn't want to be seen apparently, so she went straight on to Jean's room.

Her sister was already in bed, her face pressed into the pillow. Mary undressed rapidly, and put on her sleeping-suit, set the candle before the spotted mirror, and began brushing her hair. After awhile Jean looked up as though she had been dreaming, and said:

'Hurry up, you. It's damned cold. Come and cuddle me back.'

'Cuddle ee back?' said Mary.

When they were children Mary used to say, on a cold winter's night, 'Cuddle ee back?'; and when she was quite warm, Jean would turn over and say, 'I'll cuddle ee back now.'

'We may as well start it again,' remarked Jean, watching the strokes of the brush on the long black hair. 'For we'll probably never have anyone else to do it for us. God, isn't life a mess-up?'

'Life's all right,' said Mary. 'It's the people who're silly about it.'

'Well, what's the difference? Down Dave! Get down, curse you!'

'Life could be beautiful for every one.'

'I think it's a question of luck.'

'We can do what we like, if only we care enough about it.'

Jean thought about this, then she said:

'I don't quite understand that. I thought –' She stopped.

'By "we," I meant mankind,' said Mary quickly.

'Yes, if every one was the same. But they damned well aren't. Look at Old Jig, and compare her, say, with Aunt Edith, or Granny.'

'Granny's a darling,' said Mary, blowing at the candle, and getting into bed beside Jean. 'Nurse ee back, Jeannie?'

Jean turned on her left side, and Mary snuggled against her.

'Granny's never had to aspire,' said Mary.

'What d'you mean?'

'She's been harmonious because – well, she married happily for one thing; and she's never had to bother about her – well, she was born a "proper lady," as Nan used to say.'

'D'you think I'm a proper lady, Mary?'

'Of course you are.'

'What, when I behave as I do?'

'You behave all right, Jeannie. You're decent to other people.'

'What about old Glasseyes?'

'That's only fun.'

'I don't know. I meant it, often. Poor old chap, I think he's been really most decent. You are nice and warm on my back.'

Jean began to work her toes, a habit of hers in bed. 'Tell me if I scratch you.'

'I'll tell you all right.'

A few moments later she said:

'I know why cats pound on cushions.'

Mary did not reply.

'Are you going to sleep?'

'No,' said a voice at the nape of her neck.

'Nurse ee back?'

'It's all right.'

'You poor little dear,' exclaimed Jean, turning round. 'You're crying.'

'No, I'm not,' said the small voice in the pillow.

Jean fitted herself into her sister's bent shape, and putting an arm across her breast, held her close.

'There, my dear, don't ee worry.'

'Did he say anything, Jean?'

'He was sweet,' replied Jean. 'He sent his love to you.'

Mary asked presently, 'Did he say anything else?

'Not much, for he wouldn't wait. He said he had promised Mother he'd go, and that she'd think he didn't mean to go unless he went immediately – something like that. Get down, blast you, Dave!'

'Did he look as though he were hungry?'

'I can't tell: you know he always looks the same.'

'Did he say where he was going?'

'No – just that he was going. I expect he's gone to his cottage. He seemed rather strange – sort of excitement hidden in him, if you understand. God, I can't understand why all this fuss has come about. Old Jig going to see her lawyer, to see if he couldn't be had up for Blasphemy! Anyone ought to be able to see with half an eye how decent he is. And all he said seems to me to be common sense – although I admit I thought him a bit of a washout over some things at first. You know, patriotism and all that sort of thing. Of course, what he said applies to people of all countries.' She yawned.

'Don't you worry, Mary. Things will come all right. You two are obviously made for each other. You'll see, Mother will come round after a bit, especially if she sees that you mean to stick to him.'

'Dear Jean,' sighed Mary, smiling into the darkness, where she beheld the loved face. 'I wish you could be happy.'

'Me? I'm all right. I've finished with Howard.'

'Really?'

'In my mind, I mean. Honestly, I'm beautifully free.'

Jean was amazed at herself. She had just said it, and – it was true! She didn't care a damn about Howard!

'Since when, Jeannie?' asked Mary, delighted at this happy thing. She knew it was true, from her sister's voice.

'I don't know. It just happened. Honestly.'

Mary turned back an arm, and patted Jean.

'Good girl.'

'Damned funny,' mused Jean. 'You and me – Indel and Oudel – like the old man and woman in the weather-teller.' She yawned again.

After awhile Jean said she was tired, and turned over. They lay warm, back to back.

'Good night.'

'Good night. You're a dear.'

'Oh shut up,' said Jean, who was cherishing herself with the remembered feel of his kiss.

''Night, Jeannie.'

''Night, Mary.'

Jean was asleep soon, but Mary lay awake for more than an

hour, praying for him with her thoughts. She heard the faint slow tolls of the Ridge stable clock across the estuary, and feeling relief and hope that another day was beginning, she sank away into slumber.

Then with no knowledge of time having passed, she was alert with all her senses. Dave, pressing on her feet, was growling. She could see his lifted head and cocked ears against the oblique moonlit wall. She strained to hear what he was hearkening to, but the night was silent outside the open window. Far away she heard the barking of a dog. Billjohn! She decided that the spaniel was round at the front of the house, probably scratching at the door. He must have returned from his attraction in the village, and was seeking his master.

For a long time, it seemed – really it was five or six minutes – she listened to the spaniel barking, expecting it to cease at any moment, when he would have found the way his master had gone. But the barking went on and on, and she was about to get out of the warm bed when it grew louder. The spaniel was running round the house; she heard his panting as he passed under the window. Dave growled, and barked.

'Shut up,' said Mary fiercely, trying to kick him from under the bed-clothes. Jean woke up, and sighed.

'Mary,' she said. 'Hullo! What's the matter?'

'Billjohn's come back.'

They heard his frenzied barking round at the kitchen door.

'I'll go down and let him in,' said Mary, getting out of bed, and feeling for her slippers.

She opened the door and hurried along the landing. Round the corner she was dazed by candle-light that illumined the tall white figure of Mr. Chychester. The hollow eyes of his bearded face peered at her from his doorway.

'Confound the dog,' he said. 'It's been kicking up an infernal row under my window. I was just going down to let the beast in.'

AUTUMN

'I'll go, Uncle Suff.'

'Well, take my candle,' said her great-uncle. 'Don't bother about returning it to-night.' He thought she ought to be wearing a dressing-gown; but he said nothing, for he considered that all people who gave unsought advice or tried to reform others were interfering bores.

'Is Maddison here?' he asked, as she passed.

'No. I expect he's gone to his cottage,' called Mary quietly, over her shoulder, not wanting to wake her mother. Actually Mrs. Ogilvie, lying in bed anxious and irritable, heard what was said, and was soothed by her daughter's thought for her.

'A kennel is the proper place for a dog,' muttered the old man, as he closed his door. 'Oh well, as long as I've got a bed, I don't care where the brute sleeps.' And he got into the solid four-poster which he had brought with him from his old home.

Mary went down the stairs and through the hall, and along the passage to the kitchen. She felt as though she was walking in a dream; the air seemed thick and objects without true existence. She turned the handle of the yard door, and pushed. It would not open. With anguish she realized that it must have been locked by her mother. The rusty lock scraped back, and she opened the door. The night was cold and empty. She whistled; and hearing nothing, she called the dog's name. It had gone.

She left the door open in case it returned, and went upstairs to bed again. Jean said, sleepily:

'I heard him go off. He rattled the gate as he jumped over.'

When Mary was in bed again, and the candle blown out, Jean said, 'I've been testing myself about Howard. It's true.'

'We're growing up,' said Mary, suddenly feeling old.

'I want to go round the world. Shall we go together?'

'Yes!' Mary was warm again, so that she could not feel her body anywhere, when Jean said drowsily, 'I've finished with men. They are such silly things; they all – wear – O dear, I'm so sleepy – the same – sort of trousers.'

Lovely and comfy in bed, thought Jean, and thought no more; and in sleep she dreamed of opening her arms to a smiling form that moved to embrace and love her even as she embraced and loved him; and they glowed with light, and the sun blessed them, and never had love been so sweet. Then he struggled with her, and though she tried to hold him back he struck her, so that everything became dark, and she awoke hearing a dreadful gasping cry in the room.

'Mary!' she cried. 'Mary! What is it?'

She felt towards the shuddering form beside her. Thinking that Mary was in a fit, as once she had seen Diana, Jean sprang out of bed and felt for the candle.

'Jean!' her sister wailed in the darkness. 'Jean!'

'My God!' exclaimed Jean, 'you frightened me. What's up? I thought you'd thrown a fit.'

'O God, I had such a terrible dream,' whimpered Mary, breathing hard. 'Don't leave me, Jean.'

'I'm here,' replied Jean, 'wait a moment, I'll light the candle.' She struck a match, and the flame revealed her sister sitting up with wide eyes and ghastly face.

'Do you feel rotten?' she asked, staring at her. Mary smiled wanly.

'I'm all right,' she whispered, staring straight in front of her. The tears began to stream down her cheeks, but she was not weeping. Jean felt a cold thrill down her backbone. 'Darling,' whispered Mary, still staring so strangely at nothing. 'My darling . . . I am happy too.' And turning to her sister, without appearing to see her, she said, 'O Jean, I am so happy . . . it is so beautiful . . . everything really is so free . . . free as air and light!' The tears dropped on to the sheet, and her eyes shone.

Jean felt weak, and scared.

'Come to bed beside me,' whispered Mary. 'O Jean, I do feel so queer. So happy!'

Jean sat beside her sister, her arm round her shoulders.

'Tell me, Mary! What does it all mean?'

'I don't know,' said Mary, smiling. 'I kept thinking of Shelley, and he seemed to be gliding to and fro, laughing. Oh-h-h, my back and neck were all prickly, like a wind blowing out of my spine.'

'So was mine.'

They heard something moving in the passage, and held one another.

'O my God,' whispered Jean, glancing fearfully over her shoulder. Mrs. Ogilvie's voice said, as the door opened, 'Are you all right in here?' and she came into the room.

'What is the matter? Mary darling, lie down at once, and get covered up. Jean dear, tell me, what has happened?'

'Mary must have had a nightmare, I think,' said Jean.

'You two children are overwrought,' replied Mrs. Ogilvie, drawing her faded flannel dressing-gown closer round her body. She put her hand on Mary's forehead. 'The cry awoke me, and I wondered whatever had happened. How do you feel, dear?'

'All right,' smiled Mary. 'I had a dream, that's all.'

'What have you been eating, I wonder? You don't appear to have a temperature.'

'I'm all right now,' said Mary, smiling happily. 'It was only a dream, really, and I couldn't breathe.'

Mrs. Ogilvie was reassured, and she was about to go out of the room when the lurcher Dave, who had been lying curled up on the bed, began to growl.

'Shut up, Dave!' cried Jean, rising up to hit him. 'Shut up, damn you, dog!'

The lurcher looked at her, then over his shoulder uneasily, and jumped off the bed, making an unusual noise in his throat. He walked out of the room, tail between legs, and pattered away down the passage.

'You're shivering' said Mrs. Ogilvie to Jean. 'It is cold to-night. Ugh! There's a draught somewhere. I can feel ıt right down my back. Are you sure you are all right, Mary?'

'Absolutely all right, Mummie dear. Go back to bed, and sleep.'

'What a night,' murmured Mrs. Ogilvie, as she went out of the room, having kissed them both, and made Jean promise to fetch her immediately if Mary felt the slightest bit unwell.

'Let's hope this really is the last of the wretched business,' she said to herself; but she felt strangely disquieted.

Last Chapter

THE morning is beautiful and still, but O, so vacant, thought Mary, looking on the sunlit Burrows from the open window of Aunt Edith's bedroom. O the work in this house, I am so tired of it, there is no end of it, but at least it will help me not to think, she sighed to herself. From every pair of eyes a world was created, and the less you saw, the happier was your world, unless you were with one whose world was like your own.

She saw Uncle Suff standing by the two sunken tubs in his rock garden, his old otter-hunting hat pushed to the back of his head; he wore no collar, and his knickers hung loose and hiding his thin calves, since he had not troubled to fasten the buckles that morning. Mr. Chychester did not care what he looked like; the otter-hunting season was finished, and no one was likely to come near. He stood warm, withdrawn into himself, as a tree's sap withdraws to its roots at the fall of leaves. One day he would withdraw beyond himself, and his old clothes and body and ideas would be gone, and the air be vacant of his world.

Mr. Chychester cared about nobody and nothing as he drowsed and smoked, while the bees with frayed wings scrambled vainly for the honey long since garnered from the fading bells of the rockery heather.

Mary was doing the bedrooms for her mother and Jean had gone to Barum with Ronnie, to see him off from the Great Western Station. She moved about in her aunt's room, dusting the wooden frames of Uncle Suff's water-colour sketches; of Heanton Court, with its lawn too green and its sky too blue, and the rooks above the trees flying with wings of an unnatural shape; of Penhill point and the estuary, with four salmon-boats

397

demonstrating the art of fishing, the first waiting, the second shooting a draft, the third hauling, and the fourth landing at least a ton of fish.

Above the bed-head was an engraving of a granite cross set on a rock in a stormy sea, with a female figure clinging to it, holding a lily in its other hand; whilst winged figures, also in night attire concealing all but heads and hands and toes, floated above – symbols of man in his time-long travail transmuting physical matter into psychical energy. There is nothing new, she thought suddenly: it is only the spirit of a word or a thing that is precious.

She visualized the estuary, and the small waves running and breaking aslant the shell-strewn shingle of the Crow; and house-work seemed more unbearable. However, it must be done; and she went into the next bedroom, which was her mother's, and quickly set it right, for Mother was always so neat and methodical. There remained only Uncle Suff's, for her own bedroom could wait, with Ronnie's and Ben's, until later.

Mary had almost finished dusting Mr. Chychester's room, and was flicking the duster out of the window, when she saw the dark form of a policeman on a bicycle riding along the drive. He slowed and dismounted when he caught sight of Uncle Suff, who, blowing the dead cigarette stump out of its holder, walked across the lawn to meet him. She saw the policeman touch his helmet, and begin speaking to Uncle Suff. They spoke for about five minutes, while she waited in suspense, and then the policeman wheeled round his bicycle to return. Something that Uncle Suff said caused him to wheel it round again, and together the two men came towards the house. She finished tidying the room, constantly tip-toeing to the window to see if they had come out again, while the feeling of dread grew with the minutes. At last she heard the crunch of feet on gravel, and the policeman's 'Well, thank you very much for your kindness, zur,' before he rode away.

She went downstairs, meeting Aunt Edith in the hall.

'Now what can the constable want, I wonder?' asked Miss Chychester. 'He must be very hot in that heavy helmet and cape. However, Sufford gave him a jug of cider, and that will no doubt help to cool him.'

Mr. Chychester was picking up bone splinters left on the lawn by the dogs when Mary stopped by him, hazel stick in hand.

'These will get in the knives of the mower,' he said. 'I'm always clearing up after the dogs. Dogs and boys are untidy brutes. What time will your Mother be coming back?'

'After tea, Uncle Suff. She's going to have lunch with Aunt Georgina at Roborough.'

'H'm. She's got a very nice day for her visit.'

'Yes.'

'I was just trying to make my mind up whether or not to pick those remaining apple trees. The gales will begin very soon, I should think. The wireless said last night that a deep depression was moving in from the Atlantic.'

'Yes.'

'Are you free to give a hand, or perhaps you're off somewhere?'

'Nowhere special, Uncle Suff,' said Mary, with an anguished vision of the vacant shingle sands of the Crow. 'Couldn't I – would it make any difference if I went for a walk first?'

'Oh no, no. You go, midear; I would if I were you!'

She said almost happily:

'I'll lay lunch for Aunt Edith and you: I'll leave the meat in the safe. I'll make a salad. Do you mind having no pudding to-day?'

'Oh, don't you bother about me,' replied Mr. Chychester. 'Cold beef and salad and beer will be enough for me. Well, I think I'll go and repair the steps of the apple loft. That's more interesting than picking apples!'

'Did the policeman – want anything particular, Uncle Suff?'

'Hey? Oh, that fellow. He wanted to know if Maddison were here, that's all,' said Mr. Chychester gruffly. 'Inquiring about his dog – running about at night, I fancy.'

'Oh, I thought something had happened,' said Mary, smiling. Her cheeks grew red with relief. 'Have they got the spaniel, then?'

'Hey? Oh yes, yes, midear, they've found the spaniel.'

'Isn't he at his cottage, Uncle Suff? He doesn't have to leave for a few days yet.'

'I rather fancy there's some sort of idea he crossed over the estuary last night,' said Mr. Chychester, hastily seeking his case, and fitting a cigarette into his holder.

'Crossed over last night?' cried Mary. 'But –'

Mr. Chychester hastened to say, 'Oh, I don't suppose he went that way at all.'

'There wouldn't be any boats! The salmon fishing ended last Saturday!'

'Oh, I don't suppose he went that way. I shouldn't worry, my dear. You know what a fellow he is for the open air; he's probably in the sandhills somewhere at this moment, reading his beloved Jefferies, I shouldn't wonder.' Seeing that Mary was not happy, he added, 'Well, you go for your walk, midear, it's a beautiful day. D'ye see how the swallows are perching on the thatch? Their time must be near for flying away. Ah well, it can't always be summer.'

He watched her walking away, and wondered uneasily if he had said too much. Probably it was a false alarm; some poaching fellow had lit the flare from a boat, for devilment. Well, what had to be, would be; it was the will of Providence.

With a feeling that her uncle had not told her all, Mary walked along the inner wall of the marsh, and so to the White House. She crossed the low sandy plateau above the shore on sward made smooth and fine by the delicate nibbling of rabbits. A few flowers had outlived the wane of summer; minute crane's-bill, yellow bedstraw, ragwort, and the devil's-bit scabious, misty blue like the sky. Moths, each in a dull red flame of wings, hovered above the scabious, to dart at their shock heads and sway on the long stalks as they sipped the honey. Their red wings gleamed with green blotches as the light caught them; but those colours would pass with the bright wraith of summer, for the winds and the frosts to resolve into dust.

She passed a rusty anchor fluke jutting out of the sandy ground opposite the black hospital ship, which for an hour of a summer night had been her home in imagination. How things changed: and nothing ever seemed to make up for their going. The hospital ship had been there ever since she could remember, and now it had been sold, and was to be broken up for firewood. Well, she was glad of that, for now no one else would live in it . . .

Crossing the shingle spit of the Crow, she saw a three-masted barque being towed out by a tug, rolling and pitching in the long slow heave of the foamless rollers. Some way behind the barque many gulls were wheeling and crying, alighting on the water in an eddy of white wings, and flying up again. The water beyond the fairway was flat and blue-shining, the houses and trees of Appledore looking like a water-shadow of its own self; voices of unseen men came in distinct particles of sound, with the knocks of the shipbreakers' hammers on the *Revenge*. The bar was white with breakers, and beyond in the misty bay two full-rigged ships were waiting for the afternoon tide. How empty the shore looked, made more desolate by the tide's high jetsam of rusty tins, bottles, cabbage-stalks, bark of fir trees, sticks nibbled by rats, and bits of paper – forlorn and abandoned tokens of human endeavour.

Mary walked on, coming under the white tower of the lighthouse with its groynes clogged with roots and brushwood from the rivers and the oil-fouled corpses of sea-birds. She was looking at the beak of a bedraggled puffin when she noticed a piece of paper lying near, with its inked writing blurred by water, and partly burned. She picked it up, vaguely recalling similar pieces in the riband of jetsam beside which she had walked from the Crow; and she was trying to read it when with a shock she recognized whose writing it was.

Scanning the words, she realized that it was part of the manuscript of *The Star-born*; but how came it there, and burned? Could he have burned the book, in despair that it was based upon illusion – his old fear – and therefore worthless?

Hurrying back along her footsteps, she gathered seventeen sheets, all partly burned. She walked round the Crow, searching the tide-line; then she crossed the sandhills to the lighthouse, arriving breathlessly at the groynes. She continued the search round Aery Point, and along the flat wide sands, to the Dutchman's Wreck; and at the wreck she left the shore, unable to bear the loneliness and desolation further. She crossed the sandhills and came to the Great Field, walking between the long strip called Pillands and the splats called Gallowell, the three Thorns – Lower, Middle, and Higher – and the two Cutabarrows, and coming to Scur Cottage beside the church and the stream. The door was shut and locked: and looking through the window she saw logs beside the hearth and the ashes of a fire, and beer mugs on the table. The lamp-glass was black with smoke, and cigarette ends were everywhere on the floor. The place look terribly uncared-for!

Seeing Mules between the trees, she went into the churchyard. The sexton was digging a hole beside the grave of a child for a double-flowering cherry tree.

'Tes a butiful tree, Miss Mary, a butiful tree. 'Tes all white in spring; tes like snow, like snow, Miss Goff said, white as snow, this yurr tree, Miss Mary.'

'Yes, everyone says how beautiful Miss Goff and you have made the churchyard, Muley.'

'That's what Mr. Maddison saith, Miss Mary; Mr. Madd'zn, Mr. Madd'zn saith that. A very nice gennulman, Mr. Madd'zn, always very courteous, courteous to rich and poor alike. Very courteous. Courteous. I'll say that for'n before anyone, I will. So will my wife. Proper gennulman, Mr. Maddison.'

Seeing Miss Mary's eyes, he went on more hurriedly:

'I don't know nothing, Miss Mary. I'm only a poor hard-working man with no eddication. Ah ha!' he said, with innocent sly humour. 'Poor old Sly Fox, as Cousin Billy's widow doth call poor old Mules, 'a knoweth naught; 'a don't do much talking, tes only 'ard work I'm fit for, Miss Mary, hard work, 'ard work. That's it. I hope you'm very well, midear. Old Mules knawed ee when ee were a li'l maid hardly so high as a dog's tail, rinning 'bout you was, Miss Mary, with Master Michael; proper spark he were, dapping puddles in the road with sticks at poor old Mules; you both was. I can mind it, Miss Mary. I can mind it as if 'twere yesterday.'

He put out a hand like an earthy root and touched her arm.

'Proper, proper. Proper lady you always was, Miss Mary. I'm sure old Mules is very fond of you, Miss Mary. Very fond. Fond. Fond like. Old Mules, beggin' your pardon,' he said in an unsteady voice, looking anywhere but at her face.

Mary went back across the right-of-way to the sea-wall. At the junction of three dykes beyond the toll-gate, where hundreds of swallows were clinging to reed-maces, she met Phillip Maddison and his red-haired friend walking on the sea-wall. Warbeck bowed to her, and said gravely, 'Good morning,' and walked on. Phillip came down to her.

'Hullo, Miss Ogilvie,' he said, 'we've just come from your place.'

Mary waited for him to say more, but he said nothing.

'Did you find anyone at home?' she asked.

'Yes, Mr. Chychester – was it? An old gentleman with a grey beard.'

'That would be Uncle Suff. I'm sorry I wasn't in, or Mother.'

Warbeck descended the wall and the slope below the road, and sat down by the water-side and watched the swallows.

'Phillip,' said Mary at last, 'where is he?'

'I don't know, Mary.'

'I found this,' she said. 'Look,' and she pulled the pages, which she had arranged and folded, out of her pocket.

He took them and looked at the grassy slope behind her.

'They're burnt, you see.'

'Yes.'

She heard him draw a deep breath.

'Phillip, is anything the matter? Please tell me if there is.'

The swallows flew up in a twittering cloud, but seemed uncertain and anguished, and flew down again to the reeds in the shining mere.

'He wouldn't leave his dog, would he, Phillip? The spaniel came to the house very late last night and howled, and ran away again, barking. Poor Billjohn! so he didn't find his master. It seems strange that he forgot all about his dog, doesn't it?'

She watched Phillip picking grasses, twiddling them between finger and thumb, and dropping them again. Why was everyone so strange?

'Phillip, he hasn't been arrested, has he?'

'Arrested? Why? Have you heard anything?' he asked eagerly.

'A policeman came this morning and made inquiries about the spaniel. I got an awful scare when I saw him first! He said they'd got the spaniel. That's all I know.'

The grass-plucking ceased.

'Have you heard anything more?' she asked timidly. 'I think I ought to go and fetch the spaniel.'

'Mary,' he said, not daring to look at her face, 'I'm afraid it may be rather serious news. Please trust me as a friend.' His voice trembled; he tried to speak calmly. 'Shall we sit down?'

She sat down obediently, very pale and quiet.

'Mary, he may be at Barum, or Bideford, gone there in a boat.'

She nodded, her eyes upon his face.

He went on, with difficulty: 'They found his pack down by the North Tail this morning. Here, give me your hand.'

She gave him her hand, as though she were blind, and he clasped it.

'Mary, they found the spaniel also. Drowned.'

She sat so still that he dared to look at her, and wondered at the child-like innocence of her eyes. Suddenly she hid her face, and he heard the breath in her throat like the fluttering wing-beats of a swallow in a cage. Almost at once she became calm and looked at him.

'I dreamed a dream,' she said, in a voice that might have been of dream itself. 'I know now. Yes, he is dead.'

He saw Warbeck look round at them, then get up and walk slowly towards the toll-gate cottage.

'His spirit isn't really dead,' she said, smiling, yet with trembling, bloodless lips. 'He came to me last night. I felt so calm and lovely, and now I know why. He is free.'

'Did you see him?' he dared to ask.

'No, but I know he was there. I know he was. He came with Shelley. Shelley was drowned too, wasn't he? He loved Shelley.'

He could scarcely hear her voice; her words might have been spoken to one of the gossamers drifting by in the quiet warm air.

'Yes, he loved Shelley,' he sighed.

'He was always a strange little boy, wasn't he?' she said, smiling with ghastly lips.

'He must have burned *The Star-born* as a flare, on the Shars-hook,' said Phillip.

'Phillip, if only we had known he was sitting there, for the boats to come up with the tide! Why didn't someone tell him that salmon fishing was ended?'

'No one knew where he was going,' replied Phillip sadly, 'The last we saw of him was when he finished reading *The Star-born*, said good-bye to us suddenly, and went. That was the last time we saw him. Didn't he come out to see you? I

405

know he was bitterly remorseful for the things he had said to you, for he told me so.'

'No, it was my fault, all of it,' she cried. 'I wanted to tell him so, but he was gone. Ronnie heard him talking to Mother downstairs, and ran in to tell me, but by the time I had dressed and gone downstairs it was too late.' Piteously she added, 'He didn't even say good-bye to me.'

The wings of the rising swallows ruffled the water below them, and the air was filled with their cries.

'It is all like the ending of *The Star-born*,' mused Phillip, 'ne read it to us all through the night. It was pure beauty.'

'Ah! he never let *me* read it,' she whispered, and he was cut by the anguish in her eyes. 'Perhaps I wasn't good for him. He used to work in great stretches, and then come and see me, exhausted, and wouldn't do any more to it for weeks, sometimes months.'

They were silent, their sight unfixed from mortal objects. She felt that the day was unreal; as though the world had ceased to be, and life were awaiting, in a sunlit void, some dissolving, releasing stroke.

Silence (deare shado) wil best thy grave become.

Yes, everything was plain: he had known he was going to die almost from the first. Often he had said that he knew he had not long to live, and once he had seen Shelley rise before him from the sands of the Crow.

Twice child in age, always in innocence.

He had come to her just after the moment of drowning: she had drowned with him, the water and blackness bursting heart and throat until the last painful wrench that broke the spirit free of the body. The body . . . eyes, hair, smile – Ah, no! She must not, must not visualize or think of the body – she must think of the spirit, and all would be well. She believed, yes, she believed: no, she *knew* that he was happy and free.

Glancing at her face, Phillip thought she might like to be

alone, and said he ought to be going. Should he come and
tell her if he heard any further news?

She nodded. 'Come the back way – I shall be in the
kitchen,' she whispered out of those bloodless lips.

Phillip began laughing weakly, and then the tears came into
his eyes.

'Please don't think me callous, Mary, but when you said
kitchen, I suddenly saw him walking into the kitchen.
Wouldn't it be funny if he turned up after all? Please forgive
me laughing.'

'He would like us to laugh, wouldn't he? I said the kitchen
because I shall be alone there, I expect.' She thought of the
many times they had sat there; and her mind began to strike
wildly about the air, so she got up, and smiled at Phillip, and
whispered, Good-bye; and as she walked along the road alone
she thought: O, if he is dead, and I know he is, would that
the sea keep him for ever'

Mary began to walk faster and faster; she must get back
to the kitchen, out of the sunlight which had become so
blank and terrible. She passed through the third and fourth
gates which, swung high for a swift decisive closing,
always made visitors motoring to Wildernesse remark on the
house's extraordinary inaccessibility. The gates could not be
tied open as the marsh grazing fields belonged to different
owners. She was approaching the fifth and last gate when
she heard the noise of the gate behind clashing to, and
climbing the sea-wall, with a wild hopeful leap in her breast,
she saw only her mother getting into Miss Goff's car. She
waited by the gate, holding it open for the car, which glided
through and came to a standstill.

The door was opened, and she was pleasantly invited to get
in. Miss Goff, who had been to a committee meeting of her
Ladies' political club, on which Mrs. Ogilvie also sat, was
coming to tea.

In the house, during the meal, Mrs. Ogilvie noticed that

her daughter was quieter than usual, and wondered if it could be that she was much upset over the departure; but she decided there could be nothing in it, otherwise Mary's manner would surely be different towards Virginia. She is a dear daughter, thought Mrs. Ogilvie, with the sweet nature of her father, without his unhappy impulsiveness. How Charles had disliked poor Virginia: he had seen only her worst side: it was he who had invented the odious nickname of 'Old Jig.' Mrs. Ogilvie felt quite elated during the meal, for she was most pleased with the day's work. Ronnie had gone off quite cheerfully, after assuring her of his enthusiasm for the Navy, as she had known he would, although for awhile she had been anxious; Basil Peto, a splendid man, had been adopted as the prospective candidate; and in two days' time Benjamin was leaving for training ship *Victory*; and now that the troublesome cause of much worry had betaken itself off, Miss Goff had agreed to drop her rather drastic proceedings. Oh dear, Aunt Edith had dropped a brick!

'Where is your nice young man?' she asked suddenly, smiling at Mary, and then at Miss Goff, who happened to be looking at her. 'I have finished knitting the pair of stockings for him, but he must try them on and assure a proper length and fit before I present them to him. He gave me such a beautiful little book for my birthday, called *Songs of Innocence*, by Mr. William Blake. I shall buy a copy for Cousin Augusta, for Christmas.'

Smiling and nodding at Miss Goff, then at her niece, Miss Chychester said to Mary, 'You are not eating your bread and butter, my dear; but do not hurry, I beg of you.' She peered at her great-niece's face. 'My dear, are you feeling unwell? You are so pale, Mary!'

'Yes, you don't look at all well, Mary dear!' said Mrs. Ogilvie, with concern in her voice. 'Would you like to go and lie down, dear?'

Mary shook her head, and began to falter something to

Miss Goff about double-flowering cherry-trees blossoming before the limes came into leaf . . . and suddenly she put down her trembling tea-cup, and seemed to droop in her chair.

Miss Goff and Mrs. Ogilvie were rising to go to her when the peak-capped figure of Benjamin flew past the window on his bicycle; they heard a crash, and the tinkle of a bell; the lobby door was flung open, and Benjamin ran across the hall to the dining-room. The boy could not speak; he gaped and gasped, as though his tongue had been drawn into his belly. He held out a shaking arm, urging it in the direction of the estuary. Mary ran to him, and holding his hands firmly, led him out of the room into the hall.

'Not here, not here, Benny, please! Be quiet, be quiet! We know already! Don't make a noise! Hush! Hush!'

'It's true. It's true!' gasped Benjamin, labouring to breathe and speak. 'I saw his face in the water, looking up at me! Oh! Oh! I saw him by the Horsey Pit culvert. I saw his face looking up at me before the water rolled him over, all swelled up! It's true! Oh! God save him! I tried to pull the boat down, but it was too heavy. When I went back, he had gone! It's no use, he's dead, for ever, for ever, for ever!'

Long afterwards, as she comforted the distraught Benjamin, amidst the shocked and distressful faces that moved around her, asking questions and staring with wide eyes, Mary remembered the face of Miss Goff, which seemed to sag and loosen with the agitations of horror, and then of fear, before it became composed at the thought which she expressed in the whispered words, to Mrs. Ogilvie, 'It is the judgment of God!'

Thereafter Mary wandered away, for Miss Goff took charge, becoming busy with suggestions, one of them being that feathers should be singed and held under the boy's nose. No feathers being available, Mrs. Ogilvie hurried upstairs for Aunt Edith's bottle of smelling salts, which Benjamin was commanded to sniff; he did so, and choked, and was sick on the carpet, after which he was calmer although he sobbed for nearly an hour. He was persuaded to go to bed, but he got up again by the light of the rising moon, and crept about the house, stroking the cats, and telling them that Willie was dead, and gone for ever and for ever, and the tears would fall anew, causing the cats to flick their ears and run away a few steps. Miss Chychester spoke to him on the landing, telling him that he was a big boy, and that he ought not to cry for so long just because he had fallen off his bicycle and bent the handlebars. 'Don't tell Aunt Edith anything about it; and don't go near Mary's room – she's not at all well, and is trying to go to sleep,' said Mrs. Ogilvie to him, in a kind voice, patting his shoulder, and this trust made him feel tragically important, and his grief became controlled. He still wandered about the house, however, and was heard to address various inanimate objects in his thin, husky voice.

'Thank goodness the children aren't here,' said Mrs. Ogilvie to her Uncle after supper, a scanty meal at which only the three elders sat.

'H'm, yes. Still, it soon passes with them, that's one good thing, Connie m'dear. D'you think there'll be an inquest?'

'Oh yes, there's bound to be. I must go and see Geoffrey Lamprey about it to-morrow, to see if he can do anything to keep our name out of it. One can never tell how these things might affect the children.'

'Yes, it would be as well to make sure, perhaps. Poor young fellow, it was an accident, I suppose?'

'How could it have been anything else? Surely it won't be thought suicide? Oh dear, it's a most dreadful thing to have happened.'

Later, when they were standing by the open front door, wondering what the glow of fire in the direction of Crow Island might mean, Mrs. Ogilvie said quietly, after a long pause:

'You know, Uncle, somehow it seems to be almost a logical conclusion to his life. Thoughtless for others, thoughtless for himself. Still poor misguided boy, he's gone now. We must write to his father: Mary has the address somewhere. There's that stick of his he left here. I must send that to him.'

She thought of the few familiar relics of her own Michael, and her eyes became moist with sympathy; but it was not the face of Michael she saw, but a face that seemed so gentle, that had wanted to kiss her good-bye. Oh, why hadn't she? A fragment came to her mind, *And the greatest of these is charity.* . . . She went to find Mary, but Mary's bedroom was empty, although the bed looked as though she had been lying there, with a ruffled counterpane. A green paper-cap, folded and smoothed, was thrust under the pillow. Suddenly feeling overcome, Mrs. Ogilvie sat on the edge of the bed and wept.

Downstairs in the hall Mr. Chychester, his old otter-hunting hat, with its frayed rim, pushed on the back of his head, was standing by the table, when there came a soft knocking on the front door. Opening it with difficulty, the old man saw standing there a figure that gave him a slight shock, for it was Maddison returned! Before he could speak a voice said nervously, 'Good evening, sir. Can I speak to Miss Ogilvie, please?'

Mr. Chychester peered at the face, uncertain of the voice, until it said: 'My name's Phillip Maddison – the other Maddison was my cousin.'

'Oh ah! Won't you come in? I don't know if Mary is here. I suppose you haven't –?'

'You know about it, I expect, sir?'

'Well, yes. Is it certain?'

Phillip hesitated, to make his voice steady.

'They've found him. I've just come from the Crow. I saw Miss Ogilvie this morning, after I had left you, on my way back to the village.'

'Ah! It's an unhappy business,' muttered Mr. Chychester, and they stood still, staring at the floor. 'You'll be wanting to tell her, I suppose. Ah!' They remained still again, while the slow *tick tock* of the grandfather clock sounded loud in the empty hall.

'Is she here, sir?' asked Phillip at last.

'Eh? Mary? Oh yes. I think I heard her clearing away the supper just now.'

Phillip followed the old man, with his faded bandanna handkerchief hanging out of his pocket, into the duskiness of the hall, and stopped there, while Mr. Chychester went into the dining-room. Mary looked up as he came in.

'Oh, there you are,' said Mr. Chychester, and stopped. 'There's someone called Maddison come to see you, my dear.'

'Where?' she cried, in a voice wild with hope. 'Quick, Uncle, quick, tell me!' She stood before him, waiting, while he felt dazedly his own mistake.

'Uncle!' she gasped, clasping her hands under her chin. 'Isn't he dead after all?'

'Eh? Oh no, it's not he. It's a cousin of his, also called Maddison.'

She seemed to grow smaller again, and he wondered desperately what he should say or do; but not knowing what, he stood still before her.

'There – there, don't you worry,' he managed to say. 'He's a cousin, he says. He's in the hall, midear, waiting to see you.'

Mr. Chychester went away, closing the door behind him; and when he was alone he took out a cigarette, but forgot to light it, and stood as still and empty of thought as the air and dust of his darkened room.

Mary and Phillip were walking on the dry loose sands made dusky by the low moon, which glistened on the mud of the Bight. Sometimes a point of flame arose above the low uneven line of marram grasses before them, and when they came to the shore she saw the figure of Warbeck dragging planks of wood to the fire.

'Phillip, I must tell you something,' said Mary, stopping at the edge of the sandhills. 'It is a very terrible thing to say, but it is the truth: my mother was indirectly responsible for it happening, but she does not realize it. Jean was listening to what Mother and Willie were saying, and Mother promised to give me his message that if the spaniel came to the house, following him, would I take care of it, otherwise it might follow to the Sharshook after he had crossed, and be left there to –' her voice sank to a whisper – 'to – all alone.' She went on after a few moments: 'Mother did not give me the message. She did not realize the nets were off – that there would be no boats coming in with the tide. If I had known he was there, I would have gone at once to the lighthouse, and asked them to telephone across to Appledore for a boat. There would have been plenty of time to take him off, where he was – waiting. . .' Her voice became small, and ceased.

'I understand,' said Phillip, presently. 'It is a secret between us – and Willie.' They walked on, hand in hand.

'If she knew,' went on Mary, 'she would never forgive herself, poor dear – she didn't realize, did she? Willie would understand, wouldn't he? She – she liked Willie, really, you know. She said to me only to-night that he was something like Michael – their eyes were the same – and that war was a terrible thing. I think everyone would have liked Willie when they really understood what he meant – that is the awfully sad part about it. I am beginning to understand him now, properly,' she whispered, as though to the night. 'Yes, it is our secret – the three of us – isn't it, Phillip?'

'Yes, Mary,' said Phillip. 'Willie would not wish anyone to be hurt, would he?' and he bit his lip to prevent a hysterical flutter of breath in his throat.

'Dear Phillip, we must always be friends, mustn't we?' said Mary, pressing his hand. Together they went to the fire.

Two faces, pale and lined in the flamelight, looked towards them, then recognizing who had come, looked down again. One moved out of the glow, and came towards her, as Warbeck flung the wood on the fire, sending up a shower of sparks.

'My dear, what can I say?' said the voice of Howard.

'Words, what are words?' He put his hand sympathetically on her shoulder.

'Who is there?' she whispered.

'The Rector; and the other fellow is called Warbeck apparently. He smashed up one of the huts for that fire.'

Seeing her standing pale and silent as though lost, he suggested he should take her home.

'No one can do any good remaining here, I'm afraid. You're shivering, Mary. Come away, my dear; the others will look after him, poor fellow!'

'Where is he?' she whispered.

He said quietly. 'In the boat down there, by the water. Mary, you'd much better let me take you home. I don't think you ought to –'

She shook her head, and turned to Phillip. 'Come too,' she whispered. They went slowly down the shingle to the sea, where the waves were breaking. A thin hook of fire moved by the boat lifting and sinking in the surge. Beside the boat two men stood shadowly and still in the moonlight.

'Us got'n for 'ee, Miss Mary,' said a low anxious voice. 'Us got'n safe all right, midear. The gennulman wanted vor to burn'n, burn'n in the vire, but us got'n safe. Don't 'ee worry, Miss Mary, don't 'ee worry. It be all right, midear.'

The glimmering waves broke with regular crashes along the shore.

'Would 'ee care vor to see'n? Tes a bit wet-like still, but very quiet he lieth, the poor gennulman.'

Her hand sought Phillip's, and she went forward with him and looked into the boat, and remained there, silently, for nearly a minute, while the surge washed over her shoes unfelt; and turning with a face as pallid as the fixed white blur in the well of the boat, she whispered 'Thank you' to Mules.

'You'm quite welcome midear, you'm quite welcome. Tes for you to see by rights, and no one else, Miss Mary.'

414

Her lips whispered good-bye.

'Good-bye, midear. Good-bye,' said Mules, coming to her, and speaking in a voice strained with anxiety. 'My wife will 'ave'n laid out proper by the morning although tes only in the dead-house. Don't 'ee worry midear, old Mules will look after'n proper.'

They walked back to the fire. The flames now rose higher than the men and the sparks were lost beyond the moon. Within the fiery shell of embers, glowing with colours from sea-salts and nails in the wood, something dark was hissing and bubbling, and a bright tongue of flame flapped out of one end, as though some strange power in the fire wasting the body of the spaniel were arising with its old joyous earth-spirit.

'We should give Maddison the honour and purity of fire,' said Warbeck proudly, turning to her. 'He saw light in our world darkness. But when I go near, that madman menaces me with his hook. You see, there is a reward of five shillings.'

Howard looked at the speaker, with tightened lips. All this nonsense about light and darkness! The fellow was half-drunk.

> 'Shall I strew on thee rose or rue or laurel
> Brother, on this that was the veil of thee?'

chanted Warbeck softly, staring into the fire.

Garside moved beside her and said, 'Be brave, Miss Ogilvie! "Heaven and earth shall pass away, but My word shall not pass away." '

He looked at a star above the flames, trembling in a watery waver.

'Heaven and earth shall not pass away, but your words will,' muttered Warbeck. 'Are you praying for the departed? You will do that at the funeral inevitably, but spare his friends that violation now!'

'I was his friend, too, Mr. Warbeck,' replied the Vicar, humbly.

'I beg your pardon, sir,' said Warbeck. 'By God, but I –'

He clenched his fists, and bit his lower lip, and vainly stifling his sobs, strode towards the sea.

'It will be sometime before they can take the boat up on the tide. I think we ought to take you home now, Mary. What do you think, Vicar? Will you be coming too, Maddison, or waiting here?'

'I think I shall wait here,' replied Phillip. 'Unless Mary –' He looked at Mary, whose gaze was fixed on the fire.

A sign of wings passed in the night, and sank away in the murmurs of fire and water, and was renewed with the faint piping of birds flying out to sea. From beyond the glow of the fire they heard the voice of Warbeck:

> 'I the nightingale all spring through,
> O swallow, sister, O changing swallow,
> All spring through till the spring be done
> Clothed with the light of the night on the dew
> Sing, while the hours and the wild birds follow,
> Take flight and follow and find the sun.'

'You'd better come, Mary,' said Howard, as Warbeck came slowly into the firelight.

> 'O swallow, sister, O fleeing swallow,
> My heart in me is a molten ember
> And over my head the waves have met.'

Seeing her piteous stare upon Warbeck, down whose cheeks the tears were running, Howard breathed deeply and clenched his fists. Maudlin swine!

> 'O sweet stray sister, O shifting swallow,
> The heart's division divideth us,
> Thy heart is light as the leaf of a tree;
> But mine goes forth among sea-gulfs hollow –'

'Would you mind being quiet?' said Howard, very distinctly. 'You might at least consider the feelings of others.'

Warbeck regarded him with scorn and pride, then turned abruptly, and vanished.

'Those beautiful colours of the flames, they are the salts in the sea' said Garside to Phillip. 'His kind was the salt of the earth. Yet if everything was salt. . . .' He sighed deeply. 'That seemed to be his desire.' He shook his head slowly.

'You really should read the New Testament,' murmured Phillip.

'Let us make Money our one and only god, for ever and ever, Amen,' cried the voice of Warbeck, raging and tearing-choked, from the outer darkness. 'No one will object, except the destitute: but don't you DARE to call your god Christ!'

She cried out: 'Howard, I see it all! He was too good to live among us, and so he was taken away.'

'The legend begins,' Phillip said, as though to himself. 'If we had understood him better, he would not have needed to go away at all.'

Mary heard, and said wildly: 'Yes, that is the truth! I failed him!'

'Oh please!' said Phillip. 'I really didn't mean anyone in particular. I was thinking of myself, really!'

'Nobody has failed anybody,' said Howard. 'Nothing you or anybody else could have said or done would have made any difference. He would never have changed. Mary, dear, I'm going to take you home,' said Howard firmly, taking her arm.

As he led her away the voice was heard again, chanting sadly to the sea and the sky:

> '*Who hath remember'd me? who hath forgotten?*
> Thou hast forgotten, O summer swallow,
> But the world shall end ere I forget.'

'He did not need to change,' cried Mary, slipping her arm out of Howard's. 'It is we who must change,' and she ran down to Phillip by the edge of the sea, weeping, thinking of the darkness of men's minds, pierced in vain by the shining light of Kristos, and of the agony of Christ, at the end of the Pathway.

NOVEMBER 1924—SEPTEMBER 1928
LONDON—DEVON